Hello there!

Thank you so much for choosing to read my novel *The Toffee Factory Girls*. This is the first in a trilogy of books set during WW1. The trilogy stars three wonderful women – Hetty, Elsie and Anne. I hope you grow to love them as much as I do, and that you will follow their stories throughout the series.

Many years ago I wrote my debut novel *Belle of the Back Streets* which is about a girl who takes on her dad's rag-and-bone round after he returns from WW1. While researching that book I became aware of Horner's toffee factory in the market town of Chester-le-Street in County Durham. The factory has long since closed down, but it was where the brand of *Dainty Dinah* toffee was made. Those two words – *Dainty Dinah* – have stayed with me ever since.

I knew that, one day, I'd write a novel about a toffee factory and the women who worked there. My research into toffee production and the work of women in toffee factories has been hugely enjoyable. I've loved every minute of it and discovered some fascinating facts. In my books, while the toffee factory, brand and the women are fictional, I hope I've done justice to the hard work of factory women during WW1.

With all my best wishes

Glenda Young

Praise for Glenda Young:

'Real sagas with female characters right at the heart' *Woman's Hour*

'The feel of the story is totally authentic . . . Inspirationally delightful' *Peterborough Evening Telegraph*

'In the world of historical saga writers, there's a brand new voice – welcome, Glenda Young, who brings a freshness to the genre' *My Weekly*

'Will resonate with saga readers everywhere . . . a wonderful, uplifting story' Nancy Revell

'It's well researched and well written and I found myself caring about her characters' Rosie Goodwin

'Glenda has an exceptionally keen eye for domestic detail which brings this local community to vivid, colourful life' Jenny Holmes

'I found it extremely well written, and having always loved sagas, one of the best I've read' Margaret Kaine

'All the ingredients for a perfect saga' Emma Hornby

'Her descriptions of both character and setting are wonderful . . . there is a warmth and humour in bucket loads' *Frost Magazine*

By Glenda Young

Saga Novels
Belle of the Back Streets
The Tuppenny Child
Pearl of Pit Lane
The Girl with the Scarlet Ribbon
The Paper Mill Girl
The Miner's Lass
A Mother's Christmas Wish
The Sixpenny Orphan

The Toffee Factory Girls

Helen Dexter Cosy Crime Mysteries
Murder at the Seaview Hotel
Curtain Call at the Seaview Hotel
Foul Play at the Seaview Hotel

GLENDA YOUNG

The
Toffee Factory Girls

HEADLINE

First published in 2024 by
HEADLINE PUBLISHING GROUP

First published in paperback in 2024 by
HEADLINE PUBLISHING GROUP

1

Cataloguing in Publication Data is available from the British Library

ISBN 978 1 0354 0248 9

Offset in 11.35/14.24pt Stempel Garamond LT Std by Jouve (UK), Milton Keynes

Printed and bound in Great Britain by Clays Ltd, Elcograf S.p.A.

HEADLINE PUBLISHING GROUP
An Hachette UK Company
Carmelite House
50 Victoria Embankment
London EC4Y 0DZ

www.headline.co.uk
www.hachette.co.uk

Author's Note

Please note, in this work of fiction I have used poetic licence to best fit dates to the narrative. If you'd like to discover the real history of Elisabethville, fictionalised in this novel, I highly recommend the books *Who Were the Birtley Belgians?* by Birtley Heritage Group, published by Summerhill Books, and *Of Arms and the Heroes: The Story of the Birtley Belgians* by John G. Bygate, published by History of Education Project.

Acknowledgements

My grateful thanks go to the many local historians who provided their time, advice and help while I was researching this book.

Thank you to Gavin Purdon, local historian at Chester-le-Street and writer of the book about Horner's toffee factory, *It was Grand Toffee*. Thank you to Dorothy Hall, Alec Thompson and everyone at Chester-le-Street Heritage Group. Thank you to the staff at Chester-le-Street library and to Rosie Nichols and Julian Harrop at Beamish Museum. Everyone at Sunderland Antiquarian Society has been, as always, amazingly helpful. Thank you to Neil Sinclair for his insight and knowledge of north-east railways. Thank you to Val Greaves, Jean Atkinson and Barry Ross, and everyone at Birtley Heritage Group. Also special thanks to Birtley Heritage Group for taking me on a guided tour of what remains of Elisabethville; I highly recommend their book *Who Were the Birtley Belgians?* Thank you to Dirk Musschoot for allowing me to use his name in this novel, and for his book *Belgen Maken Bommen*.

A warm Yorkshire thank you to Peter Robinson, Tim

Kirker and Rob Heron of Calderdale Industrial Museum in Halifax for a fantastic welcome and guided tour while I was researching toffee factories in Yorkshire. Thanks also to the University of York Borthwick Archives for allowing me to view archive pictures of women workers in toffee factories.

Thank you to my agent, Caroline Sheldon, for everything, and to the team at Headline who look after me so well. Finally, thank you to my husband, Barry, for fuelling me with tea, coffee and cheese scones when I lock myself away to write.

Chapter One

Summer 1915

In a cramped upstairs room in a terraced house, eighteen-year-old Anne Wright rolled her brown hair into a bun, then pinned it neatly in place. She stood in front of the mirror, squinting at her reflection, before reaching for her glasses from the bedside table. Putting them on, she stepped back from the mirror, turning her head this way and that. She wanted to make sure there were no stray locks of hair. She had an important interview and needed to look her best. Her face was clear and well scrubbed, her cheeks pink and eyes bright.

'Miss Wright!' a voice called.

Anne's heart sank. It was Mrs Fortune, her landlady. What on earth did she want this time? Mrs Fortune was a stout woman who wore her grey hair tucked under a small black hat, no matter what time of day. Anne had often wondered if she wore it while she slept. Before she had a chance to reply or open the door, Mrs Fortune entered the room.

'Please, Mrs Fortune. How many times have I asked you to respect my privacy?' Anne said, alarmed. 'You should've knocked. I might have been undressed.'

The landlady bustled across the room with two folded towels in her arms. She laid them on a chair by Anne's bed.

'I've brought you clean towels, Miss Wright.'

'That doesn't excuse you bursting into my room,' Anne said. She tried to keep her tone light against the anger she felt. It wasn't the first time her landlady had entered without knocking. She made a mental note to find a locksmith who could provide something she might affix to the door to give her privacy against Mrs Fortune's prying eyes. Because she was in no doubt that prying was exactly what Mrs Fortune intended. She saw the woman's eyes dart around the room, then land on the perfectly made bed. The pillow was plumped and the eiderdown straight. Mrs Fortune's face dropped; she looked disappointed that she hadn't found what she'd hoped.

'Did you sleep well?' she asked.

Anne knew her landlady well enough by now. She knew that Mrs Fortune really wanted to know if Anne had broken her house rule and had a man to stay overnight. The very thought of it made Anne despair. One man had brought enough trouble to her life. She had no intention of getting involved with another. She crossed her arms and stared into the older woman's eyes.

'I slept well, as always. Now, if you have any more business with me as your tenant, please state what it is. Otherwise, I've a very busy morning ahead and I need to prepare.'

Mrs Fortune eyed Anne all the way up from her smart brown shoes, sheer stockings and brown skirt to her best cream blouse with a lace collar.

'A busy morning, you say?'

'It's none of your business,' Anne snapped. She stopped herself saying more. Oh, how she hated living in this tiny room in Mrs Fortune's house. But she had no choice; it was all she could afford.

'I have an interview, if you must know,' she said, more gently now, aware that if she upset Mrs Fortune, she might end up on the streets looking for another place to live.

Mrs Fortune raised her eyebrows. 'Where?'

'Jack's toffee factory.'

Her mouth twisted into a wry smile. 'You? A toffee factory girl?' she said sarcastically.

Anne stuck her chin out. 'What's wrong with that? I'm up to the job. I can do it.'

Mrs Fortune composed herself. 'I'm sorry, lass, but I can't see someone as slight and delicate as you, with all your airs and graces, lasting five minutes in the packing room, or the slab room. The girls there will rip you to shreds. They're tough lasses, it's hard work.'

Anne slowly removed her glasses, then took a linen handkerchief from her bag to wipe the lenses. She replaced the wire-rimmed glasses on the bridge of her nose.

'If I pass my interview today, I won't be working in any of those rooms. I'll be working for Mr Jack himself. I've applied for the position of his secretary. Look.'

She held out a folded copy of the local newspaper, the *Chester-le-Street Chronicle and District Advertiser*.

She handed it to Mrs Fortune and watched as the landlady read. When she had finished, her hand flew to her heart.

'Oh my word, lass. You'll do well if you get that job. It'd make me very proud to tell my friends that my lodger works for Mr Jack himself. Why, his toffee factory is the beating heart of our town.' But then her face clouded over. 'Although there are rumours about him, which I'm sure you'll have heard.'

Anne hadn't heard anything and was curious to know more. However, she didn't want to appear as if she was interested in hearing gossip, as she considered that common. Fortunately, she didn't have to say a word as Mrs Fortune carried straight on.

'Oh yes, the things they say about William Jack will make your hair curl. He's an odd one, all right. A maverick, they say, though I call him eccentric. Why else would he have left the comforts of his family estate in Lumley to live in the old Deanery, alone? I know I wouldn't live here in Chester-le-Street if I could afford to live in Lumley. And I hear he's built a garden at the factory for his workers to parade in at lunchtimes. He allows them an hour-long break each day, you know. A whole hour! Mind you, the toffees they make are beautiful. The best in the country, that's what everyone says.'

She made to leave, but suddenly turned and nodded at the newspaper. 'It says in that job advertisement that applicants must be able to type.'

'I can,' Anne said, although she hadn't used a typewriting machine in months. However, how hard could it be to pick up her old skills?

Mrs Fortune arched an eyebrow. 'And you'll have to

use the telephone. Not many people know how to do that,' she added.

'I have experience there too,' Anne added. She *had* used the telephone before, but she kept quiet about where and when. It was no one's business but hers.

Mrs Fortune nodded slowly, keeping her eyes on Anne. 'Well, Miss Wright, you are a dark horse. There's more to you than meets the eye.'

Anne stepped forward to usher the landlady out. 'Again, I'd like to ask for my privacy, Mrs Fortune. I always pay my rent on time, don't I?'

'Yes, but—' Mrs Fortune began.

Anne cut her short. 'And my room is always clean.'

'Yes,' Mrs Fortune added reluctantly.

'And I cook my own meals and clean your kitchen afterwards. All of that should allow me to keep my room here as my own. I'd be very grateful if you'd knock the next time you wish to come in, whether it's to deliver clean towels or ...' Anne paused, intending her next words to hit the spot, 'whatever it was you were hoping to find. Some of your previous lodgers might have broken your house rules, but not me, Mrs Fortune. I am a woman of my word.'

Mrs Fortune's cheeks coloured, then she nodded quickly and left.

Once she'd gone, Anne sat on her bed. She tore the advertisement from the newspaper, folded it precisely and placed it in her handbag. She took her coat from the peg behind the door, then checked her reflection again. She felt confident that she looked as smart as she could. There was a nervous flutter in her stomach at the thought of the interview. She'd have to tell a few white lies, exaggerate her experience, but nothing ventured, nothing gained. That was what her mum used to say. And the worst that could happen was that she'd end up working in one of the rooms at the factory Mrs Fortune had mentioned instead of in Mr Jack's office. She'd heard there were jobs aplenty there for girls now that men were leaving to go to war.

She was about to leave her room when she paused. Reaching her hand to her dressing table, she pulled open the middle drawer and rifled through her silk petticoats, pushing aside handkerchiefs and scarves, until she found a tiny square of a picture. A photograph in black and white of a baby boy. She kissed it, and a lump came unbidden to her throat. Her eyes pricked with tears. No, she couldn't cry today. She had an interview to attend. She had to be on her mettle. As she hid the picture away at the back of the drawer, she felt tears threaten again, so she shook her head, straightened up and looked at herself in the mirror.

'Pull yourself together, Anne,' she commanded her reflection.

Then she headed outside to walk to the toffee factory.

Chapter Two

At Chester-le-Street railway station, Hetty was being shoved around the crowded platform. She was surrounded by a bustle of activity as young men, little older than boys, boarded the train. Steam billowed about them. An older man was calling names, and men in the uniform of the Durham Light Infantry replied, 'Here, sir!' before stepping into the train. She knew that Bob's name would be called at any moment. She looked into his steel-grey eyes.

'Chin up, Hetty. I won't be away long. I'll be back before you know it,' he said matter-of-factly.

Hetty longed for a farewell hug or a kiss, but Bob stood straight, keeping a polite distance from her. She'd known him long enough to know he kept his feelings bottled up. Long enough to know how irritated this made her feel. She reached for his hand, but he pulled it away.

'I'd best not let myself be sidetracked by that kind of thing,' he said formally. 'Remember, when I come back, we'll get married like we planned. Our wedding might just be the thing to cheer your mum up.'

Hetty doubted that even her wedding would please her

mum, Hilda. No matter what she did, nothing was ever good enough. Not like her brother, Dan, who could do no wrong in their mother's eyes.

Another name was called.

'Grayson?'

Hetty gasped. This was it.

'Promise you'll wait for me,' Bob said.

'I promise,' she replied. 'And you, Bob?'

'I'd never go back on a promise, you know that.'

'Promise you'll write to me?'

'Of course . . . if I can.'

She yearned for him to take her face in his hands and bring her lips to his, but the moment was lost when his name was called again.

'Grayson!'

'I have to go,' he said sharply. 'Remember me always, Hetty.'

He stepped away, straightened his back and snapped his heels together.

'Here, sir!' he yelled, and climbed up into the train.

Hetty's legs felt weak as he turned his back on her. She'd thought about this moment many times since he'd signed up. She'd known she'd have to say goodbye. But now it was real. Bob was on his way out of her life and she struggled to comprehend the enormity of it. Pushing herself forward to the train window, she peered inside, desperately searching for one last glimpse. The doors slammed shut, then she heard a whistle.

'Bob!' she yelled. She banged on the window but there was no sign of him. Steam drifted along the platform. 'Bob!' she called again as the train began to move. She swallowed a lump in her throat.

Then a window opened, a head popped out and he was there. As Hetty forced her way along the platform, he held out his hand.

'Take care, Hetty,' he said.

She reached for him, but the train picked up speed and their fingertips only briefly touched. Then he waved, ducked inside and was gone.

Hetty stood rigid, watching the train snake away.

'He'll write to you, love, you'll see. My son's promised to write every day.'

Hetty turned to see a woman with a child in her arms. She wanted to thank her for her kind words, but found she couldn't speak. Around her, other women were crying, some sniffing back tears, others wailing. Some women held hands or had their arms around each other offering friendship and support. One had collapsed on a wooden bench and was being attended to by the guard.

A small black dog appeared and walked behind Hetty, trailing a tatty piece of string tied around its neck. Hetty was too upset to take any notice of it as she joined the crowd of women leaving the station. She was trying hard to hold back her tears, because she knew Bob would expect it, but now that he'd gone, she had no one to tell her to keep her chin up or be strong and brave.

Tears trickled down her face and she scrunched her eyes shut. What would her life be like without him? She felt strange inside; not lonely exactly, but lost. Despite this, however, she didn't want to go home. Not yet. Her mum would want to talk about Bob, how he'd looked when he left, what he'd said. Hetty didn't want to share their last words with anyone; she wanted to keep them to herself. She needed time to process what had happened. Bob had gone off to war without so much as giving her a peck on her cheek. His formal manner often infuriated her, but this time it made her feel unwanted and unloved. Plus, if she went home now, she knew her mum would have jobs waiting for her: cleaning the hearth, bringing in coal and water, sweeping the yard. The list went on. There was always work to do. Dan was never tasked with such chores. He was her mum's pride and joy, and while Hetty toiled in the house, he was allowed to roam the streets with his pals.

'If he's not careful, he'll end up in trouble with the police,' Hetty often warned, but Hilda always dismissed her concerns.

'He's full of youthful energy, that's all. He knows what he's doing,' she'd reply.

Hetty wasn't so sure. She'd heard that Dan had been caught stealing coal from the pit at the edge of town. But when he'd presented their mum with a barrowload of coal, telling her he'd been given it in exchange for work with a rag-and-bone man, Hilda was overjoyed.

'Such a lovely lad, so kind,' was all she'd said, while Hetty had rolled her eyes.

No, she couldn't face going home yet.

She left the station and headed into town. But with each step she took, her legs felt heavy, and she had to force herself forward. She didn't notice what was going on around her. She didn't feel the August sun on her face or hear the birds in the trees. She was lost in thoughts about Bob and fears about the war. As she neared the town centre, she didn't pay much attention to the busy stalls and noisy traders in the market square. She didn't even notice three girls from Jack's toffee factory, walking towards her in their khaki and red overalls.

'Watch out!' one of them called as Hetty bumped into her.

Hetty spun around to apologise, but the girls had moved on, laughing and chatting, taking up the width of the pavement as they walked arm in arm. She watched them go. They looked around the same age as her, but they seemed so grown up, full of life and swagger. She felt a million miles away from them. All she could think of was her life without Bob.

She reached the Lambton Arms pub and sank onto a stone wall. The pub was large; a three-storey building wrapped around the corner of Front Street. The top two floors were the living accommodation for pub landlord Jim Ireland, his wife, Cathy, and their three young boys. Her legs began to shake as the shock of Bob's departure really hit her, and she decided to sit for a while.

'Hetty Lawson! I want a word with you!'

Hetty didn't need to turn around to know who was calling. Her body tensed and she took a deep breath. The last thing she needed was a run-in with Jim Ireland, but it looked like she had no choice. She stood, pushed a lock of hair behind her ears, wiped her hands across her eyes and braced herself.

Jim was a small, stocky man with a round belly from too much beer. When he walked, he rocked from side to side. He was completely bald and his round face was pink. He wore a pair of black trousers, a white shirt with the sleeves rolled up to his elbows and a black waistcoat on top. He wobbled his way towards her.

'Where's this week's money?' he demanded.

She saw a flash of anger in his eyes. The danger of the situation forced Bob from her mind.

'Mum hasn't paid you?' she said, shocked.

'Would I be here in the middle of Front Street asking you about it if she had?'

'Mum's not well,' Hetty said, thinking quickly. Her heart began to hammer. How she hated using her mum's illness as an excuse. 'She's not been out of the house, as she's in a bad way.'

Jim glared at her. 'Bring me my money tonight.'

'I can't promise—' Hetty began, but he held up his hand.

'I want the money I'm owed. The money your good-for-nothing father racked up in debts in my pub before he drank himself to death.'

'But Jim—' Hetty tried again.

'Just bring the money, lass. And if you're late paying me again, it won't be me you'll have to deal with next time. I'll pass on the debt to my brother Frankie, and believe me, you don't want to mess with him. I've been patient with your mum since your dad died, but let's be clear about this: I want what I'm owed.'

Hetty knew all about Jim's brother Frankie. Most of the folk who lived in Chester-le-Street were aware of his fierce reputation as a drinker and a fighter. She knew that if Jim was threatening to escalate her dad's debt, she had no choice but to find the money – and quick.

'I'll sort it out with Mum,' she said, edging away.

'Aye, see that you do,' Jim replied.

Hetty was confused. Why hadn't her mum paid this week's instalment? What had she done with the money?

'Please, miss. Your dog.'

She didn't turn to acknowledge the man behind her. She didn't have a dog, so he couldn't be speaking to her. But then she felt a tap on her shoulder, and spun around to find herself looking into a pair of piercing blue eyes. His face was smooth, his hair brown. He was slim, and wore a smart black suit with an unusually wide collar. She'd never seen any of the local boys wearing such a fancy suit.

'Your dog,' he said again, offering her a piece of string. On the end of the string was the small black dog that had followed her from the station. It was sitting patiently on the pavement, its head cocked to one side.

There was an accent to the man's voice that Hetty knew meant he wasn't from Chester-le-Street. In fact, he didn't even sound English, and she wondered if he was one of the Belgians who worked at the munitions factories in the nearby town of Birtley. Her mum had warned her to stay away from the Belgians. She said they were trouble, but this man looked harmless and gentle.

'It's not mine,' she heard herself say, but he had already passed the string to her and she was too polite to refuse. Now she was holding it in her hand. 'It's not mine,' she said again, but the man was walking away.

She looked down at the dog. 'What am I to do with you?'

Chapter Three

Hetty glanced around desperately, hoping someone would claim the dog. She searched people's faces, but no one seemed interested. Women with shopping baskets strode past on their way to the market. Soldiers in uniform scurried up Front Street towards the railway station, more recruits on their way to war. No one was looking for a dog. She shielded her eyes from the sun and looked for the man with the strange accent, but he was nowhere to be seen.

She looked again at the little black dog. Its hair was short and its ears erect. It had a tiny pink nose and beady black eyes. She spotted a lamp post and thought about tying the string there. Maybe someone would walk by and rescue it. Maybe the owner would come looking for it. But in her heart, she knew she could never leave a dumb animal to fend for itself. What if it escaped and ran into the road, to be trampled under horses' hooves or the wheels of the Co-op van? She shook her head and sighed.

'Come on, I'll take you home.'

The dog looked up.

'Oh, don't look at me like that,' she chided. 'I'm not saying I'm going to keep you. You can stay until I find out who you belong to. Do you hear me?'

The animal whined in reply. Hetty tugged the string, then set off towards the riverside. As she walked, she thought of Bob and wondered where his train would be now. She had to be brave, like so many other women. If they could get through this without a man by their side, then so could she.

The dog trotted obediently at her side. She tried to figure out what she'd need to say to her mum when she returned home with it. She knew Hilda wouldn't be pleased; she'd complain it was another mouth to feed with money they didn't have. She'd call it a filthy animal and make it live in the yard – that was if she even agreed to keep it.

Hetty thought again about Jim Ireland's words about this week's instalment of her dad's debt. What had her mum done with it? Hetty worked hard each week to get the money together. She worked as a skivvy, cleaning for the town's doctor, sluicing out the waiting room and keeping his accommodation clean. It was hard, tiring work, as the doctor's house was big, over three storeys high.

Hetty's dad had died months ago. Since then, she and her mum had made a pact to pay back all their dad owed, after Jim had threatened them. Hetty decided she would speak to Hilda about the missing money the minute she walked through the door.

When she rounded the corner into Elm Street, she crouched down and ran her hands over the dog's small head.

'Now, listen to me, dog. I'm taking you in out of pity because you've been abandoned, like me. My Bob's gone to war and you've been left on the streets. I reckon we might help each other cope. But I need you to be quiet and well behaved or my mum might turn against you. She's a tricky woman. When you meet her, you'll understand. Don't say I didn't warn you, all right?'

She walked on and stopped in front of a battered wooden door. Squaring her shoulders, she pushed her feet forward in her boots. She was ready for whatever Hilda said about the dog, because she had plenty to say in return. Her mum had some explaining to do about why Jim Ireland hadn't been paid.

'Come on, dog,' she said, as she pushed the door open and stepped into the house.

Jack's toffee factory, in the centre of Chester-le-Street, employed the largest number of women in the town. The girls who worked there were considered the lucky ones, as they were paid a decent wage. However, it wasn't easy work. It was demanding and repetitive, and they had to be quick and efficient to ensure that production never stopped. In the picking room, individual toffees were picked from the slab once cut. Then every single toffee had to be precisely wrapped to display the Jack's name in blue letters, and each wrapper had to be straight and exact. This was something new girl Elsie Cooper struggled with.

With her dark hair, dark eyes and olive skin, Elsie's looks brought her a lot of attention. She'd already caught the eye of one of the men in the sugar boiling room when she'd gone on a tour of the factory with Mrs Perkins, the supervisor. She'd liked the look of the man, with his strong bare arms, and they'd exchanged a smile as she'd followed Mrs Perkins through the room.

Elsie was eighteen years old and already bored in her new job. She also hated the overall she was forced to wear. It was an unflattering khaki, with red stripes around the collar. The stripes also ran around each cuff and down the seam in the middle of the overall. Here, big round buttons closed the garment over Elsie's ample chest and hips. At the end of her first day, she'd stuffed her overall in her bag and taken it home. That night, she'd fetched her aunt's sewing basket and, with a few stitches in a cotton the closest colour she could find to the detested khaki, brought the waist in an inch on each side. Then she'd examined the hem, daring herself to take it up enough to display her shapely calves. In the end, though, she didn't think her skills as a seamstress were up to the job, so she'd left that as it was. She knew Mrs Perkins would have something to say if she discovered she'd shortened her overall. Still, pulling the horrid thing in at the waist gave it some shape at least. That ought to put a wiggle in her step next time she found herself walking through the sugar boilers' room. And she'd already made her mind up that there *would* be a next time. It'd been a couple of weeks since she'd been out with a fella. Going out with men was her only pleasure in life; the only thing that took her out of the cramped flat above a dress shop where she lived with her aunt Jean.

Elsie had quickly grown impatient with the tiny pieces of waxed paper. No matter how many times she twisted them, she couldn't get the Jack's logo straight. She knew Mrs Perkins was watching. When she saw the swish of the supervisor's blue skirt from the corner of her eye, she felt her shoulders tense. Then she felt Mrs Perkins standing at her side. She gulped. Mrs Perkins was middle-aged, a spinster, older than any of the girls in the wrapping room. She wore her long brown hair plaited down her back, and her face was always set stern. Elsie heard whispers from the other girls that it wasn't a good idea to get on the wrong side of her. If Mrs Perkins thought any of them were slacking, she'd go straight to the top, to Mr Jack himself, to complain. Elsie was terrified that the supervisor would find fault with her work and sack her. But no matter how hard she tried to perfectly wrap the toffees, as Mrs Perkins had trained her, the paper wouldn't stay straight.

'Having trouble, Elsie?' Mrs Perkins asked.

'No, Mrs Perkins,' Elsie replied quickly.

Mrs Perkins scooped up a handful of the toffees that Elsie had wrapped. She held her palm out, forcing Elsie to examine her failed handiwork.

'None of these are straight, girl.'

'Sorry, Mrs Perkins.'

Elsie glanced around and saw some of the girls listening to the exchange.

'I'll keep trying, Mrs Perkins,' she said quickly.

'No, girl, you won't,' Mrs Perkins said.

Elsie looked at her. What did she mean? Was she going to be sacked?

'You'll go and take a short break. Walk outside in the garden for a few minutes. Get some fresh air, then come back and try again.'

Relief rushed through her. She couldn't believe what she was hearing.

'You're not sacking me?'

Mrs Perkins dropped the toffees. 'Not this time. But carry on with this dreadful wrapping and I'll have no choice but to take the matter to Mr Jack. You're a quick worker, Elsie Cooper. Your nimble fingers could do well. But you must be precise. I can't send these toffees to packing in this state. They'll have to go in the bin.'

Elsie was shocked to hear the toffees would be destroyed because of her mistake.

'The bin? Surely you won't waste them?'

'Mr Jack only allows the best of the best to be sold. Never forget that his name is on each wrapper. Now, go and take a break before I change my mind. When you return, I'll instruct you again in the correct way to wrap. I'm giving you another chance. Make the most of it.'

'Yes, Mrs Perkins.'

The supervisor drifted away, leaving Elsie stunned. She abandoned the pile of toffees on the table and walked to the door. As she left the room, she felt all eyes on her. She heard girls whispering about her, and her face grew hot with embarrassment. They'd be judging her, she knew, gossiping about the girl who couldn't wrap toffees, wondering how long she'd last.

She left the factory and headed to the garden. It was a new addition, she'd been told. And while there was no doubt it was beautiful, with rows of pink and white roses neatly tended in beds, it was also an oddity. No other employer in the small market town provided a garden. But then no other employer was as unusual as William Jack. He was a wealthy man from a respected family who lived in the leafy village of Lumley nearby. Mr Jack, however, lived alone at the Deanery, a large house within walking distance of his beloved factory.

Elsie took a seat on a bench by the roses, breathing in their sweet perfume. She realised how lucky she was. Some of her friends were working as domestics, little more than servants, in big houses run by tyrant house-keepers. The thought made her shiver despite the warmth of the summer day. No, that life wasn't for her. She wouldn't skivvy for anyone. She had a dream to get away from Chester-le-Street, to explore the big cities of Durham and Newcastle. She had her whole life ahead of her and she intended to have adventures once she'd saved up some money. Until then, she was stuck here with her aunt. But what would her dreams amount to if she couldn't even wrap toffees?

Lost in her thoughts, she didn't notice a figure striding towards her.

'May I join you? I've just finished my shift and was on my way home when I saw you sitting here. You're as pretty as any rose in this garden.'

Elsie looked up. She immediately recognised him; it was the man from the sugar boiling room. She smoothed her overall, stuck out her chest, patted the back of her dark hair and wiggled along the bench.

'I'm Elsie Cooper, from the wrapping room,' she said, politely offering her hand.

'And my name's Frankie Ireland,' he replied.

Chapter Four

In the terraced house on Elm Street, Hetty's mum chased the dog outside for the third time that morning.

'If I catch that mutt in here again, I'll swing for it!' she yelled. Then she turned to Hetty, who was sitting at the kitchen table darning a pair of Dan's socks. 'Don't you know it's bad luck to have a dog in the house?'

Hetty bit her tongue as her mum continued to rant. It wasn't the first time she'd heard such harsh words since she'd brought the dog home.

'You're too soft-hearted, Hetty, that's your trouble. Taking pity on stray dogs. You need to be careful, because heaven only knows what or who you'll be bringing home next. It'll be one of them Belgiums who work in the munitions factories.'

'Belgians,' Hetty said under her breath.

Hilda sank into a chair and narrowed her eyes.

'Are you correcting me, girl?'

Hetty didn't answer. She laid her darning on her lap and looked at her mum.

'When I came home with the dog . . .' she began.

'That mangy flea-ridden mutt,' Hilda grumbled.

Hetty chose to ignore the comment.

'. . . you promised you'd tell me what you've done with Jim Ireland's money. You said you felt too unwell to explain at the time. So now you're feeling better, I'd like to know where it is. I work hard to earn that money, and you know how important it is to pay off Dad's debt. Jim's threatening to pass it to his brother Frankie if we don't pay what we owe.'

She saw Hilda flinch at the mention of Frankie's name.

'Frankie beats people up, Mum, and there's no reason he wouldn't be violent with us if he's chasing money,' she warned. 'Why won't you tell me what you did with it? Have you lost it?'

Hilda leaned back in her chair and crossed her arms. She was a small woman, thin, all skin and bones. Her sunken cheeks made her look worn and ill. Despite being only middle-aged, her shoulder-length hair had already turned grey. Her body was stooped, her shoulders rounded. Hetty looked at her for a long time, taking in her sad features, her worn clothes, and her heart went out to her.

'Look, Mum, all I'm saying is that after Dad died, you and I made a pact to repay his debt. We knew it wouldn't be easy, with you unable to work.'

'It's not my fault I've got a bad chest,' Hilda said. As if to underline her point, she began to cough.

'I know,' Hetty said. 'But the little I earn cleaning for the doctor has to keep you, me and Dan going, *and* pay Jim Ireland. You know how hard things are. All I want to know is where the money's gone.'

Hilda rocked back and forth in her seat.

'Mum?'

She was silent a long time. The only sound in the room was the ticking of the clock and the crackling of coal on the fire.

'It's gone,' she said eventually.

'Where?' Hetty demanded.

'Yesterday afternoon I went to the jug in the pantry where we keep it. I'd put my coat and scarf on ready to walk to the Lambton Arms to give it all to Jim. But it had gone. Someone's stolen it. They must've broken in when I was asleep upstairs. If you'd been here, it wouldn't have happened.'

'It's not my fault!' Hetty cried. 'Don't you dare blame me.'

She thought carefully. They'd never had anything stolen before. No one had ever trespassed into their house. Why would an intruder head to the pantry, of all places? Suddenly the awful truth dawned.

'Dan took it, didn't he?'

Hilda's body stiffened. 'I won't accuse my lad of theft. But when I asked him about it, he walked out and I haven't seen him since.'

Hetty stood. 'You know he's in with a bad lot these days. I bet one of them egged him on to take it. He's always been easily led. Just wait till I get my hands on him! He's working for the rag-and-bone man today, isn't he? I'm going to find him, and when I do, he's going to wish he'd never been born. I'll turn him upside down and shake him until all the money in his pockets falls out. And then I'm going to—'

Hilda held up her hands. 'You've got a mean streak running through you, Hetty Lawson. He's your brother, give him some credit.'

Hetty laughed out loud. 'Credit? Our Dan's neither use nor ornament. We might be related through blood, but I'm ashamed to call him family when he steals from me.'

'Now, Hetty, you've no proof it was him.'

But Hetty knew in her heart that Dan must have taken the cash.

'I'm going out to find him and get the money back.'

Hilda was silent for a few moments. When she finally spoke, her voice was quiet and small.

'He's working for Tyler Rose. You'll find him at the yard. Be gentle with him, Hetty, and don't cause a scene. You know what a gossip Tyler's wife is. If she hears you carrying on, our private business will be all over Chester-le-Street by the end of the day.'

Hetty was fired up and felt her blood rising. 'I'll kill him when I get my hands on him.'

'Just you be careful what you say about my son,' Hilda warned. 'But if you insist on looking for him, take that stupid dog with you. See if you can get a free bone from the butcher on Front Street, because I'm not paying to feed it.'

Hetty shook her head. 'Free bones for the dog? It'll soon be us begging for bones to eat. How are we to pay Jim the money that's missing? This is serious.'

'Maybe you should get yourself a proper job and earn better money, then we wouldn't be in this predicament,' Hilda snapped.

Hetty felt the sting of her mum's words. 'What do you mean, a proper job? I've *got* a proper job. Dr Gilson's pleased with my work. Anyway, why can't Dan get a job? Why is it always me who has to bear the brunt of keeping the three of us fed and the house warm? I know you're not well and can't work, and I don't blame you, of course, but Dan's of an age where he could go down the mine. He could bring in a decent wage.'

'I'll never send my lad underground,' Hilda said firmly. Then she waved her hand dismissively. 'Pah! If you had anything about you, you'd see about getting taken on at Jack's. I hear there's plenty of jobs going there now fellas are leaving for war.'

Hetty remembered the three confident girls she'd seen walking down Front Street in their khaki and red overalls. It was certainly something to think about. She'd heard the toffee factory girls were well paid and treated right. Maybe she could call at the factory to see about putting her name down, but right now all she wanted to do was to find her good-for-nothing brother.

Anne Wright was on her way to her interview. It was a fair morning with blue skies, and the sun warmed her pale face. She strode purposefully along Front Street, trying to keep the anxiety in her stomach at bay. She felt anxious about meeting the toffee factory owner, and wondered what questions he'd ask. She had experience in typing, dictation and telephone work, she was organised and diligent; there was nothing from which she would shirk. She felt confident of her skills and experience. If there were things she didn't know, she would ask and she'd learn. But if Mr Jack's questions went beyond that, if he demanded to know if she had a fella she planned to wed, or if she had any family living locally, that was when she would lie through her teeth. Her past was her own and her personal life was private.

When she reached the factory gates, she stood to one side. Women of all shapes and sizes streamed past, making their way into work. Some linked arms, some walked alone, others rode bicycles. Some women wore headscarves and jackets, but all of them had one thing in common: their overall of khaki and red. Anne already knew the factory worked around the clock, it was open all hours and production never stopped. The amount of people coming and going made her head spin. She glanced at her watch. She had ten minutes to spare before she was due to report to reception and ask for Mr Jack. She took a small mirror from her handbag and checked her reflection.

'Are you new here too, love?' a woman asked.

Anne lowered her mirror and peered through her glasses at an attractive dark-haired, olive-skinned girl. She was wearing heavy make-up and her lips were painted scarlet. The top button on her overall was open, exposing more flesh than Anne supposed it should. She noticed that none of the other girls had their overalls unbuttoned. She averted her eyes, thinking how that amount of flesh made the girl look common. She didn't reply, though, so the girl began to talk.

'I just started working here this week. I'm still feeling my way around. It's all right once you get used to it. Hard work, mind, and the overall's not flattering, but you get used to that too. Some dishy fellas work here, them that haven't gone to war yet, so you'll do all right, a pretty girl like you. My name's Elsie Cooper. What's yours?'

Anne was surprised by the girl's forthright manner, and when she looked into her eyes, she saw kindness and vulnerability. She scolded herself for thinking badly on first meeting her. She seemed harmless enough. And she was the first friendly face she'd seen since she'd moved to Chester-le-Street.

'I'm Anne Wright. I've got an interview this morning.'

Elsie raised her eyebrows. 'You don't need an interview to work here. You just put your name down, then they start you on. They need all the girls they can get now the fellas are leaving. You can come with me if you want. I'll show you the wrapping room. We wrap the toffees by hand. Every single toffee, wrapped by hand, thousands each day. It stinks to high heaven, all butter and cream. You think it's glorious at first, you want to keep licking the air it smells so good. But you soon get used to it, just like these dreary overalls.'

She turned towards the gates, but Anne hesitated.

'Come on, love, don't be shy, I'll show you where to go. You'll be in the packing room, I guess. That's where they're taking girls on. I'll introduce you to Mrs Perkins, the supervisor. She's a right old dragon, but if you keep out of her way, she's all right.'

'I won't be working in the packing room,' Anne said.

'Then you'll be in the slab room,' Elsie said. 'I can show you where that is too.'

'Not the slab room either,' Anne explained. 'I'm hoping to work for Mr Jack in his office. I have to report to reception.'

Elsie gave a long, low whistle. 'Mr Jack's office, eh? Well, I am impressed. I know where reception is, so I can take you there if you'd like,' she offered.

'That'd be nice, thank you,' Anne replied.

Elsie took her arm, and together they walked through the iron gates into the factory grounds.

* * *

Hetty was walking past the toffee factory with the little black dog. She thought about what her mum had told her that morning, about the factory taking women on. Those two girls walking through the gates looked about her age, she thought. Could she be a toffee factory girl too? If it paid more than cleaning for Dr Gilson, it'd be worth finding out. She decided to go in and make enquiries, just as soon as she'd dealt with Dan.

Chapter Five

To reach Tyler Rose's junkyard, Hetty had to walk through the railway station and cross the bridge over the tracks. Her heart felt like lead as memories of saying farewell to Bob rushed at her. Where would he be now? she wondered. In London yet? Already overseas? She balled her hands into fists as she neared the railway and forced herself not to cry. But as soon as she stepped onto the platform, the agony of him leaving without even a kiss threatened to overwhelm her. She forced her tears back and climbed the steps onto the bridge.

Tyler's yard was ahead. She saw smoke rising from a fire; he was always burning something. The soot and smoke stung her eyes. She'd thought she'd have to ask Tyler for Dan's whereabouts, but finding her brother was easier than expected, for she saw him tending the fire. He started when he saw her, looked around as if to run, but there was nowhere for him to go apart from the train lines. Hetty knew she had him cornered. If he had nothing to hide, no reason to fear being found, then why was he looking so shifty?

Dan was fourteen years old, a slight lad, wiry and

skinny like their mum. He had a mop of brown hair with a long fringe that he always pushed to one side. Freckles dotted his nose and cheeks. Hetty tied the dog to a fence, then walked through a wall of smoke. Her brother looked up, and this time when he saw her, he lifted his chin to acknowledge her, no longer startled and ready to run. It was the first time she had been to Tyler's junkyard. She knew Dan would be shocked that she'd turned up. He must surely have guessed why she was there and so she got straight to the point.

'Where's the money?'

He didn't flinch. 'It's gone.'

She felt like she'd been punched. A part of her had hoped she was wrong about him. Now, hearing the words from his own mouth, knowing that her brother was a thief, turned her stomach. Her mouth went dry and she had to force the next word out.

'Where?'

Dan nodded at the ramshackle building at the end of the yard. Hetty was shocked.

'You gave my money to Tyler?'

'I had no choice. I work for him now but I had to pay him before he took me on. It's an investment. The money will buy a new horse.'

She felt anger rising in her chest. 'You idiot!' she screamed. 'You know that money was to pay Dad's debt. Jim Ireland has threatened to turn Frankie on us if we don't catch up with the payment.'

This time she saw a flicker of fear in Dan's eyes.

'So you know about Frankie's reputation. None of us will be able to sleep easy now. He'll come into our house and take what he wants. And it's all your fault.

I can't believe you've done this. We're in real trouble.'

Dan's eyes darted around. 'I didn't think, Hetty. I just wanted a job with Tyler.'

'Tyler's taken advantage of you and should be ashamed. I'm going to have it out with him.'

Hetty was about to storm across the yard when Dan pulled her arm.

'Get off me, you idiot,' she cried.

'No, Hetty. Don't,' he implored.

She stood still and he dropped his hand.

'Sorry. I didn't mean to grab you. But I'm begging you, please don't talk to Tyler.'

He beckoned her away from the fire. Under cover of a tree beside the railway lines, he crouched down and scrabbled at the soil. Hetty's eyes opened in amazement when he pulled out a small bag and thrust it at her.

'I kept some for myself. There's about half of it left. Take it, our Hetty.'

She took the filthy bag and began to open it, but Dan stopped her.

'Don't do it here. If Tyler finds out I've kept money from him, he'll be furious. He can't know about this, it's our secret.'

Hetty looked at her brother, then shook her head. 'I'm disappointed in you, thieving from me like this. You and I used to be close, before Dad died.'

Dan hung his head. 'I'm sorry. It's just . . . these new friends I've got, they all have money, see, and I wanted some too. I wanted to be like them, to fit in.'

'So you stole from your family?' she spat. 'Do your friends steal from their families too?'

31

He bit his lip. 'I'll pay you back. I promise. I'm going to join the Durham Light Infantry, like Bob did. I'm going to fight in the war. I'll send my wages home.'

'Don't be stupid, you know you can't enlist until you're nineteen.'

He puffed out his chest. 'I can. Some of the lads say that if you're keen, you can join at fourteen. The army's desperate for troops and some recruiting sergeants turn a blind eye if you look fit enough.'

Hetty's shoulders dropped. 'Stop right now with your daft notions. You're not going to war. You're too young and that's that.'

Dan glanced over to the yard. 'I've got to get back to work. Tyler will wonder where I've gone. Take the money. I'm sorry. I swear I'll never do it again.'

Hetty put her hand on his bony shoulder. 'Do anything like this again and I'll swing for you. You might have Mum on your side; she thinks the sun shines out of your backside. But if you take as much as a sixpence from me from now on, I'll drip poison into her ear about throwing you out on the streets. I'm not living with a thief. It's a good job Dad's not here to see this.'

Dan's eyes filled with tears and he wiped the back of his hand across his face. 'I've got to go,' he said, and he walked back to tend the fire.

Hetty brushed dirt and soil from the bag of money. She decided to take it straight to Jim Ireland with an apology for it being late and a promise that she'd make up the missing amount. She sighed, stuffed the bag in her pocket and walked to the fence to collect the dog.

* * *

Anne sat in the factory reception with her back straight, knees together and feet flat on the floor. There was a large desk in front of her at which a man with slicked-back hair worked on a ledger. He'd greeted her coolly when she'd walked in and hadn't cracked a smile. She hadn't found this reassuring. Being as nervous as she was, she'd hoped for a warm greeting to help put her at ease. He had ticked her name off on a list on his desk. She'd glanced at the list and noted four more names after hers. It appeared she was the first appointment. She knew she'd be up against stiff competition for such a prestigious job. It was vital she made a good impression.

She held her handbag in her lap and gazed around. The room was an open square with a high ceiling, panelled with dark wood. Despite the warmth of the summer day, it felt chilly, and goosebumps appeared on her arms. Framed certificates were displayed on a table, awards proclaiming Jack's toffee to be the best in the country. On the wall were some of Jack's famous coloured advertisements in frames. These showed pictures of toffee tins decorated with flowers and trees; scenes of nature and wildlife for which Jack's toffee was famous. Each tin had the Jack's logo in blue in the centre and each advertisement included the same logo too. Anne admired the pictures and tins. They appealed to her a great deal with their bright colours and cheerful images. She wondered if there was a department at the factory where such things were designed. Was there an art department? She sat up straight. If she was lucky today, if she impressed Mr Jack, she might find out.

She steeled herself as a big clock on the wall ticked the minutes away. Then she heard a knock at the window behind her. The noise startled her and upset her composure. The man at the desk looked up, tutted loudly and shook his head.

'Bloody factory girls,' he muttered, before returning to his work.

Anne ignored the intrusion, but the knock came again. This time she slowly turned and saw Elsie Cooper, the woman who'd helped her earlier. Elsie beamed a bright smile, then stuck both thumbs up in the air.

'Good luck with your interview!' she yelled through the window.

'Thank you!' Anne called back.

'Miss Wright?'

She spun around, embarrassed at being caught. A portly gentleman with a curled moustache was standing by an open door. He was wearing a grey pinstriped suit with a waistcoat, and a tie in the same vivid blue as the lettering on the advertisements. He was holding a pocket watch in his hand. Anne stood up.

'Yes?'

'Come with me, please. Mr Jack and the interview panel are waiting in the boardroom.'

Anne stepped forward, then turned again to the window. She was pleased to see Elsie still there, still holding up her thumbs. She smiled back, then followed the portly man from the room.

Chapter Six

Anne stepped gingerly into the boardroom. Ahead of her, three men wearing dark suits and blue ties sat behind a long wooden table. On the other side of the table was an empty chair, which she guessed was for her. She paused behind the portly gentleman who'd escorted her from reception. She would only have one stab at this, only one opportunity to impress.

'Gentlemen, this is Miss Anne Wright, your first appointment,' he said, then he backed out and closed the door.

Anne stood rigid, not knowing if she should walk to the empty chair or wait to be called forward. She was so nervous she could almost hear her heart thumping under her blouse. In the absence of any orders, she decided to take the plunge, and set off across the luxuriously soft carpeted floor. She could feel all eyes on her with each step she took. She kept her chin raised. When she reached the chair, instead of sitting down, she looked across the table and smiled at each man in turn. Then she greeted them with a cheery 'Good morning.'

She turned to the younger man sitting in the middle. His chair had a higher back than the others, making him look like a king with his courtiers on either side. She recognised his round, cheerful face, bald head, neat black moustache and trademark bow tie from pictures in the many newspaper profiles she'd read about him in preparation for her interview. However, it was the first time she'd ever seen the colour of his tie, and it was no surprise to her that it was the blue of the factory logo. This attention to detail pleased her. He looked younger, more vibrant than his photograph. She held out her hand to him.

'Mr Jack, I'm Anne Wright. It's a pleasure to meet you, sir.'

Mr Jack seemed surprised by the gesture. He stood, leaning across the table, and shook her hand warmly.

'Good morning, Miss Wright. It's a pleasure to meet you too.' He turned to the elderly man on his right. 'Gerard, stand up and shake the woman's hand.'

The older man slowly rose from his chair, holding on to the table for support. When Anne took his hand, she noted that his skin was ice cold and papery. He had a long, thin face and bushy eyebrows, and wisps of his white hair stuck out at odd angles. She wondered if he lived alone, for if he had a wife at home, surely she wouldn't have let him leave the house in such a state. There was a glint in his eye, however, that suggested that while his body might be failing, his mind was still sharp. He sank back in his chair with a sigh, as if the exertion of standing was too much.

The man on Mr Jack's left was already waiting eagerly with his hand out, ready to shake Anne's. However, his face was set firm with no trace of a smile.

'I'm James Burl, sales manager,' he said briskly. Anne

caught the local accent in his voice. 'And Mr Gerard is our creative manager. He oversees the art and design of our packaging. In short, he's a creative genius.'

Anne couldn't fail to notice that James Burl was a good-looking man with fine features and a firm jaw. He was tall and well built, with clipped brown hair and a strong handshake. When he let go of her hand, her fingers tingled from the pressure he'd applied. However, there was a coldness about him that unsettled her.

'Please take a seat, Miss Wright,' Mr Jack said.

Anne sat straight in her chair, knees together. She set her handbag at her feet. She was ready. This was it. Their questions began and she handled each one with ease. Yes, she had office experience and had worked at management level before. Yes, she'd even worked in a toffee factory, at the Mayfair factory in Sunderland. She'd left her position there when she moved to Chester-le-Street. Yes, she agreed, Chester-le-Street *was* a wonderful market town with a beautiful river walk. However, she kept quiet about the real reason she'd moved there from Sunderland. She felt things were going well.

While Mr Jack and Mr Burl continued to ask questions, Mr Gerard remained silent. Anne kept glancing at him, concerned when his eyes closed. Mr Jack caught her gaze, turned to the elderly man and shook him by the arm.

'Gerard, wake up. This woman's damn fine. She's got a good head on her shoulders. It'll take a lot to beat her today. Makes me wonder if we should even bother to see the rest of the girls who are coming for interview.'

Anne felt flattered, but also affronted that Mr Jack was talking about her as if she wasn't there.

'Sir, of course we should see the others, it's all been arranged,' Mr Burl urged.

Mr Jack shrugged. 'Perhaps.' Then he stared straight at Anne.

'You come highly recommended from Mayfair Toffee of Sunderland,' he said. He held a sheet of paper aloft and Anne recognised the Mayfair logo. 'I know Mr Tompkins, the owner, and he speaks highly of you in his reference letter. Although he does say you left suddenly without working your notice period. I wonder where you have worked since?'

'I left due to my father's illness, which came quickly,' she said, swerving the truth.

Mr Gerard's eyes fluttered open. 'It's most commendable of you to look after your parents,' he said, then closed his eyes again. Anne carried on.

'The reason I have been out of work for more than a year since leaving Mayfair is that I was nursing my mother after my father's death. She succumbed to the Spanish flu.'

It was another lie, of course. However, if the men in front of her knew that she'd left her job at Mayfair and her rented room in Sunderland when she'd found out she was pregnant, they'd turf her out that instant. She gripped her hands together. Her reply seemed to satisfy Mr Jack. However, she could feel Mr Burl's eyes on her and saw him scratch a pen across paper, making notes. Mr Gerard was now fully asleep, his head resting on his hand propped on the desk.

Mr Jack laid down the letter from her previous employer. 'Everything seems most satisfactory, Miss Wright. But I have one more thing to ask.'

Anne forced a smile while her heart thumped. She hoped she wouldn't need to lie again. 'Yes?'

He stood, then walked out from behind the table. When he reached her, he beckoned with a curled finger.

'Come with me, Miss Wright.'

She looked at Mr Burl, wondering if he might explain what was happening. He simply indicated that she should follow Mr Jack. She stood, smoothed her skirt, picked up her handbag and excused herself from the room. She had no clue what was happening.

Mr Jack led the way along a corridor with dark panelled walls and into the room next door.

'This is my office, Miss Wright,' he said as he entered, holding the door open for her.

Anne stepped inside and gasped. The walls were covered with bright advertisements for Jack's toffee, all framed. Shelves held tins in all colours, and on Mr Jack's desk were folders and stacks of paper. But what shocked her the most was how messy the office was. Mr Jack stepped over documents and files piled up on the floor. Anne followed, picking her way across the carpet, trying not to stand on paperwork. The whole office looked as chaotic as Tyler Rose's junkyard that she'd walked past when she'd first arrived in Chester-le-Street.

Midway along one wall was a door, and Mr Jack pushed it open. 'This will be your office, right next to mine. The interconnecting door is a genius notion, if I say so myself. My own idea, of course. Burl tried to dissuade me. He reckons my secretary should work in the typing pool, not in a room of her own. But you'll hear confidential information within these walls, Miss Wright, and I need you close.'

Anne stepped into the small office, her heart skipping a happy beat at the mention of it being hers. Did that mean she'd got the job? What about the girls whose names she'd seen on the list in reception? Didn't Mr Jack have an obligation to interview them? She didn't dare ask.

She looked around the room, which was bare except for a desk and a chair. On the desk was a large typewriter. It looked brand new, without a scratch on it, and much more complicated than any she'd used before. Mr Jack waved his hand as if for her to admire it. She felt a rush of nerves. It was a monster of a machine, far bigger than the one she'd used at Mayfair. She recognised most of the buttons, but it had additional ones that she'd never seen before. In her year away from work, typewriting machines had changed and improved, and she had a lot to learn.

'My question is this, Miss Wright. Can you use this new-fangled machine we took delivery of this week? It's top of the range, of course. Only the best will do for my secretary. Think you'll be able to cope?'

'I'm sure I will, sir,' she said confidently. She wasn't going to let a few buttons defeat her.

'Very good,' he replied.

Her attention was caught by the view from the window. Outside was a pretty rose garden. She felt embarrassed when Mr Jack caught her looking.

'A splendid view, Miss Wright, and one I trust you will appreciate when you start working for me.'

Anne was shocked. Had she really heard him right?

'Me, sir?'

'Yes, you, Miss Wright. I want you for my secretary. You've got what it takes. You impressed me right from the start. It was my little test, you see. We wanted to see how you would respond, walking into the room, dealing with the factory's top brass. If you'd turned and run, you would have failed. But you didn't, Miss Wright. You walked straight to the table and shook our hands. You've already won. I want you to work for me and you'll find that I always get what I want. I'm determined and dedicated. Some may say I'm ruthless, reckless, a rebel. But all those ingredients, along with the best cream and top-quality sugar, go to make Jack's toffees the best in the land.'

Anne was overjoyed by the news that she'd been appointed. However, the speed at which her fate had been decided left her flustered.

'But sir, what about the other girls who are coming for interview today?'

Mr Jack clasped his hands behind his back and stared out of the window.

'Ah yes, the other girls,' he said, as if deciding what to do. Then he turned back to Anne. 'I assume you are able to start work today?'

'Well, yes, sir, of course.' She hadn't the money to do anything else other than walk by the river or read a book in her room in Mrs Fortune's house.

'In that case, your first task will be to greet each applicant when they arrive,' he said decisively. 'You'll break the news to them that the post has now been filled.'

Anne breathed in sharply. 'But sir, that's dreadful news to give. The girls will be in their best clothes, they'll have prepared and will be nervous. Their families will be waiting with bated breath at home to find out what happened. I can't give them such bad news then simply send them on their way. They won't think it fair.'

Mr Jack tapped his chin. 'Then what do you suggest?'

She rocked back on her heels. He really was as eccentric as Mrs Fortune had warned. The owner of a toffee factory was asking her opinion! How odd it all was. She had to think quickly, worried that he might change his mind and take back the job offer.

'I think you should . . . Well, I think it'd be good to . . .'

'Spit it out, girl. Time is money.'

She set her handbag on the desk, claiming the space as her own. She thought for a moment, an idea forming. Then she sat in the chair, looked Mr Jack in the eyes and delivered her decision.

'I'll break the news to the girls, sir. It won't be easy. I'll be gentle, yet firm. However, I can't send them away empty-handed. I insist on giving each of them something in exchange. How about the largest box of the best toffee you sell, decorated with a blue ribbon?'

Mr Jack nodded. 'Very well. Organise it. You strike me as a resourceful girl, Miss Wright. Or may I call you Anne?'

Anne opened her mouth to say that that was perfectly fine. But he had already made his decision before she could say a word.

'Well, Anne, I'll leave you to make the arrangements. Find Mr Burl in his office and tell him what you want.'

Then he stepped towards her and stuck out his hand.

'Welcome to my toffee factory.'

Chapter Seven

At the back of the Lambton Arms, Hetty rapped hard at the door. She doubted Jim Ireland would be awake. However, she was determined to pay him the little money she had. There was no answer, so she knocked again, but still no one came. She picked up a stone and flung it at an upstairs window, grimacing in case it broke the glass. But she'd aimed her shot right, not too powerful, and it glanced off safely. A few moments later, the sash window lifted and Jim's grizzled, bleary face looked out.

'Oh, it's you. What do you want?'

Hetty shielded her eyes and looked up. 'I've got your money.'

The window slammed shut. A few moments later, the door in front of her opened. Jim was wearing nothing but an old vest that came down to his knees. It might have been white once but was now badly stained. His hairy legs were bare, and Hetty looked away. She'd never seen a man's legs before, not even Bob's. She held out the small, dirty bag of money. Jim snatched it from her and peered inside.

'Where's the rest?'

'I'll bring it as soon as I can.'

He yawned. 'You're lucky you've caught me half asleep and not up to a fight. I want the rest of the money soon, and remember, this week's instalment is due in a few days.' He stepped back inside and shut the door.

How could she forget? She gathered herself and pushed her shoulders back. She felt determined to repay her dad's debt, no matter what. Her mum couldn't do it, as she couldn't work. Dan was a shirker who'd now proved himself a thief. No matter how sorry he'd said he was for taking the cash, the fact was he'd done it and might do so again. She couldn't trust him now; she could only trust herself. There was only one thing left to do. She had to find herself a better-paid job. She would head to Jack's factory to ask if it was true they were taking girls on.

She walked along Front Street, then up the narrow alley of Market Lane to the factory. As she tied the dog to the gates, a thought ran through her mind that she should have given it a name by now. However, that would have to wait; she had more important things on her mind.

Smoke was billowing from the factory chimneys. The buildings were single storey, laid out in long lines. Beyond was the railway, with sidings coming into the factory grounds. Hetty had heard this was where ingredients were delivered by train: butter, sugar and cream, and chocolate for enrobing the toffees. She'd also heard a rumour that the chocolate was delivered all the way from Yorkshire, as Mr Jack insisted on using the very best. The sidings were also where boxes were packed and loaded onto trains for delivery around the country. Hetty had even heard that toffees were sent overseas.

She marched through the iron gates with no clue where to go. The place seemed deserted; everyone must be indoors, she thought. She walked past brick buildings and across cobbled ground. Finally she saw a sign marked *Reception*, with an arrow pointing to the right. She pushed her hair behind her ears, then knocked loudly on the door.

'Come in,' a man's voice called.

She entered a large square room with a high ceiling. Four wooden chairs were lined up against a wall. A dark-haired man worked at a desk. He looked up from a ledger when she entered.

'Yes?' he barked.

It was hardly the friendly greeting she'd expected. At least Dr Gilson was kind. She wondered if she was doing the right thing thinking about changing jobs if the people at the factory were all as unpleasant as the man at the desk.

'I've come about a job,' she said.

The man lifted a bony finger and pointed at a chair. 'Sit and wait. You'll be called.'

Hetty was surprised. This wasn't what she'd expected. She sat and looked around the grand room. There was carpet underfoot, real carpet, soft and deep. The walls were panelled in toffee-coloured wood. She listened to the man scratching at his ledger and heard the clock in the room as it ticked. She looked at her hands; they were mucky from the soil from the bag of money. She wiped her palms on her skirt.

Just then, a door in the corner of the room opened and two women appeared. One of them was tall and thin. She looked severe, dressed in black. The other was fair, about the same age as Hetty. She wore small round wire-framed spectacles and her hair was neatly styled in a bun. She was dressed in a beautiful cream blouse with a lace collar, and Hetty wondered how much it had cost. The woman in black carried a large box under her arm; it had the Jack's logo on it in blue and was wrapped in blue ribbon. The girl in the pretty blouse escorted her to the door and wished her well for her future. Then she turned and walked towards Hetty. Hetty saw her gaze flicker to her dirty skirt before she looked up and smiled.

'Would you like to follow me?' she asked.

Hetty stood, wiped her hands on her skirt again and did as the woman instructed. She followed her along a narrow corridor, also lined with plush carpet. She had never seen anything like it. They walked past a lot of closed doors until the woman paused and held her arm out, indicating that Hetty should enter a room.

'Excuse the mess in here,' she said.

Hetty followed her through an office with papers and files on the floor and into a smaller room in which there was only a desk, chair and typewriter.

'My name is Anne Wright. Please take a seat, Miss Brabin.'

Hetty was about to sit down, ready to give her particulars, but now she paused and looked at Anne.

'I'm not Miss Brabin.'

Anne glanced down at a piece of paper on her desk. 'You must be. You're here for your interview.'

Hetty was puzzled. 'No, I'm not. I'm Hetty Lawson.'

Anne checked the paper again. 'Well, this is most odd. I'm afraid you're not on my list.'

'What list?' Hetty said. 'My mum said that Jack's is taking girls on now that fellas are leaving for war. That's why I'm here, to put my name down for a job. I want to work here, Miss Wright, but I don't have an interview planned.'

Anne took her glasses off, peered at the list, then put the glasses back on. 'I think there's been a mix-up,' she said. 'I'm very sorry for wasting your time.'

Hetty's heart dropped. 'So I can't put my name down to work here?'

'Of course, you can. I'll take you to see Mrs Perkins, the supervisor in the wrapping room, and she'll speak to you. I apologise again. When I saw you in reception, I thought you were waiting for an interview for the role of Mr Jack's secretary.'

Hetty's eyes opened wide. 'Me? I wouldn't know the first thing about that. I don't have an education.'

'Do you work already?' Anne asked.

'I do cleaning for Dr Gilson. He's a nice man, but I need more money. It's my mum, you see. She's not well and I have to look after her and my brother. Money's tight at home. And now we've ended up with a dog that won't leave me alone and I need to feed it, and Dr Gilson doesn't pay much, and my boyfriend Bob's left for war and . . . Oh.' Hetty clamped her hand across her mouth, embarrassed. 'I'm sorry. You don't need to hear my woes. I'm sure you're a busy lady. Just point me in the direction of this Mrs Perkins you mentioned and I'll get out of your hair.'

Anne smiled kindly. 'Let me take you to her.'

Hetty was relieved that she wasn't about to be chastised for her outburst. She'd had no one to talk to about Bob leaving, and her words had left her lips before she knew what she was saying. She composed herself and followed Anne from her office, through the disorganised larger one and back to reception.

'Jacob, I'll be back in ten minutes. I'm taking Miss Lawson to see Mrs Perkins,' Anne told the man at the desk. Hetty noticed that he didn't look up.

'Does he ever smile?' she asked once they were outside.

Anne laughed out loud. 'It's my mission to make sure he does. We can't have visitors to Jack's being greeted with such a miserable first impression.'

'Have you worked for Mr Jack long?' Hetty asked.

Anne looked at her. 'I started this morning.'

Hetty was taken aback. She'd assumed she had worked there much longer, for she seemed self-assured and in control.

'Now, where the devil is the wrapping room?' Anne said, looking around.

It was then that Hetty realised the young woman wasn't as confident as she'd first thought.

'We'll find it together,' she said.

Elsie carried a box of waxed papers to a long, wide table in the wrapping room. Next to her was Anabel. She was a pale, delicate girl whom Elsie had tried to befriend, but Anabel was shy and barely spoke. She turned up for work each morning wearing filthy clothes that stank of the tripe shop where she lived in a room at the back with her brother, Gavin. He also worked at the factory, in the packing room. On the days when Anabel stood next to her, Elsie was glad of the factory's sweet smell. The aroma of butter and cream that drifted in from the sugar boilers' room helped disguise the stench from the girl's clothes.

Elsie knew it was her own fault that she was working with Anabel today; she'd wasted ten minutes dawdling to work and had arrived late. She'd been at her station for only a couple of hours, but already her calves hurt and her feet ached. She felt a presence behind her and knew without turning who it would be. She was getting used to the way of things now.

'Good morning, Mrs Perkins,' she chirped.

Mrs Perkins looked over her shoulder. 'Good work, Elsie Cooper. Keep it up.' Then she leaned close and whispered in her ear. 'A word of caution, Elsie. Never let me catch you chatting to the sugar boilers when you should be in here. I'll dock your pay next time.'

Elsie groaned. She'd thought she and Frankie hadn't been seen. She'd have to be more careful in future, for she wasn't going to give up flirting with the best-looking fella she'd met.

'Yes, Mrs Perkins.'

The supervisor moved to the girl at Elsie's side. 'Anabel? I need a word with you about your appearance.' And she began to chastise her about her dirty clothes.

Elsie thought it unfair of the woman to embarrass Anabel in front of everyone. She walked to the girl and placed her hand gently on her shoulder.

'I'll make sure she's clean from now on, Mrs Perkins,' she said quietly. 'I have soap at home. She can bathe there if there's no facility where she lives.'

Mrs Perkins glared at her, then her nostrils flared. Elsie

held her nerve while the supervisor took a good look at her overall.

'Elsie Cooper, fasten up your top button this instant.'

Elsie dropped her hand from Anabel's shoulder and did up the button. Mrs Perkins' eyes then dropped to Elsie's waist, at the way the overall nipped in, emphasising her shapely hips. She went red in the face, then spun around and paced the floor with her hands behind her back, her skirt swishing around her legs and her long plait flying over her shoulder each time she turned. She walked to a pillar in the centre of the room, then stopped and addressed all the girls who were watching. She'd built up quite an audience by now.

'I will not have anyone in this room coming to work looking dirty or indecent!' she shouted. 'You're here to represent the highest brand of toffee in the land!'

Elsie held her head high as Mrs Perkins continued.

'I expect the girls who work in my room to be well turned out.'

She was stopped from saying more when two women entered the room. All eyes turned to look at them. Elsie recognised the taller one as Anne, whom she'd met that morning at the factory gates. She was dressed smartly in a beautiful cream blouse. The other girl, however, looked down at heel, and her skirt was covered in dirty streaks.

Anne strode confidently into the middle of the room. 'My name is Anne Wright and I'm here to see Mrs Perkins,' she announced. 'I have a new girl, Hetty Lawson, who wishes to be taken on.'

Mrs Perkins' jaw dropped and it took her a moment to

compose herself. Elsie watched with amusement as she stepped forward.

'I'm Mrs Perkins, supervisor of the wrapping room. Now, who do you think *you* are, coming in here barking your orders?'

Anne held out her hand. Mrs Perkins looked at it but made no attempt to touch it, never mind shake it. Anne dropped her hand, then straightened her back.

'I'm Mr Jack's secretary,' she said.

Elsie stifled a smile when she saw Mrs Perkins' face turn white.

Chapter Eight

Gritting her teeth, Mrs Perkins led Hetty and Anne to her desk in the corner of the room. She sat down and opened a drawer, then pulled out a cardboard folder.

'I'll leave her with you, Mrs Perkins,' Anne said, and left the room.

'Name?' the supervisor barked.

'Henrietta Hilda Lawson.'

She wrote this down.

'Address?'

'Seventy-four Elm Street, Chester-le-Street.'

'Age?'

'Seventeen.'

'Are your mother and father alive?'

'My mum is alive, but my dad is dead.'

'Can you read and write?'

'Yes.'

'Do you have nits?'

The question shocked Hetty; she thought it impertinent.

'No.'

Mrs Perkins nodded at a dark-haired girl working at a long table. 'You'll work with Miss Cooper. She's new, but a fast learner. She'll show you the ropes. Can you start immediately?'

'Yes,' Hetty said quickly, then she remembered the dog. 'I mean no.'

Mrs Perkins sighed. 'Come on, girl. Which is it?'

Hetty clasped her hands in front of her. 'I brought my dog with me, he's tied up at the gate.'

'You can't leave a dog there. What were you thinking?'

'I didn't think, Mrs Perkins. I didn't know I'd be starting straight away.'

Mrs Perkins sighed and shook her head. 'Take it home, then return quickly. Go now.'

'Thank you,' Hetty said.

She turned and walked towards Elsie.

'I've just been taken on and I'm to work with you. But I have to do something at home first. I'll be back in half an hour. Mrs Perkins said you'll show me the ropes. My name's Hetty Lawson.'

Elsie stuck her hand out. 'Elsie Cooper, pleased to meet you.' She leaned closer and whispered in Hetty's ear. 'Don't let the old dragon upset you. Her bark's worse than her bite.'

Hetty smiled, then quickly walked away. Once outside, she ran to the gates and was relieved to see the dog still there. She found herself growing fond of it and liked having it at her side as she walked. It was keeping her company while Bob was away.

'I must be getting soft, dog. I'm pleased you're still here. Come on, let's take you home.'

She ran all the way to Elm Street with the dog cantering to keep up. She planned to tell her mum the good news, then hurry back to the factory to begin her new job. She was bubbling with excitement at being taken on at Jack's. It would be big news to share with Bob, too, just as soon as she received his first letter with his address for her to reply.

She pushed the front door open and clattered into the hall.

'Mum! I've got a new job!' she yelled.

There was no reply.

'Mum!'

She opened the door into the kitchen, but what she saw there chilled her. She was so shocked, she couldn't move. At her feet, the dog growled, and Hetty gripped the string lead. Her mum was sitting by the fire, shoulders hunched. Sitting opposite was Frankie Ireland.

Frankie was a lot taller and broader than his brother. Where Jim was fat because of drinking too much, Frankie was muscled. He had receding black hair, dark eyes and a sharp, pointed nose.

Hetty's mouth went dry and she had to force her words out. 'What are you doing here?'

Frankie held up a mug and brought it to his lips. 'Me? I'm just enjoying a cup of tea with your mother.'

'Mum? Are you all right?'

Hilda nodded, then looked away. Frankie stood, his broad frame filling their small kitchen. There was a sweet, sugary smell about him that Hetty couldn't place. How odd for a man to smell that way, she thought. He set his mug on the table and looked at her.

'I came straight here from my night shift before I head home to sleep. Me and your mother have had a few words about paying your dad's debt. She knows how things stand, and now that you're here, you should know too.'

He stepped forward and ran a finger down Hetty's cheek. Her stomach turned in fear. The dog yapped and Frankie stamped his foot to scare it. The dog jumped behind Hetty but continued to growl.

'See, the thing is, it's not my brother you owe now. It's me. Jim's passed your dad's loan to me and I want it paid. You'll not find me as patient as my brother. Jim's got his pub to provide him his livelihood. All I've got is my job boiling sugar at Jack's.'

Suddenly the sweet smell made sense. However, the thought of the delicious, syrupy scent on such an evil man made Hetty feel sick. She reached a hand to the table to steady herself.

'What is it you want?' she said.

'My money, of course. And there'll be interest added. My brother's been too soft so far, but I intend to get what I'm owed, and I won't rest until the debt is paid.'

Hetty gulped. 'We paid your brother on time each week,' she said.

'Until suddenly you didn't,' Frankie sneered. 'And then you only paid him half of what was due. Well, you won't be taking any more money to Jim. From now on, it's me you'll deal with.'

'Where will we take the money?' Hetty said, trying to stop her voice quavering.

An evil grin spread across Frankie's face. 'You won't. I'll come here to collect it.'

'When?'

'When you least expect it,' he drawled. 'I might turn up tomorrow, or the day after. You'll never know for sure. See, I want to keep you on your toes. So have the money ready for whenever I arrive. I'm sure I don't need to tell you what might happen if you don't.' He aimed a kick at the dog, that leapt out of his way just in time to avoid Frankie's foot. Then Frankie turned and strode from the house.

Hetty rushed to her mum and crouched down in front of her. 'He didn't hurt you, did he?'

Hilda shook her head. 'No, lass. But I'm shaken.'

'Why did you give him a mug of tea?'

'Frankie's not the sort of man you say no to,' Hilda said sadly. 'Oh Hetty, what are we going to do?'

Hetty untied the string around the dog's neck and the animal settled at Hilda's feet.

'We'll manage, you'll see. I've got myself a job at the toffee factory.'

Hilda's eyes lit up in her sad, worn face. 'You have? Oh love, that's smashing. When do you start?'

'Right now. I needed to bring the dog home first.'

'Did you find Dan?' Hilda asked.

Hetty was careful in her reply. There was no point in upsetting her mum more than she already was. They had enough to cope with now that Frankie Ireland was on their case.

'Don't worry about Dan, I'll sort him out.'

'Don't be too harsh, he's not a bad lad,' Hilda said.

Hetty bit her tongue. She stroked the dog's head.

'Look, Mum, I've got to go. The sooner I start earning money, the sooner we can get Frankie Ireland off our backs.'

Hilda began coughing, her whole body shaking. When she settled, she looked into Hetty's eyes.

'That flaming debt of your dad's. When some fellas die, they leave their widows a pocket watch or a lifetime of happy memories. But when *your* dad died, he left a legacy we could do without.'

'We'll pay it, Mum, you'll see. I'll make Dan help. He's old enough to be responsible. It's time he grew up and started helping out. He should be bringing money in.'

'He's just a boy, leave him be,' Hilda said crossly.

Hetty suppressed the anger building inside her, as she did each time Hilda turned a blind eye to Dan's obvious faults. It'd always been that way and she knew it was unlikely to change. She'd deal with her brother in her own way. She stood and walked to the door and the dog followed.

'No, dog, you're staying here.'

The creature pattered back to lie at Hilda's feet. Hetty was pleased her mum didn't shoo it out to the yard this time.

'I'm off then, Mum.'

And with that, Hetty left. She was glad to be away from the sickly, cloying smell of sugar that Frankie Ireland had left in his wake.

Chapter Nine

Elsie leaned across the table and pulled an armful of waxed papers towards her. She reached her slim fingers to the top of the pile with her left hand and plucked a square of brown toffee with her right. Peeling a wrapper from the pile, she brought it to her right hand and enclosed the toffee in it. She made sure the wrapper went all the way around, as Mrs Perkins had shown her, and before she twisted the ends, she checked the logo on the front. It was straight and looked neat, and she allowed herself a satisfied smile. Finally she'd got the hang of putting the wrappers on properly.

Her nimble fingers worked quickly, reaching, wrapping, enclosing, checking, twisting. This was now Elsie's day. She stood for four hours straight, from eight a.m. to noon, at the table in front of her. Then there was an hour's break for lunch, a whole glorious hour in which to sit in the garden, shop on Front Street or visit the factory canteen and eat a hearty meal. After that, it was back to work until six p.m.

Talking in the wrapping room was forbidden by Mrs Perkins. If girls were caught chatting – or worse, singing

– while they worked, the supervisor would swoop by with a swish of her blue skirt and a scowl on her face.

'I demand quiet in here!' she'd yell. Then she'd storm back to her desk in the corner of the room, leaving the girls rolling their eyes at each other.

However, although Mrs Perkins discouraged the girls from talking, she couldn't stop them sending secret messages to each other. They'd devised ways to communicate in silence using hand signals. A tap on the side of the nose meant the supervisor was approaching, look out. A circular rub of the stomach meant they were hungry. Being one of the new girls, Elsie was still learning the meaning of these signals. She enjoyed trying to figure them out. It helped stop her becoming too bored, for the work hardly challenged her mind.

With the no-talking rule enforced, the wrapping room was the only quiet room at the factory. In the sugar boiling rooms where the toffee was made, the heat and noise were ferocious. The packing room was noisy too. Delivery boys waiting with horses and carts lined up at the wide doors, ready to load the toffees onto trains for their onward journeys to cities and towns.

As Elsie reached for another toffee and another wrapper, she noticed Anabel tap the side of her nose. She straightened her back. She felt Mrs Perkins at her side but didn't stop in her work, just kept reaching, wrapping and twisting.

'Miss Cooper, I want you to look after Miss Lawson.'

Elsie turned and came face to face with the girl from earlier.

'It's Betty, right?' she said.

Hetty smiled. 'Close, it's Hetty.'

'Shush, girls!' Mrs Perkins barked. 'Elsie, take her to be fitted for clogs, I'm sure you can remember where to go. And give her a quick tour of the factory and grounds. Show her the packing room and explain how to wheel the crates there. Then bring her straight back, no dawdling, and show her how to wrap. Think you can manage that?'

'Yes, Mrs Perkins.'

Elsie wondered why she'd been singled out to train the new girl. She'd only been at the factory a few days herself, and in that short time she'd thought Mrs Perkins had taken against her. First she was told off for not wrapping toffees straight, then she was warned not to go near the men in the sugar boiling room. What was the old dragon up to, giving her responsibility for training a new girl? However, she decided not to question it. Taking Hetty on a tour meant getting away from the monotonous work of wrapping and twisting for half an hour, perhaps as long as forty-five minutes if she could stretch it out.

'I'll leave you to it,' Mrs Perkins said.

'Thank you, Mrs Perkins,' Elsie and Hetty chimed as the supervisor walked away.

Elsie looked at Hetty. 'What happened to your skirt?' she said.

Hetty looked down, and when she saw the dirt, her mouth opened in shock. 'What a mess! I haven't had a minute to clean up. What must you think of me?'

Elsie shrugged. 'I think we need to get you an overall to cover it up. We'll soon have you sorted.'

'Why do I need clogs?'

'So you don't stick to the floor. All the sugar in the air falls to the ground. If you're wearing clogs and get stuck, just call for help. Someone will get you out of them and lift you away from the sticky patch.' She nudged Hetty playfully. 'There's a fella in the sugar boiling room I've got my eye on. I wouldn't mind if *he* lifted me out of my clogs and carried me off in his arms.'

Elsie glanced across the room to see Mrs Perkins glaring at her, shaking her head with a finger held at her lips. She knew what that meant.

'Come on, let's go on a tour and I'll show you what's what,' she whispered.

She linked arms with Hetty and they left the wrapping room. Elsie liked that the other girl didn't pull away, and that she seemed at ease.

'Have you got a fella?' she asked once they were outdoors.

'Yes, he's called Bob, but he's gone off to war. I don't know when I'll see him again. I'll write to him, though, as soon as he writes to me.'

'He'll be back, don't you worry,' Elsie said kindly. She pointed ahead. 'That's the stores, where we'll go to get your overall and clogs. The overall itches at first, but once you take it home and wash it, it's all right. You have to take it home on a Friday to wash at the weekend so you start the week with a clean one each Monday.'

'Do I take the clogs home?'

'No, they stay under your table. Once we've seen the factory and you know where everything is, I'll take you back to the wrapping room to show you how things work. It's simple once you get used to it. Oh, and don't mind Anabel, the girl who was standing beside me. She stinks a bit, see, as she lives in a tripe shop. She doesn't speak much, but she's got a kind heart.'

'What are the other girls like?' Hetty asked.

'They seem all right so far,' Elsie said. 'We don't get to talk much while we work, but we have a good natter in the canteen at lunchtime.'

'There's a canteen?' Hetty said, surprised.

'Girls have to sit on one side and fellas on the other. The food's not bad, and it's cheaper than any café in town.'

'Is that a garden ahead?' Hetty asked, pointing to the rose beds.

Elsie picked up her pace. 'It's gorgeous, full of roses, let's go take a look,' she said. 'They say that Mr Jack laid it out for his staff to enjoy.'

'Why, it's beautiful,' Hetty said admiringly.

A gardener was tending the roses, and as the girls passed, he raised his flat cap. Elsie caught his eye, liked what she saw and flashed him a smile.

'Morning,' she said. 'My name's Elsie Cooper from the wrapping room. This is Hetty.'

'Hetty Lawson,' Hetty said.

The gardener nodded, and the girls walked on.

'Oh, he's nice-looking, isn't he? He's got lovely brown eyes,' Elsie said.

'I'm called Stan!' a voice yelled from behind them.

She turned around and waved. 'Nice to meet you, Stan,' she replied.

'Sugar boilers and gardeners. You're man mad, you are,' Hetty teased.

Elsie stuck her chest out. 'So what if I am? I like a bit of fun as much as the next girl.'

'I didn't mean anything by it,' Hetty said quickly.

Elsie looked at her. 'I didn't think you did. I like you, Hetty Lawson, and I'd like us to be friends.'

'I'd like that too,' Hetty said.

They walked along a long bed of neatly tended pink and white roses. Elsie breathed in their sweet, peppery scent.

'Can I tell you a secret?' she said. She didn't wait for a reply, but carried straight on. 'You know what I'd really like?'

'What?' Hetty asked.

Elsie leaned in close. 'I'd like to go dancing with a Belgian man at Elisabethville,' she whispered.

Hetty stopped walking. She looked aghast at Elsie. 'You can't do that! Chester-le-Street girls aren't allowed to go there.'

Elsie tutted and dropped her arm. 'Are you a mouse, Hetty Lawson? I thought I could trust you, but now I'm not sure.'

'You *can* trust me; I won't tell a soul. But you know Elisabethville's out of bounds. It's where the Belgians live; it's their village, not ours. Anyway, how would you get in? There are gates at either end with guards on duty, and they only speak Belgian.'

Elsie wiggled her hips as she walked. 'Yes, but my body speaks a special language the Belgian men will understand.'

'You're a right one, Elsie Cooper.'

'Stick with me and we'll find fellas to have fun with.'

Hetty pulled her close. 'I don't want another fella. I just want Bob,' she said softly. 'Or at least, I always thought so. Now that he's not here, I don't know how to feel.'

Elsie looked at her. 'You'll be all right. We'll have fun together.'

'What do you know about the Belgians and their village anyway?' Hetty asked, intrigued. 'All I know is that I have to stay away from it, that's what my mum said.'

Elsie thought for a moment. 'I know it's in the next town from here, and that injured soldiers have been sent from Belgium to work in the munitions factories. They can't fight any more, but they can still work, and we need them to build shells for the war. I know they named their village after their queen. But I don't think any of them speak English.'

Hetty thought of the man with the blue eyes and the strange accent she'd met on Front Street; the man wearing the unusually styled suit who'd handed her the dog.

'I think some of them might,' she said quietly.

'They've even built their own homes there, with electricity and running water. No outside netty and tin bath for them. They've got an inside bathtub and electric lights you turn on with a switch instead of oil lamps. Can you imagine it? There's a school for the children, a hospital too, even shops and a Belgian café. And do you know the best bit of all?'

'What?' Hetty asked.

'There's a dance hall. Some of the girls talk about it in the canteen.'

'Toffee factory girls have been inside Elisabethville?' Hetty said, shocked.

Elsie nodded, and her eyes flickered with mischief. 'Oh yes, and I'm determined to get inside too.'

Chapter Ten

Over the coming days, Hetty settled into her new job. When she'd given notice to Dr Gilson, he was furious to lose her and even threatened to withhold money she was owed. She'd been angry and upset over this and ended up revealing to him a little of her circumstances at home. Once he knew the truth about Hilda being ill and unable to work, and how unruly Dan was, he relented and paid her.

'And send your mother to see me if her chest worsens,' he'd said.

Hetty had thanked him, but in her heart she knew she would never have enough money to pay a doctor's bill. Every spare penny went in the jar to pay Frankie.

She'd caught Dan eyeing the jar and warned him to leave it alone. 'If I catch you thieving again, you know I'll tell Mum. It'll break her heart if she discovers the truth about her favourite child, about what you're up to with Tyler Rose. She might throw you out.'

Dan dug his hands into his pockets. 'I've got mates, I can sleep on their floor if Mum throws me out. Anyway, I don't think she'd do that, do you?' he spat. 'I'm not doing anything wrong with Tyler Rose.'

But Hetty had heard otherwise, from the grocer at the market, who'd told her that Tyler's yard was being used to store stolen goods. Dan had sneered at her when she'd mentioned this, then slammed the door and left. He often stayed out all night and Hetty rarely crossed paths with him. But even with him out of the house, her wages from the factory didn't go far. She bought the cheapest cuts of meat from the butcher on Front Street – and occasionally, when she could afford it, scraps for the dog. At the market in town, she bought bruised fruit and vegetables no one else wanted. At home, she cooked and cleaned, and tended her mum's chesty cough.

One morning before she set off to work, she noticed her mum looking drawn.

'How are you feeling?' she asked.

Hilda raised her eyebrows. 'I'd feel better if you'd sneak some toffees out of the factory. A bit of sugar's what I need.'

Hetty was appalled. She shook her head. 'You know I can't do that. Stealing toffees is a disciplinary offence. I could be sacked.'

'Only if they catch you,' Hilda muttered.

'I won't risk losing my job. If they sack me, we'll have no money coming in. Never ask me to steal, Mum. I'm not Dan.'

'No, you're your father's daughter. And look at the state he left us in.'

Hetty gritted her teeth and turned away. 'I'm going to work. I'll be back at the usual time. I'll call at the butcher on the way home to ask if he's got cheap ham. I'll cook potatoes with it, it'll help build you up.'

Hilda waved her hand dismissively. 'Go on then.'

Hetty looked at her mum. How she wished their relationship could be different, better. They were always at odds. She couldn't remember a time when Hilda had shown her love and affection the way she showed it to Dan.

'What will you do today?' she asked.

'Not much I can do, in my condition.'

'It's warm out. You could take the dog for a walk by the river,' Hetty suggested. 'Oh, and if a letter from Bob should arrive, would you bring it to me at the factory?'

Hilda sighed heavily. 'Want me at your beck and call, delivering letters for you?' she huffed.

Hetty felt dispirited. She knew that if Dan had asked their mum for a small favour, she would have jumped at the chance to please him.

'Please, Mum?' Hetty begged. 'You could meet me at the factory gate when I finish work this afternoon. A walk there might do you good.'

Hilda tutted out loud. 'We'll see. I'm not promising anything, mind.'

Hetty left the house with a heavy heart. Nothing she did or said ever seemed to please her mum or lift her mood. Yet on the rare occasions Dan came home for a change of clothes, or a wash in the tin bath in front of the fire, Hilda's face would light up. She'd throw questions at him, interested in where he'd been and who with. She'd hang on his every word, most of which Hetty knew weren't true. Then she'd sit back in her chair with a smile on her face. Once Dan left and disappeared off to his work with the horses and the rag-and-bone man, Hilda's body would deflate. It was like the spirit had gone out of her, as if her life wasn't worth living without Dan. Nothing Hetty said ever made a difference.

As she walked along Elm Street, she felt angry at her mum, disappointed too. How dare she ask her to steal! She'd already explained to Hilda that anyone found taking toffees would be disciplined or sacked. Mrs Perkins performed checks every night at the end of the shift. She even recruited two girls to help; they were known as the searchers and were paid an extra shilling each week. Mrs Perkins and her searchers stood by the exit. Before the girls could leave, they had to turn out their pockets to prove nothing was tucked away. Anyone who carried a handbag had to open it so that the searchers could peek inside.

In the short time Hetty had worked at Jack's, she'd never taken or eaten one single toffee. It was something she'd never do, although the temptation was great, with the wonderful smell in the air that often made her mouth water and her stomach rumble with hunger. It hurt a great deal that her mum assumed she'd steal. Yes, Hilda needed feeding up, and cream and sugar would be good for her, but Hetty had never taken anything that didn't belong to her and she wasn't about to start now. She wouldn't risk losing her job, not now she knew what she was doing. Even Mrs Perkins seemed pleased with her work. She'd become firm friends with Elsie too and enjoyed seeing her each day. She wished there was another way to give her mum what she needed.

Despite the fact that she would never, ever steal, it broke Hetty's heart to see the amount of toffees thrown away. These were the misshapen ones, or those that hadn't been browned to the exact colour Mr Jack demanded. When she asked Mrs Perkins why the toffees went to waste rather than being given away to staff, the supervisor's reply was stern.

'Because Mr Jack won't let any toffees leave his factory that are the wrong colour, shape or size. Only the absolute best toffees are allowed to go out into the world, in order to protect his beloved brand.'

When toffees were thrown away, woe betide any girl who dipped her hand into the bin to retrieve one. Mrs Perkins would swoop from her desk in the corner of the room. Hetty had seen this happen more than once. Just the previous afternoon, Anabel had been unable to resist taking a reject and had popped it in her mouth. Mrs Perkins had appeared seemingly out of nowhere and the girl was chastised in front of everyone. She had been unable to apologise as her jaws were stuck together with toffee.

At lunchtime that day, Anabel sat with Hetty and Elsie on a bench in the garden and told them why she'd taken the sweet.

'I haven't eaten in two days, I'm so hungry,' she'd said in a whisper.

'But you live in a tripe shop, can't you eat tripe?' Elsie said, as if it was the answer to Anabel's problems. Hetty nudged her in the ribs and shot a warning look for her to pipe down.

'Don't you buy food with your wages?' Hetty asked gently. 'What about your brother? He works in the packing room and must earn a good wage. Doesn't he help to buy food?'

Anabel dropped her gaze. 'He's not eating well either. He almost passed out yesterday. We're so hungry. I don't know what to do.'

Hetty and Elsie shared a concerned look. Hetty laid her hand on Anabel's arm.

'Where does your money go, Anabel?'

Anabel took her time before she replied.

'To the man who runs the tripe shop, to pay for our room,' she said quietly.

'All of your money goes to him?' Hetty asked.

Anabel nodded. Hetty banged her fist against the arm of the bench.

'It's so unfair! You can't work if you don't eat. We can't have you and your brother fainting from hunger.'

Anabel turned to face her. 'Then what am I to do?'

'Come home with me after work tonight. You can eat with me and Mum. It'll just be cheap ham and potatoes. There won't be a lot of it, as I can't afford much.'

'Why not?' Elsie asked forthrightly.

Hetty looked at her friend. How she wanted to tell her about Frankie Ireland's threats and the debt her dad had left. But she didn't want her new friend to know too much about her life in case she thought badly of her.

'Things at home are a bit tricky,' she said softly.

'Anabel could always come to my flat for tea instead. You could come too,' Elsie offered.

Hetty was surprised to hear this, as Elsie rarely spoke about home. Their conversation topics usually involved fellas at the factory who Elsie had her eye on. Or her plans to smuggle herself into Elisabethville to dance with a Belgian man. In return, Hetty had talked about Bob and how she was waiting for his first letter, which she was sure would turn up soon. They'd shared their fears about the war, joked about going dancing while wearing their work clogs, and discussed which colour roses in the factory garden they preferred. Hetty's was the delicate white, while Elsie's was the showy pink. But one topic they rarely touched on was their home life. All Hetty knew about Elsie was that she lived with her aunt above a dressmaker's shop.

'Won't your aunt mind if we turn up for tea without warning?' she asked.

'Won't your mum?' Elsie replied, then she shrugged. 'Aunt Jean will be out tonight.' Then she scratched her head and thought for a moment. 'Sorry, no, tonight she'll be in. No, we can't go there tonight.'

Hetty wondered why not, but she kept quiet as Elsie continued.

'I know what we'll do instead. I'll buy ham on the way home, enough to feed us all, and we'll take it to your house, Hetty, if you're sure your mum won't mind. The baker on Front Street sells the most gorgeous sponge cake. I could buy one of those too.'

Hetty guessed her mum wouldn't be happy about her bringing two friends home from work. But Elsie had promised a feast, with ham and cake. It had been a long time since there'd been enough money for cake in the Lawson house.

'Could we, Hetty? Please?' Anabel begged.

Hetty thought about it.

'Anabel, could I speak to Elsie alone?' she asked.

Anabel's stomach rumbled with hunger as she stood from the bench and walked off. Hetty turned to her friend with a stern expression on her face.

'What are you looking at me like that for?' Elsie cried. 'Don't you want a feast for tea?'

'I want to know where you get the money to buy ham and cake on a whim. You're my friend, Elsie. Is there something I should know?'

Elsie crossed her arms and stared at the roses.

'Elsie? What is it you're not telling me?'

'Can I trust you?' Elsie asked.

'Of course,' Hetty replied.

'It's my aunt . . . she's got two jobs,' Elsie began hesitantly.

'Really? She must work very hard,' Hetty said.

Elsie uncrossed her arms and sat up straight, then leaned in close. 'You mustn't tell anyone what I'm about to say. It's top secret.'

'Why, does she work as a spy?' Hetty teased. But when she saw the serious look on Elsie's face, she shut up. 'I'm sorry, go on.'

'She works on the market by day, selling cottons and threads. And by night, she . . .' Elsie paused, 'she entertains men in our room above the shop.'

Hetty was confused. 'Entertains men? You mean she sings to them?'

Elsie's serious demeanour lightened for a moment and the trace of a smile flickered on her lips, but then her face turned earnest again.

'No, she's . . . well, she's more intimate with them than that. Do you understand what I'm saying? They pay her to spend time with her . . . in her bedroom.'

Suddenly the penny dropped.

'Oh,' Hetty said, taken aback.

'So, do you still want to know more about me? Because

that's the top and bottom of it, Hetty Lawson. My aunt's a common tart. It means she earns enough to give me money to buy ham and cake. Still want me to come to your house for tea when you know how the food's been paid for?'

Hetty was shocked, but she needed to look after her mum, and she wanted to help Anabel. If she didn't have to pay for tea herself, there'd be extra money to give to Frankie Ireland. The faster they paid him, the quicker he'd disappear.

'Yes, I'd like you to come to my house.'

'I can't stay long,' Elsie said, beaming. 'I've got a date with a fella.'

Hetty looked at her. 'Who is it? Someone at the factory?'

'Just someone I've got my eye on,' Elsie teased, then turned away. Hetty got the hint.

'If you don't want to tell me, that's your business,' she said. 'But can I ask you something else?'

'You can ask me anything, but I can't promise I'll answer.'

'There are two things you mustn't mention to my mum while you're at my house. She's a bit set in her ways, and that's putting it mildly.'

'What sort of things shouldn't I say?'

'First of all, don't say what your aunt does at night. If Mum asks, tell her she works on the market during the day, nothing else.'

'And the second thing?' Elsie asked.

'Don't mention Elisabethville and that you want to go dancing with Belgian men. Mum's old-fashioned, and she doesn't understand things the way you and I do.'

Hetty slid her arm through her friend's. Her mouth was watering at the thought of ham and cake for tea. They stood from the bench and went in search of Anabel to give her the good news.

Chapter Eleven

The rest of their lunchtime passed quickly. In the canteen Elsie treated herself to a cheese roll and a glass of milk. However, Hetty had brought her own food, unable to afford to buy anything at the counter. She unwrapped a cloth to reveal a slice of egg pie and a tomato. The pie was squashed after being in her pocket all morning, and it didn't smell good. A glass of water stood on the table in front of her.

'I wish we were allowed to sit next to the men,' Elsie sighed. 'I don't understand why they're kept on one side and us girls have to stay on the other.'

Hetty looked across the vast room, where long tables were set up with seats either side. The canteen was always busy, with the clatter of plates and glasses mixing with the chatter of friends catching up on news. She was about to take a bite from her pie when Elsie nudged her.

'Look over there. It's Anne, the girl who works for Mr Jack.'

Hetty looked where Elsie was pointing. Anne's hair was neatly tied in a bun and she wore her small wire-framed spectacles. She was dressed today in a dark patterned blouse and a dark skirt. She brought an air of calm to the busy canteen as she glided past tables to the serving counter.

'I wonder how much she gets paid?' Elsie whispered.

'A lot more than us girls on the factory floor, I'd bet,' Hetty replied.

A few moments later, Anne appeared at Hetty's side carrying a tray of food.

'May I join you both?' she asked.

Hetty was surprised that someone as high up as Mr Jack's secretary wanted to sit with them. But then she remembered how friendly and welcoming Anne had been when she'd met her on her first day.

'Yes, of course,' she said. 'Shuffle up, Elsie.'

Elsie moved along to make space. When Anne sat down, Hetty couldn't resist peeking at the food on her plate. Her stomach rumbled at the sight of roast beef with all the trimmings. Potatoes and gravy steamed next to green beans and carrots. She looked at her own squashed pie and sighed as Anne picked up her knife and fork and began to tuck in.

In between mouthfuls, Anne spoke to the girls.

'How are you getting on at work?'

'Oh, just fine, Miss Wright,' Elsie replied.

'Please, call me Anne.'

Hetty licked her lips as she watched Anne cut into beef in thick gravy. The last time she'd eaten beef and gravy was before her dad died. They hadn't been able to afford it since.

'We're having ham and cake for tea,' she said. The words tumbled out before she realised she'd said them.

'I'm sorry?' Anne said.

Hetty felt Anne and Elsie's eyes on her. She sat up straight.

'I mean . . . the food in the canteen is good, isn't it?'

Anne nodded. 'Yes, it is, but I've spoken to Mr Jack about taking liver and onions off the menu. It doesn't seem to sell.'

Hetty's eyes opened wide. 'Do you really tell the factory owner what to do?'

'It's all part of my job. Mind you, I'm not sure how much he listens. But when he asks my advice, I tell him the truth. We've been in talks this morning about how best to improve production. It might involve moving some of you girls from the wrapping room to the slab room in the coming months.'

Hetty knew about the slab room. She'd visited it when Elsie took her on the guided tour.

'It's hot in there,' she said, remembering the fierce heat she'd experienced. It was a noisy room too, with women working either side of the long, wide metal slabs where the hot toffee was poured from big metal pans. It flowed out of the pans boiling and bubbling, snaking like lava, spreading out as it slowly cooled. Then a metal tray called an equaliser was placed on top to ensure the right thickness was achieved. Hetty recalled the smell of the slab room too; the rich, buttery scent of freshly made toffee was divine. Her mouth watered at the thought. But it was also dangerous work, as the toffee had to be cut by hand with long, sharp knives. Two women took hold of each knife, one at either end, and together they brought it down, cutting the toffee into even shapes.

'I'd much prefer to stay wrapping toffees rather than making them,' Elsie said, echoing Hetty's thoughts.

Anne laid her knife and fork down and faced the two of them. 'We'll all have to make sacrifices to keep the factory going. There's a war on, girls. I'm sure there are worse things than moving to work in the slab room.'

'Suppose so.' Elsie shrugged.

Anne began eating again, then she looked at Hetty and gave a cheeky wink. 'Anyway, how's the old dragon treating you in the wrapping room?'

Hetty's jaw dropped. She thought only the girls in the wrapping room used Mrs Perkins' nickname.

'I'm sorry, I'm not sure who you mean,' she replied. She was unsure what was going on; was Anne setting her a test?

Anne leaned in close. 'It's all right. I know that's what everyone calls Mrs Perkins. I'm learning quickly what goes on. Well? Is she treating you well, or do you have any complaints?'

'No complaints,' Hetty said quickly. And it was true. She had discovered that Mrs Perkins' bark really was worse than her bite, as long as you did your work.

'She keeps us in line,' Elsie said.

'She's firm but fair,' Hetty added.

Anne nodded. 'That's good to hear. But if either of you has concerns about the way she treats you, come and tell me, in confidence.'

She scraped up the last of her food from her plate, and placed her knife and fork neatly on it. Then she pushed her chair back and stood, removing the blue napkin from her knee and smoothing her skirt.

'Good afternoon, ladies, I must return to work.'

'Don't you take your full lunch hour?' Hetty asked. 'You've only been here for a fraction of that.'

'I've already been for a walk around the garden,' Anne replied. 'I like to get some fresh air before I come in for my lunch. Now remember what I said: if you have any concerns, come and see me. My office door is always open.' She glided away.

'Her office must be draughty if the door's always open,' Elsie whispered.

Hetty pushed her shoulder against her friend's and smiled. 'She seems nice, though. She's very pretty.'

'Nah, she's too plain, hides away behind her glasses. She'll never get a fella at the factory looking like that.'

'Maybe she's already got a fella – or perhaps she doesn't want one?' Hetty said.

Elsie tutted out loud. 'Don't be daft. Every girl wants a fella.'

Anne sat in Mr Jack's office, poised with her notepad and pencil, ready to take dictation. Mr Jack paced between his desk and the window. She knew him well enough by now not to hurry him along or interrupt his thoughts. He would speak when he was ready. His office was tidy now and organised since she'd started work. On her first day, she'd sorted out the piles of paper littering the floor, and they were now neatly placed in cardboard folders and filed away in cabinets. Awards and certificates strewn around the room when she'd arrived were now polished and displayed in a cabinet behind his desk. All the better for visitors to appreciate.

She watched as he strode to and fro. He was a short man, much shorter than Anne, who towered above him when they stood together. His bald head shone in the sunshine filtering through the window. His blue bow tie sat neatly at his throat. His round, chubby face with its black moustache didn't make him look handsome, at least not to Anne. However, she appreciated his cheerful countenance and optimistic outlook. She found him a most agreeable employer. He was unlike anyone she'd worked for before, as not only did he listen to her ideas, but he even asked her for advice on factory matters.

The only fly in the ointment was Mr Burl, the sales manager. He was brusque in his manner and rude to Anne when their paths crossed. He often had meetings with Mr Jack to which Anne was called to take notes, so she met him a few times each week. However, she appreciated the wages she was being paid by Mr Jack and tried not to let Mr Burl's attitude disturb her. The money she was earning was far more than she'd earned at the Mayfair factory. If she was careful and saved up, she might be able to take a trip to see her son. The thought of it filled her with hope.

She forced herself to concentrate on her work, for it wouldn't do to let her emotions get the better of her. She looked up when Mr Jack stopped pacing.

'Ready, sir?' she asked. She sat straight in her seat, ready to take notes.

'I have decided to fight,' he declared.

Anne wasn't sure if he wanted her to write this down. She'd been expecting him to dictate a letter to their chocolate supplier in Yorkshire.

'We have a new competitor, Anne,' he said gravely. 'There's a factory on the Scottish borders that hasn't been of concern until now. However, they've been ramping up production over the last year. And now they've created a very pleasing toffee that may damage our sales once it becomes commercially available.'

She decided it was best to start taking notes.

'We need to employ new tactics to rise above this competition. And do you know what these tactics will be, Anne?'

'No, sir.'

'We will fight, with toffees as weapons. We will fight in confectionery shops and in grocery stores all across the nation. We need to design new packaging to attract new buyers, give people a treat. I need to speak to Mr Gerard this week to discuss designs, labels, tins. I need to speak to Mr Burl to discuss new ways to sell. We will win this toffee war, Miss Wright. Oh yes, we will reign supreme.'

'Yes, sir.'

'There is one more thing I intend to do. I have an idea to sell our toffees where no other confectionery manufacturer does. If I can get them in there, it'd make us unique. Think of the publicity we'd garner.'

Anne was becoming used to hearing Mr Jack's oddball ideas and was curious to discover his most recent plan. He strode towards her and looked her square in the eye.

'What do you know about the Belgian village in the nearby town of Birtley?'

She laid her pad and pencil on her knee. 'Elisabethville? Well . . .' She racked her brains to remember what she'd read in the local newspaper.

Mr Jack resumed his pacing. 'I need to know if there are shops there. What kind of goods do they sell? And where do these goods come from?'

Anne looked into his dancing eyes and was caught up in his excitement. 'And is there a sweet shop where our toffee can be sold?' she added.

'Exactly!' Mr Jack cried. 'There's only one way to find out. We must discover who's in charge of buying supplies for Elisabethville. Draft me an introduction letter, which we'll send today. Better still, you can deliver it by hand.'

'With a box of our best toffees wrapped in blue ribbon?' she suggested.

Mr Jack smiled at her. 'I knew I was right to take you on . . . whatever Mr Burl says.'

Chapter Twelve

Anne was about to ask Mr Jack what he'd meant by his strange comment when there was a knock at the door.

'Come in,' he called.

The door opened, and her stomach dropped as James Burl stormed in, red in the face.

'Mr Jack, we need to talk. I've just heard about the new toffee factory on the Scottish borders. They say the quality is as good as ours. This could seriously jeopardise our position in the market. Our shareholders will be furious!'

Mr Jack walked behind his desk and sat in his chair. He nodded at Anne.

'I'm about to ask Miss Wright to set up a meeting for us to discuss this. But now that you're here, why don't we speak about it now instead of waiting? Anne, fetch Mr Gerard.'

Mr Burl rocked back on his heels. 'But sir, I'm—'

Mr Jack raised an eyebrow. 'Too busy to discuss the future of our factory?'

Mr Burl's jaw was set firm. 'Never too busy for that, sir.'

'Then take a seat,' Mr Jack said. 'Anne, would you bring coffee, please? Then I'll need you to take notes at the meeting.'

'Of course, sir,' Anne replied. 'However, you've just asked me to type up an introduction letter and take it to Elisabethville. If we wait until after your meeting for me to do that, it may be too late. The supplies officer at the military base may keep office hours, the same as we do here at the factory.'

'Good point,' Mr Jack said. He jumped from his chair. 'Burl, you fetch Gerard. Anne, I'll need you here to take notes at the meeting. Instead of going to Elisabethville yourself, send one of the factory girls. I want the Belgians to appreciate our workers' distinctive overalls.'

Mr Burl coughed twice. 'Sir, do you really think a factory girl should be sent on such a vital mission? I could send one of my salesmen instead; they're upstanding, clean and polite.'

Anne shot him a look. 'As are the girls on the factory floor, Mr Burl,' she said firmly.

'Anne's right, Burl,' Mr Jack said, then he turned to Anne. 'Pick a girl to represent the factory, and make sure she's well scrubbed. Tie her hair with blue ribbon and give her money for the bus fare to Birtley. We don't want her walking there. She'd arrive a sweaty mess. Do you have anyone in mind?'

Anne thought of the girls she'd met so far. There was Anabel, who was pretty and fair, but also small, with a strange odour of tripe. Plus, Anne doubted if she would know which bus to take to Birtley and whether she could cope with the errand. Then there was Elsie, with her seductive looks and shapely figure. It was on the tip of her tongue to suggest Elsie when she remembered that Mrs Perkins had complained to her twice about the girl flirting with one of the sugar boiling men when she ought to be at work. She decided not to offer Elsie's name, otherwise it might look as if she was rewarding behaviour that Mr Jack might not approve of. Then another face came to mind.

'I'll send Hetty Lawson. She's a local girl, hard-working and presentable.'

'I'll trust your judgement, Anne. Thank you.'

Mr Burl left the room, muttering darkly. Once he'd gone, Mr Jack dictated his letter, and Anne typed it up on paper with the factory logo in blue. She'd made sure she learned what each unfamiliar button on her typewriter did, and her fingers flew across the keys. She pulled the paper from the machine and Mr Jack signed it. Then she neatly folded it into an envelope that also had the Jack's logo on it.

'I'll call at the stores to pick up a box of best toffee and take it to Miss Lawson with instructions on what to do,' she said.

Anne made her way to the wrapping room with the letter and a box of toffees. Mrs Perkins stood from her desk when she entered.

'Miss Wright, how may I help you today?'

'I'm here to see Hetty Lawson. Mr Jack wants her sending out on business. She'll not be back for the rest of the day.' She turned away, leaving Mrs Perkins in shock.

Hetty and Elsie were standing with their heads together, whispering. When they saw Anne approach they jumped apart.

'Hetty, I need you to come with me. Mr Jack wants you to leave the factory this afternoon to conduct business for him.'

'Me?' Hetty said, confused.

'He's chosen you specially,' Anne said, smiling.

Hetty glanced at Elsie, who looked as gobsmacked as she felt.

'I'll meet you at the factory gates after work,' she whispered. 'I want to help carry the ham and cake. We'll wait for Anabel too and all walk home together.'

Elsie nodded in reply.

'Back to work, ladies,' Anne said to the other girls at the table. They had all stopped working and were watching the exchange, wondering what was going on.

Hetty had to walk quickly to catch Anne, who was now striding from the room. It was then that she noticed the box of best toffee under the other girl's arm. What was going on?

'What business am I being sent on?' she asked. 'I'm not in trouble, am I?'

'On the contrary, Hetty. You've been given a special task, one that could bring more orders to the factory if it succeeds.'

'Really?' Hetty breathed. 'But what if I get it wrong?'

'Believe me, you won't. Have some confidence in yourself,' Anne said kindly.

When they reached the factory gates, Anne turned to Hetty and inspected her from her worn boots all the way to her fair hair.

'You look presentable enough, but something's missing.'

Hetty watched as Anne reached into her skirt pocket and pulled out a length of blue ribbon.

'Here, tie this in your hair.'

She did as instructed, and Anne beamed her approval. She handed over the toffees.

'You're to take the bus to Birtley from Front Street; it goes all the way without you needing to change. Alight at the crossroads with Station Road, and it's just a short walk from there. Here's the money for the fare.'

'But where am I going?' Hetty asked.

Anne clamped her hand against her forehead. 'Oh, I'm sorry, didn't I say? It's been a mad rush today. Sometimes I don't know whether I'm coming or going. Once Mr Jack gets an idea in his head, things move at quite a pace. You're going to Elisabethville, Hetty. Seek out the sentry at the gate and ask him to give this letter and the toffee to the person responsible for buying supplies. That's all you need to do. Do you understand?'

Hetty's head spun. 'Elisabethville?' she gasped. She bit her lip. 'My mum said I should never go there. It's where the Belgian people live. What if they don't speak English? What should I do?'

Anne laid her hands on Hetty's shoulders and looked her straight in the eye. 'It's perfectly safe. I wouldn't send you if it wasn't. The sentry will speak English. He'll also speak French, Dutch and Walloon, but I think English will do for you.'

Hetty began to feel panicked. 'What's Walloon?'

Anne dropped her hands to her sides and smiled. 'You've nothing to fear, Hetty, and everything to gain. Remember, the future of the factory is at stake. Are you ready to face your task? Mr Jack is depending on you.'

Hetty gulped. 'He is?'

'We're all depending on you. Now go and catch the bus to Birtley.'

Hetty touched the blue ribbon in her hair and nodded. Then she turned and walked through the gates, her stomach churning with nerves and her heart beating a little too fast.

Chapter Thirteen

Gripping the box of toffee, terrified she might drop it, Hetty walked down Front Street as if in a dream. She had to force her feet forward to keep moving. All her instincts were telling her to turn around. She wanted to go back to Anne and tell her she couldn't do this; it was too big a task. Oh, why had Anne picked her? Elsie had more confidence; she would have lapped up the chance to visit the Belgian village.

She felt sick. For a moment, she thought she might faint. She slowed down and breathed deeply. She noticed people walking by on the street, taking in her overall and the box of toffee. She knew they'd be wondering why a toffee factory girl was walking the streets when it wasn't lunchtime. Their prying eyes made her feel conspicuous, and by the time she reached the Co-op at the bottom of Front Street, she wanted to run inside and hide. But just as she was considering this, she heard the roar of a bus engine. She turned, saw the Birtley bus and knew she had to get on. She didn't have the nerve to defy Mr Jack.

The door opened, and she stood to one side while a woman got off.

'All aboard,' the conductor shouted.

Hetty stepped inside and took a seat downstairs by the window. The conductor was at her side immediately, and she handed over the coins Anne had given her. She knew the journey would be short, less than ten minutes. This did nothing to calm her racing heart, knowing her task was just minutes away. She ran through in her mind what she would say. She'd smile and look the sentry in the eye, if she dared. She was there to represent Jack's toffee factory. She understood what an honour it was to have been chosen. But that didn't mean she wasn't nervous, and her stomach was in knots. She couldn't wait to write and tell Bob about this.

She felt a lump rise in her throat. She knew she was being silly, emotional, but she also knew exactly what was causing it. She was absolutely terrified of what lay ahead. As for what her mum would say when she told her where she'd been, she didn't dare think about that. Hilda had warned her many times to stay away from the Belgians. There'd been whispers that local girls weren't safe with them. Anyone with any sense knew those rumours had been put about by local men worried that their girlfriends would have their heads turned by the newcomers. Still, it was a rumour that Hilda repeated when she warned Hetty to stay away. And now Hetty was on the bus to the very place her mum had told her to avoid, on a mission for the toffee factory owner.

She wondered why Mr Jack had chosen one of the girls from the factory instead of one of the office men. She'd seen those men sitting in the canteen at lunchtimes. They wore dark suits and smart ties, and their hair was neatly slicked back. They were studious types who smoked pipes, read newspapers and carried briefcases. Surely any one of them would have been better at conducting business.

Since Hetty had started work at the factory, she'd heard people say that Mr Jack was eccentric. She remembered Anne's words earlier, that once he got an idea in his head, she didn't know whether she was coming or going. Hetty didn't think she would enjoy working for him directly; besides, she liked working with Elsie, whispering while they worked and gossiping at lunchtime. She began wondering who Elsie was going on a date with after their feast of ham and cake when the bell rang and the conductor called out.

'Alight here for Station Road!'

Hetty was startled. She had been so lost in her thoughts, she hadn't been paying attention. She jumped up and hurried off the bus with the box of toffee under her arm.

As soon as she stepped onto the street, she was caught up in a crowd jostling and shoving to get on the bus. It was a busy stop, right next to the munitions factories. She pushed her way through and out the other side, and crossed Station Road. As she walked along Durham Road, the bus she'd been on went sailing past. Ahead of her she saw the sentry on the gate, standing to attention. This was it. She had no choice now but to do as Mr Jack asked. What was it Anne had said? The future of the toffee factory depended on her.

She hid behind a wall to compose herself. She tightened the blue bow in her hair and made sure her khaki and red overall was straight. Then she inspected the toffee box and adjusted its ribbon before stepping out and approaching the gate. The sentry didn't turn to look at her, but kept his gaze ahead. She looked at his boyish face. He appeared ordinary enough; what was there to be frightened of? Why, he was young, not much older than Dan. She walked towards him as confidently as she could and held out the box. This time he moved his head. He looked at the box, then at Hetty, puzzled.

'What is your business?' he said in a clipped accent.

Hetty began to reply, but the words she'd practised came out too fast. It was as if she couldn't get rid of them quickly enough before running back to the bus stop and far away from this place.

'I'm here from Jack's toffee factory in Chester-le-Street. My instructions are to make sure this letter and this box are given to the person in charge of buying supplies. Thank you very much and good day.'

She shoved the box forward, then took the letter from her pocket and held that out too. The sentry made no attempt to take either of them.

'Please, you must take these. I have to go,' she said.

'Goods and supplies are to be taken to the south gate,' he instructed. 'This is the north gate.'

Hetty wondered what to do. This wasn't going to be as easy as she'd hoped.

'But I don't know where the south gate is,' she mumbled.

'Is there a problem?' a man's voice said.

Hetty looked beyond the iron gates, where a pair of blue eyes stared out. She stepped back in shock. She'd seen those eyes before, and that brown hair and gentle, kind face.

'Frans, let the woman inside,' the man ordered.

The guard opened the gate and indicated that Hetty

should enter. But her feet felt glued to the ground. To be sent to Elisabethville on official business for Mr Jack was one thing, but to enter the Belgian military camp was quite another.

'Am I really allowed in?' she asked, shocked.

The man in front of her smiled. 'Normally you would need an authorised pass to gain entry. But as I'm here, I will vouch for you. I will take you to the supplies office. Come.'

Hetty cautiously stepped across the threshold and the gate closed behind her with a clang. Despite still being in the county of Durham, she was now on Belgian soil, under Belgian law. She didn't know what to do.

'Come with me,' the man said. There was a warm smile on his face, and Hetty took comfort from it.

She stepped forward, expecting to feel different, out of place, but she felt exactly the same. She took another step, then another. The ground under her feet held her weight just as it had done on the other side of the gate. The air smelled the same, birds flew overhead, and she could hear noise from the road as buses and trams trundled by. Being inside Elisabethville wasn't so different to being in Birtley or Chester-le-Street. This gave her the confidence to walk alongside the man. She was puzzled by his appearance, for he didn't wear a soldier's uniform, as the guard had. He was dressed in the same black suit with the wide lapel that she'd noticed him wearing on the day she'd met him.

He smiled again. 'My name is Dirk Horta. How is your dog?'

So he had recognised her too.

'Oh . . . the dog's fine, thank you. Well, he's not really

mine, but I suppose he is now. I think he was a stray when you handed him to me.'

'Stray?' Dirk asked.

'Lost, unwanted,' Hetty explained. 'My name is Hetty Lawson.'

'You have business with the supplies office, Hetty?'

'I have to deliver a letter and a box of toffees to the person in charge of buying supplies,' she said proudly. 'I'm here to represent Jack's toffee factory.'

'Ah yes, the famous Jack's toffees of Chester-le-Street,' Dirk said. 'We even knew of Jack's in Belgium before we came here. Some of my colleagues buy the toffee from the Co-op store in Birtley.'

Hetty was surprised to hear this, and she tucked the nugget away to tell Anne.

They walked in silence for a few moments, giving her time to take in her surroundings. There were long rows of one-storey wooden huts, with windows and doors. Dirk caught her looking.

'This is the living accommodation. The rows of huts are for soldiers who live with their families. I live over there, in the accommodation block for single men.' He pointed to a large wooden building with steps leading to a wide door.

Between some of the rows of huts, Hetty saw laundry strung on washing lines, drying in the sun. The trousers, shirts, pants and socks looked the same as any she'd seen. The familiarity helped ease her fears about being inside the military base.

'Do you work in a munitions factory?' she asked, curious.

Dirk shook his head. 'I work there,' he said, pointing at

a small building. To Hetty's eyes it looked like a chapel. She wondered if he was a vicar.

'It's a school,' he explained. 'I instruct the boys. My sister, Gabrielle, teaches the girls in their school on the south side of the village.'

Hetty was impressed. She'd never met a teacher before, other than those at the school she'd attended.

As they walked, Dirk asked her about the toffee factory and the work she did there.

'You don't really want to know about me,' she said, bashfully, but when she turned her eyes to him, she was surprised to find herself under his intense gaze.

'I want to know everything about you, Hetty Lawson,' he replied earnestly. 'Tell me about Chester-le-Street, about where you grew up and where you went to school. Tell me . . .' He paused, and smiled at her. 'Tell me all about you.'

Hetty was taken aback. No one had ever showed such an interest before.

'Don't be daft, you'll get bored if I talk about myself like that,' she replied.

Dirk paused and turned to her. 'I don't think I could ever get bored with you.'

And so Hetty began to talk. When Dirk asked about the dog, and what she'd decided to call it, it occurred to her that she still hadn't named it. She hadn't thought she'd be keeping it and had simply kept on referring to it as *dog*. When she told Dirk this, he started to laugh, and she found herself caught up in his infectious cheerfulness. How was it possible, she thought, that she so felt at ease with him, as if she'd known him for a long time? She felt comfortable with him in a way that she hadn't done with anyone, perhaps not even Bob. Bob was a serious man, efficient and organised. She couldn't imagine him befriending a lost girl in the way Dirk had befriended her. When that thought popped into her mind, it felt like she was being unfaithful, and her gut twisted. She shook her head to chase the feeling away, and the smile fell from her lips.

Dirk stopped suddenly in front of a wooden hut. 'Here is the supplies office. Some inside speak English very well. Give them your letter and your box and you will be warmly received. But remember, if you need to return to Elisabethville, you will need a pass from Jack's toffee factory, which needs to be authorised.'

Hetty pushed the box of toffees under her arm and stuck her hand out. 'Thank you for looking after me and showing me the way,' she said.

Dirk reached for her hand, all the while keeping his eyes on hers. 'I hope to see you again, Hetty Lawson.'

Hetty felt heat rise in her neck. But instead of pulling her hand away, she held Dirk's gaze for a while. She didn't seem able to look away. It was as if she was falling into the blue of his eyes.

Chapter Fourteen

Hetty left the letter and the toffees with a tall, thin man with cropped hair. Fortunately for her, he spoke good English. His eyes lit up when she handed over the box of best toffee. Task completed, she left the supplies building and headed back to Elisabethville's main street to retrace her steps and leave.

She pushed her shoulders back and strode up the long, narrow street towards the sentry on guard at the gate. As she walked, she noticed the street names on signs at each corner. She hadn't spotted them on her way into the village because she'd been engrossed in talking to Dirk. Now she marvelled at the wonderful names: Boulevard Prince Leopold, Boulevard Princesse Marie-José, Rue de Liège, Place Albert 1, Place Georges 5. She wondered if the streets were named after real people. Was Leopold a real prince? Marie-José a princess? Who were Albert and George? There were more signs pointing to Rue de France and Rue de L'Yser. How very grand the street names sounded, a world away from plain old Elm Street.

Before she reached the guard, she took one last look back at Elisabethville, or at least that was what she told herself. In her heart, she knew she was hoping to see Dirk. Perhaps he might wave goodbye if he saw her. Perhaps she might pluck up the courage to speak to him. But there was no sign of him. She was surprised by how disappointed she felt. She reprimanded herself for being so silly. What good could come of meeting him again? She had Bob and that was that.

She thanked the sentry, then headed to the bus stop on Station Road. On the journey back to Chester-le-Street, she thought about Dirk's blue eyes and warm smile. His charming accent when he spoke English and the way he listened intently to her answers when he asked her about her work. As the bus neared Front Street, she tried to push thoughts of him to the back of her mind. Well, it wasn't as if she'd ever see him again. Instead, she turned her attention to meeting Elsie and Anabel and shopping for ham and cake. She'd need to apologise to her mum when she turned up with two friends, and hoped that Elsie's offerings would cheer her up.

She found the girls waiting at the gate as planned. Elsie threaded one arm through Hetty's and the other through Anabel's, and the three of them set off. As soon as Hetty told them where she'd been sent by Mr Jack, Elsie wasted no time in firing questions at her.

'Well? What was Elisabethville like? Did you see any soldiers? Did you find the dance hall? Do you think it'd be easy to sneak in one night? My friend Winnie in the packing room says she and her friend go on Saturday nights. Their Belgian boyfriends smuggle them in. Do you think we could get in too?'

'I didn't see a dance hall,' Hetty said, remembering the strange buildings and street names she'd encountered.

'I don't know how Winnie sneaks in to go dancing. I was told I needed an official pass from Jack's before they'd let me in again. And no, I didn't see any soldiers.'

She kept quiet about Dirk; she wanted to keep him as her secret. If she told Elsie about him, her friend would want to know details, and Hetty thought it best to forget him. The only problem was, she couldn't seem to get him out of her mind.

'It was a proper village,' she carried on. 'Streets and houses with washing strung up, a hospital, café and school.'

The girls walked to the butcher's first to buy ham, then to the baker's for a round, deep sponge cake dusted with sugar. Hetty carried the cake, Elsie carried the ham and Anabel walked between them. Hetty noticed that Anabel looked exhausted; her face was pale, her skin almost translucent, and she was dreadfully thin.

'You're quiet, Anabel. Is everything all right?' she asked.

'I'm very grateful to you both for taking me in and feeding me,' Anabel said.

'It's my pleasure to do this for my friends,' Elsie said proudly.

'And it's my pleasure to take you both home to Mum. I have to warn you, though, she can be prickly,' Hetty said. She crossed her fingers and hoped Hilda wouldn't mind hosting Elsie and Anabel.

'I need to leave before six o'clock to get ready for my date,' Elsie said.

Hetty wondered again who she was meeting and why she hadn't revealed who it was.

When they reached Elm Street, Hetty braced herself. The dog ran along the hall to greet her the minute she walked through the door. Hilda was sitting by the fire, wrapped in a shawl. Hetty thought she looked drawn and quite ill. She wondered in that instant how wise it had been to bring strangers to the house when her mum wasn't feeling well.

'Mum, these are my friends from work, Elsie and Anabel. I thought we'd cook tea. Elsie's brought ham and she even bought this cake,' she said as cheerfully as she could.

'Nice to meet you, Mrs Lawson,' Elsie said politely. Anabel hid behind Elsie and didn't say a word.

Hetty held out the box containing the cake and opened the lid, presenting it like a prize to her mum. Hilda peered inside, then looked suspiciously at Elsie.

'You bought this, and the ham? Why? We don't need charity here.'

'Mum!' Hetty scolded. 'Elsie bought it as a treat.' She leaned towards her mum and whispered, 'The money we would've spent we can put in the jar.'

Hilda sighed heavily. 'I suppose you're right. Peel the potatoes while I put the kettle on the fire. I'll make a pot of tea for your friends. What's wrong with the little one hiding behind Elsie?'

Anabel stepped out.

'She's shy,' Elsie said.

Hilda sniffed the air. 'There's a strange smell coming off that ham. It's almost like tripe.'

As Hetty and Elsie smiled at one another, Anabel disappeared behind Elsie again.

'Don't just stand there, girls, help Hetty with the potatoes,' Hilda ordered.

The three of them bustled around the small kitchen,

peeling potatoes, frying the ham in a pan on the fire, drinking tea and chatting. Hetty noticed how animated her mum became once she got used to her friends being there. Hilda's mood lifted further when the ham and cake proved a success. It was the most delicious food Hetty had eaten in months.

After the meal, Hilda threw questions at the girls, wanting to know all about them. Hetty shot Elsie a warning look, a reminder not to mention her aunt's night-time work or that she wanted to go dancing with Belgians. But then Hilda turned to Anabel.

'And what do you do at the factory?'

Anabel looked nervously from Hetty to Elsie before she replied.

'I work with Hetty and Elsie in the wrapping room,' she said.

'I expect you girls keep each other company all day,' Hilda said.

'Usually we do, but not today,' Anabel continued, more confidently now. 'Hetty was sent on a special mission for Mr Jack. She went to Elisabethville.'

Hilda's eyes grew wide, and she turned to Hetty. 'Tell me you didn't go there! How many times have I told you to keep away from those men? They're different to us, Hetty. They have their own language, their own rules. Why did Mr Jack send you, of all people?'

Hetty felt affronted. 'Why shouldn't he have picked me? I'm as good as anyone else.'

'She's right, Mrs Lawson,' Elsie said.

Hetty was heartened that Elsie was defending her. But she knew from the look on her mum's face that she was horrified about where she'd been. Suddenly the mood in the room darkened. Hilda crossed her arms and stared frostily at Hetty. At Hetty's side, Elsie shifted uncomfortably.

'Well, I really should be going. I've got . . . er, something to do tonight. Thank you for your hospitality, Mrs Lawson.'

Anabel stood too. She thanked Hilda, then Hetty showed both girls out.

'Enjoy your date,' she whispered to Elsie.

She returned to her mum in the kitchen and braced herself for an argument. When Elisabethville had been mentioned between them before, Hetty had always heeded her mum's words about never venturing there, though she'd never truly understood what the problem was. Now that she'd been there and seen it for herself, she realised it wasn't so different to their own life. Yes, the people spoke a different language, but some also spoke English. They were good people, hard-working, she'd seen that. School teachers, nurses, doctors, administrators, and hundreds of them worked in the munitions factories. They were making shells to send to British troops, to soldiers like Bob, to help win the war. She was ready to defend Elisabethville this time, but before Hilda could say a word, the dog had darted past Hetty, along the hall and out to the street. The front door was ajar, and Hetty realised she hadn't closed it properly after Elsie and Anabel left.

'Dog!' she yelled. 'Come back here, now!'

She walked to the door, ready to go out to retrieve the animal. She saw Elsie and Anabel walking away, then spotted Frankie Ireland walking towards them. She knew what Frankie was coming for, and she and her mum had a small payment waiting. Then she saw a curious thing. Elsie peeled away from Anabel, and as the younger girl walked on alone, Elsie stopped to talk to Frankie. She greeted him warmly, then snuggled into his side as he slid his arm around her and they turned and walked away together.

Hetty was confused. She knew that Elsie was keen on one of the sugar-boilers, but why on earth did it have to be *him*?

Chapter Fifteen

The next day, Hetty arrived at work before Elsie. At her side, Anabel yawned, then tapped the side of her nose in warning. Mrs Perkins was coming. Hetty stood up straight.

'Where is Miss Cooper this morning?' Mrs Perkins demanded.

Hetty knew it was a question the supervisor didn't expect her to answer. Even if Hetty knew where her friend was, there was no chance she would tell. Elsie was more than capable of getting herself into trouble; she had no wish to add to that.

'I don't know, Mrs Perkins.'

Mrs Perkins turned to Anabel. 'Do you know her whereabouts?'

Anabel shook her head and Hetty saw her bottom lip quiver. She really was a sensitive girl. The supervisor tapped her bony fingers on the table.

'Anabel, come with me. You're working in the slab room today, they haven't enough girls in there.'

Hetty wished she knew how best to help the young girl. Despite the fact that Anabel had eaten well the previous night, when they'd feasted on ham and cake, she looked exhausted, as if she hadn't slept.

'Yes, Mrs Perkins,' Anabel said obediently.

'Could I go in her place?' Hetty offered. The thought of Anabel working in the heat of the slab room concerned her, plus the fact that she wasn't strong enough to use the cutting knife.

'No, you may not,' Mrs Perkins snapped. 'You'll stay here to do what you do best. When Elsie arrives, send her to me immediately. If she's flirting with one of the sugar boilers again, she'll be in trouble.'

'Yes, Mrs Perkins,' she muttered.

Mrs Perkins strode away with Anabel in tow. Hetty looked at the big clock on the wall. Elsie was now ten minutes late. She tried to concentrate on her work, enclosing the toffees and twisting the paper. She often thought the wrapped toffees looked like butterflies with paper wings. Then she found her mind returning to her visit to Elisabethville, and to Dirk. She shook her head. No. That wouldn't do. She forced herself to think about Bob. Solid, dependable Bob who was fighting for king and country. How proud she'd been of him when he'd signed up to the Durham Light Infantry.

She felt someone push past, breathing heavily. She guessed who it would be.

'Mrs Perkins wants a word with you for being late.'

'Oh crikey!' Elsie groaned. 'Couldn't you have covered for me and said I wasn't well?'

Hetty looked at her friend. 'Don't ask me to lie.'

Elsie didn't even bother picking up wrappers and toffees. 'I suppose I'd better go and see the old dragon.'

'And when you come back, I've got some questions for you.'

Elsie looked puzzled. She disappeared to Mrs Perkins' desk in the corner of the room. When she returned a few moments later, she was red in the face.

'Well, what did she say?' Hetty said.

Elsie reached for a toffee, then a wrapper, and her fingers began wrapping and twisting.

'She's put me on a warning. If I'm late again, I'll have my pay docked,' she whispered.

Hetty sucked air through her teeth. 'Serves you right for being late.'

Elsie looked at her. 'Well, who got out of bed the wrong side this morning?' she teased. 'You're in a bad mood. What did you want to ask me?'

A girl across the table tapped the side of her nose in warning. Hetty and Elsie kept quiet as Mrs Perkins strode by. When Hetty was sure she was out of earshot, she took a deep breath. She knew there was only one way to tackle Elsie, and that was head-on. There could be no skirting around, no subtlety where her friend was concerned.

'Are you courting Frankie Ireland?'

Elsie's hands never stopped working, wrapping, enclosing, twisting.

'Well? Are you?' Hetty insisted.

There was silence between them until Elsie finally spoke.

'What if I am? What's it to you?'

Hetty looked at her. 'He's dangerous, Elsie. He's a villain. Everyone knows it. He beats people up.'

Elsie shrugged. 'He's never laid a finger on me.'

Hetty turned back to her work, wondering how much more to say. It was on the tip of her tongue to mention her dad's debt, and Frankie's veiled threats to her and her mum if they couldn't pay. But she knew her mum wouldn't want their private business known. Instead, she swallowed her words and concentrated on her work.

'He's not a good man, Elsie. You need to watch out.'

The girl across the table who'd indicated earlier that Mrs Perkins was coming now tapped her left ear. Hetty didn't know what that meant, but she saw alarmed expressions on some of the girls' faces as they looked behind her. When she turned around, she saw Anne from Mr Jack's office. Was a tap on the ear the secret signal to indicate someone from the management office had entered the room? She vowed to find out. She was learning something new every day.

She was surprised to see Anne in the wrapping room, but even more surprised when Anne walked straight to her.

'Mr Jack was pleased with your work yesterday, Hetty. Already this morning he's received a hand-delivered letter from the supplies office at Elisabethville. They've confirmed they'll take our sweets for their general store.'

Hetty could feel all the girls' eyes on her, and she wished Anne had chosen a less public place to speak. She stiffened when she heard the word 'Elisabethville' being whispered around her. She'd be the topic of gossip for the rest of the day, possibly even the week.

'Mr Jack has asked me to personally thank you for your sterling work,' Anne continued, and shook Hetty's hand.

She was about to walk away when Elsie stepped forward. 'Anne, may I speak to you, please?' Without waiting for a reply, she pushed her chest out. 'If Jack's are now selling toffee to Elisabethville, I'd like to volunteer to deliver them there.'

Anne's face broke out in a smile. 'Can you drive a horse and cart, Elsie?'

'Well, no, but—'

'Then could you deliver twenty boxes at once, carrying them in your bare hands on the bus?'

'No, but—'

'Then you know fine well you can't deliver toffees to Elisabethville. Let's leave the deliveries to the boys with the carts. Your skills are better used in the wrapping room,' Anne said kindly.

Elsie followed Anne as she left the room. Hetty looked around. There was no sign of Mrs Perkins, so she dropped the toffee and wrapper she was holding and headed after her friend. She wanted to know what Elsie wanted with Anne. Was she jealous that Hetty had been to Elisabethville? Hetty hoped they wouldn't fall out over this.

Outside the wrapping room, Anne was looking at Elsie with a frown on her face.

'Why have you followed me? You should return to work before Mrs Perkins realises you've gone. You can't work in delivery, Elsie. The horses need a lot of looking after, and believe me, they stink. I can't believe an attractive girl like you wants to muck out horses. What is it you really want?'

When Elsie spotted Hetty, she gently pulled her forward so she was standing beside her.

'Hetty deserves more than just Mr Jack's kind words for the important work she did yesterday.'

'Elsie, no!' Hetty gasped. 'I'm sorry, Anne. I didn't put her up to this.'

Anne stood firm and narrowed her eyes. 'Go on,' she said carefully.

Elsie took her cue. 'If she's sent back to Elisabethville on more business for the factory, shouldn't she have her own pass to get into the camp?'

'You don't need to talk about me as if I'm not here,' Hetty chipped in. 'I can speak up for myself. Anne, I'm sorry about this. I don't want anything. Mr Jack's thanks are enough.'

Anne put her hands on her hips, then looked at Elsie. 'You're not very subtle, are you?'

Elsie's mouth twitched in a mischievous grin.

Anne thought for a moment.

'I wasn't going to mention this yet, but as you've forced the issue, I might as well tell you both now. Mr Jack and I were talking this morning about how successful Hetty's mission was. Sending a girl in her overall with the blue ribbon on the box proved to be the thing to get the Belgians interested. He believes if we send more factory girls on small delivery errands, it would be a wonderful publicity stunt. Leave it with me to think about, but I'm not making any promises.'

Then she smiled at Hetty and Elsie.

'You two will be the death of me.'

Chapter Sixteen

Anne walked away from the girls, heading back to her office, where she had letters to type for Mr Jack. But just as she was about to enter reception, the sound of a siren filled the air. She stopped dead. Where was it coming from? She looked around, puzzled, and saw women and men running from the wrapping room, the sugar boiling room, the packing room. They were all heading to the slab room. Anne ran with them. Her heart skipped; was the siren to do with the war? Were bombs falling near the factory? She'd been warned by Mr Jack that it could happen.

A crowd blocked the entrance to the slab room.

'Let me through, I'm from Mr Jack's office!' she cried. She pushed and shoved forward, the crowd parting for her at the mention of the factory owner's name.

'What's going on? Why the siren?' Anne gasped.

'There's been an accident, lass,' a man behind her said. 'The siren always goes when someone's been hurt.'

She peered into the room. A scene of chaos was unfolding. Men ran this way and that, women were crying, and on the floor lay a pile of crumpled rags. Anne focused. She could see a pair of spindly legs sticking out, a twisted arm, a clump of hair. It wasn't rags at all. It was a girl.

'She collapsed!' a woman cried. 'She complained about feeling weak. The poor lass looked half starved. She must have passed out from exhaustion.'

'Who sent her here? She's far too young for the work!' another yelled.

Hetty and Elsie arrived, pushing forward to see what had happened. Hetty could hardly get her words out.

'Oh no . . . it's Anabel,' she cried. 'Mrs Perkins sent her to the slab room this morning. I offered to come in her place because Anabel was tired. She wasn't strong enough to be working in here.'

Anne marched to where a small group of women were tending the girl on the floor.

'I'm from Mr Jack's office. What happened here?' she asked.

Her question was answered when one of the women crossed herself. Another put her hands together to pray. A thin young man barged forward, his face twisted with shock and grief. He flew to Anabel's side and collapsed. Anne heard whispers around her that he was the girl's brother, Gavin. The crowd at the door was jostling, trying to see into the room. She knew she had to take control. Mr Jack would expect it.

She strode briskly to the door with her arms outstretched. 'Everyone out. Back to work. Now!' she ordered.

When Hetty and Elsie turned to leave too, Anne grabbed their arms.

'Not you two, I need you to help make sure everyone leaves. Herd them all out.'

The girls didn't hesitate to help.

'Mrs Perkins!' Anne yelled when she spotted the supervisor in the crowd. 'Go to Mr Jack's office and tell him what's happened. The siren will have alerted the doctor. He should be on his way now.'

'Too late for the doctor,' a woman muttered.

As the crowd slowly dispersed, Anne knelt on the floor next to Anabel's body. Gavin was cradling his sister's head in his lap as tears streamed down his face.

'How could this happen?' he wailed.

A stocky man knelt beside Anne and put his hand on Gavin's shoulder. 'She was carrying a bucket of vanilla essence, and we all know how heavy those buckets are. She dropped it. The poor lass had no strength. She was exhausted. She could hardly keep her eyes open from the minute she was sent here. She dropped the bucket, tripped over and banged her head on the floor. The lasses thought she'd just fallen, they tried to help her up, but . . .'

He stopped speaking, his voice broken by tears. He squeezed Gavin's shoulder again.

'I'm sorry for your loss, lad.'

Anne forced her gaze from Anabel's lifeless body and gulped back her tears.

'Me and the lads will carry the lass to the doctor's room,' the stocky man continued, speaking to Anne now. 'Although there's nothing he can do for her now, poor thing. I'll take Gavin to the canteen and give him brandy for the shock. I'll sit with him a while before I send him home.'

Anne glanced at Gavin. He was weeping, holding Anabel in his arms.

'I want to carry her,' he sobbed. 'Let me carry my sister.'

Anne was shaken by the sight of it. She'd known accidents happen when she'd worked at Mayfair. Toffee factories were dangerous, with the boiling sugar and sticky floors. An accident was one thing, bad enough under any circumstances, but the death of a young girl was another thing entirely. It shouldn't have happened; no one should be killed at work. She was determined to speak to Mr Jack about it, because she never wanted this to happen again. The thought of Anabel losing her life because of being exhausted was too awful to bear.

She saw Hetty and Elsie waiting by the door, wiping away tears. The crowd was slowly moving away, some crying or wringing their hands. Brisk footsteps heralded the arrival of the factory doctor, who bustled into the room with his black bag. Behind him was Mr Jack. Anne explained what had happened, and the doctor immediately attended to Anabel, sadly confirming her death.

Anne watched as Gavin lifted Anabel's tiny limp body and walked from the slab room holding her carefully in his arms. Her heart broke into tiny pieces. Respectfully and quietly, the doctor followed him from the room, along with the man who had promised Gavin a glass of brandy to help numb his shock. Anne and Mr Jack headed to their office. However, they didn't get further than reception. Mr Jack slumped into a chair, held his head in his hands for a few moments, then looked straight at Anne.

'Do you know where the dead girl lived?'

'She lives . . . lived at the back of the tripe shop on Front Street,' Anne replied.

'Take a box of best toffee there, with my heartfelt regards to her mother.'

'Toffees at a time like this?' she said, shocked.

'It's what we always do when something like this happens.'

She sat next to Mr Jack and smoothed her skirt. 'Sir, if I may suggest something?'

'Go on,' he said.

'The girl does not have a mother. She only has her brother, Gavin, who also works at the factory. He is heartbroken. We can't send him toffees, what use will they be? We should help pay for her funeral, at least.'

Mr Jack's face dropped. 'Pay for the funeral?'

Anne nodded. 'A young girl died while working for us. She was exhausted. We can't carry on as normal, sending gifts to her brother and pretending none of this is our fault.'

Mr Jack's normally cheerful expression soured. 'What are you suggesting?'

Anne looked across the room at Jacob sitting behind his desk, working at a ledger. His long, thin face was set in its usual frown.

'I'm suggesting we need to ensure our girls are looked after better, sir. They're taking on men's jobs and aren't used to heavy work. Anabel collapsed. Why did nobody notice the state she was in? Why was she moved to the slab room if she couldn't do the work? What I'm saying is that we have a responsibility to keep our workers safe . . .'

She paused, then raised her eyes to Mr Jack. She worried

she'd gone too far, telling him what she thought, what she felt in her heart.

He stood and began to pace. Across the room, Jacob lifted his gaze from his ledger, for just a second, to give Anne the faintest nod of his head.

As she watched Mr Jack stride back and forth, she worried that he might be forming a plan to get rid of her, to sack her for speaking out. Then he suddenly stopped in the middle of the room.

'I'll speak to the board as a matter of urgency. And yes, we'll pay for the girl's funeral, of course.'

'But don't send any toffees, please,' Anne said.

'Flowers instead?' Mr Jack asked.

She nodded. 'Flowers for the funeral, with a note of heartfelt sorrow. I'll arrange it.'

'Come with me. I need to speak to Mrs Perkins, and I want you at my side when I do.'

He marched out of reception into the factory grounds. Anne ran to keep up with him as he headed to the canteen. Inside, she saw Gavin being tended to by the stocky man from the slab room. Two more men sat opposite, and another next to him, with his arm draped across Gavin's shoulders. On the other side of the canteen were some of the women from the slab room, many in tears. Hetty and Elsie were there too. Anne saw Hetty leave her seat and head towards Gavin.

'Miss Lawson! Where the devil do you think you're going?' a voice cried.

Mrs Perkins was red in the face, furious that Hetty was crossing the forbidden divide. She strode across the floor to catch and chastise her. Then Mr Jack stepped forward. Silence fell. Mrs Perkins' face dropped. She'd had no idea he'd entered the room.

'Come with me, Anne,' Mr Jack ordered.

Anne followed him to where Gavin was being consoled by his workmates. She watched as a chair was pulled away from the table for Mr Jack to sit on. She was flabbergasted. She looked at Hetty and Elsie. From their expressions, she could tell they couldn't believe what was happening. Neither could the women from the slab room. Everyone watched in awe. Even the women serving food and drinks at the counter set down their teapots and plates to watch this unprecedented event.

'Mrs Perkins,' Mr Jack snapped, 'I need to speak to you in my office. We need to talk about the welfare of girls in your room. And I will not allow you to chastise this young woman . . .' here, he pointed at Hetty, 'for crossing the canteen under the distressing circumstances we've suffered today.'

He looked around the large room.

'In fact, I think there will be some changes in here.'

'Sir?' Anne asked, surprised.

'Women on one side, men on the other? It was a rule my father brought in when he built this factory. But times have changed. Our boys are heading to war and more girls are working for us. We need to look after them all. There will be changes throughout the factory. Anabel's death will not be in vain.'

He put his hand on the table, then stepped up to stand on a chair. The room had fallen silent.

'From now on, there will be no demarcation in here. Men and women will sit next to each other. There will be no divide in this room.'

He struggled to clamber down, and Anne offered her

hand to steady him. Then he did a most peculiar thing. He pulled out another chair, indicating that Anne should sit down. She heard a man behind her gasp, and there was the sound of something being dropped and smashed behind the counter.

'Anne, please be seated,' he said.

Anne knew everyone was watching. This had never happened before at Jack's toffee factory. She was about to become the first woman to sit on the men's side of the canteen. She looked at Hetty and Elsie. Both gave encouraging nods. With her heart beating nineteen to the dozen, she sat next to Mr Jack.

Chapter Seventeen

Anabel's funeral was held at St Cuthbert's church on Ropery Lane. The day was cool as the weather was turning from the warmth of summer into early autumn. Hetty, Elsie and Anne attended the service to pay their respects. They sat at the back of the church with other factory girls who'd known Anabel. Gavin sat at the front with Mr Jack.

Once the service ended, the girls walked in silence to the factory. Anne had headed off alone, but was soon caught by Hetty and Elsie. She was pleased when Hetty linked arms with her on one side and Elsie on the other as they headed back to work.

After Anabel's death, life at Jack's factory began to change in subtle ways. Mrs Perkins was disciplined. At Anne's suggestion, Mr Jack also brought in new measures to ensure no one went hungry to the point of exhaustion. He dropped the already low prices for food and drinks in the canteen and offered a free glass of milk with each meal. And for the first time in the history of the factory, he allowed toffees to be eaten at work. Misshapen toffees, those of the wrong colour or wrapped wrongly were no longer thrown out but were separated into baskets instead. One basket was placed in the canteen for workers to help themselves to at break times, and others in the wrapping room, the slab room and the packing room. Not only that, but new safety rules were put in place.

'We must protect our girls!' Anne insisted if Mr Jack flinched when she recommended a new procedure or suggested an idea he wasn't keen on. He always came around to her way of thinking in the end.

During those weeks, Hetty was called to Anne's office to have her photograph taken. It would be used on her authorised pass to allow her to return to Elisabethville. She sat perfectly still with her hands in her lap and stared at the camera. She'd been told to keep her face motionless, which was hard as she was so excited. She was the only factory girl who'd been asked to have her picture taken for a pass, much to Elsie's chagrin.

One early autumn day, as Anne walked into the wrapping room to speak to Hetty and Elsie, she saw Elsie pick a toffee and pop it in her mouth. When she reached her, she tapped Elsie on the shoulder, and the girl almost jumped out of her skin.

'You should only eat toffees from the basket. You're lucky it was me who saw you and not Mrs Perkins.'

Elsie's mouth was gummed with toffee and she couldn't reply.

'I keep telling her not to steal them,' Hetty whispered.

Elsie swallowed hard. 'I'm not stealing. I thought one of them looked a bit odd.'

Anne laughed out loud. 'Oh, you're terrible, Elsie Cooper. Anyway, it's not you I've come to see. It's Hetty.'

Hetty's eyes opened wide. 'Me? Am I in trouble?'

'Of course not. Unless you've been stealing toffees too?'

'I would never do that.'

'Then come with me. I've got something for you. Mrs Perkins knows you'll be away for a while; I've already cleared this with her.'

As soon as Anne's back was turned, Elsie popped another toffee in her mouth.

'Where are we going?' Hetty asked as they walked.

Anne noticed her anxious tone.

'My office. Don't worry. It's something you might like.'

Anne strode confidently across the cobbled yard to reception. She felt a chill through her thin blouse and rubbed her arms.

'Autumn's coming in, I can feel it in the air.'

Hetty shivered. 'I don't know how we'll get through this winter. It's our first since my dad died, and Mum hasn't the money to buy coal for the fire.'

'Your wages must help at home, surely?' Anne said.

'Yes, a little . . . but we have debts to be paid,' Hetty said.

'I wish we could offer higher wages for you girls,' Anne said kindly. 'But with the war on, everything is so uncertain.'

'My Bob's at war. He's in France . . . I think,' Hetty said.

Anne looked at her. 'I didn't know you had a boy-friend. I expect he writes often. You must miss him a lot.'

There was a beat of silence before Hetty replied.

'I'm sure his letter's on its way,' she said, clearly trying to convince herself.

As they entered the reception, Jacob nodded tersely.

'I'm determined to get him to smile if it's the last thing I do,' Anne whispered as they walked past his desk.

In her office, Anne took her seat behind her desk.

'Please sit, Hetty,' she said.

She pulled open a drawer and removed a small piece of card. She held it up for Hetty to see.

'Do you know what this is?'

Hetty peered at it. 'Is that really what I think it is?'

'Yes, it's your pass to Elisabethville. It states officially that you, Henrietta Hilda Lawson, are authorised to enter the Belgian village of Elisabethville for the purpose of delivering sweets from Jack's toffee factory. The pass has been signed by the Chief Constable of County Durham as well as by Mr Jack. It's also been authorised by the administration of Elisabethville. It gives your age and birth date, even the colour of your eyes and your height, and there's your photograph, for identification. Now, I want to read some words to you from the bottom of the card. They're important.'

Anne cleared her throat.

'"This pass is strictly for the use of the person to whom it is granted and it is to be shown to any police officer who may ask for it."'

She raised her eyes to Hetty, letting the importance of the words sink in.

'Do you understand? You must guard it with your life, and never lend it to anyone. If it's found in the wrong hands, it will be a matter for the police.'

Hetty gulped. 'I'm honoured that Mr Jack thinks

highly enough of me to send me back to Elisabethville on factory business.'

Anne passed her the card. She watched as Hetty turned it in her hand and ran her fingers over it.

'The pass will stay in my office until you need it. I can't allow it to be given to you in case someone else gets hold of it.'

Hetty handed it back. 'I understand.'

'When Mr Jack decides he'd like you to return to Elisabethville, I'll let you know. He may ask you to take more toffee to the supplies office or deliver special promotions to the sweet shop. Think you'll be up for the job?'

Hetty smiled widely. 'I know I will. Thank you, Anne. And please thank Mr Jack too.' She shifted in her seat. 'But . . . why me, Anne? Oh, it's not that I'm not grateful. I am. I was frightened at first, but once I got there, it wasn't so bad. In fact the people were friendly.'

Dirk's open face and blue eyes flashed through her mind.

'But I'm not as pretty as the other girls. You could have sent Elsie instead.'

Anne leaned back in her seat. 'Yes, Elsie's charms are obvious,' she began. 'But Mr Jack wants only one girl to go to Elisabethville on business. There's something special about you, Hetty. You're polite and hard-working. And you must never do yourself down; you're as pretty as any of the girls. You do the toffee factory proud. Speaking of which, you'd better go back to work, or Mrs Perkins will be complaining that I'm keeping you away for longer than necessary.'

Hetty stood. 'Thanks again, Anne.'

Anne stood too. 'I hope a letter arrives from Bob soon,' she said.

Hetty bit her lip. 'It'll come when it's ready, I'm sure. In the meantime, I enjoy spending time with Elsie at work. In fact, we're planning a picnic one Saturday, on a day when the weather holds. Would you like to come? I'm sure Elsie won't mind. It'd be fun with the three of us. I have a little dog, and he'll come too. He's friendly and rarely barks.'

Anne picked up a pen and ran it through her fingers. 'Oh, I'm sure you don't want me tagging along.'

'I wouldn't have asked otherwise,' Hetty said.

Anne smiled. 'Well, if you're sure . . . You know, Anabel's death made me realise that life's too short to say no to invitations from people I like. We should all seize opportunities when they're presented. So yes, I'd love to join you. Will you let me know what day you'll be going and if you'd like me to bring picnic food?'

Hetty began counting on her fingers. 'Elsie's planning to bring beef sandwiches, boiled eggs, lemonade, and chocolate cake from the baker on Front Street.'

Anne raised an eyebrow. 'My word, I'm surprised she can afford all of that on the wages she's paid.'

'Her aunt helps her,' Hetty replied, then she clamped her mouth shut.

Chapter Eighteen

Two weeks later, Hetty woke to a cold autumn Saturday. She and Elsie had agreed in advance that if the weather was good, it'd be the day of their picnic. She had told this to Anne the previous day and had given her instructions to meet them outside the Rectory. She was looking forward to walking around the pretty riverside park with its gardens and walkways. However, before she left Elm Street to meet her friends, she had her mum and Dan to deal with.

Dan had been spending more time at home lately, and Hilda was overjoyed. Hetty, however, was less happy. Dan spent his days sleeping, then went out at night, often not returning until the early hours. He told Hilda he was working for Tyler Rose at the junkyard, but Hetty wondered what sort of work he did in the dark. She suspected he was involved in more thieving. When she broached the subject with him, he slammed the door on her and stormed up to his room. And each time she tried to speak to her mum, Hilda became irritated at her for speaking ill of her beloved son. Hetty swung between bouts of anger at Dan, mixed with concern for her mum suffering with her bad chest, and a desire to escape them both. Work at the factory became her refuge.

There'd still been no letter from Bob, not even an official card to say he'd arrived safely. Hetty kept up to date on the war by reading the local newspaper, copies of which were kept for staff at the factory canteen. She scanned each news item, searching for a mention of the Durham Light Infantry. She wondered about visiting Bob's sister in Durham. She was his only living relative, but Hetty didn't know her well enough and didn't want to worry her. And what if she did visit only to discover that Bob had written to his sister and not to her? What would that tell her about her place in his life? Would it confirm she was as low on his list of priorities as she feared she must be? No, she wouldn't visit.

She crossed her fingers and hoped a letter would come soon. But with each passing day, when the postman delivered the mail and there was nothing from Bob, her thoughts turned more to Dirk. Her little black dog proved a welcome distraction, but even the dog made her think of the blue-eyed Belgian. She kept hoping Mr Jack would send her back to Elisabethville on business now that her official pass was in Anne's office. She'd already decided she'd pluck up the courage to speak to Dirk if she saw him when she returned. And if there was no sign of him when she delivered toffee to the supply office, she'd ask for him by name – Mr Dirk Horta, the school teacher – and enquire if he might be free.

As Hetty washed and dressed that morning, she felt a lightness at the thought of spending the day with her friends, away from her mum fussing over Dan when he finally crawled out of bed. Downstairs, she toasted bread on the fire, then buttered slices for herself and her mum and brewed a pot of tea.

'How long will you be out today?' Hilda asked. She didn't wait for a reply, simply carried straight on. 'Don't forget you've got the yard to swill and the kitchen to clean. Oh, and your dog's starting to smell. Wash him outside with rainwater from the barrel, but don't use my best soap.'

Hetty gave a wry smile. She knew they didn't have best soap.

'The dog doesn't smell,' she huffed. 'I might be out all day if the rain keeps away.'

There was a banging at the door. Hetty stiffened and looked at her mum.

'Are you expecting anyone?'

Hilda's eyes grew wide. She shook her head. 'Are you?' she asked.

Hetty set her mug of tea on the table. Her heart felt heavy and her legs weak as she made her way along the hall. She leaned close to the door but didn't pull it open.

'Who is it?' she asked.

'Get this bloody door open, now!' Frankie Ireland yelled.

Feeling sick with nerves, Hetty pulled the door open. 'We've got your money, Frankie,' she said nervously.

Frankie teetered from side to side. Hetty wondered what was going on until the stench of stale beer reached her. He was drunk. She wondered who was selling beer to him at this time of day. But then his brother did own a pub. Perhaps Frankie helped himself. She took a step back.

'Give me the money,' he said. His words were slurred.

He leaned against the wall while Hetty went to the pantry to empty the jug. Hilda stayed where she was, pinned to her seat, too scared to move. Hetty handed over the cash.

'Where's the lad?' Frankie muttered.

Hetty wondered who he meant. 'Bob? He's at war,' she said.

'Not him. Your brother. I need a word, in private.'

She shook her head. 'No!' she said defiantly.

Frankie's arm swung out, but his movements were clumsy and she had time to jump back. His fist missed her cheek by inches.

'How dare you!' she screamed. 'Get out of my house.'

He tried again, but missed completely this time and stumbled into the wall. He steadied himself, then grabbed hold of Hetty's arm. She tried to twist away, but his grip was too strong. He leered at her, breathing beer fumes in her face. She turned her head, but he squeezed her chin with his other hand and forced her to look at him.

'Where's Dan?' he growled.

Hetty knew better than to argue. She was in too much pain for that. 'Let go of my arm and I'll tell you.'

Frankie loosened his grip.

'He's in bed. I'll get him,' she said.

But before she could move, Frankie swung his hand to the stair rail and began to climb.

'No, I'll go,' Hetty said. 'You're not going upstairs in my house.'

Frankie lashed out again, and this time almost caught her in the chest. She stepped back and watched him climb the stairs.

'What do you want with our Dan? He's done nothing wrong. Leave him out of this. It's me and my mum you deal with here, not him.'

Frankie ignored her and continued up the stairs, walking slowly and carefully. Hetty stood at the bottom, listening. She heard voices, Frankie's voice dominating Dan's. She heard Tyler Rose mentioned, money too. Then there was scuffling, footsteps on the landing. A few moments later, Frankie and Dan headed downstairs together.

'I'm going out, Mum!' Dan yelled as they pushed past Hetty and out to the street.

Hetty returned to the kitchen and sat opposite her mum.

'What's our Dan got himself involved in?' she asked, although she doubted Hilda would know the truth, or that Dan would've revealed it.

'He's a good lad, Hetty love. Let him have his fun.'

Hetty fumed with anger. 'Fun? Frankie just tried to hit me! Dan's heading out with the fella who's taking every penny I earn. He's got himself involved with one of the biggest crooks around. Plus, he's working for Tyler Rose, who's involved in all kinds of crime. I've heard he uses his junkyard for storing stolen goods. Fun? You've got no idea! You've protected Dan for too long.'

She patted her side and the dog came running.

'I'm going out. I don't know when I'll be back.'

She stormed along the hall, slamming the door behind her as she left.

She was still angry when she reached the Rectory, but the walk in the fresh air had helped calm her a little. For the first time since she'd left the house, she unclenched her fists and slowed her pace. The dog ran at her side, chasing birds that Hetty knew it would never catch. But just as she was beginning to relax, she saw Elsie. She'd been looking forward to the picnic for ages; it was the first time she and Elsie had spent a day off work together. But it felt like it had already been spoiled because of Frankie. She knew she had to talk to Elsie about it, otherwise what had happened that morning would fester.

Elsie gave a cheery wave as Hetty drew close, but she couldn't bring herself to wave back.

'What's wrong with you this morning?' Elsie teased. 'You look as miserable as Mrs Perkins.'

Hetty threaded her arm through her friend's and pulled her close. She looked from left to right to ensure that Anne wasn't on her way. When she saw the coast was clear, she began to speak.

'How's Frankie treating you?'

Elsie pulled her arm away. 'Why?'

'I saw him this morning, he came to my house.'

She shrugged. 'So? I know all about your dad's debt. Frankie told me. That's his business. It doesn't affect our friendship, does it?'

'There's more to it than that,' Hetty said gently. 'He was drunk when he turned up. He took the money we had for him, then he woke my brother and took him out with him. I think there's something murky going on involving Frankie and Dan.'

She paused, unsure how much else she should reveal.

'There's something else . . . Frankie was violent with me. He tried to hit me, Elsie. Has he ever lashed out at you?'

Elsie looked at her hard. 'What are you implying? He treats me all right.'

'I wasn't implying, I was saying,' Hetty said.

'Listen, Frankie might not be as upstanding as your Bob, but at least he's here. When was the last time Bob wrote to you?'

Hetty's mouth opened in shock as Elsie continued.

'Frankie takes me to his brother's pub. Sure, he's no angel – I've heard things about him – but all I know is how he treats me. And I'm fine.'

Hetty looked at her friend for a long time. Then she gently put her hands on Elsie's shoulders. Elsie stared at the ground, and when she raised her eyes, there were tears in them.

'I'm sorry, I shouldn't have said that about Bob, it was cruel,' she said softly.

'Just be honest with me about Frankie,' Hetty pleaded.

Elsie pushed her shoulders back. 'He hasn't laid a finger on me.'

'If that's what you're telling me, I have to believe you,' Hetty said. 'But if he ever does . . .'

'He won't!' Elsie snapped.

Hetty stepped back and let her hands fall. 'Then let's not talk of him again,' she said.

She pressed her back against the Rectory wall, and Elsie did the same. Hetty reached for Elsie's hand and they stood side by side in silence, the dog at their feet.

'I've got everything for the picnic,' Elsie said at last. 'Aunt Jean even gave me enough money to buy bottles of beer.'

Hetty wrinkled her nose. 'I'm not sure I like beer.'

Elsie laughed out loud. 'Me neither. Maybe Anne likes it.'

Hetty looked along the lane. 'Where is she, anyway? She's late.'

'Let's go and look for her. She hasn't lived here long; she might not know where the Rectory is.'

Hetty helped Elsie carry the heavy picnic basket and they turned the corner to Front Street.

'Look!' Hetty gasped. She pointed at the bus stop outside the Co-op. She was stunned to see Anne, dressed in a smart coat and hat, climbing aboard the Durham bus.

Chapter Nineteen

On Monday morning at the factory, Hetty began picking and wrapping the moment she arrived. A new girl called Beattie had replaced Anabel, and Hetty was explaining the secret communication methods to her. Beattie was a tall, stout girl with thick arms and a cheerful round face. She told Hetty she'd been working on her family farm near Beamish but had jumped at the chance of getting away from pigs and cows.

Hetty glanced at the clock; Elsie was late again. Fortunately, there was no sign of Mrs Perkins, who'd been called to join a meeting in the slab room. Hetty guessed her friend would be with Frankie, stealing kisses in the narrow lane that ran behind the factory. The lane wasn't overlooked by any windows and provided a perfect secret place for lovers to meet. At night, as there were no street lamps there, it was rumoured that stolen goods changed hands. Some of the factory girls were scared to walk alone there, for fear that men waited in the dark.

When Elsie finally rushed into the room, Hetty turned to greet her. Elsie slipped her shoes off and pushed her feet into her clogs.

'You're lucky the old dragon isn't here to catch you coming in late again,' Hetty said.

Their hands reached automatically for toffees and wrappers.

'Were you with him again?' she asked, not looking at Elsie, keeping her concentration on her work.

'If you mean Frankie, yes, I was. Listen, Hetty, I'm sorry again about what I said to you about Bob. It's been bothering me ever since. We had such a nice picnic and I don't want anything to come between us. We're still friends, aren't we?'

'Of course we're still friends. I'm just worried about you, that's all.'

'Well, don't be,' Elsie said firmly. 'I'm a big girl. I can look after myself. Did you see Anne this morning on your way into work?'

'I looked for her but didn't find her,' Hetty replied.

'We should find out why she didn't join us at the picnic, and why she was on the Durham bus.'

'It's none of our business,' Hetty said, although she was curious.

'Girls, be quiet!' Mrs Perkins was behind them. They'd been so busy talking that they hadn't noticed the other girls giving them the warning sign.

'Sorry, Mrs Perkins,' they muttered. The supervisor headed to her desk with a swish of her blue skirt.

At lunchtime, in the canteen, Anne sat next to Stan Chapman, the gardener. She was going over the planting plans for the following spring that Mr Gerard had drawn up.

'He's asked for more daffodils, to brighten the flower

beds. As cheery as you can make them.'

Stan scratched his head as he studied the plans. He was a thickset man with hands like shovels, a broad chest and strong arms. His face was open and honest, weather-beaten and ruddy from years working outdoors doing the job he adored. His thick brown hair was cut short and his eyes were hazel brown. He pointed at the plans on the table between him and Anne.

'And more tulips here?'

'Think you can make it work?'

'I'm sure I can.' He folded the plans away. 'Well, I'll be off, Anne. I've got a mountain of leaves to deal with. This time of year, leaves fall quicker than I can sweep them. Mind you, they all go on the compost heap; you can't beat leaf mould to help improve the soil. You can let Mr Jack know that my team of lads will start planting the spring bulbs before the end of the month.'

He put on his flat cap, then stood and strode away. As he reached the door, Hetty and Elsie entered. Stan raised his cap at Elsie and they exchanged a smile.

'You shouldn't go making eyes at him,' Anne heard Hetty say.

Elsie shrugged. 'He's a good-looking man. What's wrong with a bit of flirting?'

'Isn't Frankie enough for you?'

She nudged Hetty playfully. 'You're just jealous,' she teased.

The girls made their way to the counter. Anne managed to catch Hetty's eye and waved. Once they'd been served, the pair of them joined her at her table.

Anne inspected Elsie's tray of food. 'Let me know what the steak pie's like. I found a new supplier for the meat; they're cheaper than the one we've been using so far.'

She looked at Hetty's tray too, saw an empty plate and kept quiet. She watched as Hetty pulled a squashed bread bun from her overall pocket and laid it on her plate. While Elsie tucked into pie and peas, Hetty picked at her sandwich, making each mouthful last as long as she could.

'Where were you on Saturday?' Hetty asked. 'We waited for you at the Rectory, just like we agreed. You missed a good picnic.'

Anne shifted in her seat and took a moment before she replied.

'I'm sorry, girls. My landlady, Mrs Fortune, had trouble laying a new rug. She made me stay and help her. I'm her only lodger, so I could hardly say no. It took half the morning to put right, and by the time we'd finished, I didn't think it worth joining you. Besides, I didn't know where on the riverside you'd be by then. There was no way of letting you know. Maybe next time I'll come.'

She picked up her mug of tea and took a long drink. She felt her neck and face redden, and thought she saw Elsie nudge Hetty, but perhaps it was just the way she was eating her pie, with her elbows poking out. She turned away to gather herself and looked around the canteen, wondering how best to change the subject.

'Isn't it wonderful that men and women can sit together now?' she said cheerily. 'Look over there: Anabel's brother, Gavin, is surrounded by girls from the wrapping room.'

Elsie and Hetty carried on eating, and when they'd finished, they quickly excused themselves.

'We want to get some fresh air with a walk in the garden before we head back to work,' Hetty said.

'Just a moment, before you go,' Anne said.

Hetty stopped and turned. 'Yes?'

'Mr Jack would like you to return to Elisabethville tomorrow, first thing. You can collect your pass and the toffees he wants you to take. Think you'd be up for the task?'

Hetty beamed with pride. 'I know I will. Thank you.'

As they left the canteen, Elsie turned to Hetty.

'Anne lied to us about missing our picnic. We saw her on the Durham bus on Saturday, as clear as day. It was definitely her. Why would she make up a tale about her landlady and a rug?'

'It's odd, I agree,' Hetty replied. 'Maybe she was being polite and letting us down gently because she didn't really want to come. Yet she sounded keen when I invited her.'

Elsie hooked her arm through Hetty's and pulled her close. 'Or maybe she's got a secret fella she doesn't want us to know about and she was spending the day with him. Anyway, enough about Anne, let's talk about you going to the Belgian camp. Do you think I could come with you this time?'

'No,' Hetty said sharply. 'This is factory business. I won't disobey Mr Jack.'

Elsie dropped her arm. 'Then you must tell me all about it when you come back. I want to know what the Belgian men look like, how tall they are and what clothes they wear. I want to know if I'd stand a chance with them if I could get someone to smuggle me in for a dance one Saturday night.'

Hetty laughed out loud. 'First of all you're courting Frankie. Next you're making eyes at Stan the gardener, and now you're thinking about Belgian men. You're incorrigible, Elsie Cooper!'

'Someone mention my name?' A man's voice came from behind them.

Stan removed his flat cap and winked at Elsie. Hetty took the hint.

'I'll see you back at work, don't be late,' she said as she turned away, leaving Elsie and Stan to talk.

She kicked leaves along the ground as she walked, enjoying the crunching sound under her feet. Her heart felt light and a smile made its way to her face. She was going back to Elisabethville. She tried to pretend it was the honour of being chosen to represent the toffee factory that was making her so happy. But deep in her heart, she knew the real reason.

Anne made her way back to the office. Mr Jack was in Yorkshire that day; he'd travelled by train from Chester-le-Street station and wasn't due back until the following day. While he was away, she was taking the opportunity to update his filing system.

She began work straight away, forcing herself to concentrate on papers and folders. However, her thoughts kept turning to the lie she'd told Hetty and Elsie. She reassured herself that there was no way either girl could have known where she'd been. She wouldn't tell anyone the real reason she'd missed their picnic. It was her secret alone.

Her journey to Durham had taken an hour by bus, but it had been worth it, for she had seen her boy. Oh, how she'd longed to hold him, but she'd always known that wasn't possible. It was never part of the deal when she'd sold him to Peter Matthews and his barren wife, Ruby. She wasn't even supposed to know where the family lived. However, Anne was clever, efficient and organised. She made enquiries and easily discovered their address. Once she knew where her boy was, she travelled to Durham whenever she could afford the fare. The Matthews' house was on the outskirts of the city, under a railway bridge. She positioned herself behind trees at the back of the house and peered over the wall for a precious glimpse. This time, she'd seen him twice when Mrs Matthews had walked past a window with the child in her arms, and had thought her heart would burst.

As she sorted papers on Mr Jack's desk, she knew she had to get a grip on her emotions The child wasn't hers any more. She'd sold him before she moved to Chester-le-Street. There wasn't the option to keep him; she couldn't possibly have raised him alone. The shame of it would have killed her, and she'd have been shunned by all. As for the child's father, she hadn't seen him since the night she told him she was pregnant.

After she'd left Mayfair toffee and moved out of Sunderland, she'd nursed her ailing parents and hidden herself away. She'd hoped and prayed that after she'd had the child, she could persuade his father to come home. Sadly, it hadn't worked out, for the baby's father couldn't be found. Not only had she lost the man she thought she loved, she'd ended up selling her son. Some days she took a no-nonsense view of it. She had a good job now and a future to look forward to. But on other, darker days, the sense of loss overwhelmed her. Saturday had been one of those days.

She straightened her glasses and returned to her work, filing the receipts for the cheaper meat that Mr Jack had bought for the canteen. But as she lifted a folder from the desk, another one underneath caught her eye. It was marked *Strictly Confidential* in Mr Jack's handwriting. This was unusual, as it was Anne who labelled his files. She glanced at the door; it was closed, and no one was expected. She quickly opened the file and scanned the contents. What she saw chilled her to the bone.

Chapter Twenty

Anne's heart raced as she read. The papers in the folder were handwritten accounts that she'd never seen before. This was odd, as Mr Jack always said he gave her full sight of all papers. Now she wondered if this was true. Why would he have kept this from her when its contents were so important?

She sat in his chair with the open file in front of her on the desk. She was engrossed in the columns of figures, trying to work out what they meant, when the door was flung open and Mr Burl walked in. She jumped up and closed the folder, but she wasn't quick enough. She pressed her feet into the carpet and stood up straight.

'Mr Burl, how may I help you?'

He didn't speak for a moment, just stared at the folder.

'I came to collect some papers Mr Jack left for me on his desk.'

Anne gulped. 'Papers?' she squeaked. She guessed immediately which papers he'd come for.

He walked forward and picked up the file she'd been reading.

Anne stood her ground. She and Mr Burl had never got on. He was rude to her, even in front of Mr Jack, and his manner was always abrupt. She'd seen him be courteous to Jacob in reception and patient with his secretary, a meek woman called Meg, but never to her. She eyed the folder in his hand.

'Mr Jack trusts me with everything in his office. I had every right to read it,' she said. She was surprised how confident her words sounded, as inside she felt nervous.

'Well, that's as may be. But you certainly shouldn't have been sitting in his chair. You're taking advantage while he's away.'

'I would never take advantage or abuse my position,' Anne said firmly. 'I sat down to read, that's all.'

Mr Burl's shoulders seemed to sink, and his face looked defeated. 'I understand that,' he said, more gently now. He tapped the folder with his finger. 'The contents don't make easy reading. The factory's facing hard times, Anne. I'm sure Mr Jack must have explained.'

Mr Jack had told her no such thing. She was shocked and hurt, both by the bleak news of the factory's finances and by the fact that Mr Jack had kept it from her.

'The war has brought uncertainty to the country. Not just to our toffee production but to manufacturing of all kinds. Money is being poured into munitions and weapons, and of course we must have those. But times ahead will be hard.'

'Will jobs be cut?' Anne dared herself to ask.

'It's possible,' Mr Burl said carefully. 'But I can't say any more. The board will be meeting once Mr Jack returns. You'll be taking notes, as always, so you'll find out what's going on. In the meantime, I'd be grateful if you wouldn't mention our conversation outside of this room.'

She glared at him. 'I'd never do that,' she said. 'What is discussed within these four walls always stays here.'

Mr Burl's tone turned dark again. 'Ah, but I know you're friendly with two girls from the wrapping room. I've seen you in the canteen with them. I know how gossip starts.'

Anne stepped forward, trying to keep her temper in check. 'What is it I've done to deserve your anger, Mr Burl? I know you told Mr Jack he was wrong to employ me. Why do you dislike me so much?'

He gripped the file tightly. 'Remember Miss Brabin?' he said.

She racked her brains. The name sounded familiar, but she couldn't place it.

'No, I thought you wouldn't,' he continued with a touch of sarcasm. 'She was due to be interviewed for the role of Mr Jack's secretary on the day you were given the job. The day Mr Jack asked you to let the other girls know they hadn't been successful. I managed to stop her from setting off from home for her interview so that she didn't waste her time.'

'I don't understand,' Anne said.

Mr Burl stuck his chin out. 'Miss Brabin is my fiancée.'

Suddenly it all made sense. Anne stood straight with her hands clasped in front of her. 'I won't apologise for Mr Jack's decision to employ me.'

Mr Burl turned away without another word and headed out of the door with the folder under his arm.

Once he'd left, Anne turned to the window and looked out across the gardens. She had much on her mind.

She saw Stan the gardener sweeping fallen leaves. A factory girl was with him, and they were laughing and chatting. She peered to see who it was and then laughed out loud.

'Of course it's Elsie Cooper, who else?' She hoped Mrs Perkins wouldn't catch Elsie shirking when she should be at work. But that wasn't her concern. Mr Jack and the factory were. More importantly, the factory's finances and its future, her future, lay heavy on her mind.

She turned from the window and resumed her task, sorting papers into date order and placing them carefully into folders. Her nimble fingers worked quickly, and soon everything was filed away. There was a knock at the door, and she braced herself in case it was Mr Burl again. Then she remembered that he'd barged in without knocking last time. She knew he wouldn't have dared do that if Mr Jack had been there.

'Come in,' she called.

Jacob's tall, stooped figure hovered in the doorway. 'Miss Wright, there's a visitor in reception for you.'

Anne followed him along the corridor and was pleased to see Hetty. She greeted her warmly and asked her to follow her to her office.

'This is a nice surprise,' she said. 'I wasn't expecting to see you until tomorrow morning, to pick up your pass for Elisabethville. Please, take a seat.'

She looked across the desk and remembered the meagre lunch that she'd seen Hetty eating.

'How are you, Hetty?'

'I'm better now that there's free toffees with their nutritious cream and vanilla. Elsie can't stop eating them. Every time I look at her, she's got a toffee in her mouth.'

Glenda Young

'How is Elsie? I saw her chatting with Stan in the gardens just now.'

'Oh, she's fine. She likes Stan, you know. But she's already got a fella called . . .' Hetty sat up straight. 'I'm sorry, I'm not here to talk about Elsie. I don't want to waste your time; I know you must be busy.'

Anne waved her hand dismissively. 'Mr Jack's away in Yorkshire, meeting the chocolatier. What can I help you with?'

Hetty leaned forward. 'I was hoping to collect my pass now. That way I could go straight to Elisabethville in the morning, direct from home. It'd save me a long walk from home to the factory then back to the bus stop. Might that be possible?'

Anne pulled the top drawer of her desk open, found Hetty's pass and handed it across the desk.

'I don't see why you can't have it now. You will look after it, won't you? Don't let it out of your sight. I want to remind you of what I told you before, Hetty, because it's serious business. If it ends up in someone else's hands, it could be a matter for the police.'

Hetty put the pass into her overall pocket and patted it down. 'I'll guard it with my life.'

Anne stood. 'Come with me to see Jacob in reception. He'll give you a box of best toffee to take, and we'll wrap it with blue ribbon as before. Would you wear the blue ribbon in your hair again too?'

'Of course,' Hetty said.

She paused, and looked at Anne.

'You know, if you didn't want to come on the picnic with Elsie and me, I do understand.'

Anne quickly composed herself.

'I told you why I couldn't come. I had to help my landlady with her new rug.'

'Yes, of course,' Hetty said quickly.

Once the ribbon had been tied around the box, Anne said goodbye to Hetty and returned to her office, feeling sick over telling more lies.

Hetty couldn't keep the grin off her face when she returned to the wrapping room. She carried the box of toffee carefully. It was her ticket to return to Elisabethville, and it felt as precious as jewels. First thing in the morning, she would take the bus to Birtley, and this time she was determined to find Dirk and speak to him.

Chapter Twenty-One

The following morning, Hetty woke earlier than usual, excited for the day ahead. She turned over in bed and glanced down at the floor, relieved to see the box of toffee intact. She'd been worried it might've been nibbled by mice. From under her pillow she pulled the piece of card, her pass to Elisabethville. She'd hidden it there with Anne's words ringing in her ears about how important it was not to lose it. She leapt out of bed and drew the curtain back. It was a dark autumn morning, but the dreary day did nothing to dampen her excitement. She washed quickly in cold water from the bowl and jug in her room, then dressed in her overall. She brushed her hair and tied the blue ribbon so that the bow fell neatly at the side of her face. When she stepped out of her bedroom, the dog jumped to attention on the landing, where it had spent the night.

'Downstairs, dog,' she called, and it bounded ahead.

In the kitchen, Hetty found her mum sitting by the fire drinking a mug of tea. 'Is there enough in the pot for me?' she asked.

Hilda shook her head. 'No. Dan drank the last of it.

He needs his strength building up for his work.'

'Oh? And I don't?' Hetty said.

Hilda pursed her lips, and Hetty knew she'd gone too far.

'Sorry, Mum. I'll make some fresh. So, our Dan's got up early for work. Well, that's something, I suppose.'

Hilda looked at the ribbon in Hetty's hair. 'Why do you look like you're dressed up to attend Durham Miners' Gala? Where did you get money for ribbon?'

Hetty lightly touched the bow. 'Mr Jack paid for it. I'm being sent on a mission for him this morning. He likes me to wear the blue ribbon when I represent the factory.'

Hilda raised her eyebrows. 'A mission? I bet I can guess where he's sending you. It'll be the Belgian village again, I expect.'

Hetty decided to keep quiet until her mum ran out of steam.

'It's not safe for you to go there, Hetty. I'm surprised at Mr Jack sending a young factory girl. Why did he pick you? What's so special about you?'

Hetty filled the kettle and put it on the fire, then sliced bread to toast. All the while, Hilda didn't stop to take a breath.

'I heard some girls go dancing in Elisabethville on Saturday nights. What's the world coming to when local girls have their heads turned by strangers? It's not right, I tell you. No good will come of it. You need to stick with your own kind. Be grateful you've got Bob. He might not be my cup of tea, but he's better than nothing.'

Hetty bit the inside of her cheek to stop herself from

saying something that would turn Hilda's words even more sour.

'Mind you, our Dan will prove quite the catch when he finds the right girl.'

She concentrated on toasting bread, trying to tune out her mum's words as they rattled on.

'Speaking of Bob, why hasn't he written yet? Doreen's daughter Barbara, who lives at the end of Victor Street, well, her fella's in the Durham Light Infantry and she's had two letters so far. It sounds to me as if Bob's forgotten you already.'

This proved too much for Hetty. 'For goodness' sake, will you just shut up!'

Hilda folded her arms and narrowed her eyes. 'Don't you raise your voice to me, girl.'

But Hetty wasn't prepared to back down. 'Don't say things about Bob that aren't true. There's a war on and letters might be lost. Now, please, drop the subject.'

She ate her toast quickly and gulped down her tea, then stuck her arms into a heavy old coat that had once belonged to her dad. She buttoned it to her neck, then picked up the box of toffee. Hilda looked at her.

'Bring some of the reject toffees home tonight.'

Hetty sighed. 'You know I can't. Yes, we can eat them at work now, but we're not allowed to take them out of the factory. If I'm caught by the searchers with toffees in my pockets, I could lose my job.'

Hilda shivered by the fire and began to cough.

'Has Dan brought coal?' Hetty asked. She was worried about how they'd get through the winter.

Hilda shook her head. 'He's too busy working to bring coal home now.'

'I can't afford to keep buying it, Mum. You know how I'm fixed. Every spare penny goes to Frankie Ireland.'

Hilda looked into the fire. 'Your bloody dad and his drinking,' she hissed. 'I always said he'd be the ruin of us.'

Hetty sat down. 'Dad was a good man underneath it all. Yes, he had problems and got himself into debt at the Lambton Arms. But he was a decent man and I loved him.'

She waited for Hilda to soften, to admit she'd loved him too, but she never said a word. Hetty stood.

'I've got to go. I have to catch the Birtley bus and don't want to be late.'

'Watch what you're doing,' Hilda said.

Hetty bent down to scratch the dog behind the ears, then left the house.

Outside, the day was dark and cold with a bitter chill on the breeze. As she waited for the bus outside the Co-op on Front Street, leaves drifted slowly to the ground. She stood with her back straight, her chin tilted. She was on official business for Mr Jack, proud to be representing the toffee factory again. She told herself the nerves she was feeling were brought on by the thought of heading back to Elisabethville, but she knew what they were really. She thought about Dirk's blue eyes, his friendly smile and open face. And that was when the butterflies in her stomach took flight and made her smile.

The bus arrived and she clambered aboard. She sat in the same seat as last time, downstairs by the window, and all the while kept the box of toffee on her knee, holding it with both hands. There was no letter to deliver this time, just the toffees, and she was to hand them to the supplies officer she'd met before. It was an easy task and one she was looking forward to. She patted her pocket, reassuring herself that her pass was still there.

When the bus reached the crossroads at Station Road, she alighted. This time she walked confidently across the road to the sentry at the gate. She was nowhere near as nervous as she'd been last time.

'Good morning, I'm here to make a delivery from Jack's toffee factory to the supplies office,' she announced.

The guard eyed her coolly. 'You must show authorisation,' he barked.

Hetty pulled the pass from her pocket and handed it over. The guard looked from the card to her face.

'You need to enter by a different gate, on the south side,' he said.

This time she wasn't fazed. She knew exactly where to go after Dirk had shown her last time.

'It's all right, I can enter here now I know where the supplies office is,' she said. 'I have been here before.'

The guard handed her pass back and she tucked it safely in her coat pocket. He opened the gate, then stood to one side and allowed her to enter before returning to his position. Hetty was now inside Elisabethville, and this time she was on her own.

She walked along the main street, past the lines of huts where families lived. No washing was strung out today. She walked past the accommodation block for single men, where Dirk lived. Two men strolled by, talking in a language she didn't understand. She kept her eyes peeled in case she saw Dirk. She passed a shop, and after a few more minutes, she spotted the supplies office. Before she entered, she tightened the bow in her hair, pressed her shoulders back and put a smile on her face.

'Aha! My toffee factory girl!' a voice cried as she entered.

She was relieved to see the man she'd dealt with last time.

'A present from Mr Jack, hand-delivered to show how much he values your business,' she said, repeating the words Anne had asked her to say. She handed over the box and the man shook her hand.

'Do you enjoy your work making toffee?' he asked. His English was good, but his accent was heavy and Hetty struggled to understand. He repeated his question.

'Yes, I enjoy it very much,' she replied.

She made to step out of the office, then stopped. She forced herself to say the words she'd practised many times.

'I wonder . . . do you know of a Mr Dirk Horta, and if so, where I might find him?'

She couldn't believe she'd asked such a direct question, but the words were out before she realised she'd said them. She rocked back on her heels as if the force of them had knocked her for six.

'Dirk? The school teacher? Do you have business with him?'

Hetty didn't want to lie. 'Yes . . . I . . . No, I don't have business with him. I wanted to thank him for his help in guiding me the last time I was here. I was a little nervous, you see, and Dirk . . . I mean Mr Horta . . . helped me at the gate.'

The man glanced at a clock on the wall. 'Classes begin in twenty minutes. If you hurry, you might find him at the school. I'm sure he would welcome a visit from such a pretty toffee girl.'

'Thank you,' she said.

She smoothed the ribbon in her hair as she left the office. Underneath her dad's coat, her heart was beating fast. Retracing her steps to the main avenue, she walked past the shop, then saw the building that Dirk had said was the school. The door was open. She stepped inside. There was a small square vestibule with another door leading from it.

'Hello?' she called.

There was no reply, so she knocked on the inner door and waited. Still no one came.

'Hello?' she called again.

This time the door swung open and she was met by a tall, slim, handsome woman dressed in a white blouse with a brown striped scarf at her neck. Her fair hair was swept up on the top of her head. There was something familiar about her pale face and blue eyes.

'Hello?' she said.

Hetty breathed a sigh of relief. 'Oh, you speak English.'

'Yes, I do. I'm Gabrielle Horta, how may I help?'

Hetty stood stock still. Of course. Dirk's sister. 'I'm looking for Dirk Horta. I was told he might be here.'

'Yes, my brother is here. But who are you?'

'My name's Hetty Lawson, I'm from Jack's toffee factory.'

Gabrielle's face lit up with joy. 'Oh, so *you're* the toffee factory girl,' she said warmly. 'My brother has talked fondly of you.'

Chapter Twenty-Two

Hetty followed Gabrielle into a large room where chairs were set out in rows. At the desk at the front sat Dirk. Her heart leapt when she saw him.

'My brother, you have a visitor,' Gabrielle said.

Hetty was grateful she'd spoken in English; it made her feel as if she was being included.

Dirk looked up, and when he saw her, he leapt from his desk, knocking papers to the floor. Hetty saw his face blush red. He picked up the papers, then extended his hand.

'How do you do?' he said politely. 'It's nice to meet you again.'

Gabrielle laughed. 'Nice? You're all he's talked about.'

Hetty felt her cheeks burn. She shook his hand. 'I just wanted to say thank you for your help last time I was here.'

Gabrielle stepped forward and gently touched her on her shoulder. 'I must go to work now. It has been nice meeting you, toffee girl.'

'Her name is Hetty,' Dirk said, gazing into Hetty's eyes.

As Gabrielle drifted away, Hetty realised she was still holding Dirk's hand. Neither of them seemed able to let the other go. Finally she released her hand and took a step back.

'I mustn't keep you from your work, and I have to return to the factory. I simply wanted to say hello before I left. I've been delivering a toffee box to the supplies office.'

'And I'm very pleased you did,' Dirk replied.

She liked the sound of his voice. His accent had a musical lilt to it that appealed a great deal.

'I must go, really,' she said, and made to leave.

Dirk cleared his throat. 'Hetty?'

She met his gaze. 'Yes?'

'We . . . er . . . we have a dance in the village centre on Saturday night. Would you like to come?'

Hetty's eyes opened wide. 'Me?'

Dirk nodded. 'I'd like it very much if you would. I'm not much of a dancer, but perhaps you could show me the steps.'

She laughed out loud. 'I can't dance either, so we could help each other.'

'I'd like that, yes,' he said.

She knew she should leave. She'd be in trouble with Mrs Perkins if she stayed away too long.

'I must go,' she said again.

'You must, yes,' Dirk replied. But still Hetty couldn't move her feet to take her to the door.

'So you will come to the dance?' he asked again.

She didn't hesitate. 'I'd love to, thank you. I have a pass now if I need to show it to the guard.'

'I think you should be all right without the pass, as

you're my guest. It's not just girls who come for our dances, you know, we also have local men who bring their wives. Elisabethville is a lot more friendly and welcoming than your newspaper suggests.'

Hetty had read the letters of complaint from locals about the high standard of accommodation at Elisabethville, with running water and electricity. They were petty letters with jealous remarks, the type Hilda would write if she was able to articulate her misplaced anger.

'I don't agree with those letters,' she said.

Dirk gave a sharp nod. 'That's why I like you, Hetty Lawson.'

Hetty looked into his blue eyes again. It felt as if she'd known him all her life. She felt comfortable. It was as if this second meeting had been on the cards all along. She couldn't explain it, but she felt at ease with Dirk in a way that she'd never felt with Bob.

'I like you too, Dirk Horta.'

He stood to attention. 'Then that's settled. I will see you on Saturday night.'

Hetty managed to push her feet forward until she found herself outside on the wide avenue.

'I'll see you on Saturday,' she said.

They said goodbye and Hetty walked off. When she was halfway up the avenue, she turned to look back. Dirk was still at the schoolhouse door, watching and waving. She waved back, with a beaming smile on her face.

It was while she was sitting on the bus heading back to Chester-le-Street that Hetty's doubts set in. How could she even think of meeting Dirk again? She had Bob. He was overseas, fighting to save the country, one of the thousands of brave boys and men. He'd never raised his hand to her, not like Frankie Ireland. He didn't drink much. In fact, he had no bad habits Hetty could recall. What would it say about her as a person – as a woman – if she danced with another man? Would she end up like Elsie Cooper, flirting with everyone she met? Would she get herself a bad reputation? How would she explain to her mum that she was falling for another man?

She gasped at where her thoughts were leading, because she realised that she *was* falling for Dirk. He'd been on her mind constantly since the first time they'd met. It'd been heartening to hear from Gabrielle that he had spoken fondly of her. Was it really wrong to fall for him? To dance with him, even kiss him? He was Belgian and she was English, but where was the harm in that? She knew Hilda would find plenty to say.

She felt conflicted. What if Bob found out she'd been dancing with Dirk? What if someone saw her and wrote to tell him? Would they know Bob's army address when even she didn't know it? Might they tell his sister? There was the tiniest possibility that the news might reach him and break his heart. No, she couldn't do it. She wouldn't go dancing. How foolish she'd been to even contemplate it. She'd had her head turned by a pair of blue eyes and a kind face. That was all it had been. She had to pull herself together. She'd promised Bob she'd wait for him and that was what she'd do. But even as she thought this, she knew in her heart it wasn't what she wanted. Bob was safe, dependable, reliable . . . and dull.

She bit her lip as she alighted from the bus, her mind in turmoil. She walked up Front Street as if in a daze. She tried to push thoughts of Dirk and Elisabethville to the back of her mind, but it proved impossible. She already knew how much she wanted to see him again, to be held in his arms at the dance. She wanted to get to know him, to hear his lovely accent. And yet how wrong it felt too. Shouldn't she be grateful for what she had and make the most of it instead of reaching for something unknown? Oh, it was all so hard.

She turned up Market Lane towards the factory gates and saw her mum there with the dog. Her heart quickened at the sight, and she broke into a run.

'Mum? What's happened? Why are you here?'

Hilda tutted out loud. 'What a fine greeting that is for your own mother.'

Hetty's shoulders slumped. 'I didn't mean it like that. I got a shock, that's all, seeing you here. Is everything all right at home? Dan's not in trouble, is he?'

'Dan can look after himself, he's a fine boy,' Hilda said.

'Then what is it?' Hetty said, irritated that her mum was defending Dan again.

Hilda dug in her pocket and pulled out a brown envelope. 'This arrived for you. I thought you'd want to see it. I asked that miserable fella in the factory reception if he knew whether you were back from the Belgian village yet, but he said . . .'

As Hilda rattled on, Hetty stared at the envelope. She recognised Bob's writing on the front, and traced the words where he'd printed her name. *Miss Henrietta Lawson, 74 Elm Street, Chester-le-Street, County Durham, England*. The envelope was stamped and franked with official markings.

'. . . and I've been waiting here by the gate with your

dog for half an hour. Then you turn up and ask me why I'm here. That's all the thanks I get for bringing your letter after I've been standing in the cold air with my bad chest.'

Hetty looked at her. 'What? Sorry, Mum. I didn't catch what you said.'

Hilda sighed loudly, deliberately. 'You always did have cloth ears. You're not like our Dan. *He* listens to me. I'm going back home where it's warm. It's too cold to be standing outside.'

'Thank you for bringing the letter,' Hetty said. But Hilda was already walking away with the dog.

Hetty glanced through the gates. No one was about, so she ducked behind a brick wall and ripped open the envelope. Inside was a small card. She felt deflated that it wasn't a letter, a long, loving one full of plans and dreams for their wedding when he returned. She'd hoped it would contain all the words he'd left unsaid on the day he'd pulled away from her at the railway station. Instead, it was a card printed with standard phrases, with Bob's only contribution, it seemed, crossing out irrelevant words. *I am quite well*, it stated in official type. Underneath that, thankfully crossed through in pen, was ~~I have been admitted to the hospital~~. Then, infuriatingly, another line crossed out the card's final words: ~~Letter follows at first opportunity~~. Hetty glared at it with tears in her eyes. The card was as square and solid as Bob, revealing nothing.

'I am quite well,' she said out loud. She couldn't believe it. *Quite well*. Was that all she deserved? She was relieved he wasn't in hospital, of course. That was good news. Even better, there was a return address to write to; at least she had that now. She read the card again, and tears sprang to her eyes. That was Bob all right. Official, to the point, blunt, obtuse. There was no *Darling Hetty* – not even *Dear* – and no sign of the word *love*. The man she thought she cared for hadn't even put a kiss on the card. Bob's missing words gave her yet more reason to think about Dirk.

Chapter Twenty-Three

Later that week, Anne was called to take notes at a board meeting. The boardroom was grand, with its ceiling and walls panelled in caramel wood. She always felt as if she was being enrobed by toffee whenever she entered the room, which was perhaps Mr Jack's intent.

She was the only woman at the table. Mr Jack sat at the head and she was on his right-hand side. Mr Burl sat on his left. Next to Anne was Mr Gerard, the creative manager. She enjoyed Mr Gerard's company whenever he called at her office. Despite his advancing years, he always had a mischievous grin and a twinkle in his eye, and his mind was very sharp. He was constantly coming up with new and exciting ways to market Jack's toffee. Mr Burl, however, considered him something of a relic, and Anne had even overheard him suggest to Mr Jack that he was too old to be of use. However, Mr Jack had been firm, and she was relieved to hear that there were no plans to retire Mr Gerard.

Mr Jack brought the meeting to order. Jacob wheeled in a trolley with dainty cups and saucers rattling on top. Each cup bore the company logo in blue. Anne saw Mr Jack glance at the trolley.

'Must we always drink from such small cups at our meetings?' he sighed.

She made a note to obtain a price for large mugs. She stood to help Jacob serve coffee to each man. Then she sat down, adjusted her glasses and concentrated on her notepad.

Once the meeting began, her pencil rarely left the page. She worked furiously, recording the proceedings in shorthand, to type up later that day. But what she heard concerned her, especially when talk turned to the threat of sugar rationing.

'With fewer men in the workforce, industry is starting to run at reduced capacity. This will have a knock-on effect to all parts of the supply chain. Added to that, naval blockades might reduce food imports into the UK. That would, of course, include sugar,' Mr Jack said gravely.

'Surely it won't happen?' Mr Burl said.

Mr Jack nodded. 'The chocolatiers in York fear that it will,' he said.

Around the table, a low murmur started. Mr Jack raised his hand.

'Gentlemen, please. Let us return to our agenda. There is no use in becoming anxious about sugar rationing until we know for sure when, or if, it will happen.'

The murmur quietened, then Mr Gerard raised his hand.

'Gerard?' Mr Jack said.

Anne waited with her pencil poised in mid-air and looked at Mr Gerard's long, thin face, his bushy eyebrows and his wispy white hair. He rarely spoke at meetings, preferring to listen to others, and she was intrigued as to what he would say.

'I fear sugar rationing will happen sooner than we think. This war will rumble on, gentlemen, and we must be prepared. The confectionery trade will be one of the first to suffer once sugar becomes scarce. Mr Jack, with all due respect, sir, I beg you make preparations. And believe me, it won't just be sugar that will be rationed, but cream and milk too.'

Mr Gerard looked around the table, letting his gaze rest on each man in turn.

'Times will be tough, gentlemen,' he continued. 'We could face our most difficult challenge in the history of Jack's toffee factory.'

A silence fell across the table. Mr Jack slowly nodded.

'Mr Gerard has a point. We must prepare, just in case.'

He pointed to a stocky man whose waistcoat was straining under the bulk of his hefty stomach.

'Smith, I want you and your team to draw up a set of emergency accounts so that we know where we stand if sugar rationing should begin. Call your friends at the Yorkshire toffee factory, make discreet enquiries. If anyone else at the table has contacts elsewhere, find out all you can. I'll enquire too. We must keep on top of this, as Mr Gerard recommends. Good work, Gerard. You're right, of course. My father took you on as a creative genius when he opened this factory, and you've stood by me ever since. I am indebted not only to your creativity in marketing our toffee, but to your valuable insights into the confectionery business.'

The rest of the meeting was taken up by a discussion of production figures and marketing plans before the conversation made its way back to war. The possibility of laying off workers if sugar rationing began was debated.

Anne thought of Hetty and Elsie. She would never put her own job in jeopardy by repeating anything heard in confidence at the board meeting. This meant she couldn't warn her friends that their jobs might be in danger. With her free hand, she crossed her fingers under the table, hoping the girls would be spared.

When the meeting ended, Mr Jack and Anne left the boardroom together. They walked along the wood-panelled corridor with its thick carpet underfoot. Anne expected Mr Jack to enter his office, but he kept going.

'Follow me, Anne,' he said.

He led the way through reception and out to the yard. The bitter wind hit her hard. Her thin blouse was no protection against the autumn chill.

'Sir, it's cold. Allow me to collect our coats.'

He nodded, and she quickly walked back inside to collect her own coat and hat and take Mr Jack's over-coat from the stand in his office. She returned outside to find him standing in exactly the same spot she'd left him. He didn't turn when she offered him his coat. He seemed lost, in a trance. She knew him well enough by now to realise he was deep in thought. She lifted his coat and gently, automatically, placed it across his shoulders. She'd never done anything so intimate before, and she stepped back in horror once it was done. It felt like she'd crossed a line. An unspoken rule had been broken. She immediately chastised herself. She should never have been so forward. However, Mr Jack seemed to neither notice nor care.

Anne knew little about Mr Jack's home life other than what everyone at the factory knew. He lived in the

Deanery in Chester-le-Street, away from his family's home in Lumley village. It was understood by all that he wanted to be close to the factory. What little she had learned about him so far had come from Mr Gerard. He'd confided in her that Mr Jack was engaged to a society girl of whom his father highly approved. He didn't say whether Mr Jack himself was as happy with the arrangement, but his knowing looks suggested to her that the engagement didn't sit as comfortably with Mr Jack as his father might have liked.

'Come with me, we're going for a walk,' Mr Jack ordered.

She wasn't at all surprised by the factory owner's decision to take a walk after such a difficult meeting. She knew this was his way of processing what had been discussed. However, he'd never asked her to accompany him on one of these walks before. She put her coat on and pulled her hat onto her head. Then she fastened the buttons of her coat and stuck her hands in her pockets.

'Where to, sir?'

'We're going to the railway line.'

Anne was puzzled. Why would he want to walk all that way? But he had already set off at a brisk pace, and she had to hurry to catch up with him.

When they reached the rail yard, he stopped and pointed ahead. 'See that, Anne?'

Anne peered at bare tree branches. 'Sir?' she said, confused.

'The railway, Anne,' he said.

She could see the railway line clearly, but didn't understand why she was being asked to look. Mr Jack stared ahead as he spoke.

'Do you know, Anne, in Yorkshire there's a toffee manufacturer who's going all out to promote himself as the King of Toffee. He's even written a declaration to the effect, which every damn newspaper has printed.'

'I've heard of him, sir, but the Chester-le-Street newspaper refused to print his declaration. Your factory is one of the biggest and most important employers in town. Our local newspaper would never print anything from any company that goes in competition against us.'

'Very good,' Mr Jack said, nodding his head. 'Did you know also that the same man, this self-styled King of Toffee, sails wooden boats shaped like swans down the River Ouse in York?'

'I didn't know that,' Anne said, wondering where Mr Jack was going with this.

'Oh yes, his swan boats are painted with his factory name. Everyone in the city turns out to see them. Free toffees are given away at the end of the ride to those who wait along the riverside. The boats are a spectacle. It's free advertising, of course. The King of Toffee is ahead of me in his race to have the best gimmick. Well, it's time for Jack's to have a gimmick too. Pressure from the threat of sugar rationing, losing men to the war, training girls up, it's all taking its toll. Speaking of which, Burl told me he caught you reading the confidential accounts while I was away. I'm sure you now realise how perilous a state the factory might soon be in.'

Anne felt her face grow hot. She should have known that Mr Burl would have told Mr Jack he'd caught her reading the file. She'd not had a chance to speak to Mr Jack about it since his return from York, as preparations for the board meeting had taken up his time.

'Sir, I—'

'No need to say anything,' he said. 'I had planned to discuss the figures with you. But we need to do something, Anne. There's new competition from the toffee factory on the Scottish borders as well as this York Toffee King. We need a publicity stunt to put Jack's on the map for all the world to see. I just wish I knew what to do.'

Anne frowned. 'Why did you bring me to the railway?' she said. 'We could have discussed this in your office.'

Mr Jack delved into his coat to reveal his pocket watch. 'Because in thirty seconds' time, the train to London will rattle past our factory.'

Sure enough, right on cue, the engine steamed past pulling a long line of carriages. Anne could see the passengers' faces as the train went by.

'See that, Anne? That train was full of people on their way to London. Not only that, but by my reckoning, seven trains pass our factory each day on their way to London or back. There are also sixteen local trains that pass through and stop at Chester-le-Street station. Plus another five passenger trains that don't stop.'

'That's a lot of trains,' Anne said.

Mr Jack turned to her, his eyes shining. 'It's much more than that. It's a lot of opportunities for advertising toffee.'

'How, sir?' she asked.

Mr Jack began pacing the cobbled railway yard. 'The Toffee King of York might have his swans. The Scottish factory might offer new flavours, but we're going to have something to beat them all.'

He pointed at the factory chimneys reaching up to the sky.

'We're going to put the Jack's logo on both chimneys, so that every single person on every single train that travels past our factory knows exactly what we do. I want the name of Jack's toffee to be on the lips of every passenger who travels on the East Coast line. I don't know why I didn't think of it before.'

He paused and tapped his fingers against his chin.

'Mind you, after this morning's board meeting, with the talk of sugar rationing, and of course our current financial position, I wonder if we can afford to pay for this gimmick.'

Anne looked at him. 'Surely, Mr Jack, the real question is: can we afford not to?'

Chapter Twenty-Four

On Friday, the factory whistle blew at six p.m. For the girls in the wrapping room, this signalled the end of their working week. They weren't due back until eight a.m. on Monday. For others at the factory, including the sugar boilers and the workers in the slab room, shifts of workers would continue to come in throughout the weekend. Hetty and Elsie walked from the wrapping room together.

'What are you doing this weekend?' Elsie asked.

Hetty bit her lip. For days she'd wrestled with her decision over whether to see Dirk again. She'd looked deep inside her heart and examined her feelings, turning things over this way and that. In the end, she'd decided she had to see him. If she was still eaten up by guilt over Bob, then she wouldn't meet him again. The excitement of being invited to the dance was burning inside her. She felt as if her heart would burst if she didn't tell someone.

'Promise you won't tell anyone where I'm going on Saturday night?' she whispered.

Elsie pulled her close. 'Where?'

Hetty shook her head. 'Promise me,' she said.

Elsie crossed her heart. 'I promise.'

'I'm going dancing at Elisabethville.'

Elsie's eyes opened wide. 'No! How did you manage that? Is someone smuggling you in?'

Hetty shot her a look. 'Of course not. And if there's a problem getting in, I'll have my official pass with me.' She patted her coat pocket. 'Anne says she trusts me to keep it over the weekend because I need to go to Elisabethville first thing on Monday morning. Mr Jack wants me to collect paperwork from the supplies office. Anyway, I've been invited to the dance by someone in the camp, so all being well I won't need it.'

Elsie looked at her. 'Well, you kept that a secret. Is he nice?'

'Very nice.'

'Is he Belgian?'

Hetty nodded. She saw a look on her friend's face that she'd never seen before.

'I'm shocked at you, Hetty Lawson,' Elsie said, but the mischievous smile around her lips suggested otherwise. 'I wish you could get me in too.'

Hetty ignored the comment, knowing how precious her pass was.

They reached Market Lane, where Elsie went one way and Hetty the other.

'Come here and let me hug you,' Elsie said.

Hetty was surprised by the request. 'This isn't like you.'

'I'm just so happy for you, my friend,' Elsie replied.

Hetty stepped into her embrace, then pulled away, waved farewell and set off down Front Street. She felt someone at her side, and when she turned to see who it was, she was pleased to see Anne there.

'Doing anything nice at the weekend?' Hetty asked.

Anne shook her head, mumbling something about her landlady and her rug.

'My word, she's really having trouble with that rug,' Hetty said, wondering if she dared say more. It seemed as if Anne was fobbing her off rather than reveal what she had planned. 'Will it take up all of your weekend?'

Anne began to walk faster. 'I can't stop, Hetty, I've got things to do,' she called over her shoulder. She was soon lost in the throng of factory girls walking home.

At home on Elm Street, Hetty cooked tea while Dan lazed by the fire. It was a simple meal of pie and peas with mashed potato and gravy. Neither her mum nor Dan thanked her for her hard work and the food she'd provided, but Hetty never expected anything else. There was one slice of pie left to feed the dog, who lapped it up greedily.

'Is Frankie's money in the jar if he calls tonight?' she asked.

'As it always is,' Hilda replied sternly.

Hetty saw Dan perk up. She shot him a look. 'Don't even think about taking it,' she hissed.

Her Friday night was filled with chores and cleaning. Frankie arrived late for his money, and when he disappeared, he took Dan with him. Hetty watched them walk away in the dark, wondering what devilment they were up to. That night she slept fitfully, too excited about the dance on Saturday night.

The next morning, the first thing she did was remove Bob's card from the mantel and place it on her bedroom floor, propped up against the wall. She'd been given a chance to enjoy herself with Dirk for one night. It was only a dance, after all. Dirk was a friend, someone who'd been nice to her. It wasn't as if she was being unfaithful. Or so she told herself.

The day dragged by as she watched the minutes count down to the time when she'd leave home to catch the bus to Birtley. She brushed her hair and tied it with the only decoration she had, the piece of blue ribbon Anne had given her at work. She wore a blue dress that fell below her knees. It was her best dress, with a scalloped neck and three-quarter sleeves, and it floated as she walked. Bob had never liked it; he said the colour didn't suit her and complained that it showed too much of her neck. Hetty hadn't worn it since his cutting remarks, but now she put it on with pride. So what if Bob didn't like it? His opinion didn't count now. He was hundreds of miles away and he hadn't even put a kiss on her card. What was important was that *she* liked the dress, that *she* thought she looked pretty.

When she was ready, she put on her dad's coat and went to face her mum.

'Where are you going, all dressed up?' Hilda cried.

'I'm out dancing tonight with some girls from the factory,' Hetty replied. She crossed her fingers against the half-truth. But she knew that if she told her mum where she was going, she might not be allowed out.

'Don't be late back,' Hilda warned.

Hetty kissed her, then walked out of the door.

On the bus to Birtley, she began to feel conflicted again. How difficult this was. She thought she'd made up her mind, and yet the doubts kept creeping in. Yes, she wanted to see Dirk and go dancing with him. Yes, she wanted to know him better and spend time with him. He was all she could think about. And yet a part of her wanted Bob too. But she wanted a version of Bob she knew she was unlikely to find. She wanted a Bob who would write long, loving letters. A Bob who would – should – have kissed her when he went off to war, instead of telling her to keep her chin up and be strong. Couldn't he have spared one single second to add a kiss on the card, to tell her he loved her and missed her?

She alighted at the crossroads on Station Road and headed for the gate. However, this time she wasn't alone. Men and women, some single, some in couples, showed passes to the guard and he allowed them to enter. Hetty dug in her pocket for her own pass. With rising panic, she realised the pass wasn't there. She tried the other pocket, but that was empty too. Her heart filled with dread.

'I don't understand,' she gasped.

'Excuse me, please,' a voice said behind her.

She stepped to one side as a couple walked past, and she scrabbled in her pockets again, turning the linings inside out. Telling herself to stay calm, she forced herself to think carefully about where the pass could be. Perhaps it had fallen out of her pocket on the bus. What if it ended up in the wrong hands? She remembered Anne's warnings that that would be a matter for the police.

'What is wrong, miss?' the guard asked.

Hetty was on the verge of tears. 'I've lost my pass. I swear I had it before I set off from home.'

But then she remembered that she hadn't checked her coat pockets before she left. She cast her mind back to the last time she'd seen the pass. Her mind was racing, and she forced herself to take long, deep breaths. She definitely remembered putting it in her coat pocket after Anne had given it to her. It was still there when she'd entered the wrapping room. None of the girls knew about it, and even if they had, she felt sure they wouldn't have taken it. Then a thought hit her.

She rocked back on her heels and put her hand on the gate to steady herself. She remembered Elsie hugging her as they'd left the factory the previous day. Oh no . . . it couldn't be, could it? Had Elsie taken the pass from her pocket? Her blood ran cold, her fear and panic intensifying. If she had taken it and was caught, they'd both be in serious trouble.

She looked through the gate at the men and women streaming into a long, low building on Elisabethville's main street. She saw lights and heard music, and through a window she caught sight of people dancing. A tear rolled down her cheek, then anger built up inside her.

'Wait until I see Elsie,' she muttered to herself. 'I'll give her what for. How dare she do this?' She wiped her hand across her eyes.

'Are you all right, toffee girl?'

Hetty looked into the kind, gentle face of a woman she recognised. She stood up straight and tried to pull herself together, although it was hard when she was feeling so wretched.

'Gabrielle? What are you doing here?'

'Why, I'm going to the dance. I wanted to clear my head first with an evening walk around Birtley. But why are you out here by the gate? I thought Dirk had finally plucked up the courage to invite you to the dance. He said you had a pass.'

Hetty told her about the missing pass and how worried she was. 'I need to go home right now.'

Gabrielle gently laid a hand on her shoulder. 'And what would you do there? If your pass has been lost, you can sort things out on Monday, first thing. Now don't worry. Tonight is for dancing. I'll vouch for you with the guard on the gate and tell him you're my guest.'

Hetty dried her eyes as Gabrielle spoke to the guard, who allowed them to enter. When they reached the dance hall, she stopped at the door and peered in nervously.

'I must look a mess after all that crying,' she said.

Gabrielle scrutinised her. 'Nonsense. You look very pretty, especially with your blue ribbon. My brother is a lucky man. Now, come inside and we'll find him.'

Gabrielle stepped inside, but still Hetty hung back. She knew that once she crossed the threshold of the dance hall, she would finally have the answers to the questions her heart had been asking about Dirk and Bob.

'No, I can't do it,' she whispered to the night air. 'Bob depends on me, he needs me.' Slowly she turned away from the bright lights and the music and began to retrace her steps. But then she stopped dead. Ahead of her, showing a pass at the gate, was Elsie. Hetty put her hands on her hips.

'Elsie Cooper!' she yelled. 'I want a word with you!'

Chapter Twenty-Five

Elsie froze. Then she plastered a smile on her face, stuck her chest out and strode confidently forward. She took Hetty by the arm and pulled her to one side, but Hetty shook herself free.

'I thought you were my friend!'

'Shush, keep your voice down,' Elsie said.

'I'll do no such thing,' Hetty yelled. 'I'm warning you, you've gone too far. Just look at you! You've even styled your hair the same as mine so you'd look like me in my picture. You might have fooled the guard on the gate because it's dark tonight, but you won't get away with this. You and I are done, Elsie. Stealing from a friend, why, it's the lowest thing a person can do. I could get into serious trouble.'

Elsie bit her lip. 'Look, I'm sorry, all right? No one will find out.'

'Why did you do it?' Hetty demanded.

'Because . . .' Elsie struggled to find the words. She couldn't face telling Hetty the truth about why she'd taken her pass. She was afraid that if she did, her friend would never speak to her again. 'Because I wanted to see for myself what goes on here. Because you had a pass and it didn't seem fair that I didn't have one too.' She reached for Hetty's hand, but Hetty pulled it away sharply.

'You knew I was coming here tonight to meet someone. You could have ruined everything, as well as stealing something that didn't belong to you.' Hetty held out her hand. 'Give it to me.'

Elsie dug into her handbag, brought out the pass and handed it over. 'I just wanted a bit of excitement.'

Hetty stuffed it into her coat pocket. 'Doesn't Frank give you enough excitement?' she snapped.

Elsie raised her eyebrows. 'Do I need to remind you that you've already got Bob?'

The girls glared at each other. Then a voice called Hetty's name. Elsie spun around to see a slim man with brown hair. She grinned at Hetty as if their argument had never happened.

'Oh, he's a dish!' she whispered.

'I don't know if I'll ever trust you again,' Hetty said, then she turned and made her way over to the man behind them.

Elsie watched them engage in conversation. She saw the man offer his arm to Hetty. Hetty hesitated, then took it, and they walked into the dance hall together.

Elsie stood alone. She felt rotten about what she'd done, but after what she'd discovered in the last few days, she was determined to have fun tonight. She was desperate for one last fling before the truth became common knowledge. Stealing Hetty's pass was the only way she could have entered Elisabethville.

When she saw two men walking towards the dance hall

together, she flashed a smile, stuck her chest out and wiggled her way towards them.

'Which one of you would like to dance with me first?' she said.

The men looked at each other, confused but smiling, then replied in a language she didn't understand. Elsie wasn't going to let that stop her. She linked arms with the pair, and the three of them walked into the dance hall together.

Hetty took Dirk's hand and stepped onto the dance floor. They began moving slowly, tentatively, trying not to step on each other's feet. It felt to Hetty as if everyone was watching her, judging her for dancing with a man who wasn't her boyfriend. But when she looked around, her anxiety was quelled, because no one was watching, of course. Everyone was dancing, smiling, enjoying the music from the band on stage. It was music Hetty wasn't familiar with, although the beat of the drum propelled her feet forward as if they had always known how to dance this way, her blue dress floating around her.

After a while, she began to feel comfortable with her surroundings, and with being held by such a gentle man. They didn't speak as they danced, for they would have had to shout to be heard over the music, and the words they wanted to say deserved quiet respect. Instead, she let Dirk lead her in the dance, and every now and then she dared to lay her cheek against his.

When the music stopped, the couples on the floor parted to applaud.

'Would you like a drink, Hetty?' Dirk asked.

She nodded and walked with him to the side of the room, where bottles of beer were lined up.

'Beer?' he offered.

Hetty shook her head. She didn't like beer. In truth, she was afraid of it because it had been her dad's downfall. 'A soft drink, please. Lemonade if there is some.'

Dirk disappeared. Another tune began, and Hetty watched the dancers go by. She saw Gabrielle in the arms of a tall, handsome man with a dark moustache. Then she saw Elsie dancing with a short man wearing a black suit and tie. Her stomach twisted as she watched. She'd been betrayed by her friend. Elsie stealing her pass had hurt her deeply. She doubted their friendship could recover from such disloyalty.

Dirk returned with two glasses, one filled with beer, the other with lemonade. Hetty's thoughts turned from Elsie's betrayal, and she found herself thinking of Bob again. Before she'd seen Elsie outside, she'd decided not to enter the hall and instead go home. But then Dirk had turned up. In that moment, when she'd seen him, she'd realised she wanted to be with him. She felt certain of it. She walked to a line of chairs along the wall. Dirk followed, and they sat next to each other watching the dancers. Each time Elsie and her man danced past, Elsie looked across at Hetty and mouthed the word *sorry*, but Hetty turned her head and pretended she didn't notice.

'Your friend?' Dirk asked. 'It seemed you were arguing before.'

Hetty shrugged. The last thing she wanted was to spoil tonight by talking about Elsie. 'She's my friend, yes. We were just talking, that's all.' She put an end to the subject and took a sip of lemonade.

Dirk asked questions about her life, family and work, and they fell into easy conversation. While his English was good, he stumbled over some words. Hetty was keen to help him learn when he said the wrong word or used the wrong tense, and he was grateful for her advice. When a jaunty tune began, he offered his hand again, and once more they were dancing.

The room became a blur of lights, music and people enjoying themselves. Hetty had never experienced anything like it. Dirk brought more lemonade, and between dances they sat away from the band. He told her about his home town of Ghent in Belgium. He explained that when the opportunity had come to live and work in England, he'd jumped at the chance to carry on his teaching profession abroad. Their conversation flowed, despite bumps in translation and some words Hetty didn't understand when Dirk lapsed into Flemish. She was so engrossed in what he was saying that she even forgot about Elsie. However, she never forgot about Bob. He was at the back of her mind and guilt pricked her all night.

The last dance was announced. Couples gravitated to the floor, and Hetty and Dirk joined them. Dirk held her close, and she laid her head on his shoulder as they gently swayed to the music. When the final note had died away, the hall began to empty. Slowly people made their way back to the avenue, to the guard on the gate and to Station Road to catch their bus to Chester-le-Street, Newcastle or Durham. Hetty began walking too, with Dirk at her side. The night was cold, and she shivered despite her coat.

The gate was just a few steps away, and when they reached it, Dirk stopped and took her hands. In the moonlight, Hetty looked into his blue eyes.

'Will I see you again?' he asked.

She squeezed his hands. 'I'd like that very much.'

She forced herself to focus as she felt another stab of guilt. She'd once imagined that Bob would return from war, they'd get married and that would be that. And yet here in front of her was the most attractive man she'd ever met, asking to see her again. All night long she'd tested herself, wondering if she could let Bob go, asking herself what she wanted. At each stage of the evening – wearing the blue dress that Bob didn't like, getting on the bus to Birtley, walking towards the guard at the gate, overcoming her reluctance to step into the dance hall – she had willingly forged ahead, fully aware of the consequences of each step she'd taken. She bit her lip. If she agreed to a second date, there could be no going back to her old life, waiting for Bob to return. Being with Dirk made her happy, which was more than being with Bob had done.

Dirk stepped forward. 'May I kiss you?' he asked politely.

Hetty's heart flipped as his lips gently brushed hers.

Chapter Twenty-Six

The following Monday at the factory, Hetty concentrated hard on her work. Dirk's kiss ran through her mind; she'd thought of little else since Saturday night. She closed her eyes, remembered his lips brushing hers and sighed.

'What's got you all dreamy-eyed this morning?' Beattie whispered.

'Nothing,' Hetty replied, keeping her gaze on the toffee she was wrapping. It was a secret she wouldn't share with Beattie, for she didn't know the girl well. It was the sort of thing she would have told Elsie, but she wasn't sure if she wanted to speak to her again after she'd stolen her pass. It stung her each time she thought of it.

There was a space at Hetty's right-hand side where Elsie should have been.

'Elsie's late again,' Beattie said, as if Hetty hadn't noticed.

Hetty glanced at the clock, guessing that Elsie would be with Frankie out in the lane. She shrugged. What Elsie did now was her own business. Beattie tapped the side of her nose; the warning that Mrs Perkins was on her way. Hetty straightened her back and focused on picking, wrapping and twisting. To her surprise, she saw Elsie follow the supervisor into the room. While Mrs Perkins walked to her desk, Elsie took her position at Hetty's side. The girls didn't speak or even look at each other as Elsie slipped her boots off and pushed her feet into her clogs.

'Ask her what she was doing with the old dragon,' Beattie whispered to Hetty.

Hetty didn't pass the message on. She was determined not to be the first to break the silence. But as Elsie picked her first toffee from the table, she put a hand on her stomach and lurched forward. Hetty was alarmed.

'Elsie? You all right?' she whispered.

Elsie turned away, gripping her stomach with one hand and clamping her other hand across her mouth. Hetty was stunned to see she was leaving the room. She glanced at Mrs Perkins, who was deep in conversation with two girls at her desk.

'If the old dragon asks where I am, tell her I've gone to the ladies' room,' she told Beattie.

She quickly followed Elsie outside and found her sitting on a bench in the garden. Elsie looked up as she approached.

'What's wrong?' Hetty asked. She sat down next to her.

Elsie shook her head. 'Nothing,' she said quickly.

Hetty looked at her, and for the first time she noticed how grey Elsie looked. It was the first time she'd seen her without her trademark powder and rouge. She seemed suddenly young and vulnerable. Her hands gripped the bench and her eyes were watering. Hetty noticed that her overall was dirty, too; it clearly hadn't been washed over the weekend. The buttons across her chest strained and the material pulled tight around her stomach and hips. Hetty had already noticed her eating too many toffees lately. It looked like the extra sugar and cream had finally caught up with her.

Elsie reached for her hand. Surprised by the bold gesture, Hetty let her hold it. The anger she'd felt earlier began to subside as she realised how quiet Elsie was. It was most unlike her.

'What is it, Elsie?' she asked.

'I don't deserve you as a friend, Hetty Lawson. I did a terrible thing stealing your pass, and now you're sitting here being nice and it's more than I deserve. I'm sorry, really I am. I just wanted a bit of excitement at the dance, because . . .'

'Because what?' Hetty said gently.

Elsie turned to face her fully.

'Because it was the last dance I'll ever go to. I'm going to have a baby. There, I've said it. Now you know.'

Hetty's mouth fell open in shock and she rocked back in her seat. She couldn't speak.

'What?' she said when she could finally get a word out. 'Are you sure?'

Elsie nodded.

'Is it Frankie's?'

She nodded again, and tears rolled down her cheeks.

'Will he marry you?'

Elsie pulled her hands away and wiped them across her eyes. 'He doesn't know.'

Hetty reached her arms out to Elsie and the girls hugged for what seemed like for ever.

'Hetty Lawson and Elsie Cooper! What are you two doing out here?'

They snapped apart, horrified to see Mrs Perkins.

'Sorry, Mrs Perkins,' Hetty said. She reached for Elsie's hand and helped her to stand. 'Elsie's not feeling well. I was looking after her.'

Elsie stood too, scrubbing at her tears.

'If she's not well, take her to the factory doctor,' Mrs Perkins ordered. 'Don't let me see you taking time out of the wrapping room again. Elsie, I've already caught you once this morning lingering outside and I had to usher you indoors. Poor Beattie's doing the work of three girls in there.'

Hetty held Elsie's hand as they walked back to the wrapping room.

'Are you sure . . . you know, about what you've told me?' she whispered.

Elsie nodded. 'I had to tell Aunt Jean, she caught me being sick. She knows someone who'll help me, see. That's why I haven't told Frankie, in case this woman she knows can solve the problem I've found myself in.'

Hetty narrowed her eyes. 'It's dangerous, Elsie. The women who do that sort of thing . . . I've heard of girls dying after having it done.'

'What choice do I have?' Elsie said sadly.

'Maybe Frankie will do the right thing and marry you.' But even as Hetty said it, she knew she wouldn't wish Frankie Ireland as a husband on anyone.

Elsie rubbed her cold arms to ward away shivers from the stiff wind. Hetty put her arm around her friend's thickening waist.

'Come on, let's get inside.'

'You're one in a million, Hetty Lawson. I can't tell you

how sorry I am about your pass. I'll never do anything like that again.'

Hetty gave a wry smile. 'I wasn't going to forgive you, you know. But I won't drop you as a friend after what you've just told me.'

'You mustn't tell anyone, please.'

'I won't,' Hetty reassured her. 'Your secret's safe with me.'

'Then are we friends again?' Elsie said softly. 'I know you must hate me for stealing your pass. I wish I'd never done it.'

'We're friends,' Hetty said. 'But don't you ever betray me again.'

'Friends for ever,' Elsie promised.

They walked on and reached the door to the wrapping room.

'Where did Mrs Perkins go?' Elsie said, looking around.

'I have no idea. She's like a ghost. She turns up when you least expect her,' Hetty replied.

This made Elsie smile.

'You looked happy at the dance, Hetty. I saw you dancing with that good-looking man. Are you going to see him again?'

Hetty felt herself blush. She wanted to see Dirk more than anything. 'It's complicated. There's Bob to deal with first,' she said quickly, hoping to change the subject. She didn't feel comfortable talking about her feelings for Dirk while she was still trying to make sense of them. But then Elsie patted her stomach.

'If you want my advice, take happiness where you find it. You never know when your life will be turned upside down.'

Once Elsie had gone inside, Hetty waited a moment by the door and turned to look at the garden. There were no flowers, just long, narrow empty beds. Spindly bare rose branches twisted out of the soil. She saw Stan the gardener walk by pushing a wheelbarrow. He raised his cap and waved.

'Take happiness where you find it,' she whispered to the breeze, then she followed Elsie inside.

Anne was doing her best to take notes while Mr Jack held a heated conversation with Mr Burl and Mr Gerard. Though Mr Gerard rarely spoke at the larger board meetings, preferring to listen to everyone else, when it was just the three men, his conversation was animated. The topic currently under discussion was innovation, new ways to publicise toffee. Mr Jack's idea of having the factory name emblazoned on the chimneys overlooking the railway line had been approved, despite Mr Burl's objection. He remained convinced that it wasn't the right time to spend money on publicity and promotion.

'There's a war on, in case you've forgotten!' he exploded.

Mr Jack leaned forward with his elbows on his desk and glared at him. 'All the more reason for us to spend money on advertising now. Don't you see?'

Mr Gerard tapped his pencil against the arm of his chair. 'He's right, Burl. We need to position our toffee as the best in the land. We need to beat the competition from the new factory in the Borders. And we need to show the Toffee King of York that we're a force to be reckoned with. Because if rationing starts and people can only afford one treat, we want that treat to be *our* toffee. No one else's. We want Jack's toffee to be on everyone's lips.'

'And in their mouths,' Mr Jack added, amused by his own little joke.

Mr Gerard stood carefully and slowly from his seat and walked past Mr Jack to look out of the window. Anne knew by now that he was the only member of staff allowed to get away with such maverick behaviour. He'd been at the factory longer than anyone else and Mr Jack valued him greatly. She scribbled quickly when he began to speak.

'What we need is something that'll put us on the map!' he cried excitedly. 'Yes, we've got chimneys. That gives us free advertising to the railways, but we need something else, something more. Something better.'

'What's better than advertising on chimneys?' Mr Jack said, affronted. 'I thought my idea was first rate.'

Mr Gerard's eyes shone with excitement. 'We need a woman!' he cried.

Anne almost dropped her pen.

'Have you gone mad?' Mr Burl said.

Mr Jack raised a hand to quieten him. 'Carry on, Gerard.'

'A woman. The prettiest we can find. The sweetest girl for the sweetest toffee,' Mr Gerard continued. He was fired up now and pacing the floor. 'We'll put her face on our toffee tins. She'll be irresistible, with a face to cheer the nation as we fight the war.'

'And where, pray tell, are we going to find a woman who'll be able to do that?' Mr Burl snapped.

Mr Gerard spread his arms wide. 'Why, right here in the factory, of course.'

The three men looked at Anne. She shrank back in her seat and shook her head.

'No . . . don't look at me like that. I'm not going on any toffee tin. Besides, I'm not pretty enough.'

'Don't do yourself down, Anne,' Mr Jack said. He pulled at his shirt collar before he carried on. 'On the other hand, I can't let you spend time with Mr Gerard's design team having your likeness drawn when I need you to run my office.'

She felt a burst of pride at his words. She caught Mr Burl looking at her with a sneer, and returned her gaze to her notepad.

'We can market the toffee as a new brand and include different flavours. Raspberry and mint have proved our bestsellers so far. But we'll need a name for this toffee with a woman's face on the tin,' Mr Jack said. 'Any suggestions, Gerard?'

'Juicy Julie . . . Fruity Frances . . . Minty Melanie,' Mr Gerard began muttering under his breath, trying names out loud. But Mr Jack shook his head.

'They sound like the sort of loose women who'd frequent the Lambton Arms. We need a more regal name. Something memorable to emblazon on the tin.'

'The tin . . . the tin . . .' Mr Gerard was muttering again. 'The tin of toffee . . . tin of toffee . . .'

Anne watched him pace the floor, repeating the word *tin* over and over again. And as she listened, an idea began to form.

'Tin of toffee,' she said out loud, playing with the phrase. 'Tin o toffee. Tin a toffee.' Then she ran the words together. 'Tina toffee.'

Mr Gerard threw his arms out wide. 'My word, she's got it! Tina Toffee. I like it a lot.'

'It's terrible,' Mr Burl said, but no one took any notice.

'Make the name more regal,' Mr Jack demanded.

'Princess Tina?' Mr Gerard offered, but Mr Jack shook his head.

'I don't like it. Burl, do you have any suggestions?'

'I suggest we scrap this idea and take the government's money to renovate our slab room to manufacture munitions instead. It's what's coming, mark my words.'

'How about Lady Tina?' Anne said softly.

The three men turned to stare at her.

'Sorry?' Mr Jack said.

She sat up straight in her seat. 'I said "Lady Tina", sir. How about calling the new brand Lady Tina Toffee?'

Mr Gerard walked to her and kissed her on the cheek. 'Anne, you're a blooming marvel,' he said.

Mr Jack nodded approvingly. 'Perfect. Lady Tina Toffee it is. All we need now is a girl from the factory to be the face of the brand. Anne, I will leave that task to you. I trust you to find the perfect girl.'

Chapter Twenty-Seven

The first thing Anne did was to talk to Mr Gerard about how to find the right girl to be the face of the new brand. She felt proud to have been given the task. She threw herself into the challenge, knowing only too well it was a displacement activity, a way to stop herself dwelling on her son. With help from the creative men in Mr Gerard's department, a poster was created announcing a competition to find the face of Lady Tina. It caused much excitement when it was put up on the canteen wall, with girls gathered around it. Many put their name forward, and Anne arranged to meet each one. However, she was disappointed that neither Hetty nor Elsie had entered the competition.

On the appointed day for her to meet the girls who'd nominated themselves, Mr Jack was away on business and Anne had his office to herself. Over thirty girls arrived en masse in reception, sending Jacob into a spin.

'Miss Wright, I can't cope with all these silly chattering girls!' he complained.

'Do calm down, Jacob. They're excited because they think they're in with a chance to be the face of the new brand. Send the first one in to see me, and once she leaves, ensure the next one comes straight in. I'll be spending ten minutes with each, no more. The girls will be out of your hair and back at work in no time. Now go and be polite to them all.'

He scowled, then turned to leave the office. But she wasn't finished with him yet.

'Oh, and . . . Jacob?' she said.

He stopped with his hand on the door. 'Yes?' he said, without turning.

'It wouldn't harm you to smile at the girls. That's if you can manage it, of course.'

A few moments later, there was a knock at the door and a short young woman entered. She looked presentable, Anne thought, but she kept scratching her head, a sure sign of nits. Anne crossed her name off the list when she left. More girls followed. Some were too old or too young. Some looked unhealthy or had bad teeth, and that was not the message that Jack's toffee wished to promote. Anne was polite and asked each girl the same questions about their family background and how long they'd worked at Jack's. Of the thirty girls she saw, she ended up with four on her shortlist for Mr Jack to meet. The girls she chose all had strong features she felt sure would work well. One had big brown eyes and a demure look, which she thought would appeal to their buyers. She inserted a new sheet of paper into her typewriting machine, ready to type up the shortlist, then paused. There was something she had to do first.

Anne entered the wrapping room and walked straight to Elsie and Hetty. They had their backs to her as she drew near, but she could tell they were whispering to each other, deep in conversation. When she appeared at their side, she saw that Elsie was chewing toffee again. It was no surprise how much weight she'd put on. But despite the fullness of her face, Elsie's looks still beat all the girls Anne had shortlisted. She'd be a perfect model for Lady Tina, with her olive skin, dark eyes and full lips.

Anne gently took her by the arm and drew her to one side. 'Did you see the poster, Elsie?'

Elsie bit her lip. 'Yes.'

'But you didn't put your name forward. I hoped you would. There's still time before I draw up the shortlist for Mr Jack.'

'I can't,' Elsie said quickly, her eyes darting to Hetty.

'Any reason why not?' Anne asked. 'There'd be extra money in it for you, a bonus paid when the toffees go on sale.'

'No, Anne, I can't, really. Excuse me, I need to return to work.'

Elsie turned away and faced the table of toffees and wrappers. Anne was confused but stayed silent. From the little she knew of Elsie Cooper, she was surprised she didn't want to be in the spotlight. However, it seemed as if the girl had made her decision and Anne had to respect that. She looked at Hetty.

'You must've seen the poster too, Hetty. Didn't you want to enter the competition?'

Hetty blushed red, and the toffee she was wrapping fell from her fingers. 'I'm far too shy,' she mumbled.

'But you'd be perfect for it,' Anne said encouragingly. 'Especially after your visits to Elisabethville on business for Jack's. Why, you're already an ambassador for our toffee. Having your face on the tin would be the next step.'

Hetty raised a hand to her cheek as if trying to hide. 'No, I haven't the confidence.'

'But you had the confidence to go to Elisabethville,' Anne said gently, trying to change the girl's mind. 'You had the confidence to train Beattie when she started work here.'

'That's true, you were great,' Beattie chipped in.

Anne lowered her voice. 'And you had the confidence to keep the girls in the wrapping room calm after poor Anabel died. The way you coped was admirable. Mrs Perkins kept me informed of what went on in here. She speaks highly of you. In fact, she's asked Stan to plant a rose bush in the garden to honour Anabel's memory, and I understand that was your idea. Anyone else at the factory would have made a song and dance about suggesting it, but not you. You're humble, kind and the sweetest person I've met here. Now do you understand why I wish you'd entered the competition to be the face of Lady Tina?'

Hetty glanced at Elsie. 'I'm not as pretty as the other girls,' she said softly.

'It's about more than looks, Hetty. It's about character and stamina. It's about a face our customers feel they can trust. They want to see a girl on our tins who looks like their best friend. The final choice will be Mr Jack's. He'll choose who he thinks best represents the brand. But if you're not on the shortlist, there's no chance of winning. And as I've told Elsie, there's a small bonus for the winner once the new brand is launched.'

Anne noticed that Hetty perked up at the mention of the financial incentive.

'Please, Hetty, reconsider. Let me add your name to the list.'

'Go on, do it, Hetty,' Beattie chirped.

'She's right, you should enter,' Elsie said sagely.

Hetty wavered, looking from Beattie to Elsie. 'All right, you can put my name forward,' she said at last.

'Now are you sure?' Anne asked. 'Don't let me railroad you into doing something you're not happy with.'

Hetty hesitated a moment. 'How much will the bonus be?'

'I'll discuss it with Mr Jack and let you know,' Anne replied, hoping the girl wouldn't change her mind.

'I'll do it,' Hetty said, firmly this time.

Beattie and Elsie clapped their hands with glee. Anne felt a rush of relief. She headed back to her office, where she typed up the list of five names, with Hetty's at the top.

When the factory whistle blew at the end of the day, Hetty linked arms with Elsie and they headed to the yard and out through the gates. They stopped on Front Street and huddled in a doorway.

'What does your aunt Jean say about the woman . . . you know, the one who can fix things for you?'

Elsie looked towards the market square, where the stallholders had started to pack up.

'Well?' Hetty asked.

'She can't find the woman who normally does these things and there's no one else she knows so . . . I'm keeping my baby,' Elsie said softly. 'I've told Frankie. He said he'll marry me. Aunt Jean threatened him; she said that if he didn't do the right thing, she'd tell the police about him. She knows . . .'

Hetty felt her friend stiffen at her side. 'What?'

Elsie sighed heavily. 'Oh, you were right about Frankie. He steals things and sells them. And he doesn't mean to hit me, Hetty, honestly, he doesn't. It's just that his temper runs away. You should see him afterwards; he's broken and crying and swears he'll never do it again.'

Hetty was horrified. She dropped her arm from Elsie's. 'You told me he didn't hit you.'

'I was ashamed to admit it. He says he loves me, so what am I to do other than marry him? I don't have a choice with his baby on the way. Anyway, he says we can move into his room at the Lambton Arms once we're wed. I'll have a husband and a baby. It won't be so bad, will it?'

Hetty narrowed her eyes. 'You've got the rest of your life to think about getting married and having babies. And if you get married, you'll have to leave the factory.'

'I've already thought about that,' Elsie said sadly.

'Oh Elsie. I can't let you live with a man who hits you!' Hetty cried.

Elsie shifted in the doorway. 'Shush, keep your voice down. Don't say that. He just . . . lashes out. Sometimes I can sense when his temper's changing and then I get out of his way. Anyway, I don't see a lot of him. If he's not at the factory, he's working for Tyler Rose.'

'Doing what?' Hetty asked.

Elsie shrugged. 'He won't tell me what they're up to, but he mentions your brother.'

Hetty felt anger building up. Anger at her mum for always taking Dan's side even though he was involved in something dangerous and seedy with Tyler Rose. Anger at having to continue to give money to Frankie when the full amount must surely have been paid by now – she'd suspected for a while that he must be adding interest to the debt. And anger at Dan for being involved with Frankie. She didn't know what was going on with her brother, but she was determined to find out and stop it.

She felt anger at herself, too, for not being able to help Elsie escape Frankie's clutches. Her head reeled at her friend's news. Being pregnant by him was bad enough, but now Elsie was set on marrying him. She thought about what lay ahead for her. Elsie wasn't moving far, just to the Lambton Arms, but Hetty wondered if she'd see her again. Would they walk arm in arm once Elsie wed Frankie and had a baby to care for? Or would Frankie keep her locked away in the pub? Hetty felt sick at the thought.

She walked home slowly, despite the bitterly cold day. It felt like snow was on the way, and she pulled her dad's coat tight. She had much on her mind and she wanted to think before dealing with Hilda. As she walked, she let her mind turn to Dirk again. She'd thought of little else since dancing with him at Elisabethville. At the end of that night, after they'd kissed, they'd arranged to meet for a walk in the riverside park. Hetty smiled at the thought of it. Deep inside, though, it still felt like she was betraying Bob. She knew there was only one thing to do.

Chapter Twenty-Eight

As Hetty rounded the corner of Elm Street, she made her decision. That night, after she'd cooked tea, she would write to Bob to tell him the truth and call things off with him. She could hear her dad's voice in her head urging her to be honest. She couldn't carry on with Bob while she had feelings for Dirk. She wasn't that sort of girl. Yes, it might break Bob's heart to receive her letter, especially when spirits were low in the war. But she had to do it, otherwise her relationship with Dirk would be based on a lie.

Bob was away fighting. Who knew when, or if, she might see him again? Even if by good fortune he returned from war uninjured, a hero, what would that mean for her? She'd be stuck with the same old Bob, dull and unloving. That wasn't the life she wanted. Hadn't Elsie advised her to take happiness where she could? She wouldn't saddle herself with a man she didn't love, who couldn't even put a kiss at the end of a card. By contrast, Dirk spoke to her with kindness, with patience and with humour too. More than anything, she enjoyed his company, which was more than she could say about Bob.

She opened the front door and stepped inside, feeling a lightness in her heart now that she'd made her decision. She would write to Bob that night and post the letter the next day.

'Mum, I'm home!' she yelled along the hallway. The dog bounded to her, jumping at her knee until she bent down and scratched him behind his ears. She walked into the kitchen, surprised to find her mum stirring soup in a pan on the fire.

'You felt well enough to cook? That's great news,' she said.

'Why? Because you won't have to start peeling potatoes and carrots the minute you walk through the door?' Hilda snapped.

Hetty sat down and warmed her hands by the fire. She chose to ignore her mum's cutting remark, being used to such comments by now. She doubted Dan would have received the same welcome if it'd been him walking in. Thoughts of her brother made her wonder where he was.

'Is Dan eating with us?'

'He's out,' Hilda said, not taking her eyes off the bubbling pan.

'Where?' Hetty asked.

Hilda shrugged. 'Frankie Ireland called earlier for his money. I gave him what we had in the jar. He took Dan with him when he left, then the two of them came back here. They said they were dropping something off in Dan's room.'

Hetty frowned. 'Did they say what it was?'

'I didn't ask. I'm just pleased Dan's got a job,' Hilda said.

'Oh Mum, for goodness' sake!' Hetty cried.

Hilda stopped stirring the soup and held the wooden spoon close to Hetty's face. 'Don't you dare speak to me like that!'

'Dan hasn't got a job, Mum. If he's involved with Frankie Ireland, he's up to no good. Surely you see that?'

Hilda turned back to the soup. Hetty stood up.

'Where are you off to? Your soup's ready. Butter some bread and set the table.'

But Hetty didn't reply. She stormed upstairs, with the dog running behind.

'Hetty!' Hilda yelled, but Hetty paid her no heed.

Blood rushed in her ears as she ran to Dan's room and flung the door open. Standing with her hands on her hips, she looked around the room, wondering where her brother would hide whatever he and Frankie had left there. His bed was unmade, the eiderdown messy and the pillow on the floor. The only furniture was a chest of drawers, and she strode towards it. She pulled each drawer out, but all she found were Dan's shirts, vests and socks. She slammed the drawers closed. She peered behind the thin curtains to see if anything was hidden on the windowsill, but there was just a brown apple core. From the corner of her eye she saw the dog disappear under the bed.

'Here, boy,' she called, expecting the animal to come out. When it didn't, she knelt down and peered beneath the bed. What she saw made her blood run cold. There were tins and tins of best toffee from Jack's, wrapped in blue ribbon.

'No!' she gasped.

The dog was pulling at a ribbon, unable to resist the sweet aroma from the boxes.

'Here!' she said sharply.

She couldn't believe her eyes. She counted twelve boxes. They were the best and most expensive toffees Jack's sold. Her jaw dropped in shock. So this was what Frankie and Dan were up to. Her mind raced, trying to make sense of it. Frankie must be stealing the toffees from work and getting Dan to hide them in his room. She banged her fist on the floor.

'Dan! You idiot!' she hissed.

'Hetty, get down here now. Your soup's ready,' Hilda called up the stairs.

Hetty sat on the bare floor of Dan's room, gathering her thoughts. Now that she knew Frankie was stealing from the factory, she had to do something, but what? Elsie was relying on him marrying her for the sake of the baby. She couldn't break her friend's heart by telling her about this. But then who should she tell? Mr Jack himself?

'Hetty! Your soup's getting cold,' Hilda called.

Hetty returned slowly downstairs. Her mind was working overtime, trying to decide what to do. Then an idea came in a flash. She walked into the kitchen to find her mum buttering bread.

'Have you got cloth ears? I was calling upstairs for you,' Hilda said.

But Hetty wasn't listening.

'I'm going out.'

Hilda banged her spoon on the table. 'I've spent all afternoon cooking and this is all the thanks I get. If our Dan was here, he'd sit and eat with me. But not you. Oh no, you think you're too high and mighty since you started work at the toffee factory. Where are you off to anyway?'

Hetty shoved her arms into her coat and pulled her dad's scarf from the peg by the door. Hilda was still muttering complaints when she left.

Hetty ran along Elm Street, heading for the Lambton Arms. She didn't know if that was where Frankie Ireland would be, but it was the only place she could think of to look. A plan was forming in her mind, and while it didn't sit easy with her – in fact it made her feel sick – she hoped it would solve all their problems.

When she reached the pub, she knocked hard at the back door and waited. Jim opened up, his round face looking flushed.

'Oh, it's you, what do you want?'

Hetty pushed her feet to the ground, determined. 'I need to speak to Frankie.'

She saw Jim grip the door handle. 'He's not here.'

Hetty glared at him. 'Where is he?'

'Jim? Who's there?' a woman's voice called.

Jim glanced nervously behind him. 'It's nothing, Cathy love. No one.'

His wife bustled to the door, drying her hands on a tea cloth. She was a short, stocky woman with dark curly hair swept back from her face. She eyed Hetty suspiciously.

'We're not in need of any barmaids.'

'I'm looking for Frankie,' Hetty said.

The woman's eyes grew wide. 'I should have known. He's always got girls coming here. He's upstairs.'

Jim's face dropped, but he pulled the door open for

Hetty to step inside. She followed Cathy to the foot of the stairs.

'First room on the right. You might want to knock before you go in, just in case there's a tart already there,' Cathy said.

Hetty fumed at the woman's words. She wanted to protest that she was no tart, but she kept her mouth shut. The fewer people who knew her business, the better. She climbed the stairs slowly, taking her time, trying to calm her racing heart in preparation. She knocked at Frankie's door.

'Come in!' he yelled.

She hesitated, not daring to enter at first. Then she pushed open the door and stepped inside, gripping her hands in front of her skirt.

'I know what you're doing, Frankie.'

Frankie's face fell. 'What the hell are you doing here?'

She forced herself to move forward, swallowing hard. There was a sweet toffee smell in the room that made her feel sick.

'I know you're stealing from the factory.'

Frankie banged his fist against the wall. 'Bloody Dan and his big mouth!' he cried.

'Leave my brother out of this. He doesn't know I'm here. Dan didn't tell me what was going on, I found out for myself.'

Frankie lunged towards her, but Hetty was too quick. She stepped to one side.

'The way I see it, Frankie, is that you've got a choice. I can either tell Mr Jack what's going on and you'll be sacked on the spot. Or . . .' she paused, 'I can keep my mouth shut.'

'And what's in it for you if you keep quiet?' he leered.

She straightened her spine. 'If I keep quiet about this,' she began nervously, 'I want my dad's debt considered paid in full.'

Chapter Twenty-Nine

Frankie rocked back on his heels. 'You're full of yourself, aren't you? What makes you think I'd agree? So what if I help myself to a few boxes of toffees. I'm not the only one who does.'

Hetty paused with her hand on the door and looked him in the eye. 'What's it to be, Frankie? My dad's debt paid off or do I go straight to Mr Jack in the morning? Now you've told me that others steal too, I could mention that to him while I'm there. That could put you in trouble with your workmates. I wonder what they'll think of you then?'

Frankie glared at her and she had to force herself not to run. She was terrified he might lunge for her again. But when she saw his shoulders sink, she knew she'd given him something to think about. She decided to strike another blow.

'And leave our Dan out of this,' she added. 'If I find out that our house is being used to store stolen goods again, I won't go to Mr Jack next time, I'll go straight to the police.'

'All right!' Frankie yelled. 'Keep your bloody gob shut and consider your dad's debt paid.'

Hetty felt her heart flutter. Finally, after months of scrimping and saving every spare penny, going without food, without coal, they were free. Her legs turned to jelly and she had to hold the door tight. All she had to do now was appease her conscience over not telling Mr Jack about his employees stealing. Then Frankie stepped towards her and poked a fat finger against her cheek. The sweet, sugary smell of him was at odds with how evil he was. She failed to understand what Elsie saw in him.

'Don't come here again,' he hissed.

Hetty stood rigid. Then, with all the strength she had, she moved away and walked out. She heard the door slam behind her. At the top of the landing, she hung on to the banister as her legs began to tremble.

'You all right up there, lass?' Cathy called. Hetty opened her mouth, but no words came out. Slowly she made her way down the stairs, let herself out of the back door and walked home in the cold, frosty night.

She hated herself for making the pact with Frankie to keep quiet about the thefts. However, the relief that the debt was paid off was overwhelming, and she walked home with a hand trailing against the walls and windows of shops and pubs, anything to steady her shaking legs.

When she arrived home, she was surprised to hear her brother's voice coming from the kitchen. Dan was a nuisance, a layabout and now, it turned out, a thief. But he had no father in his life to show him right from wrong. He only had men like Tyler Rose and Frankie Ireland, both operating outside the law. Hetty knew she was the only decent influence in his life. Dan was her little brother and she wanted to protect him, to give him a chance to make something of himself. She had to believe he had good in him somewhere.

She took off her coat and scarf and entered the kitchen. Dan was sitting at the table, slurping soup from a bowl. In his hand was a chunk of bread. Hilda was standing next to the hearth. The dog walked to Hetty and whined.

'Oh, the wanderer returns,' Hilda complained. 'You're here one minute and the next you're rushing out with not a word about where you're going or when you're coming back. Well, if you want soup, there's none left. Dan finished it.'

'Sit down, Mum,' Hetty said firmly.

Stunned into silence, Hilda flopped into a chair. Dan put his spoon down, stuffed the bread into his mouth and looked at Hetty.

'What's going on?' he asked.

'I've been to see Frankie Ireland,' Hetty began.

Dan began to chew faster. Hilda looked at her, puzzled.

'Why? We've already paid him this week.'

'Dad's debt is fully paid now. It's over. Frankie won't bother us any more.'

Hilda's mouth opened and closed. It was Dan who spoke first.

'Why?' he asked.

Hetty crossed her arms. 'You ought to know better than to be mates with him. He's dangerous, Dan. I thought Tyler Rose was a bad influence on you, but Frankie Ireland's worse. You should stay clear of him. He beats women up, he's violent and he . . .' she paused and glared at her brother, 'he steals. You know what I'm talking about.'

Dan swallowed hard. Hilda stood up and wagged her finger at Hetty.

'Now don't you give our Dan a hard time. It's not his fault he has to work with the likes of Tyler Rose. At least he's out there being useful.'

'Useful, my backside,' Hetty muttered under her breath. 'Don't I get any thanks for bringing you the news that the debt's paid? We can keep every penny I make at the factory. We can eat ham on a Sunday, cook eggs for breakfast whenever we like. I can afford to buy a box of best toffee to bring you from work.'

Hilda narrowed her eyes, then looked her up and down. 'And what did you offer Frankie in exchange for him writing off the debt?'

Hetty was appalled at what her mum was suggesting. She bit the inside of her cheek to stop herself from exploding. 'Do you really think so little of me? Do you think I'd stoop to . . .' She couldn't continue, the words burning in her throat. 'The debt's finished, that's all you need to know,' she said firmly, then she turned to face Dan. 'I don't want anything in this house that shouldn't be here.'

'What's that supposed to mean?' Hilda chipped in.

Hetty nodded at her brother. 'Our Dan understands, don't you?'

He acknowledged her with a nod of his head, then rose and walked out of the room. Hetty followed him to the hallway and caught him by his arm.

'I want the stolen toffees gone by tomorrow morning. And don't you dare bring anything like that home again. If I lose my job because of this, Mum will never forgive you. You're her golden boy. You wouldn't want her to think badly of you, would you?'

Dan made to head up the stairs, then paused. 'You think you're so bloody perfect,' he leered. 'But I know something about you.'

'What are you talking about?' she hissed.

He puckered up his lips and made kissing sounds, then turned and ran upstairs. Hetty chased him, just like she used to do when they were children, playing catch. This time she stormed into his bedroom to find him pulling toffee boxes from under his bed.

'What do you know about me?' she said. 'And keep your voice down so Mum doesn't hear.'

Dan sat on the floor with his back against the bed. He pulled an open box of toffees onto his knee. There was something about the scene that disturbed Hetty. They were toffees that she or Elsie or Beattie, or any of the hundreds of other girls at the factory, had wrapped. He dipped his hand into the box and pulled one out. Hetty slapped his hand and the sweet fell to the floor.

'You can't treat me like a child,' he sulked.

'Then act like an adult and tell me what you know,' she demanded.

He shrugged, infuriating her even more.

'Dan, tell me!' she cried.

'All right, leave me alone,' he huffed. 'I know about you kissing a Belgian man. You were seen, our Hetty. And by all accounts you looked very cosy. I wonder if you've told Bob. Maybe I should write to him to let him know? Or maybe I should tell Mum? She's always telling you not to go to Elisabethville.'

Hetty stood in front of her brother, towering over him. 'I'm older than you and what I do is my business,' she said firmly. 'At least I'm not breaking the law. Now get rid of those toffees. Get them out of our house.'

She walked out of Dan's bedroom fuming with anger and crossed the landing to her own room. Sinking onto her bed, she put her head in her hands. Her stomach rumbled with hunger as she sat alone in the darkness. She wondered who had seen her with Dirk. Probably one of Dan's friends who'd been at the dance. She felt tears prick her eyes, then turned her gaze to the fireplace. The fire in her room hadn't been lit since her dad died; there hadn't been money for coal in any room but the kitchen. Well, at least from now on they could afford to buy coal and food, maybe even a goose at Christmas.

Her gaze settled on Bob's card on the floor, propped against the wall. If Dan knew the truth about her and Dirk, others might too. Word would spread, and there was nothing she could do about it. The girls at the factory would know she was cheating on her boyfriend who was away fighting. Tongues would wag and heads would shake. Hetty knew what she had to do. She wiped her eyes on her sleeve, then picked up Bob's card and her notebook and pencil and walked downstairs to the kitchen, where there was light from the oil lamp and heat from the fire. Her mum was sitting by the fire with her eyes closed and her head tilted to one side. Above her she heard Dan scrabbling around in his bedroom. She sat at the table and began to write to Bob.

The next morning, she was woken by howling wind and rain lashing at her bedroom window. She dressed quickly and prepared a breakfast of oats. There was no sign of Dan, so she checked his bedroom and was relieved to see the toffee boxes gone. All, that is, apart from one, left in

the corner of the room with toffee papers discarded in a
trail to his bed.

When she was ready to head to work, she kissed her
mum goodbye. She was happy to see a smile on Hilda's
face, the first one she'd seen for months.

'Now that Dad's debt has been paid, things will be all
right, Mum, you'll see,' she said reassuringly. She stuffed
her letter to Bob in her pocket, intent on taking it to the
post office during her lunch break. She had no clue how
to send a letter overseas and hoped the postmaster would
help.

Hetty's letter to Bob left Front Street post office that
evening on its long journey to the Western Front. It was
one of thousands to be taken by a fleet of army lorries to
Folkestone. From there it would be transported by boat
across the Channel. Then it would travel by train.
However, that evening at Folkestone, one sack of letters
fell between boats in the harbour. It went unseen in the
darkness, to be left behind. What Hetty would never
know was that her letter to Bob was in that sack.

Chapter Thirty

Anne strode through the factory gates, girls teeming past her on their way into work. Some were headed to the wrapping room, others to the slab room or packing room. But one of them was standing still in the middle of the cobbled yard. She couldn't see who it was, as the girl had her back to her. When she reached her, she was surprised to discover it was Elsie. Her face was deathly white and her eyes were glassy, as if she'd been crying. Anne laid her hand on her arm.

'Elsie, are you all right? You look dreadful. Do you need to see the factory doctor? I could take you there now.'

Elsie pulled away and Anne let her hand drop.

'Elsie?' she said, concerned.

But Elsie walked off without a word.

In reception, Anne forced a cheery hello towards Jacob. Elsie was on her mind; she was worried about the girl, but she knew she had to be on her mettle once in her office and concentrate hard on her work. Jacob grunted his usual reply. She paused by his desk and looked at him.

'It wouldn't hurt to say good morning, Jacob. Come to that, what's so wrong with a smile?'

He grimaced. It made Anne laugh out loud.

'Well, that's a start, I suppose,' she said as she walked briskly into her office.

Her morning was busy, filled with typing and filing and organising meetings for Mr Jack. She arranged to meet Mr Gerard to help oversee the new signs going up on the chimneys that overlooked the railway. Then she was called to take notes at an urgent meeting in Mr Jack's office, where she heard distressing news from one of the sugar boilers. He told Mr Jack, in strictest confidence, that boxes of best toffee were being stolen. The name on everyone's lips as the thief was Frankie Ireland, a man Anne had never heard of. However, apart from gossip and rumour, there was no proof that Frankie was the culprit.

When the meeting ended, Anne presented Mr Jack with the list of girls she thought suitable to be the face of Lady Tina Toffee.

'Who's the prettiest on this list?' he asked bluntly.

'Ethel MacDonald,' Anne quickly replied, thinking of the girl with the brown eyes and demure smile.

To Anne's shock, Mr Jack crossed out Ethel's name.

'Sir?' she said, surprised.

'We don't want pretty; we want trustworthy and honest to be our Lady Tina. Send the remaining four to my office after lunch so I can meet them all.'

'Yes, sir,' she replied.

Mr Jack checked the list again. 'This Henrietta Lawson, at the top of the list. Isn't she the girl you sent to Elisabethville to deliver toffees? The girl we authorised a pass for?'

Anne nodded.

'Interesting,' Mr Jack muttered as he returned to his desk.

At lunchtime in the canteen, Anne sought out the shortlisted girls to ask them to come to her office that afternoon. She found three of the girls, but couldn't see Hetty. Finally she found her huddled in a corner with Elsie, with their backs turned to the room. Anne didn't like to interrupt, but she needed to speak to her. She stood behind them and coughed loudly to announce her presence. Hetty turned around, but Elsie stayed where she was with her face to the wall.

'Sorry, girls, I don't mean to bother you, but Mr Jack would like to see Hetty this afternoon. He wants to meet the girls I've put forward to be the face of the new brand.'

When Hetty didn't respond, Anne carried on.

'You do still want to be included in the competition, don't you?' she said, worried in case Hetty had changed her mind. As Hetty hesitated, Elsie turned round, and Anne noticed she'd been crying. She sat at Elsie's side and laid her arm around her shoulders.

'What's happened? Has someone upset you?' she whispered.

Elsie shook her head. 'I'm fine, or at least, I will be once I get used to what's going on,' she replied.

Anne looked at Hetty, worried, but the other girl gave nothing away.

'Look, I don't mean to stick my nose in where it's not wanted,' she continued. 'I know you two are good friends, but I'm here for you too, Elsie. If you need help, let me know. I'm speaking as your friend, not as

Mr Jack's secretary. Anything you tell me stays with me. In confidence.'

Elsie shook her head. 'I can't tell you.'

Anne took Elsie's hands in hers. 'Try me,' she said. 'There's more to me than you know. Maybe I can offer advice.'

Elsie glanced at Hetty, who nodded. 'Tell her,' she whispered.

In that moment, the truth dawned on Anne. The way Elsie's face had filled out, and the way her bosom strained against her overall . . .

'When's your baby due?' she whispered.

'I don't . . . I don't know . . .' Elsie began, tripping over her words. 'I've only recently found out I'm expecting. I think I'm about two months gone.'

'Her aunt tried to find someone to . . . you know . . . sort things out, but she couldn't. So she's going to have the baby. She's getting married, Anne. To one of the sugar boilers.'

Anne bit her tongue. She'd been in Elsie's position, but her baby's dad hadn't offered to stand by her the way Elsie's had. Her boyfriend had disappeared. She felt the familiar stab of rage as she did each time she thought of him.

'Is he a good man?' she whispered.

Elsie closed her eyes, so Anne looked at Hetty instead. She was dismayed when Hetty shook her head. Anne softened, but knew she had to point out the reality of what this would mean for Elsie.

'If you get wed, you know the rules.'

'I'll have to leave the factory, I know,' Elsie said sadly.

'When you're ready to share your news, tell Mrs Perkins first and she'll pass it on to Mr Jack. But you can trust me to keep quiet.'

Tears streamed down Elsie's cheeks. 'I don't want to leave. This factory is everything. It's all I've got,' she whispered.

Hetty gently stroked her arm. 'You'll have a baby to care for and a husband to look after. You won't have time to think about us.'

Elsie turned her tear-stained face to Anne. 'What did you mean before, when you said there was more to you than we know?'

Anne straightened in her seat. She adjusted her glasses, then glanced behind her. When she was sure no one could overhear, she began to speak.

'I can't tell you here, but perhaps we could meet after work one day. We could go for tea on Front Street. My treat.' She clasped her hands in her lap and felt Elsie and Hetty staring at her. 'I owe you an explanation about why I didn't turn up for the picnic.'

'We saw you on the bus to Durham,' Hetty said softly.

Anne felt her stomach twist. She should have known someone would have seen her. Chester-le-Street was too small a town not to go unnoticed.

'I think it's only fair that I share something about myself, since you, Elsie, have been so honest with me. Let me tell you later this week, outside of the factory. How about Thursday for tea, if you're both free?'

Elsie and Hetty nodded. Anne stood.

'Don't worry, Elsie. We'll get through this, all three of us. Hetty and I will help you in every way we can.'

'Thanks, Anne,' Elsie replied.

'Oh, and Hetty? Don't forget that Mr Jack wants to see you this afternoon. Come to his office at two o'clock.'

Anne left the girls huddled in the corner of the canteen. She'd never had anyone to talk to about her baby. She couldn't tell Mrs Fortune, or she'd be thrown out on the street. She certainly couldn't tell Mr Jack or Jacob or any of the men she worked with, for they wouldn't understand. There was also the possibility that she would never have been appointed to work for Mr Jack if she'd been honest about her personal life. No one wanted the shame of an unmarried mother on their hands. No, there was no reason for the men to know. She thought about Hetty and Elsie, remembered their eager faces, waiting to hear what she would tell them. Finally she had friends she could trust.

Chapter Thirty-One

At two o'clock that afternoon, Hetty presented herself at reception. She straightened her spine, lifted her chin and smiled. When Jacob didn't respond, she coughed loudly to get his attention. He looked at her and arched an eyebrow.

'I'm here to see Mr Jack. Anne asked me to arrive at two p.m.'

'Very good. Take a seat,' he replied.

Hetty sat in a chair along the wood-panelled wall. Two other girls walked into reception together, then a third one on her own. Hetty smiled and said hello, taking in their neat clothes and tidy hair. She couldn't help but compare herself. Looking at their clear skin, slim waists and delicate features, she suddenly felt lumpen.

The clock on the wall ticked as the girls waited in silence. Hetty clasped her hands in her lap. She still wasn't sure what she was doing here. It had only been the financial bonus for the lucky winner that had persuaded her to enter the competition. Even though she didn't have to pay Frankie Ireland any more, the extra money was much needed at home, as there was still only her wages coming in. Despite what Hilda said about Dan having work, Hetty had never seen him bring a penny into the house. He brought the odd bucket of coal, stolen from somewhere. And whenever he did, Hilda treated him as if he'd brought gold.

Lost in her thoughts, she didn't notice the door open in the corner of the room. When she heard a name being called, she looked up to see Anne standing there. The girl sitting next to her followed Anne from the room.

Hetty sat patiently as the other two girls were called. Waiting to see the factory owner made her feel dishonest. She shifted in her seat. How could she even think about being the face of a new toffee brand when she knew about Frankie Ireland and the thefts? It wouldn't be right. She stood, determined to walk out and forfeit her chance, but at that moment, the door opened again and Anne called her name. Hetty gulped, turned around and followed her along the carpeted hallway.

'Don't be scared,' Anne said as she showed Hetty into Mr Jack's office.

Hetty stood in front of Mr Jack's desk.

'Please sit, Miss Lawson,' he said.

She sat on a hard-backed chair facing Mr Jack. Anne sat on his right-hand side with a notepad in her hand. She gave Hetty a reassuring smile, which helped to quell her nerves. Hetty noticed that Mr Jack's bow tie was the same blue as the ribbon she wore when she visited Elisabethville. She took in his cheerful round face, neat moustache and bright eyes. He looked at her and beamed.

'Now then, Miss Lawson. I understand you're highly thought of at Elisabethville when you've been there on business for us.'

'I am, sir?' Hetty said, surprised to hear she'd been talked about.

'Oh yes. They admire your confidence. Orders for toffees from the Belgians have been steady since your first visit. Would you be willing to go back again?'

'Any time,' she said quickly, thinking of Dirk. 'I mean, yes, sir. I would be willing to return.'

Mr Jack nodded approvingly.

'Miss Lawson, I need to ask you a question.'

Hetty sat up straight as he continued.

'Why would you like to be the face of Lady Tina?'

Hetty looked at Anne, unsure of what to say. She'd only entered the competition because Anne had encouraged her, and of course there'd been the chance to earn money. But she could hardly tell Mr Jack that.

'Well, sir, it's because . . .' she began hesitantly, then paused, not knowing how to carry on. She couldn't tell a lie; it wouldn't sit right with her, and she felt sure Mr Jack would see through her straight away.

'It's because Hetty Lawson is one of the best workers in the factory, sir,' Anne chipped in. 'She's honest and decent. A good friend and mentor to the girls in the wrapping room.'

Hetty opened her mouth to speak, but nothing came out. She felt tears prick her eyes.

'Sir, I'm just a factory girl, the same as any other,' she said quietly.

'Don't be modest, Miss Lawson,' Mr Jack replied cheerfully. 'You've a certain quality I admire. In fact, I believe you may be exactly what we're looking for.'

'Me, sir? But—'

He held up his hand to stop her saying more. Hetty

saw Anne shake her head in a warning to keep quiet. Mr Jack stood and paced the carpet. Each time he passed Hetty, she sensed his eyes on her face and felt herself reddening.

'Yes, I believe we've found our Lady Tina. Anne, set up a meeting for Miss Lawson with Mr Gerard's department, who will capture her likeness for the artwork. I want her face on the new tins as soon as possible.'

Hetty laid a hand on her chest to try to calm her racing heart. She was flabbergasted at the news.

'Are you sure you want *me*? The other girls were prettier and much better groomed,' she said, trying to make sense of what she'd just heard.

'I'm always sure when I make a decision, Miss Lawson,' Mr Jack said firmly. 'Just ask my father. When he first handed this toffee factory to me, I made changes he didn't approve of. But I knew what I was doing and I was proved right. Even he conceded he was wrong, in the end.' A sadness clouded his face. 'If only he would concede the same on personal matters . . . Oh, but now I'm rambling. The point is, I like you, Miss Lawson,' he continued, more cheerily this time. 'I admire your spirit and especially your enthusiasm for returning to Elisabethville on factory business.'

Hetty gulped.

'I also admire your looks, of course. They're exactly what we need to entice customers to buy our new brand. Your face will cheer up the nation as it suffers during this war. You'll be in everyone's home, under everyone's tree at Christmas. You'll be on the shelves of confectionery shops across the land. You'll be famous, Miss Lawson.'

Hetty felt her neck and cheeks growing hot. 'I'm not sure I want to be famous,' she muttered.

'No one outside of Chester-le-Street will know it's you, Hetty,' Anne said kindly. 'To everyone else in the country you'll be Lady Tina, the girl on the tin, that's all.'

'Anne's right,' Mr Jack said. 'Only those in the factory will know your identity. Oh, and local people, of course. We'll have a celebration in the canteen to unveil our new brand. We'll get the local newspaper involved; they'll give us free publicity. Anne, make a note to call the editor tomorrow.'

Hetty's head whirled with what she'd heard. Nothing seemed real. She had to grip the arms of her chair to help bring herself down to earth.

Mr Jack was still speaking. 'Honesty and integrity, Miss Lawson, are qualities we admire at Jack's, and I think you've got those in spades.'

Frankie Ireland and the stolen toffees never left her mind. She felt sick. How could she be the face of a new brand when she knew such terrible things? Yet she couldn't tell anyone; she'd made a pact. Her head swam. She couldn't go through with this. It was impossible. She tried to stand to leave the room, but her legs were shaking. She opened her mouth, ready to tell Anne and Mr Jack that she couldn't be the face of Lady Tina. She had to give this up right now and turn down the bonus because of the terrible secret she kept. But before she could say a word, there was an urgent knock at the door.

'Enter!' Mr Jack yelled.

Hetty saw a handsome man with fine features and a firm jaw. He was tall and well built, with clipped brown hair.

'Burl? What is it? Do you have news?' Mr Jack demanded.

'Yes, sir. We've found the thief. It's one of the girls from the wrapping room. She's admitted everything to Mrs Perkins. Her name is Elsie Cooper.'

Chapter Thirty-Two

Hetty couldn't believe what she'd heard.

'Elsie? No!' she cried.

Anne leapt to her feet. 'Mr Burl, are you sure it's Elsie Cooper? She's a friend of mine. I know she'd never do such a thing.'

Mr Burl looked affronted at being challenged. 'That's the name Mrs Perkins gave me. Miss Cooper is in reception now.'

Hetty's feet felt glued to the floor. She wanted to push past Mr Burl and run out of the room, but she couldn't move with the shock. Had Elsie really been involved in helping Frankie steal the toffees? Surely not. She was foolish and flirty, but she wasn't a thief. But then Hetty recalled her stealing her pass to Elisabethville. Was her friend guilty of worse crimes too?

Mr Jack stood up. 'Very good, Burl. You may leave.'

Mr Burl headed to the door, but before he left the room, Mr Jack called him back.

'Burl, just one moment.'

Hetty realised her legs were still shaking. Mr Jack walked towards her and laid his hand on her shoulder.

'I'd like you to meet our Lady Tina.'

Mr Burl nodded sharply at Hetty. Then he looked her over as if inspecting a piece of toffee from the slab, deciding whether to send it to the reject basket.

'Very good, sir. Nice choice,' he said, then he turned and left the room.

Hetty's head was still reeling over Elsie. She tried to make sense of it. Was Elsie really a thief, or was something sinister going on? Was Frankie forcing her to take the blame?

'I'm sorry you had to overhear that exchange, Miss Lawson,' Mr Jack said. He seemed almost embarrassed. 'We've, er . . . had a few problems with certain items going missing, but now it seems the culprit has been caught. I think you should return to work. Please, not a word to anyone there. If Mrs Perkins complains that you've been away too long, just let Anne know.'

Hetty didn't know if she was coming or going.

'You'll make a fine Lady Tina,' Mr Jack said as he escorted her to his office door.

In reception, Elsie looked up when she heard the door open and was stunned to see Hetty walking towards her.

'What's happened?' Hetty asked.

Elsie wiped her hand across her eyes and stared ahead, too embarrassed and ashamed to look Hetty in the eye.

'Did you help steal the toffees?' Hetty asked sternly. 'Come on, Elsie, tell me. Or are you taking the blame for Frankie?'

Elsie stayed quiet. She was worried that if she started to speak, she would end up in tears.

'Elsie, for goodness' sake!' Hetty cried. 'If you take the blame for this, you'll lose your job. Mr Jack will sack you.'

Elsie laid her hands on her stomach. 'I'll have to leave anyway,' she said.

'Please, Elsie, I'm begging you. I know you took my pass for Elisabethville, but I can't believe you'd steal from the factory. I know you're doing it for Frankie.'

Elsie closed her eyes and wished Hetty could understand just a fraction of what she was going through. Her aunt had taken her in after her parents died when she was young. Jean was generous with her cash when she had it, allowing Elsie to buy food and drink, but she was less generous with her love and affection. Elsie had a baby on the way and now she was about to lose her job. But she had a man who said he loved her, and that meant the world to her. Despite Frankie's faults, which Hetty kept pointing out, and despite the fact that his temper ran away with him on occasion, she knew she couldn't bring up her baby alone. She needed someone by her side, and he was the only person she had.

'He told me he'd marry me within the month if I took the blame,' she confessed. 'While you were out of the wrapping room, I confessed to Mrs Perkins. Don't you see, Hetty? I don't have a choice if I want a future for my child. My aunt has made it clear she isn't going to help. She doesn't want a crying baby in the flat. She says it'll put the men off and they'll go elsewhere to pay for pleasure. Anyway, I can't raise a baby somewhere strange men are coming and going at night; it's too dangerous.'

In the corner of the room, the door opened and Anne appeared.

Glenda Young

'Elsie?' she said softly. 'Mr Jack is ready to see you.'

As Elsie stood up and walked towards her, she knew she couldn't tell the truth. To do so would mean she'd end up alone.

Inside Mr Jack's office, it was Anne who asked Elsie to sit. Mr Jack's normal procedure when disciplining or sacking an employee was to leave them standing. Elsie was grateful for the seat, for her legs were weak and she felt sick. She felt too ashamed to raise her head, unable to look at Mr Jack or Anne. When Mr Jack began to speak, she heard his voice rise and fall. Words including 'serious offence' and 'a matter for the police' floated around her. She felt numb and couldn't react. That is, until she heard Frankie's name.

'It was brought to my attention that one of the sugar boilers, a man called Frankie Ireland, was suspected of stealing. When questioned, he said the thefts were instigated by you, Miss Cooper. Is that true?'

This time Elsie looked up. She saw Mr Jack watching her with a serious expression. Anne stood behind him, to his right-hand side.

'Please, if I'm to be sacked, just sack me,' Elsie pleaded. 'This is the worst thing that's ever happened in my life.'

She expected Mr Jack to ask her to leave his factory and never darken its doors again. However, Anne stepped forward.

'Sir, if I may, I'd like to speak up on Elsie's behalf.'

Elsie wondered where this was leading.

'This is most unusual, Anne,' Mr Jack said. 'Miss Cooper has confessed to Mrs Perkins. I don't see what else there is to say.'

226

Anne moved to stand beside Elsie and laid her hand gently on her shoulder. 'Elsie Cooper is a hard-working girl, and a ray of sunshine in the wrapping room. If . . .' She paused, letting the word hang in the air. Underneath Elsie's overall her heart was beating fast. She gripped the arms of the chair. 'If Elsie is guilty, I beg you not to sack her.'

'Nonsense!' Mr Jack exploded.

Both girls were startled by his outburst.

'There is no place for thieves in my factory,' he said, more controlled now. 'Miss Cooper, collect your belongings from the wrapping room and leave this instant.'

Elsie made to stand. It was nothing less than she'd expected. A lump came to her throat. However, she couldn't rise from her seat as Anne was pressing hard on her shoulder to keep her in the chair.

'Sir, I beg you. Do not sack this girl.'

Mr Jack narrowed his eyes at her. 'Why not? She's a thief!'

Elsie's gaze darted from Anne to Mr Jack. The pressure of Anne's hand was almost painful now. She closed her eyes to squeeze away tears.

Anne continued. 'I don't believe for one moment that she stole from us, or that the thefts were her idea. I beg you to keep her on at the factory until more investigations are carried out to determine who the real thief is. Elsie will be on her best behaviour during the next few days while the sugar boilers are questioned. I will personally see to it that she isn't left unsupervised at any time.'

Mr Jack fiddled nervously with his bow tie. 'But she confessed,' he repeated.

'I beg you to give her a chance while an inquiry is held to find the real thief. Mr Burl's men could begin looking into the matter today.'

Elsie sat rigid as Anne and Mr Jack discussed her as if she wasn't there. She was too scared to speak, terrified that if she said the wrong thing, she could land Frankie in trouble. If he found out she'd told the truth to Mr Jack, he'd call their wedding off and she'd be left on her own. She glanced at the carpet. There was silence as she waited for Mr Jack's verdict. She heard him sigh heavily.

'Very well, Anne. I trust your judgement. Miss Cooper?'

Elsie forced herself to look up.

'You may return to work while the matter is invest-igated thoroughly. I will advise Mrs Perkins to never let you out of her sight.'

She felt Anne at her side, helping her rise from her seat.

'Thank you,' she said.

Anne held her arm, escorted her to the door and out into the corridor.

'Why did you help me?' Elsie said once they were outside.

'Because I like you, Elsie, and I know you weren't involved. This sugar boiler, Frankie Ireland, he's the real culprit. Everything I've heard about him from the men in the boiling room . . . well, they say he's a nasty piece of work. He's violent too. I wouldn't want to be the poor woman he returns home to at night.'

Elsie thought she was going to faint. She put her hand against the wall to stop herself from falling.

'Elsie? Are you all right?' Anne sounded panicky.

Elsie took a moment, but still couldn't find it in her to admit that Frankie was her man.

'I appreciate what you've done for me, letting me keep my job,' she said instead.

Anne patted her arm. 'That's what friends are for.'

Elsie walked out into the cold day, glancing towards the wrapping room, where Hetty and Beattie and the other girls would be picking and wrapping toffees, twisting waxed papers. Mrs Perkins would demand to know what she was doing back there, and she'd have to explain. Hetty would want to know why she hadn't been sacked. The rest of the girls would make up their own stories about why she had been taken to Mr Jack's office, and gossip would be rife. No, she couldn't face returning right away. Instead she walked to the garden, gulping down cold air, trying to stop herself crying. She didn't deserve Anne's kindness and she felt wretched.

She sat on a wooden bench with her head in her hands and thought about her baby, about Frankie, about their life together at the Lambton Arms. When they were wed, when the baby came, Frankie would change and treat her better . . . wouldn't he?

'Penny for your thoughts,' a voice said.

She opened her eyes to see Stan the gardener. She quickly wiped her eyes and sat up straight.

'My word, you're not looking so good,' Stan said, concerned. 'You look perished, too. Here, take my jacket or you'll catch your death.'

He took off his jacket and handed it to her. Elsie accepted it gratefully and draped it across her shoulders. Then he sat on the other end of the bench, keeping a respectable distance between them.

'Shouldn't you be indoors, at work?' he said.

She turned to look at him, taking in his ruddy weather-beaten face and the concerned look in his brown eyes. How easy it would be to tell him the truth, she thought. He'd offered her nothing but friendship and kindness. He'd never forced a kiss on her, the way most men would, the way Frankie did. He always smiled and waved when he saw her in the factory grounds. And when they spoke at lunchtimes in the canteen or when passing in the gardens, he listened and made her feel important, as if he really cared. How she'd love to confide in someone who wouldn't judge her. Under Stan's coat, she rubbed her arms and felt the sting of her bruises. No, she couldn't tell anyone the truth for fear of what Frankie might do next. In silence, she stood and handed Stan his coat, then walked quickly back to work.

Chapter Thirty-Three

On Thursday, Anne packed up to leave her office at the end of the day. She draped the cloth cover over her typewriter to keep the dust off overnight. She made sure her desk was tidy, with confidential papers locked out of sight. She lifted her coat from the peg on the back of her door. Then she took her scarf, wrapped it around her neck and placed her brown velvet hat on her head. She picked up her handbag and walked into Mr Jack's office. He was at his desk, reading papers Mr Burl had given him earlier that day. Anne noticed that his face was set firm.

'Goodnight, sir,' she said.

Mr Jack looked up, distracted. 'What? Oh yes, of course. Is it that time already? My word, doesn't time fly?'

He placed the papers on his desk and tutted out loud, shaking his head.

'This doesn't make good reading. It's the financial projection for the next twelve months. This damn war, it's going to put us out of business if we let it. That's why it's essential we keep one step ahead of our competition.'

He smiled warmly at Anne.

Glenda Young

'Speaking of which, how's our Lady Tina doing?'

'Hetty has met with Mr Gerard's team and they've drawn her likeness. They'll soon have samples of the artwork for you to approve. I understand it will include pink and white roses, to represent those in our garden.'

'I like the sound of it, Anne. Mr Gerard is a genius.'

'Actually, sir,' Anne began cautiously. 'It was my idea. The roses, I mean. I suggested it to Mr Gerard and he liked it. But of course the final decision will be yours.'

She wondered if she'd gone too far, telling Mr Jack about her input. After all, she hadn't worked at the factory long, and he might not think she had the right to offer suggestions. But he seemed amused. He leaned back in his seat and looked at her. For the first time since she'd begun working for him, she felt she was being appraised. He'd never looked at her in such an inquisitive way before. It was as if he was seeing her for the very first time.

'You look pretty, Anne. I mean ... you look very smart,' he said, before returning his gaze to the papers.

Anne was stunned to hear this. He had never commented on her appearance before. She didn't know how to react. She pulled herself together and told herself he was only being polite. However, she felt slightly uncomfortable. Those were the first words he'd ever said to her that weren't to do with paperwork, figures, finances, design or anything to do with toffee.

'I'm taking tea out this evening,' she explained.

'Then you must go. I expect there'll be a young man waiting for you,' he said, lifting his gaze to meet hers. 'I hope he treats you well. It's important to find the right partner in life, the one person who suits you well. I wish my father understood this. He's arranging for me to be

232

wed, Anne. Did you know? Oh, I'm sure you must have heard gossip in the factory.'

'No, sir!' Anne cried, then gave a nervous cough. It felt as if a line had been crossed. In that moment, she saw Mr Jack for the man he was instead of the factory manager who employed her. She wondered if he was seeing her in a different light too. Why else had he commented on her appearance, even suggesting she had a boyfriend taking her to tea?

'I have heard no such gossip,' she went on calmly. But in the back of her mind a little bell rang about something Mr Gerard had told her. She wondered why Mr Jack was choosing to confide in her about his upcoming wedding.

'Sorry, Anne. I have no wish to keep you from meeting your young man.'

She straightened her spine. 'There is no man, I am meeting two friends,' she said.

Mr Jack began adjusting his tie. Anne had seen him do this in board meetings, when he felt anxious about factory finances, or under strain from too many demands. She wondered if letting his guard down had upset him. Perhaps he was regretting being so familiar.

'I'd better go, my friends will be waiting,' she said, excusing herself.

'Yes, very good,' Mr Jack said, formal again, as if the last few minutes hadn't happened. 'I'll see you tomorrow bright and early.'

Anne left the room with her heart thumping under her blouse. She wasn't sure what had just happened, but she felt uneasy. As she walked along the hallway and into reception, she was lost in her thoughts. How odd it had been for Mr Jack to speak so candidly. Most unlike him. She ran through the events of the day, wondering if it was possible that he'd had a meeting involving alcohol from the canteen that afternoon. Had it loosened his tongue?

She walked past Jacob and called out goodnight, and he grunted in reply. Something had changed between her and Mr Jack, but she was hard pressed to say what it was. It certainly wasn't desire on her part. With his short legs and bald head, she didn't consider him handsome. Yet there was something about him, something warm and friendly, cheerful and calm. Something that made her feel safe. That was it, she decided. Because she felt safe working with him, maybe he felt the same, and that was why he'd allowed himself to open up.

She thought about Mr Jack's father arranging for him to marry. It seemed strange that a man of his age would have no say in who he wed. But then Mr Jack and his family were different to local folk. Maybe all their money had turned them peculiar.

Her thoughts whirled as she opened the door to the yard and the cold wind hit her. There was sleet in the air, icy, biting into her face. She saw Hetty and Elsie, heads down, waiting for her by the gates, and rushed over to them.

'Sorry I'm late, girls. Mr Jack kept me. Come on, let's get out of this sleet and into the café.'

The three of them huddled together as they ran across the road to a tea shop called Lambton Café on the corner of Front Street and High Chare. A bell jingled above the door as they entered. Hetty shook raindrops from her nose and Anne dabbed her wet face with a linen hand-kerchief.

Elsie edged her way to a table at the back of the café, away from the other customers, two elderly ladies sipping from china cups. Once the girls had removed their wet coats, hung them on their chairs and smoothed their hair, they sat down. A young, miserable-looking waitress dressed in a green apron walked over to them and slapped three menus down.

'We've got no cheese and the bacon's off,' she announced sharply as she took a small pad and pencil from her pocket. She stood at the table next to the girls while they read the menu.

'Three rounds of sandwiches, then fruit cake with tea? My treat,' Anne suggested.

'Thanks, Anne,' Hetty said.

'It's very generous of you,' Elsie added.

She rounded up the menus and handed them to the waitress. 'We'll have three rounds of ham sandwiches, three slices of fruit cake and—' she began.

'Three teas, I've got it,' the waitress interrupted as she scribbled in her pad. 'Will there be anything else?'

Elsie shook her head.

'Good,' the waitress snapped. 'Because we close in an hour and I want you out by then.' She nodded at Elsie's khaki and red overall. 'I know what you toffee factory girls are like; you'd sit here for hours if you could.' And with that she walked off.

'She wasn't very friendly,' Elsie muttered.

She looked across the table at Anne, whose glasses had steamed up. Anne rubbed at them with her handkerchief, then slid them back on. Elsie leaned forward.

'You said you had something to tell us, after I told you about . . . you know,' she said. She didn't want to mention the words *pregnant* or *baby*. The two ladies at the far table looked old, but Elsie was worried their hearing might still be first rate.

The waitress appeared with three small teapots and china cups on a tray. She set them on the table with a jug of milk, then walked away. Once she was out of earshot, Elsie tried again.

'Come on, Anne. We have to make the most of this hour. What did you want to say?'

She watched as Anne poured milk into cups, lifted the lid of her teapot, gave the tea a stir, then picked up the tea strainer.

'I know what you're going through,' Anne said quietly. 'I've been there too.'

Under the table, Elsie gripped Hetty's hand.

'You were pregnant?' Hetty whispered.

'Shush,' Elsie warned her, nodding at the two ladies.

The girls leaned in over the table, so close their heads were almost touching, and Anne began to speak.

'Elsie, you were honest with me this week and I want to be honest with you. If we're to be good friends, we need no secrets between us.'

She began to tell them about her baby boy. Elsie took in the news, asking questions about the birth, about what had happened afterwards and where her child was now. Anne even told them how she'd spied over the wall of her son's new home, hoping for a glimpse of him.

'I'm not proud of myself,' she said, eyes downcast. 'I know the child is no longer mine. But there are some days I miss him so much I'm raw with pain. That's why I'm here for you, Elsie, as a friend, as someone who's been through what you're going through. Let me help you if I can.'

Elsie reached across the table and took Anne's hand in hers. Then she brought Hetty's hand from under the table. Hetty reached for Anne's other hand, completing the circle.

'Let's have no more secrets,' Anne whispered.

Elsie thought about Frankie and shifted uncomfortably in her seat.

Chapter Thirty-Four

Anne gently dabbed her eyes with her linen handkerchief.

'Did you . . .' Elsie glanced at her quickly before she continued. 'Did you give your child a name?'

Anne shook her head. 'No. I didn't trust myself to do that. I knew I'd have to hand him over the moment he was born. If I'd named him, it would've made my heartache even worse. I had to steel myself all the way through my pregnancy. I needed the money and I knew I couldn't keep him. And yet now, he's all I think about. I can't stop, somehow. I know I can't have him back. I'm a single woman living in a rented room. I have no husband, no boyfriend, no one. My parents died. I'm alone. I shouldn't even call him my son.' She wiped her eyes again.

'This couple you gave your son to, are they good people?' Hetty asked.

Anne slid her handkerchief into her bag. She lifted her teacup and took a long sip.

'They live in a big house in Durham, they have money. Mr Matthews is a chief engineer. He works high up in a factory. On the wages he earns, my boy will never go hungry.'

'Then be reassured he'll grow up big and strong,' Hetty said. 'Not like the scruffy kids who live around here.'

'He'll be looked after well, I know,' Anne said, resigned. 'It's a good job I enjoy working for Mr Jack at the factory. It stops me from dwelling too much.'

She took another sip from her cup.

'But enough about me. What about you, Elsie, what will you do?'

Their conversation was interrupted when the waitress sidled to their table carrying a tray of sandwiches. Plates were laid down without a word and she disappeared again. Anne picked up a sandwich and leaned towards Elsie.

'Are you sure you want to marry your fella?' she whispered.

She saw Elsie look at Hetty, as if for reassurance.

'What is it?' she asked.

'I've got to marry him, I've no choice.' Elsie shrugged. 'I want my baby to be respectable, to have a proper mum and dad. I know I'll have to leave work once I'm wed, although I don't know what I'll do for money.'

'I'm sure Jim Ireland and Cathy can find work for you in the pub,' Hetty said.

'I've never worked in a pub before,' Elsie replied sadly.

'What's your fella called?' Anne asked.

Elsie stiffened and picked at her sandwich.

'Elsie?' she said, wondering why the girl wouldn't answer.

It was Hetty who spoke first. 'Elsie, tell Anne the truth. We're friends now, the three of us, and we just agreed we shouldn't have secrets.'

Elsie took her time finishing her sandwich. 'You won't like it when you hear his name,' she said at last.

Anne frowned. 'Why ever not?'

'It's Frankie Ireland.'

The sandwich fell from Anne's hand and her jaw dropped in shock. 'But he's the sugar boiler who's suspected of stealing. What are you doing with him?'

Suddenly the penny dropped. She could have kicked herself for not putting two and two together before.

'So that's why you confessed to Mrs Perkins that you were the thief. You were covering for him.'

Elsie groaned. 'Frankie will kill me if he finds out I've told you.'

Anne sat back in her seat, reeling.

'She's not kidding,' Hetty added. 'Frankie's a violent man. He beats her.'

Elsie's face flushed red and she glared at Hetty. 'He's got a bad temper, that's all,' she said quickly. 'Anne, please. Keep this to yourself. You said we shouldn't have secrets. Well, now I've told you the truth about Frankie and my baby. You think your life's a mess. You should try being me. When I marry Frankie, I'll move to live with him at the Lambton Arms.'

Anne sucked air through her teeth. 'Oh, that's a rough pub. You know, he's in a lot of trouble. Another sugar boiler came forward to confirm that Frankie had stolen the toffees after word got around that you'd confessed. It's not looking good for him; he's going to be sacked.' She watched Elsie's face as the news sank in.

'I hope he knows how to pull pints at the pub, then,' Elsie said.

'Doesn't it bother you that he's a thief?' Anne asked.

Elsie shrugged. 'Of course it does. But he'll change when the baby comes. My baby needs its father.'

There was silence at the table for a few moments before Anne turned to Hetty. 'Is there anything *you'd* like to share?'

Elsie perked up and nudged Hetty playfully. 'Hetty's the most stable of us all. She's got a steady home life, a family and her own fella. He's gone off to fight in the war.'

'I've known Bob a while,' Hetty began. 'But the truth is, he's not my boyfriend any more. I wrote to him to call things off. There's . . . well, there's someone else now. A Belgian man called Dirk.'

'I knew it!' Elsie cried.

'Shush, keep your voice down,' Hetty said, nodding at the elderly ladies.

'Where did you meet him?' Anne asked.

'On Front Street, he handed me a dog on the day that Bob went off to war. It's a long story. Then, I met him again at Elisabethville, when you sent me on factory business the first time. He helped me when I turned up at the wrong gate.'

'Have you kissed him?' Elsie whispered.

Hetty nodded. 'Just once. I'm spending Saturday with him; we're going for a walk along the river. That's if it doesn't rain or snow.'

'What do your parents make of him?' Anne asked.

'I've only got my mum, and to be honest, we don't really get on. We never have. She's always made me feel like I'm second best to my brother. I used to get on great with my dad, but he died months ago. He left me and my mum in debt.'

Anne noticed Hetty's gaze flick across the table to Elsie, and wondered what was being unsaid.

'Does your mum like Dirk?' she asked.

Hetty shook her head. 'She hasn't met him yet. I can't take him home.'

'Why not?' Elsie asked.

Hetty dreaded the harsh words her mum would yell at her if she told her she was dating a Belgian man.

'Mum is intolerant of people outside her small world. She wouldn't understand why I was dating a Belgian when I could have my pick of Chester-le-Street boys. But I feel strongly for Dirk, that's why I had to write to Bob to call things off. I'm not the kind of girl who'd string a fella along. A clean break was best. This way, Bob can get on with his life; he might even meet a nice girl overseas.'

Anne raised her eyebrows. 'Meet a nice girl?' she said. 'He's out there fighting a war. You make it sound as if he's at a tea party.'

Hetty dropped her gaze. 'Bob's not a bad man, he's just, well . . . dull.'

Anne raised her teacup. 'Here's to saving ourselves from dull men,' she said, smiling. Hetty and Elsie smiled too, and clinked their cups against hers.

'What's Mr Jack like to work for?' Hetty asked, pushing her plate away.

Anne was about to reply when the waitress appeared with three slices of fruit cake. She set them down on the table and removed the empty plates.

'Anyone want more tea?' she asked.

The girls shook their heads.

'Good, because we're closing in twenty minutes.' She turned and walked away.

'She'll never get top marks for being nice to her customers,' Elsie said.

'She doesn't need to, she's the owner's daughter,' Hetty replied.

Elsie raised her eyebrows at this information, then turned to Anne. 'Well? What's Mr Jack like?' she asked.

Anne thought for a moment, trying to figure out how best to describe him.

'It's hard to say,' she said. 'He's a fair employer, who treats me well. Of course, he makes me work hard, but I don't mind. He can be eccentric at times. Do you remember when he strode into the canteen after Anabel died and announced that men and women could sit together? Well, that's what he's like. He gets a notion in his head and he goes ahead and does things straight away. He's impulsive, I guess.'

'He keeps his home life very private,' Elsie noted.

'He certainly does,' Anne agreed. 'There's nothing I can tell you in addition to what everyone at the factory already knows. He lives apart from his family. Their house is sprawling, in its own grounds, and his is modest by comparison.'

'It's still four times as big as our house on Elm Street,' Hetty pointed out. 'And he lives there alone.'

Anne picked up her cake and bit into sweet, soft fruit. There was a lot more about Mr Jack she could say after their peculiar exchange earlier. However, despite being the one to suggest they kept no secrets between them, she kept quiet. She remembered the charged moment when he'd told her she looked pretty. Him opening up to her like that, then talking about his upcoming wedding, well, it felt as if something had shifted. She still wasn't certain what had happened between them; all she could gather was that something had.

She felt a touch of anxiety when she thought of seeing him the next day at work. He might want to confide in her again, tell her more about his wedding and his father. On the one hand, she felt important and trusted knowing personal things about him. But on the other, it made her uneasy. It wasn't as if she could offer advice. She decided to face him the following day in the same way she always did: friendly, efficient and polite.

'What happened to your baby's dad?' Hetty asked.

The question pulled Anne from her reverie.

'He ran as fast and as far away as he could the minute I told him I was pregnant. I've not seen him since.' She could feel her shoulders tense when she thought about him. 'I'd rather not speak about him,' she added, turning her attention back to her cake.

'Is there a new man in your life now?' Elsie asked.

Anne pushed her glasses to the bridge of her nose. 'Don't be silly. I haven't got time to waste on a man. I don't care if I'm single for the rest of my life. I've got my work at the factory. Anyway, where am I going to find a decent fella in Chester-le-Street? They're all miners or toffee men.'

'Ooh, got your sights set somewhere higher, have you?' Elsie teased. 'What about Mr Burl? He's handsome. I've seen him in the canteen at lunchtime. He'd make a good catch, if that's what you're after.'

Anne thought of ill-mannered Mr Burl. 'No, he's not

my cup of tea,' she said quickly. 'I'm happy to concentrate on work and leave men out of my life. They cause too much pain and I won't suffer again.'

The waitress sauntered across to them and slapped their bill down. 'Sup up,' she said. 'We close in five minutes.'

Chapter Thirty-Five

Elsie was hard at work the next day when Hetty arrived in the wrapping room.

'My word, will wonders ever cease?' Hetty teased as she slipped her boots off and put her clogs on. 'This is the first time in weeks you've been here before me.'

Elsie ignored her and carried on picking toffees with one hand and wax wrappers with the other. She was so adept at the job now that she could do it quickly, without thinking. Every toffee she placed on the tray to go to the packing room was perfectly wrapped, with the blue logo exactly in the centre. She sometimes felt as if she could wrap toffees in her sleep. The gentle noise of waxed papers being twisted whispered around the room. It was a pleasing sound that Elsie liked, and it helped calm her mind. As her pregnancy progressed, she no longer ate toffees from the reject baskets, as she couldn't face the taste. Even the sweet smell in the wrapping room made her feel sick.

'Elsie?' Hetty whispered as she began working. 'You're quiet this morning. What's up? Are you feeling all right?'

Elsie was about to reply when she noticed Beattie

tapping her finger against the side of her nose. Mrs Perkins was on her way. She stayed quiet and carried on with her work. When she saw Mrs Perkins engrossed in paperwork at her desk, she leaned across to whisper to Hetty.

'What are you doing on the first Saturday in December?'

'Why?' Hetty replied.

'I want you to come to my wedding.'

Hetty dropped the toffee she was holding. 'What?' she cried.

Beattie glared at them. 'Girls!' she hissed. 'Be quiet or Perkins will be over here.'

Elsie and Hetty returned to their work, moving slightly closer together. Their shoulders were touching and their faces were turned to each other, to ensure their words went unheard by anyone else.

'Yes . . . yes, of course I'll come,' Hetty said.

'Frankie's been sacked,' Elsie told her. 'Mr Jack dismissed him last night when he turned up for his night shift. Frankie's sister-in-law, Cathy, knows I'm pregnant. Frankie must have told Jim. She told Frankie she won't let us live in the pub or set Frankie on behind the bar unless he does the decent thing and marries me. He's already got Aunt Jean on his case, who's threatened to call the police on him, she knows one of the inspectors at the station, he's a regular visitor to her flat. Frankie's got no choice. Both Aunt Jean and Cathy are a force to be reckoned with.'

Hetty recalled Cathy's words about Frankie taking women into his room. She'd referred to them as tarts. She decided not to tell Elsie about this, because she knew that no matter what she said about Frankie, Elsie would choose to believe her own version of him.

'Anyway, Cathy's on my side,' Elsie continued. 'She even reserved the first available date at the register office for us.'

'Blimey,' Hetty said. 'It's all happened so fast. It's a lot to take in.'

'You were probably hoping Frankie would drop me now he's been sacked and I don't have to take the blame for the thefts.'

'No!' Hetty gasped.

'It's all right, I know what you think of him; you've told me often enough.'

Elsie stiffened and concentrated again on her work when she noticed Mrs Perkins leaving her desk. She kept one eye on the supervisor, however, and when she was sure she was out of earshot, she resumed their conversation.

'All you need to know is that it's my decision to marry him and have his child.'

'Are you sure about this?' Hetty said, glancing at Elsie's stomach. 'Because it might not be too late for your aunt to find someone to do something about your situation.'

'It *is* too late,' Elsie said, keeping her voice level. 'I want to marry him, Hetty, I want to give my child the chances I never had.'

There was a beat of silence between them as Mrs Perkins made her way back to her desk. Once she was working on her ledger again, Elsie began to whisper once more.

'My aunt's not coming to the wedding. She washed her hands of me when I got together with Frankie. She's relieved I'm someone else's responsibility now. She's never wanted me. She thought giving me money to spend when she had it would make up for her years of neglect.

It'll just be you on my side, and Jim and Cathy on Frankie's. Then we'll go to the Lambton Arms for a drink.'

'How did Frankie take the news about being sacked?' Hetty whispered.

Elsie dropped the toffee she was holding, and her eyes filled with tears. Frankie had taken the news badly. He'd turned up drunk at the Lambton Arms, where she'd been waiting for him, and had continued drinking despite her pleas for him not to. Then when they'd gone up to his room, his temper had flared and he'd lashed out.

She didn't have a chance to reply to Hetty, though, for Mrs Perkins swanned up to them, inspecting their work. Their conversation was over for now. Elsie gritted her teeth against the pain from the fresh bruises all the way down her right-hand side.

Anne poured coffee into a large mug with the Jack's logo in blue. She handed it to Mr Jack, who turned it around in his hands, admiring it.

'This is the perfect size, Anne. I knew I could trust you to order correctly. It seems to me that there's not much you can't do.'

He sipped his hot coffee as Anne poured herself a cup.

'Anne, I want to discuss the guest list for the launch of Lady Tina,' he said.

Anne sat in the chair on the opposite side of his desk. She set her coffee cup down and took up her pencil and notepad. Since she'd arrived at work that morning, Mr Jack had treated her as he did every day, with respect and politeness. There was no mention of his softening towards her the previous day, and for that, she was grateful. His personal comments had been a one-off, she decided, unlikely to happen again. But as she waited for him to tell her who he'd like invited to the launch, she noticed he was staring into space. This wasn't the Mr Jack she had grown to know. He was usually fizzing with energy and raring to go.

'Sir?' she said.

Her voice brought him down to earth. He picked up his mug, took a long drink, then snapped back to his usual self.

'Ah yes. The Lady Tina launch.'

Anne sat with her pencil poised, waiting.

'I want the most important dignitaries invited from County Durham and beyond. We'll put on a tour, then unveil the new brand.'

She scribbled notes as fast as she could while Mr Jack laid out his plans.

'We'll make it a Christmas launch. Ask the canteen to prepare accordingly. We'll offer a seasonal buffet for staff and guests. Ensure there are enough tins of Lady Tina to hand out to everyone, staff included.'

'Everyone, sir? That's very generous,' Anne said.

Mr Jack leaned back in his seat and lifted his mug again. The earthy aroma of coffee filled the office, and Anne breathed it in. It was a scent she liked very much. It made the office feel cosy and warm against the cold, dark winter's day. She thought about Hetty and Elsie working in the draughty wrapping room.

'There's a file in the drawer where you'll find the addresses of those to be invited.'

He tapped his fingers against his chin.

'Ah, I've just realised there's one person whose name

isn't typed on the list but handwritten at the bottom. You'll need to type up his name. He used to be the chief engineer at the Durham factory where they make the tin for our boxes, but is now the new owner. His name is Matthews. Peter Matthews. Make sure you invite all the wives too. I understand Mr Matthews' wife is called Ruby.'

Anne dropped her pencil in shock.

Chapter Thirty-Six

There was a knock at the door. Anne was glad of the interruption, as her heart was beating wildly after the shocking news Mr Jack had just given her. She picked up her pencil and turned to see Jacob, who was looking unusually flustered.

'Sir, you have a visitor,' he said, but no sooner had the words left his lips than he was pushed aside by a woman.

She was tall and willowy, and trailed a sickly lemon scent as she swanned into the room. Her dark eyes were exaggerated with pencil and shadow and her lips were scarlet. Her hair was neatly tucked under a squat black hat, although a few blonde tendrils escaped around her handsome face. She wore a green fitted jacket with matching skirt and gloves. Her feet were clad in short black boots with sharp heels. She looked very well-to-do, Anne thought, with her expensive clothes.

She walked straight to Mr Jack and kissed him on his cheek, leaving a smear of red lipstick there. Then she pulled a lace-edged handkerchief from her bag and dabbed his cheek until the colour had gone. Anne was dumbfounded. She guessed this must be Mr Jack's fiancée, for who else would be so familiar? She was too young to be his mother, and a sister would never have kissed him so intimately. She felt as if she was interrupting a personal moment, intruding in their private space. She gathered her notepad and pencil and stood from her chair.

'Please, Anne, remain seated,' Mr Jack said, fiddling nervously with his bow tie. He turned to the woman standing by his side, who was now looking at Anne with a quizzical expression.

'So you're the famous Anne,' she said with a wry smile. 'I've heard so much about you from William.'

William? It took Anne a moment to realise she was talking about Mr Jack. Anne had never addressed him by his first name, although she'd typed it often enough. The woman laid a green-gloved hand on Mr Jack's shoulder, as if claiming him as her own. Anne didn't know what to say. Mr Jack straightened in his chair and patted the woman's hand.

'Anne, I'd like you to meet Miss Lucinda Dalton.' He paused. 'My fiancée.'

Anne stood and offered her hand across the desk. Lucinda took it, and Anne felt the soft, silky material of her thin gloves.

'It's a pleasure to meet you,' she said. She wished she could say something else, something nice, but she knew absolutely nothing about Lucinda Dalton. She decided to stick to safe territory. 'It's very cold outside, isn't it? Would you like a mug of hot coffee?'

Lucinda waved her hand dismissively. 'What a darling girl you are. Isn't she darling, William? How right you were to employ her. But no, I won't accept your offer. George is waiting at the factory gates with the Aston

Martin. He's driving Mother and I to Newcastle to begin the hunt for my wedding gown.'

She turned away from Anne, leaving Anne staring at the back of her green jacket. Blonde hair cascaded stylishly from under Lucinda's smart black hat.

'I just called by our little factory to remind William that we're hosting Lord Crimdon for dinner. You won't be late, William, will you?'

Mr Jack shook his head. 'No, dear.'

Lucinda glanced back at Anne. 'Anne, my darling, be a good girl and make sure he leaves the office at six p.m. prompt.'

She bent low to kiss Mr Jack again. This time it was Mr Jack who pulled out a handkerchief to wipe away the lipstick smear.

'Thank you for calling to see me, my dear. Perhaps allow me more notice next time,' he said tersely.

Lucinda spun around, smiled at Anne through gritted teeth, then glided out of the office as quickly as she'd come in. The overpowering lemon scent followed her, lingering after she'd left.

Anne was gobsmacked by what had just happened. Mr Jack seemed embarrassed, and coughed nervously as he gathered papers in front of him on his desk.

'Right, where were we?' he said, back to business, as if the last few moments hadn't happened.

Anne couldn't believe it. While Lucinda had been in the room, she'd witnessed a meek, cowed side to Mr Jack that she'd never seen before. She'd only ever known him as the titan of the toffee factory, assertive and in control. She remembered what he'd told her the previous day about his father choosing the girl he would marry. Was

Lucinda his father's choice? Did Mr Jack really have no say? She was lost for words.

When Mr Jack spoke again, she forced herself to concentrate. He looked at the clock on the office wall.

'You must remind me to leave at six o'clock sharp, Anne,' he said briskly. But then his face clouded over. 'It wouldn't do to be late,' he muttered, almost to himself. 'It'd upset Lucinda and there's too much at stake. Although Crimdon's a fool of a man.'

Anne wasn't sure she'd heard him correctly. Was he giving her an instruction?

'Sir?' she said, hoping he would repeat what he'd said so that she could take the appropriate action.

'Nothing, Anne. Ignore me. Now then, let's get back to business. Could you start drafting an invitation to the Lady Tina launch and arrange a meeting with Gerard and Burl?'

'Yes, sir. Will that be all for now?' Anne said, forcing herself back into professional mode.

Mr Jack looked across the desk and they held each other's gaze for a few seconds longer than necessary. He opened his mouth as if to speak, but snapped it shut again. It seemed to Anne that something was on his mind. Was he considering confiding again? She waited a moment in case he said more, but when he stood, she knew the moment had passed. Whatever was on his mind would stay there for now. However, she didn't like feeling so uncomfortable. Working for Mr Jack was a job she adored. She felt at home in the toffee factory; it suited her down to the ground. The last thing she wanted was any kind of bad atmosphere between her and her employer when things had been straightforward so far.

'Mr Jack,' she said, addressing him firmly.

He paused and looked at her. 'Yes?'

Anne braced herself for what she was about to say.

'I, er . . . I wanted to clear the air, sir. Between us, I mean. I fear something has changed and I rather wish it hadn't.'

She waited for him to respond. She worried she'd gone too far. Perhaps she'd imagined the shift between them? She looked at Mr Jack and was relieved to see a tiny smile make its way to his lips.

'You're a good woman, Anne Wright,' he said kindly. He strode to the door and grasped the handle to open it, but then stopped and turned to her. 'I apologise for Miss Dalton's behaviour, and her comments. She isn't used to a working environment and has no notion of how to behave. She's a lady of means, you see. Her family is one of the wealthiest in Durham, and she's never had to work a day in her life.'

Anne pressed her feet into the carpet and gripped her notepad in her hands. She thought of the most complimentary thing she could say about Lucinda, as it seemed that Mr Jack needed cheering up. His fiancée's visit had plunged him into a strange mood.

'She seems a very forthright woman,' she said.

He took his time to reply.

'Forthright,' he said sadly. 'Oh, she's that all right. My father thinks she's the right match for me. I just wish I agreed.' And with that he left the office.

Anne was speechless and in shock for the second time that morning. Mr Jack's mention of Peter Matthews had already upset her. Now her head was spinning after Lucinda's visit. She headed to her own office and sat down. She pulled the cover from her typewriter, then returned to Mr Jack's office to search for the file of dignitaries to be invited to the launch. Her eyes scanned the pages of names and addresses, and sure enough, added to the end of the list, scrawled in pen, were Mr and Mrs Peter Matthews. Their address was horribly familiar. It was the house where her baby lived, where she'd looked over the wall hoping for a glimpse of him.

She felt sick to her stomach at the thought of coming face to face with the couple at the launch. They'd recognise her, of course. They'd hardly forget the face of the girl whose baby they'd bought. She contemplated not posting their invitation, claiming it had got lost in the post. Well, there was a war on and such things could happen. Letters went missing every day, she heard herself murmur, practising the words she'd say to Mr Jack in case she dared follow her plan. But then she thought better of it. She felt her breath quicken when she thought of Mr Matthews again and fear ran through her. What if he told Mr Jack the truth about buying her child from her? She shook her head to rid herself of the notion.

'Come on, Anne. Pull yourself together. You're not a coward and you won't run from this. Besides, Mr Jack's relying on you to send out the invitations. You can do this! Acknowledging your past is the best way to face your future. You want to get on with your life, don't you? Well, make a start right now.'

And with that, she wound a sheet of cream paper with the Jack's logo in blue into her typewriting machine.

The following day, Hetty rose early, excited about the day ahead, for she was due to meet Dirk. The first thing she did was glance out of the window to check the weather. The arrangement she'd made with Dirk was that if it was raining, snowing or too windy for a stroll, they'd meet the following day instead. However, when Hetty pulled her bedroom curtain aside, her heart lifted. The sky was clear. There was a touch of frost on the ground and the sun was low in the sky, but there wasn't a cloud to be seen.

She dressed quickly, in a skirt she'd laid over a chair in her bedroom the previous night. It was her favourite skirt, a blue velvet, though Bob had said the style didn't suit her. She felt as if a weight had been lifted from her shoulders. She didn't need to worry about pleasing Bob any more. Now she could do what she wanted. If she wanted to wear her favourite dress for a dance or her favourite skirt for a walk, she would.

Before she headed downstairs, she opened her handbag and pulled out two bags of toffee she'd bought at work. She couldn't afford bags of best, so she'd bought the plainest, cheapest toffee Jack's sold. But it was treasure that she could finally afford. Without her dad's debt hanging over her, she could spend a little of her wages on things she wanted. She kept hold of one packet of toffee to give to her mum, hoping it would put a much-needed smile on her face. The other she stuffed into her pocket; it was a present to give to Dirk.

Chapter Thirty-Seven

Hilda was toasting bread on the fire. She looked up sharply when Hetty entered the room.

'Where are you going, wearing your best skirt?' she demanded.

Hetty shrugged. 'Out for a walk.'

She still hadn't told her mum about calling things off with Bob, because she knew she would want to know all the ins and outs. She'd tell her when she was ready. She also hadn't mentioned Dirk. Her mum might eventually understand why she didn't want to continue with Bob, but Hetty knew she'd struggle to accept Dirk. Hilda was narrow-minded and critical of those outside the enclosed world of the market town where she'd lived all her life.

Hetty held out the packet of Jack's toffees in their blue wrappers. She waited, with her hand outstretched, hoping for a smile. But Hilda just sniffed, then turned away.

'Don't you want them?' Hetty said, feeling dejected again. She should have known better than to expect anything else. If it had been Dan offering her a bag of sweets, Hilda's face would have lit up and she'd have given him a hug. 'I bought them specially for you,' she continued.

'Took your time about it, didn't you? My friend Doreen has been getting toffees for months from her daughter who works in the slab room.'

Hetty dropped her hand. 'Doreen's daughter steals them, Mum, she doesn't buy them. I told you I wouldn't steal. It's more than my job's worth. If Doreen's daughter gets caught, she'll lose her job. Anyway, how does she get past the searchers at the factory door with stolen toffees?'

Hilda slid the crisp brown toast off the toasting fork. She inspected it for burnt bits, then scraped them off with her fingers.

'She wraps greaseproof paper around her stomach, then spreads warm toffee on. It cools down and hardens, then she pulls her overall down and walks past the searchers. They're none the wiser. When she comes home at night, she gets Doreen to smash it off her with a hammer.' Hilda sneered. 'Now why couldn't you have come up with that idea?'

Hetty sat down and glared at her. 'It's not funny. She could get scalded if the paper tears. Anyway, stop encouraging me to steal. Dad will be turning in his grave.' She could feel her temper rising. 'I bought you those toffees from my hard-earned wages. If you want stolen goods, you're asking the wrong child. You should speak to our Dan. He's always up to no good.'

Hilda jabbed the toasting fork in Hetty's direction and Hetty moved sharply back. 'Leave my lad out of this. He's doing his best.' She lowered the fork, speared another slice of bread and placed it over the fire.

'Mum,' Hetty said, more calmly now, 'Dan's out all hours of the night, running wild. When he does come home, he treats this place like a doss house. He's got you at his beck and call and—'

'Enough!' Hilda yelled.

Hetty stood, smoothed her skirt down and picked up her dad's coat and scarf.

'I'll be off then,' she said, affronted. 'I'll leave your toffees on the sideboard. I hope you enjoy them.'

The dog had been lying by the fireplace, but now it stood and followed Hetty out of the room. Hetty left the house with tears in her eyes. Her heart felt heavy. No matter what she did to please her mum, nothing was ever good enough. As she walked along Elm Street with the dog at her side, she pulled the scarf to her chin and snuggled her face down in its folds, then stuffed her hands into her pockets, feeling the bag of toffees there. When she reached Front Street, she crossed the main road and headed to the riverside. She'd arranged to meet Dirk by the bandstand. Her heart skipped a beat when she saw him. She quickened her pace, waving and smiling when he acknowledged her.

They walked side by side with the River Wear flowing next to them. The air was bitterly cold, the sun hadn't yet melted the night's frost and Hetty shivered. She was grateful for Dirk's company and easy conversation. It helped take her mind off her mum and Dan and stopped her worrying about Elsie, too. She hated what Frankie was doing to her friend; the way he treated her was dreadful, but Hetty didn't know how to help. Whenever she broached the subject, Elsie insisted she was fine and knew what she was doing. Oh, but he was drinking, lying, thieving . . . even hitting Elsie when his temper exploded. What else was he capable of?

The dog came running towards them, and Dirk's eyes lit up.

'Is that . . . could it really be the same dog?' he asked. 'The one that brought us together on Front Street?'

He bent low and began stroking the creature behind its ears. The dog rolled over in submission with its legs in the air, making both Hetty and Dirk laugh.

'Yes, it's the same dog. I took it home on the day you handed it to me and it's now part of the family. I often think it's the only one who understands me at home.'

They resumed their walk, chatting amiably. Hetty pointed out landmarks along the river. In return, Dirk told her more about his life in Ghent. He spoke fondly of his sister, Gabrielle, who was engaged to an ex-soldier who also lived at Elisabethville and worked at one of the munitions factories.

'What about your parents?' Hetty asked.

'They are still in Ghent,' he replied. 'They own a small shop in the town square selling chocolates. The sweetest chocolates. I remember their taste and smell. My stomach rumbles at the thought.'

'Oh, I nearly forgot!' Hetty cried. She pulled the bag of toffees from her pocket and handed them over. 'These are for you, my treat.'

'My treat?' Dirk said, confused.

'A little present. My gift to you,' Hetty explained.

He took the bag. 'May I open them now?'

'You can open them whenever you like.'

A wooden bench on the riverbank came into view. When they reached it, Dirk slowed down and asked Hetty if she would like to sit. He opened the bag of toffees and peered inside, then brought it to his nose and breathed in the aroma that Hetty knew only too well.

'It is a beautiful smell,' he said. 'You are very lucky working in the factory all day.'

Hetty laughed out loud. 'I don't know about lucky, but it's a job I enjoy. See those toffees? They're all wrapped by girls in the wrapping room. Every single toffee that Jack's factory makes, whether it's a best toffee or a plain, flavoured with vanilla, mint or fruit, they all get wrapped by hand. That's my job; that's how lucky I am.' She sighed. 'I wrap and twist all day.'

A look of concern passed over Dirk's kind face. 'Does it make your fingers hurt?' he asked.

Hetty nodded. 'Sometimes, but I'm used to it now. Just like I'm used to the smell of the sugar and cream that go to make the toffee.'

Dirk laid the bag of toffees between them on the bench, then turned to Hetty and gently took her hand, enclosing her small fingers in his big, warm ones. That was all it was, just holding hands by the riverside on a cold, frosty day. But there was something special about it. Hetty couldn't explain it, yet she knew she wanted to capture the moment in her heart. Dirk's touch made her feel cosy and safe. She felt comfortable, able to be herself in a way she never could with Bob. Talking to Dirk wasn't hard work like it was with Bob, and he asked questions about her, wanting to know more. More importantly, he listened when she replied. He seemed decent and honest. He wasn't like Frankie, who'd force himself on a girl, get drunk and hit her. He was gentle and kind. Her heart tripped over itself as she looked into his blue eyes.

'Hetty?' he whispered. 'I have something important to ask you.'

She saw a mischievous smile reach his lips. 'What is it?' she asked.

He released her hand, picked up the bag of toffees and offered it to her. 'Would you join me in enjoying one of your toffees?' he said.

Hetty grinned. She dipped her hand into the packet and brought out a wrapped sweet. Dirk did the same, then they both turned to look at the river. The low winter sun was on Hetty's face, Dirk was by her side and she could hear birdsong from above. She felt content. That was it, she decided. Being with Dirk made her happy.

Slowly she unwrapped her toffee. How strange it felt to be doing it. She wondered if she'd wrapped this one, or whether it might have been wrapped by Elsie, or Beattie, or one of the hundreds of other girls in the wrapping room. She smoothed the waxed paper against her leg, along her blue velvet skirt, then raised her eyes and looked across the river at the grand turrets of Lumley Castle on the opposite bank. A robin landed on the grass in front of them, and she marvelled at its colour and its tiny stick legs. Dirk had seen the bird too, and nudged her.

Hetty held the toffee between her finger and thumb and gave it a tiny squeeze. It wasn't too soft, nor too hard. It was just as it should be. She turned to Dirk, saw him pop his toffee into his mouth. She reached along the bench for his hand. Their fingertips touched again, and she allowed herself a satisfied sigh.

Chapter Thirty-Eight

As blustery November turned to icy December, preparations for Christmas began. The shops along Front Street changed their window displays, offering marzipan fruits, iced loaves and jam tarts dusted with sugar. One day in early December, in the reception at Jack's factory, with the coal fire burning brightly as snow fell outside, Anne decorated the wide windowsills with sprigs of holly and silver baubles with the Jack's logo in frosted blue. When it was done to her satisfaction, she put her hands on her hips and looked across the room at Jacob. He had his head down, as usual, updating the visitors' book.

'What do you think, Jacob?' she said, glancing at her handiwork.

He raised his head, appraised the room with an arched eyebrow, then nodded sharply. Anne knew him well enough by now to know that his taciturn response was the only one she was likely to receive.

She was about to return to her office when the main door swung open and an elderly man walked in. He wore a long black overcoat and a matching black hat with a wide brim. There was a covering of snow on his hat, melting fast in the warmth of the room. He was a short man, with a long, narrow face and a tidy white moustache and beard. Anne stepped forward, ready to greet him, puzzled as to who he was. She wasn't expecting anyone that morning; there were no appointments in Mr Jack's diary. However, before she had a chance to say anything, the man thrust his hand out to her.

'You must be the delightful Miss Wright. I've heard a lot about you.'

Anne shook his hand, taking in his features. There was something about him that looked familiar. She thought about the way he'd stepped confidently into the room and put two and two together.

'Why, you must be Mr Jack senior. What an honour to meet you,' she said. 'Let me take your coat and hat.'

'No time for that, my girl. And call me Albert, please. Now where's this son of mine? In his office, I expect.' He turned to Jacob. 'Jacob, my boy. How the devil are you? Still looking as happy as ever.'

Anne had to bite the inside of her cheek to stop herself giggling.

Albert marched towards the corridor that led to his son's office. Anne followed, having to quicken her pace to keep up with him. She marvelled at the energy of the sprightly old man.

'I hear William is keeping you busy with the launch of a new brand,' he said as they walked. 'I understand you've been pivotal in the competition to find a girl to represent Lady Tina.'

'Oh yes, sir. We have a wonderful girl, Henrietta Lawson, whose likeness has been captured for the tins,' Anne replied.

When they reached Mr Jack's office, Albert didn't knock; he just pushed the door and walked in unannounced. Anne was at his shoulder and saw Mr Jack look up in shock. She stepped forward, positioning herself between father and son.

'May I bring coffee, sir, for you and your father?' she asked.

Mr Jack nodded sharply, and she retreated into the corridor.

When she returned a few minutes later pushing a small trolley with a coffee pot on it, Mr Jack's office door was closed and she heard raised voices from within. She stopped outside the door. Albert's voice was irritated and loud.

'You didn't have the decency to go to dinner with Lord Crimdon after the woman arranged it. What's wrong with you, lad?'

'Crimdon's a fool, Father. You know it and I know it. He thinks confectionery is a soft business. I have nothing in common with him.'

'Lucinda's parents are terribly angry with you for leaving her to cope with Lord Crimdon alone. After all she'd done to arrange for you to meet him! They have asked me to express their anxiety about your upcoming wedding. And if you must know the truth, I'm anxious too, because you know how serious things are. You can't afford to lose Lucinda's family money. The factory needs it!'

Anne couldn't believe what she was hearing. Suddenly everything that Mr Jack had said about his father choosing Lucinda as his bride-to-be made sense. She thought of the confidential finance figures she'd found on his desk. She remembered the threat of sugar rationing discussed at the board meeting. However, from what Albert was saying, she wondered if the factory was in a much deeper financial hole than Mr Jack had told her – or the board.

'Ah, so that's the reason you're here!' Mr Jack yelled. 'Heaven forbid you should visit to give me the benefit of your business advice or suggest how to get out of this hole we find ourselves in. No, all you care about is that I marry that woman so that your precious factory will be saved by her family's fortune. You know I don't love her and I don't want to marry her.'

'Oh, stop being petulant, boy. You sound like the moody teenager you used to be, not the businessman you are now. It's you who's got the factory in a mess. I should never have left my place on the board. I could have kept an eye on you if I was still attending meetings. This financial hole is your making.' Albert's tone was serious and grave. 'I've already told you that I don't understand why you're launching a new brand while the country's at war. I warned you it wasn't a good idea, but you're going ahead with it anyway. This could be the most foolhardy thing you've ever done. I know Gerard has warned you about sugar rationing; I read it in the minutes of the board meeting that are mailed to me at home. And yet you chose to ignore him. Without sugar, there can be no toffee. I'm already hearing from friends in Yorkshire that they're turning over confectionery factories to make munitions. Instead of gums, they're making guns. Mark my words, it won't be long before that happens here.'

'The country will always need confectionery, Father, and when people turn to toffee for comfort, for treats, they'll turn to Jack's.' Mr Jack's tone was slow and deliberate. 'With Gerard's help we're positioning the new brand to be the only one that people will buy. Ah, but you know all of this already if you've read the board reports. What's the point of saying more when you never listen? Your old ways of running this factory are dead and gone. It's my turn now. When you handed over the reins, you said you'd trust me to manage things my way. With respect, I ask you to let me get on with my job.'

'This new brand of yours, Lady Tina, won't save the factory,' Albert shouted. 'The only woman who'll save you is Lucinda Dalton with her family fortune. For some reason, she dotes on you. Make the most of it, son. Take her money to keep this place afloat.'

'But it means marrying her, Father. And I . . .' Mr Jack faltered. 'I can't bear it. You know how I feel. I don't love the woman and I don't think I ever will.'

'Love?' Albert scoffed. 'Don't tell me the feelings you have for Miss Wright are clouding your judgement.'

Anne's mouth fell open with shock. Her heart was beating so fast and hard she feared Mr Jack and his father might hear it on the other side of the door. Mr Jack had feelings for her! She didn't know what to think. Suddenly his more intimate, confiding manner made sense.

'Keep your voice down!' Mr Jack cried, but Albert continued as if he hadn't spoken.

'Love's got nothing to do with this. It's about money, boy. Money, power and status.'

'No, it's about people, Father,' Mr Jack countered. 'It's about keeping the sugar boilers in work and the boys who work in packing; the girls who work in the wrapping room and the slab room. It's about looking after the gardeners who tend the roses in the factory grounds. It's about the women who run the canteen. It's about giving a good life to the people who work here . . . and that includes me. I have my future to think of and I don't see it with Lucinda. You know she doesn't make me happy.'

Anne gasped. She was aware that her legs were shaking, and she laid her free hand against the wall. She was afraid she might collapse.

'Happiness has no part to play when the future of the factory is at stake,' Albert said gravely. 'You know what needs to be done. Either you marry Lucinda and take the money her father has offered to invest, to tide you over until this damn war is done. Or you allow your heart to rule your head, fall for your pretty secretary and see the factory close and Jack's toffee go out of business. Is that what you want? For your precious sugar boilers and wrapping girls to be out on the streets with no work?'

'Of course not!' Mr Jack snapped.

'Then think carefully about how you treat Lucinda,' Albert said. 'Your wedding has been announced. Invitations have been sent. It's too late to turn back. Please don't give me any reason to return here to speak to you again at Lucinda's parents' request. You're old enough to know better.'

Anne heard more noise from within. Footsteps. She jumped back and moved the trolley aside. The door opened and Albert appeared, putting on his hat. He walked away without acknowledging her.

She watched him go, then waited a few moments before she wheeled the trolley into Mr Jack's office. Her head was reeling, her heart beating wildly. How could anything be the same any more? She tried to keep calm, as if she hadn't heard, as if she didn't know, and forced herself to go through the motions. She needed time to process what she'd learned. With trembling hands, she poured coffee into a mug, added cream and two sugars, then placed the mug down on Mr Jack's desk.

'You heard all that, I expect?' Mr Jack said.

Anne didn't respond. To say yes would be to admit she'd been listening at the door, and she felt her face grow hot with embarrassment. But to say no would be to lie, and she couldn't do that.

'Sit down, Anne. I'd like to speak to you,' he said gently.

Anne sank into the chair where Albert had been sitting just moments ago. 'I don't have my notepad and pencil, sir. I should get them,' she said, but Mr Jack shook his head.

'Make no notes about what I'm going to say next,' he said. 'I don't want this written down. It isn't factory business. It's personal.'

She shifted in her seat and looked him in the eye, bracing herself.

'I don't know how much of my conversation with my father you overheard. But I know you will have listened. It's what I would've done. You're an intelligent woman, Anne. You know what's going on in the factory, sometimes before I do. So I'm not going to insult you by pretending you didn't hear what you did. My father wants me to marry Miss Dalton in order to keep the factory afloat, and I . . . well, my heart tells me otherwise.'

He paused.

'Anne, I believe I'm falling for you.'

Chapter Thirty-Nine

Anne heard a catch in his voice. She knew there was only one way to react and that was with honesty and truth. It was what he deserved after he'd opened his heart. Mr Jack straightened his blue bow tie.

'Anne . . . would you take tea with me one afternoon?'

'Oh,' she said, taken aback. 'Tea? Would you like me to invite Mr Gerard and Mr Burl or the men from the board?'

Mr Jack leaned forward. 'No, Anne, this isn't business. It would just be you and I. It would give me a chance to explain what you've overheard. It would give us a chance to talk . . . about the factory and what lies ahead.'

Anne was surprised to feel a twinge of disappointment to hear the factory mentioned. After what had just happened, she'd hoped to clear the air between them. She knew in her heart that she didn't feel the same for Mr Jack as he did for her. She didn't find him attractive, for a start. She'd have to let him down gently but firmly. She wondered if she should take a few days away from work, or even start looking for a new job elsewhere. She had a lot to take in now she knew his true feelings. However,

Fill

there was something about him being open and dropping his defences that led her to believe she could do the same with him. Even if she wasn't in love with him, she knew now she could trust him. She already admired and respected him.

'Ah yes, the factory, of course,' she said.

'Would you take tea at my home, Anne?' he asked again. 'I have a housekeeper, we would be chaperoned.'

'At your home . . . are you sure? People might talk if they find out.'

'Let them talk. If I've learned one thing in my time running this factory, it's that people will talk about me no matter what. I feel I can trust you. You've become more to me than my secretary. You've proved yourself invaluable. In fact, I'm not sure how I used to run this place without you.'

'Thank you, sir,' she replied. 'You know how much I love working here . . . for you.'

'Then come for tea this weekend. We have much to talk about, not least Lucinda Dalton, and what I'm sure you must have overheard my father say about my feelings for you.'

There was a sharp knock at the door and Mr Gerard popped his head into the office. He had a question for Mr Jack, cutting short their conversation. Anne returned to her own office, too stunned to do anything other than sit and stare at the wall.

The next morning when Hetty arrived at the factory, Elsie was already hard at work. Hetty sidled up to her, slid her boots off, pushed her feet into her clogs then gently nudged her in the ribs.

'Morning, Elsie. You all set for your big day tomorrow?'

Elsie didn't speak, just kept picking and wrapping toffees, twisting the ends and placing them on a metal tray. Hetty looked at her friend; she was pale, with dark circles under her eyes. She watched her for a few seconds. Elsie usually worked quickly, without thinking; she was one of the fastest wrappers in the room. But that morning, her right arm was slow.

'You all right?' Hetty asked.

Elsie still didn't reply. Hetty began work, sliding a pile of unwrapped caramel toffees covered in chocolate towards her.

'What time do you want me to arrive at the register office tomorrow?' she whispered.

'Nine o'clock,' Elsie replied.

'Blimey, that's early,' Hetty said.

'Gets it over with,' Elsie said dully. 'Are you bringing your Belgian fella?'

Hetty hadn't given this a thought.

'No . . . I haven't asked him. We're still getting used to each other.' She leaned close to Elsie. 'Are you sure you're all right? You seem quiet. Is your arm all right? It looks like you're holding it funny. Does it hurt?'

'I'm fine,' Elsie snapped.

Hetty got the message that Elsie didn't want to talk, and began concentrating on her own work. Then she looked around the table at the other girls.

'Where's Beattie this morning? Anyone know?'

Those girls who dared defy Mrs Perkins' no-speaking rule answered her, but no one knew where Beattie was. Hetty returned to work and was soon lost in the soothing rhythm of picking and wrapping, twisting and placing.

It was sometime later when Beattie arrived, running into the wrapping room with her coat flying. Her stockings were laddered and one of her knees badly scraped. Everyone stopped what they were doing and stared. Mrs Perkins spotted her and marched across the room.

'Look at the state of you, Beattie! What happened?' The supervisor spun around.

'Get back to work, everyone.'

Girls turned back to their tables, to their toffees and wrappers. However, those closest to Beattie and Mrs Perkins were eavesdropping. Beattie was flustered, crying, and Mrs Perkins led her to a seat. Hetty watched as Beattie sat down with the supervisor towering above her. She nudged Elsie to alert her.

'What happened, Beattie? Did you fall?' Mrs Perkins said, concerned.

Beattie shook her head. 'I walk to work along the back lane, Mrs Perkins. I always go that way, each morning and at night when I finish work. But it's so dark there at this time of year.' Her words were coming out in great gulps between her tears.

'So you fell in the dark?' Mrs Perkins said. 'Come on, I'll take you to the factory doctor. You'll need a dressing on that knee.'

Hetty watched as Mrs Perkins held her arm out for Beattie, but Beattie didn't move. She put her head in her hands and began to sob. Hetty had never seen her so vulnerable; she always seemed strong and capable, with her thick arms and stout frame.

'I didn't fall, Mrs Perkins. I was pushed. Someone . . . a man . . . pushed me down in the dark.'

Hetty dropped the toffee she was wrapping. She turned to Elsie and gasped.

'He tried to . . . he tried to grab me, Mrs Perkins. But I swung my bag at him. I thumped him.'

'Did you see who it was?' Mrs Perkins asked.

Beattie shook her head. Mrs Perkins crouched in front of her and said something that Hetty couldn't hear. Beattie shook her head, then she was led by Mrs Perkins from the room.

Once they had left, the girls in the room who'd heard what had happened began whispering. Hetty heard others admit that they too had been chased along the lane in the dark. Others said they'd seen a man waiting under the railway bridge at the end of the lane. It was a man they felt sure didn't work at the factory, as those who'd seen his face hadn't recognised him. Hetty began to feel angry when she heard the girls' tales. If it hadn't been for Beattie being attacked, none of their stories would have come to light.

'I've got to do something about this,' she declared.

'What can you do?' Elsie replied. 'You're just a toffee factory girl. Leave things alone. If anyone should do something, it's Mr Jack. He should put lamps in the back lane to make it safe for girls who walk that way.'

Hetty mulled this over, then she dropped the toffee she was wrapping and headed for the door.

'Hetty! Come back!' Elsie cried.

Hetty knew that a lowly factory girl like her couldn't directly bring the matter to Mr Jack's attention. But she knew someone who would. She walked as quickly as she could in her clogs across the cobbles, and pushed open the door to reception. Enveloped in the warm glow of the fire, she stood in front of Jacob's desk with her back straight and her hands clasped.

'Yes?' Jacob said, arching an eyebrow.

'I need to see Anne Wright. It's urgent,' she said. Her words sounded more assertive than she felt.

Jacob slowly closed the ledger he was working on and unfolded his tall frame from behind his desk. He pointed a long, bony finger at a chair along the wall. 'Sit there and wait.'

Hetty chose the seat closest to the fire and felt the warmth spread into her body. A few moments later, Jacob returned with Anne.

'Hetty? Please come through,' Anne said.

As soon as they were out of earshot of Jacob, she stopped and turned to Hetty.

'What's wrong? Is Elsie all right?'

Hetty thought of Elsie's arm that morning. 'I think so. But it's Beattie I'm here to see you about. She was attacked this morning in the back lane. Some of the girls say they've been followed there too. It's not right. Is there anything you can do? Mrs Perkins doesn't know I'm here; she took Beattie to the doctor.'

She took a breath, aware that her words were tripping over themselves.

'I'm sorry, Anne. I'm scared for the girls. I didn't know what to do. Something needs to change. There need to be lamps in the lane. It might stop men loitering around. Do you think you could ask Mr Jack?'

Chapter Forty

The next day, Elsie woke early. Frankie's snores had kept her awake half the night and she hadn't slept well. She had a headache, and squeezed her eyes shut, willing herself back to sleep for another few minutes. Half an hour later, she was still tossing and turning, so she clambered out of bed and placed her feet on the cold bare floor. As carefully as she could, afraid of waking Frankie and suffering the consequences, she tiptoed from their bedroom.

She shivered in the cold air as she walked to the bathroom. She felt sick; it wasn't a great start to her wedding day. At the toffee factory, she'd worked with many girls who'd been engaged to be married. They'd looked forward to their big day, planning and preparing. They'd spoken of choosing flowers, making dresses with their mums, sisters and friends, even about what food would be on the menu for their wedding tea. But Elsie had none of that planned. She couldn't afford it, for a start, and Frankie hadn't offered to pay.

After her workmates had married, Elsie hadn't seen them any more. The law had obliged girls to leave the factory once wed. However, now that war was raging and men were signing up to fight, things had changed drastically. It wasn't just in the confectionery business where even married women were being called up to replace men. With the high demand for weapons, more munitions factories had opened and were taking on women. Elsie had been relieved to learn that she would be allowed to stay at work after her wedding. It meant she would be away from harm, away from Frankie, for a few hours each day.

'Elsie? Is that you, pet?' Cathy's voice drifted along the hallway as Elsie came out of the bathroom in the darkness. 'Are you all right?' she whispered.

'I couldn't sleep for wedding nerves,' Elsie replied.

'Come downstairs with me. I'll put the fire on, we can have a cup of tea,' Cathy offered.

Elsie followed her to the small kitchen at the back of the pub. Cathy gave her a blanket to wrap around her shoulders while she worked quickly to build a fire with paper, sticks and coal. Flames were soon roaring in the hearth and a kettle of water was placed there to boil.

Cathy and Elsie sat close to the fire. For a long time, neither of them spoke. Finally Cathy busied herself making tea and offered a mug to Elsie.

'Get that down you, girl, it'll do you good. You've been looking pale lately, I've been worried about you. You know I'll do my best to feed you while you're living here. But . . .' She faltered.

Elsie looked at her. Cathy's dark shoulder-length hair was flattened against one side of her head where she'd slept on it. She looked bleary-eyed and exhausted.

'I'm sorry to be a burden on you,' Elsie said.

Cathy laid her hand on Elsie's arm. 'You're not a burden. If you were, I'd never have agreed to let you live here. But there's something wrong and I can't hold my tongue. I need to speak to you, woman to woman.'

Elsie took a long sip of tea. She knew what was coming.

'Me and Jim have lived in this pub for over fifteen years,' Cathy began, looking at Elsie. 'And it's an old pub, love. With old walls and old floors and . . . Well, what I'm trying to say is that noise travels in a place like this. You and Frankie, your room is just along the corridor, and we can hear everything. When Frankie raises his voice, we hear every word. And when you cry out, we hear you scream.'

'He just loses his temper, that's all,' Elsie said quickly, jumping to Frankie's defence. 'I can handle him.'

Cathy glared at her. 'Can you?'

Elsie looked into the fire. She gave a long sigh. 'I have no choice,' she said.

'Oh, you've got a choice, girl,' Cathy said darkly, leaning forward. 'You can leave now. I'll help you. All you need do is pack your bag.'

Elsie was taken aback. Leaving Frankie wasn't something she'd ever thought about. As far as she was concerned, if she wanted the best for herself and her child, she was stuck with him for life.

'There are places where girls in your condition can go.'

Elsie rubbed her sore arm as Cathy continued.

'I know a woman who runs a house in Ryhope. She'll take you in.'

'Where's Ryhope?' Elsie asked. She couldn't fully grasp what Cathy was suggesting. Running away from

Chester-le-Street, leaving Frankie behind, had never been in her plans.

'It's a small village on the south side of Sunderland. You can take the train there. You must be able to afford a ticket, surely, from your factory wages? Don't you understand, Elsie? I'm offering to help you get away from the brute. You can't want to spend the rest of your life with him. He's rotten to the core. Even Jim says it. He doesn't want Frankie around our kids, and neither do I.'

Cathy glanced at Elsie's stomach.

'Have you thought about what he might do to your child when he loses his temper once it's born?'

This had preyed on Elsie's mind. She nodded. Tears pricked at her eyes. 'He'll be different when the baby comes. It'll calm him,' she said, but she knew she was trying to convince herself.

'He won't change, love,' Cathy said gently. 'Men like him never do. Get away from him now. He's snoring his head off upstairs and he'll have a hangover when he wakes after all the ale he drank last night. Get some clothes, your bag. I'll give you the address of Miss Gilbey's house in Ryhope. She'll look after you. She'll train you for domestic work while you're pregnant, help keep you out of sight. No one will know you there. Once the baby's born, she'll help you find a job. She'll even find someone to buy your baby.'

Elsie gulped back tears. 'How do you know all this?' she whispered.

Cathy leaned back in her seat. 'My sister went through it. She was the same as you, pregnant by a rotten fella who mistreated her. He wouldn't marry her. She worked at Jack's factory, in the slab room, years ago. She's married now, to a respectable man who doesn't raise a finger to her.'

She glanced at the clock on the mantel.

'You've got four hours of freedom before you're due at the register office. Use the time wisely. I'm offering you the chance to escape. Jim will understand. He's with me on this.'

'But . . . you insisted on arranging my wedding to Frankie at the register office. Why would you do that if all along you wanted me to leave him?' Elsie asked, puzzled.

'Me and Jim are decent people. When Frankie said you were coming to live here, I wanted things to be respectable. My reputation's on the line as landlady of this pub. I know some around here think the Lambton Arms is rough, but if folk didn't think I'd done the right thing, they'd have taken their custom elsewhere. Arranging for you and Frankie to be wed on the earliest date was the least I could do. I knew Frankie wouldn't organise it, and I can only imagine how your head must've been spinning. But now I know what a monster he is. Me and Jim have heard you crying yourself to sleep every night since you moved here. I can't bear it any more. You've got to get away. Go now, before it's too late.'

Elsie's mind reeled. She understood what Cathy was saying. Part of her wanted to leap out of her chair, run up the stairs, pack her bags and go. But she didn't seem able to move. Her legs were heavy, she felt stuck to the chair. She laid her free hand on her stomach.

'I can't go,' she said sadly. 'My baby needs a dad. I can't do this on my own.'

'Miss Gilbey in Ryhope will help you,' Cathy urged.

But Elsie shook her head. 'I never had a dad and I can't let my baby grow up without one. It needs me *and* Frankie, don't you understand?'

Cathy stood and held her hand out to help Elsie from her chair. 'Elsie, please, be strong, for your sake and your baby's. You can do this.'

Elsie bit her lip. She knew what Cathy said made sense. Frankie was a bad man. Hetty had told her so already, although she'd chosen to believe she could change him in time. Even her aunt Jean had warned her against him. Her arm was black and blue from where he'd thrown her against the wall in the worst fight they'd yet had. His temper was getting worse, the beatings came more often. She put both hands on her stomach when Cathy began speaking again.

'Come on, Elsie, let me help you. I'll walk to the railway station with you once you've packed your bag. We'll wait for the first train. I'll make sure you know how to reach Miss Gilbey's house.'

Elsie thought of Hetty and Anne. She'd miss them terribly if she left. She thought of her aunt Jean and the men who came to her flat. There'd been so many men over the years. What she needed now, more than anything, was stability, a home of her own.

'I can't leave him, I won't,' she cried.

Cathy was silent for a moment before she dropped her hand. 'Then you're a fool, Elsie Cooper,' she said darkly.

She set her mug on the hearth, then placed both hands on Elsie's shoulders and looked her in the eye. Elsie felt her breath catch in her throat.

'If Frankie lays a finger on that baby when it's born, you come straight to me, you hear?'

Elsie nodded.

'Right then,' Cathy said, all businesslike now. 'I don't approve of your decision and I'll never understand it. But that doesn't mean I won't help you. Come on, dry your eyes, we've got a wedding to get through.'

Chapter Forty-One

It was a short walk from the Lambton Arms to the register office on Front Street. Elsie lowered her eyes to the pavement. She couldn't face seeing anyone she knew who might ask where she was going. She clung to Frankie's arm. He stank of stale beer and smoke from the night before. He hadn't even washed before leaving the pub. He hadn't shaved either, and his hair was sticking up on one side. Ahead of them were Cathy and Jim, holding hands. Elsie noticed that Cathy was dressed in her good skirt and overcoat. Jim wore a black hat and coat, as if attending a funeral.

When they reached the register office, Hetty was waiting. Elsie forced a smile at her friend.

'Thanks for coming,' she said.

She noticed Hetty take in Frankie's dishevelled state. He peeled away from Elsie and followed Jim and Cathy through a sturdy door.

'Are you all right?' Hetty asked.

Elsie shook her head. 'No . . . but I will be. I have to be, for this one,' she replied, laying her hand on her stomach.

'You look nice,' Hetty said.

Elsie touched the red felt hat that Cathy had loaned her. 'Thanks, so do you.'

'Did you invite Anne?' Hetty asked.

'No, just you. I like Anne, but you're my best friend. Come on, let's get this over with.'

The wedding ceremony was simple and quick. There were no flowers, no hymns or prayers. Proceedings were overseen by a small, thin man in a black suit and tie. He had a pinched face and oiled black hair, and wore glasses that slid to the end of his nose. At the end of the short service, he turned to Frankie.

'You may now kiss your bride,' he directed.

Frankie lunged at Elsie and in full view of everyone started fondling her backside, smothering her lips with his rank-smelling breath. She pulled back.

'You may leave once you've signed the register,' the registrar said.

Outside in the cold winter day, Elsie turned to Hetty. 'Will you come to the Lambton Arms for a drink?'

'Of course,' Hetty said politely.

The small party walked to the pub, where Jim lit the fire in the downstairs bar. He opened a bottle of whisky and poured each of them a drink. The smell of it turned Elsie's stomach and she pushed her glass away. Jim and Cathy sat on stools at the bar; Elsie and Hetty were at a small table, and Frankie sat between them.

'I've never had whisky before,' Hetty said.

'It'll put hairs on your chest,' Frankie joked, laughing out loud.

Elsie saw his gaze land on Hetty's blouse, and she felt

uneasy. Then a movement under the table caught her attention. She turned just in time to see Frankie lay his hand on Hetty's knee.

Hetty started, pushed her chair back and gathered her coat and hat. 'I must go,' she said, standing. Elsie noticed her hands fumble nervously as she fastened her coat.

She felt sick. How dare Frankie do this?

'Hetty, please,' she said, but her friend was already leaving.

'What was so urgent?' Jim asked.

Elsie looked up to see Cathy shaking her head. She knew she'd seen what Frankie had done. Frankie slid his chair close to her and laid his arm around her shoulders, forcing her head towards his.

'Come here, Mrs Ireland,' he said, and kissed her full on the lips.

Elsie heard Jim give a little cough.

'Me and Cathy have got work to do upstairs,' he said. They left the bar and disappeared. Frankie called after them.

'Don't I even get congratulations on my wedding day?' he yelled, but there was no reply.

Elsie swallowed hard. She knew she had to be strong in what she said next. She couldn't let Frankie get away with what she'd just seen. It was unthinkable . . . and on their wedding day too. She knew she had to confront him.

'You had your hand on Hetty's leg.'

'No I didn't,' Frankie spat, without missing a beat.

'Don't lie to me. I saw you. That's why Hetty left. You scared her off,' Elsie said.

Frankie narrowed his eyes. 'She started it, little bitch. She was looking at me, flirting. She was asking for it.

Anyway, she's a tidy piece, not like you with your bloated belly.'

Elsie suddenly felt sick and afraid. Frankie was acting as if he was still drunk from the beer of the night before. She wanted nothing more than to get away from him, terrified in case he lashed out.

'I need some fresh air,' she said. She was intent on leaving the pub, walking along Front Street, catching up with Hetty, apologising for what had happened. 'I need to get out.'

But Frankie wouldn't let her. He pinned her down in her seat with his forearm across her shoulders. With his free hand, he gripped her arm tight. She struggled, but it only made him angrier. When he squeezed harder, she tried to scream. He clamped his hand across her mouth to stifle her cries. She could hardly breathe. Her arms were pinned to her sides as he pressed down, intent on hurting her, silencing her.

This time, though, Elsie wouldn't be cowed. Her arms might be restrained, but her legs were free. She kicked out and caught his shin hard. He yelped in pain, reached down to rub his leg, and in that instant, she stood and ran to the door. Frankie was behind her, pulling her back before she could open it. She screamed, yelling for Cathy and Jim. He threw her to the dusty floor. She screamed again and again.

As she lay helpless on the floor, Frankie started to kick her. When she couldn't take the pain any more, she stopped crying and screaming and blacked out. The next thing she knew, Cathy was at her side. She could hear Jim yelling, saw him wrestling with Frankie as Cathy bent over her, telling her everything would be all right. Elsie felt sick, dizzy, her vision blurred. Then there was silence, no more Frankie.

Jim and Cathy's faces came into focus, asking if she was all right, could she sit up, could she manage a sip of brandy for the shock, a nip of whisky for the pain. She couldn't speak in reply, couldn't form words. The shock of what had happened hit her hard when she opened her eyes again and saw the doctor kneeling by her. She heard Cathy telling him she was worried, concerned for the baby. She saw the blood before she felt it. It pooled around her legs as she lay on the floor. She heard the doctor say there was no baby any more. Frankie had kicked it out of her.

Elsie was laid up for a few days in Frankie's room at the Lambton Arms. Frankie, however, was nowhere to be seen. Cathy looked after her, brought her beef tea and sweet cakes to help build up her strength. She provided a shoulder to cry on and helped dry Elsie's tears. She also wiped away the blood running down Elsie's legs when Elsie was finally able to walk. On the third day, Hetty visited, having been told by Cathy what had happened. Elsie was sitting on the bed as a coal fire burned in a small hearth in the room. Hetty had brought a bag of best toffee and handed them to Elsie, but she put them to one side.

'I can't chew toffee, my mouth's swollen,' she said.

Hetty gently hugged her friend. 'The girls at work are asking about you. Don't worry, I won't tell them what happened.'

'You can tell Anne. We can trust her,' Elsie said.

'What'll you do, Elsie? I mean, where will you go once you recover? What if Frankie comes back? Will you . . .'

'Will I go back to him?' Elsie said. 'No, I'll never go back. I was foolish to think I could change him. There's no going back after what he did. Not after he killed our child.'

'But you're still married to him,' Hetty said grimly.

'In name only,' Elsie said. 'I hope I never see him again. Cathy says I can stay here for a few days, but she wants to rent out the room and I need to move on. I'll probably go back to Aunt Jean, for now.'

'And Frankie? Where's he gone?'

'I don't know. Jim says he won't let him in the pub if he returns. Has Mrs Perkins asked questions about me at work?'

'She's curious, that's all. I told her what Cathy advised me to say, that you weren't well and were being treated by the doctor. Does it . . . I mean . . . do you still hurt, Elsie?'

Elsie reached for Hetty's hand and silently nodded, then began to cry.

Chapter Forty-Two

That night, after Hetty left, Elsie eased herself out of bed. Her legs still felt weak, but the pain was subsiding and she was able to dress herself for the first time in days. Carefully she pulled on her coat and hat over her clothes and began to descend the stairs. She took care not to alert Cathy and Jim, who were downstairs in the bar. If they caught her leaving the pub, she was afraid they might try to stop her.

She let herself out of the back door and walked along Front Street. From there she made her way slowly down to the river. She held on to railings and walls as she went, scared that she might fall. She breathed deeply, pulling cold air into her lungs. At first she felt dizzy and had to keep pausing to catch her breath, and to stop her heart racing. But once she began walking again, as long as she did so carefully and slowly, she managed to reach the river. All she'd wanted was to take a breath of fresh air, alone. Hetty's visit had strengthened her resolve to get outside, but she knew she couldn't do so in daylight. She had to wait until evening so that darkness hid her bruised face. She pulled her scarf up to hide the worst of it and buried her chin inside her coat collar. When anyone approached her, she turned her face away.

The river flowed fast and noisy, splashing over rocks. She sat on a bench and closed her eyes, breathing in the night air and listening to the sound of the water. Then she opened her eyes. The night felt like a dream, with moonlight on the water and the turrets of Lumley Castle on the opposite bank. She slowly raised herself to standing and took a step forward. How easy it would be, she thought. How simple to step into the water. There would be no more pain. No more heartache over her dead child. No more Frankie. Nothing. She took another step, and her feet left the pathway. Now she was on the grass. Two more steps, that was all it would take. She'd let the water flow over her and give in to it fully. She'd allow herself to be dragged under and down. She wouldn't have to think any more . . .

'Elsie!' a voice cried.

She didn't hear it. All she could hear was the sound of the river calling her. She took another step. This was it. One more and she would be in the water. She closed her eyes and stepped forward.

'Elsie! What the hell are you doing?'

She closed her eyes and gave in, for she no longer cared. It felt as if she was flying. Her legs were light, her arms floating. She was being carried in a man's arms from the river to the path, where she was gently laid down on the ground.

'Elsie, it's Stan Chapman. You know me, I'm the gardener at Jack's factory. Are you all right, love? Is there anyone here with you? Elsie? Elsie, speak to me.'

Elsie began crying, and her body shuddered with sobs.

Stan lifted her again and carried her to where a gas lamp illuminated the path. There he set her down on a bench. Elsie slumped forward with her head in her hands.

'What happened to me?' she said, looking around. 'Stan? What are you doing here?'

Stan gave a sigh of relief. 'Thank heavens you're all right. I dread to think what would have happened if I hadn't been here. I always walk my dog here at this time of night. I'd heard you weren't well; you know how gossip spreads at the factory. But what happened to you? Your face is all bruised.'

Elsie put her hand to her cheek. It was still sore.

'Stan, could you help me home, please? I'm staying at the Lambton Arms.'

'That dump?' Stan said, then checked himself. 'Sorry, Elsie. Yes, of course I'll help you. Here, hold my arm. We'll walk slowly. Don't worry, I'll take good care of you now.'

He whistled, and a large brown mongrel bounded up.

'Patch! Heel,' he ordered, and the dog walked at his side.

Elsie took his arm and let him guide her back to the pub.

'You mustn't tell anyone what happened at the river,' she pleaded as they walked. 'They'll cart me off to the funny farm if they find out.'

'Your secret's safe with me,' Stan said, and he patted her hand. 'But if you want my advice . . .' He paused. Elsie knew he was waiting for her to speak, to prove she was listening to him.

'Go on,' she said.

'Well, I'd say you need to speak to a friend. Now, I'd

be willing to listen, but if it's women's troubles you need to speak about, another lass might be best. Mind you, I can talk all day about varieties of roses if you'd care to listen some time.'

For the first time in days, Elsie smiled. 'Thanks, Stan. I've got two friends I can talk to at work.'

They reached the Lambton Arms and Stan insisted on seeing Elsie inside. She didn't want Cathy and Jim to see her, so they walked around to the back.

'I'll be fine from here, Stan. Thank you for everything. And thank you to Patch.'

'You weren't really going to walk into the river, were you?' he said hesitantly.

She shrugged, then winced with pain.

Stan raised his cap. 'Goodnight, Elsie. I hope to see you at work soon. Take care of yourself. And remember, talk to your friends about what's on your mind. Don't bottle it up. It won't do any good.'

Elsie opened the door and stepped inside, then collapsed in a heap. She sat there for some time trying to work out what had happened. She was afraid of where her mind had been leading her.

'I've been cooped up in Frankie's room too long,' she whispered to herself. 'I need to get away. I need to stand on my own two feet.'

She pulled herself up to standing, clung on to the banister and began to climb the stairs. It proved more difficult than she'd expected. Her legs ached and her head swam. When she reached Frankie's room, she took off her coat and scarf, fell onto the bed fully clothed and fell fast asleep.

* * *

The following Monday, she felt strong enough to return to work. The bruises on her body were hidden by her clothes. However, those on her neck were still visible, so she wore a scarf to disguise the worst of them. When Hetty saw her, she left the toffees she was working on and walked to her.

'Do you still hurt anywhere?' she asked, keeping her voice low.

Elsie shook her head. 'I'm fine now,' she said.

'Then come here and let me hug you.'

A mischievous smile made its way to Elsie's lips. 'Are you sure you want to hug me after the last time, when I stole your pass?'

Hetty embraced her friend warmly. 'It's good to have you back,' she said.

Elsie pulled away. 'It's good to be back. Thank you for visiting me and bringing those toffees. I've finally been able to eat them now my jaw doesn't hurt so much. I'm living back at Aunt Jean's, by the way.'

'Is she looking after you?'

Elsie tutted. 'As much as she ever did. But I'm fine, honest. Just a little battered and bruised.' She tapped the side of her head. 'Not least in here. I keep going over what happened and blaming myself.'

'You must never do that,' Hetty said firmly. 'Frankie is evil. None of this was your fault.'

Elsie gave a wry smile. 'Try telling my brain that.'

'Have you seen him since it happened?'

She shook her head. 'No, and I meant what I said when you came to visit me at the pub. I never want to see him again. Did you tell Anne what happened, about me losing the baby, I mean?'

Hetty nodded. 'She won't tell anyone. We're the only ones who know.'

'And Stan the gardener,' Elsie confided.

Hetty looked askance at her friend. 'Stan? What's he got to do with it?'

'He doesn't know about the baby, but he knows I wasn't in my right mind. He found me one night by the river and took me back to the Lambton Arms. I'll tell you about it sometime.'

Hetty took hold of Elsie's hand and walked with her across the wrapping room. The other girls were staring at Elsie, wondering what had happened and why she'd been away.

'Don't be so bloody nosy,' Hetty called to them. 'Elsie's back and that's that. Now get on with your work before I report you to Mrs Perkins.'

Elsie winked at her. 'Thanks, Hetty.'

Later that week, Anne was typing out the speech that Mr Jack was due to give at the Lady Tina launch. Her relationship with him had now settled into one of friendship and trust. After he'd admitted his true feelings, she'd accepted his invitation to take tea at his house. It had been a perfectly respectable event. The tea and cakes had been high quality from a baker in Durham. The smoked salmon sandwiches sublime. Mr Jack's elderly housekeeper was discreet. However, his home, Anne thought, needed a woman's touch. It was lifeless, with no prints on the wall, no flowers in vases. There had been no Christmas tree.

They had taken tea in his study, which had a large, sturdy desk overlooking a lawn. While they ate, Anne told him politely but firmly that she didn't feel the same for him as he felt for her. She was relieved that he seemed to take the news with good grace and politeness. However, their conversation afterwards felt somewhat strained.

Meanwhile, arrangements for Mr Jack's wedding to Lucinda Dalton were forging ahead. It was to take place the following summer. Anne had now received an invitation, along with Mr Burl and Mr Gerard, to attend the reception after the ceremony. It was to be held in the grand ballroom at Lumley Castle.

She did her best to remain upbeat and professional in her dealings with Mr Jack, but she noticed he'd become withdrawn. She often found him staring into space, with his fingers interlaced under his chin.

'Your speech for the launch tomorrow, Mr Jack,' she said, laying the typed papers in front of him.

'Thank you, Anne,' he said.

He opened a drawer in his desk and pulled out a small blue velvet bag fastened with a silver drawstring.

'I have a small gift for you. A Christmas gift. I trust you will like it.'

She was surprised by his gesture. She wasn't aware of other members of staff receiving a Christmas gift. She knew then that this was personal, a gift from him to her.

'I'll open it on Christmas morning,' she said.

'Could you open it now? Please?' he asked.

He looked so forlorn that Anne didn't have the heart to refuse. She looked at the velvet bag. It was the exact shade of blue of the factory logo. Gently she opened the drawstring. Inside was a heavy silver brooch with a blue stone in the centre. She gasped.

'Why, sir, it's beautiful,' she said. 'I don't know if I can accept such a gift.'

Mr Jack stood and walked round the desk towards her. He laid his hand gently over hers and she felt the warmth of his skin. When she looked into his eyes, she saw a depth of sadness she'd never seen before.

'Please accept it. Always know that whatever happens, I will always care deeply for you. I just wish things had been different. Perhaps if we'd met years ago, before the war, before the talk of sugar rations. Before Lucinda's father wanted his share of the factory. Perhaps if I'd only . . .'

Anne looked down at Mr Jack's hand resting on hers. 'You're engaged to Lucinda Dalton. When you marry, it'll be the best thing for the factory.'

'But not the best thing for me,' Mr Jack replied.

Anne patted his hand affectionately, then turned away and walked to her office. When she reached it, she closed the door, sat down and put her head in her hands.

After a few moments, she brought the brooch from the velvet bag and pinned it to her lapel, where it glistened in the light from the fire in the small hearth. Glancing out of the window, she saw snow falling. She tried to make sense of the heaviness she felt. Was it the season, she thought, making her feel sentimental . . . or was it something else?

Chapter Forty-Three

The following day, there was excitement in the air at the factory. It was the launch of the new brand of Lady Tina toffee. Everyone was in high spirits. Work was being called to a halt at precisely ten o'clock for staff to assemble in the canteen to hear Mr Jack's speech.

Hetty arrived at work wearing her blue velvet skirt. She'd washed her hair specially the night before. When she walked into the wrapping room, the girls applauded and she felt herself blush. She rolled her eyes and told them to be quiet, but secretly she enjoyed the fuss. She was pleased to see Elsie already at work, picking and wrapping toffees.

'Is your mum coming to the launch?' Elsie asked.

Hetty began picking and wrapping too.

'I asked her to, but she said she's going shopping to buy a Christmas gift for Dan.' She had been disappointed, but not surprised, when her mum had told her this.

'It's a shame your Belgian fella can't come. I'm sure he'd have loved to see you praised by Mr Jack in front of everyone.'

'Dirk's teaching today, he can't leave the school. I'll

take him a tin of Lady Tina when I see him at the weekend.'

'It sounds like you two are getting on well. You seem to see him every weekend now.'

Hetty smiled. 'We get on well. He's a decent man.'

'I wish I could find a decent man.'

'What about Stan the gardener?' Hetty asked. 'I don't mean you should go courting him now, just when you're ready, and you will be, in time.'

'I could do a lot worse than Stan . . . when I'm ready,' Elsie replied. Hetty saw a smile play on her lips.

Just then Beattie bustled to the table and stood at Hetty's side. 'You'll never guess what Anne's just told me,' she said, eyes wide with excitement. 'Mr Jack's paying for street lamps to be installed in the lane at the back of the factory.'

'That's great news,' Hetty said.

Elsie winked at her. 'You're a good woman, Hetty Lawson. You got that sorted. If your face wasn't already going on the new tins, you'd deserve a medal for all you do.'

Hetty thought her heart would burst with pride.

Anne was running through last-minute launch preparations. She was fully prepared for what lay ahead. Dignitaries were arriving and the Mayor was on his way. The editor of the local newspaper was arriving with a photographer and a reporter. She checked her paperwork, reread Mr Jack's speech in case of any errors, then smoothed her hair against her head. She wore her best skirt suit, with the blue brooch from Mr Jack pinned to her lapel. She straightened her glasses, then walked into Mr Jack's office.

'Sir, we need to make our way to the canteen. It's almost ten o'clock.'

Mr Jack presented himself for inspection. 'Will I do?'

Anne looked him over, all the way from the polished shine of his shoes to his smart suit to his pleasing, open face and round bald head. His dark eyes twinkled with the same excitement she felt. However, she noticed his bow tie wasn't straight.

'May I adjust your tie, sir?'

He tilted his chin, and her fingers worked quickly to straighten the bow.

'I think we're ready,' she said. She handed over a folder of paperwork. 'Your speech, sir.'

Mr Jack took the folder, then nodded at her. 'I don't know what I'd do without you,' he said.

It was on the tip of her tongue to tell him she would always be happy working for him. But she held back. Ever since he'd presented her with the brooch, she'd been trying to make sense of her feelings. He'd never been anything more to her than her employer. But now . . . quite unexpectedly, she found herself thawing towards him, getting to know and understand him, as a man. A man who'd laid his heart open. She found that extremely attractive. She straightened her spine and nodded at the door.

'Let's go and launch our new brand.'

She followed him from the office, feeling nervous. However, it wasn't the thought of meeting the dignitaries or the Mayor that caused her anxiety. It wasn't the newspaper editor, for she could handle him and his reporter, make sure they asked the right questions and spoke to the right people. It was the thought of coming face to face with Mr and Mrs Matthews. And what if they brought the child with them? She shook her head. No, surely they wouldn't do that.

'Are you all right, Anne?' Mr Jack asked as they made their way across the cobbled yard.

'Fine, sir,' she said, pulling herself together.

They entered the canteen to a rapturous round of applause. The noise took Anne by surprise. She hesitated at the door while Mr Jack strode confidently to the makeshift stage at the front. Mr Burl and Mr Gerard were already seated there next to the Mayor. Anne quickened her pace to catch up. When Mr Jack took his place on the podium, she stood to one side with her copy of his speech. Efficient and organised as ever, she had typed two copies, in case anything happened to the original. Mr Jack had praised her for her advance planning. He'd said it was one of the many things that he admired about her.

She looked at the factory staff seated in rows. She searched for Mr Jack senior, but was surprised she couldn't find him. A front-row seat that had been reserved for him was empty. The vast room was packed full. Those who couldn't find seats were standing at the sides and along the back of the canteen. Christmas streamers in the factory colours of blue and white hung across the ceiling. Sprigs of holly decorated the tables. She focused on the front row again and saw Hetty in the middle. Elsie was next to her, and she smiled at them both.

On stage, the Mayor began his speech. Anne heard his voice rise and fall, his tone serious as he spoke about the war and factory work, and about the importance of Jack's toffee to the people of the town. As he went on, she gazed into the crowd, this time deliberately seeking Mr Matthews and his wife. For if she knew where they were, she could relax. One face ran into another. Men in suits and ties, with oiled hair and stern expressions. Women in fancy hats and smart coats. Next to them, the factory girls wore their overalls of khaki and red. Then her heart stopped. She gripped the speech in her hand, as if for support. Her breath caught in her throat. She looked away, thinking she'd made a mistake. Perhaps it wasn't Matthews, just someone who looked like him. But when she looked again, she knew in her heart it was him. At his side was his wife, and she was staring straight at Anne. Anne held firm. If she faltered now, she'd never forgive herself for crying in public. She pressed her feet to the floor, straightened her spine and tilted her chin.

A round of applause went up when the Mayor finished speaking. Now it was Mr Burl's turn. While he read from the speech his secretary had typed, Anne kept glancing at Mr and Mrs Matthews. She saw that Ruby Matthews had alerted her husband to her presence, and now both of them were looking at her. She felt her face growing hot, but stood her ground, determined not to let her emotions show. Instead, she took in Mrs Matthews' expensive-looking coat and hat and Mr Matthews' smart suit. She'd always known they had money, that her boy would want for nothing. She took comfort from that as her breathing returned to normal. The worst was over now. She had faced her fears and conquered them over seeing the Matthews again.

Up on stage, Mr Gerard had begun to speak. Anne forced herself to concentrate on his words. He spoke of the new brand as if Lady Tina was a living woman, describing her as delicate and creamy, delicious and sweet.

Next came the moment that everyone was waiting for. It was time for Mr Jack to speak, then reveal the face of Lady Tina. Anne noticed Hetty fidget in her seat. She was aware how excited she must be. Anne had already seen the artwork, of course, having been given advance proofs by Mr Gerard's team, and she'd approved it with all of her heart. At Mr Jack's request, she'd kept the details secret. She crossed her fingers and hoped Hetty would like it too.

The applause died down as Mr Jack moved to centre stage with the typed speech in his hands. Anne turned to watch him, feeling proud to work for such a well-respected man. Her heart fluttered with something else too, and in that moment, she wondered for the first time if she could bring herself to feel for him the way he felt for her. Could she . . . should she let herself fall for him? Their relationship had deepened to one of mutual admiration and respect. She'd grown closer to him than she'd ever expected. The truth of it was that she liked him; he was a thoroughly decent man. Oh, he wasn't as handsome as Mr Burl, and yes, it was true he was much shorter than her. When they walked together at the factory, she knew they made an odd sight. But when she sat at his side in meetings, or across his office desk, their height difference didn't matter.

She mulled over this while he spoke. She knew his speech off by heart, and was aware that he'd soon be coming to the end. After that, it would be the grand unveiling of the Lady Tina artwork, then a presentation to Hetty. Then she saw Lucinda walking onto the stage. She gasped in horror. This wasn't supposed to happen. When she'd planned the launch with Mr Jack, he'd made no mention of Lucinda joining him. In fact, he'd made no mention of her at all other than to say she was meeting the florist that morning to discuss arrangements for her wedding bouquet. What was she doing here?

Anne watched in amazement as Lucinda made her way across the stage to Mr Jack. He didn't notice her at first, as he continued with his speech. It was only when she was right by his side that he spotted her. Anne saw his eyes grow wide, and a look of surprise flitted across his face, followed by a forced smile. She recognised that smile, hiding gritted teeth. She'd seen him employ it in difficult meetings when he wanted to get his point across to a truculent board member. To her horror, he paused, waiting while Lucinda settled herself behind him in the seat he'd vacated, between Mr Burl and Mr Gerard. A shiver ran down Anne's back as she realised that Lucinda was publicly staking her claim to Mr Jack and the factory.

Chapter Forty-Four

Anne was pulled out of her reverie by the sound of applause. Mr Jack's speech had finished and the canteen filled with noise as everyone clapped and cheered. He was still standing centre stage and raised his arms to quieten everyone down.

'Ladies and gentlemen, we now come to the moment you've all been waiting for, the launch of Lady Tina. As you know, we modelled Lady Tina on one of our factory girls after a competition was held to find the girl who would best represent the new brand.'

He turned to smile at Anne.

'The idea to name the brand Lady Tina came from my secretary, Miss Wright. Please, Anne, come up to the stage.'

Anne hadn't expected this; it wasn't part of the plan. But she knew she had no choice. She forced her legs forward, shaking with nerves, afraid of tripping up the steps. However, she needn't have worried, for Mr Jack was there, holding his hand out, helping her up. A respectful round of applause filled the room as she walked forward and stood at his side. The photographer from the local paper rushed forward, positioning his camera. Anne shuffled back a few steps so that she was behind Mr Jack, where she felt more comfortable, but she was beaming with pride.

Standing there in front of everyone, she saw her life more clearly than before. The only way to face her future was to seal up her past with love. Her child would be given a good life with Peter and Ruby Matthews. They were people of standing. Why, they must even employ a nanny at home to care for him. Was that who was looking after him now?

Meanwhile, Mr Jack was still speaking.

'. . . and the factory girl we chose to represent the new brand is Miss Henrietta Hilda Lawson. Hetty, please join us on stage.'

Anne stepped forward to help Hetty climb the steps, just as Mr Jack had helped her. She felt even more confident once her friend was on stage by her side. Another round of applause filled the room.

'And now it's time to unveil the artwork for our Lady Tina brand,' Mr Jack said proudly.

He walked to the side of the stage, where a large easel was draped in a white cloth with the Jack's logo in blue. A hush fell over the room.

'Ladies and gentlemen, it is an honour to proudly present to you the latest brand of toffee from Jack's factory. I give you . . . Lady Tina!' He whipped the cloth from the easel to reveal the picture underneath.

Hetty gasped when she saw it. 'Why, it's beautiful.'

'It is indeed,' Mr Jack said. 'Mr Gerard and his team have done us proud. They've done you proud, Hetty, too.'

Hetty couldn't believe her eyes. Her face was right there. She looked fresher in the artwork than she knew she did in real life. Fresh and pretty, with creamy skin with a blush of pale pink. There was no denying it was her, though. She felt as if she was looking into the past, at a picture of herself from days gone by. They'd darkened her hair in the artwork to contrast with her eyes and pale skin. But most surprising of all was that they'd painted her wearing a bonnet. A beautiful bonnet of purple and green, with a purple ribbon tied under her chin. Lady Tina's lips had been picked out in cherry red, much darker than her own. Around her face was a bouquet of pink and white roses with delicate leaves spreading to the edges of the tin.

As for the tin itself, Hetty saw, it was most unusual, like nothing Jack's had produced before. It wasn't square or round like tins usually were. This one was lozenge-shaped, with rounded edges, giving it a softer, more feminine look. Finally, under her image, the words *Lady Tina Toffee* were written in blue. She had never seen anything so beautiful. She wanted to trace her fingers over it, to inspect it from top to bottom, side to side. She wanted to inspect every brushstroke, but she knew she couldn't touch it; it was forbidden. She had to drink it all in with her eyes.

'It's really me,' she whispered.

'Yes, indeed. We're pleased with how it turned out,' Mr Jack said. 'It's a very striking image, I'm sure you'll agree. One of the best Mr Gerard has produced.'

Hetty saw Mr Gerard smile in appreciation of the remark. By now, the ladies who worked in the canteen were walking amongst those seated, handing out tins of the new toffee with Hetty's face on the front. A murmur of appreciation went up in the room, as the tins were inspected; some were even opened and the new, creamy toffees were popped into mouths. Hetty turned to smile at Anne, and slid her arm around her friend's slim waist. Then she looked out at the audience and saw Elsie beaming with pride, clapping her hands and cheering.

'Well done, Hetty. It's gorgeous! You look amazing! You'll be in all the shops around the country,' Elsie yelled.

Mr Jack smiled kindly. 'Not just around the country. Lady Tina will be going around the world, my dear, the world.'

Hetty didn't have time to feel nervous about the remark as the photographer from the newspaper popped up again. He positioned Mr Jack and Hetty next to the artwork, then he asked for Mr Jack to be photographed alone; then with both Hetty and Anne. As they were being shuffled around, a strange aroma reached Hetty: the overpowering scent of citrus. She turned to see the tall, well-dressed woman who'd arrived late on stage, and who was now pushing her way forward, almost knocking Hetty to one side.

'As Mr Jack's fiancée, and an investor in this factory, I should be photographed too,' the woman said, forcing her way through to Mr Jack.

As more pictures were taken, Mr Burl took to the stage and brought the room to order.

'Ladies and gentlemen, we hope you enjoy your gift of Lady Tina Toffee. And we sincerely hope that you will tell your friends and family about it. Not only that, but if you have business contacts who'd like to supply it,

I would be happy to talk to you over the buffet the canteen has prepared. Speaking of which, the food is now ready, and those who'd like to are very welcome to stay for a Christmas drink and bite to eat. Thank you all so much for coming.'

Another round of applause filled the room, signalling the end of the formal launch. Those who worked at the factory knew they had to return to their stations in the slab room, the sugar boiling room, the packing room, the wrapping room and the railway yard. Five men left to make their way to the lane at the back of the factory, discussing the installation of street lamps. As the factory girls and men poured out of the canteen, it left space for the visitors to mingle with the factory's top brass and their teams. Many of the dignitaries' wives made a beeline for the artwork.

'I wonder where I might buy a bonnet just like this and have my portrait painted in the Lady Tina style?' one said.

Hetty braced herself when she saw a group of women walking towards her, but when they veered away to speak to Lucinda Dalton instead, she felt disappointment mixed with relief.

'I wouldn't know what to talk to them about anyway,' she muttered to Anne.

Elsie joined them. 'It looks incredible, Hetty. You must be enormously proud.'

Hetty nudged her. 'I'll be glad of the bonus Mr Jack promised.'

'I'll make sure you get it before Christmas,' Anne said.

Elsie hugged Hetty. 'I'll see you back at work.'

Hetty watched her go, then noticed Anne glancing around the room as if she was looking for someone.

'You seem distracted, Anne. Do you need to go back to work too?'

Anne shook her head. 'No. I'll stay here for a while. I'll go and grab us both a mince pie and a glass of sherry. We need to celebrate your special day. Are you pleased with the artwork?'

'I love it.'

'Your mum will be proud when she sees it,' she beamed.

Hetty picked up a tin and ran her fingers over the girl in the bonnet. 'I hope so,' she replied dully.

'Stay there, don't move,' Anne said. 'I'll be back in a second with food.'

Hetty watched as she moved into the crowd. Some of the visitors now had glasses and plates in their hands; many stood in groups, chatting. Laughter filled the air. She waited by the artwork, politely answering questions from those who wandered by. She spoke to the Mayor, unsure if she should curtsey. She dipped her knees slightly, just in case. Left on her own again, feeling slightly nervous, she looked again for Anne. It was while she was looking that she glanced through the open canteen door. Outside she saw Elsie – and looming over her was Frankie Ireland.

Chapter Forty-Five

Hetty couldn't let Elsie handle Frankie alone. She had to head outside. A gentleman in a top hat was walking towards her, ready to ask questions about the artwork. But Hetty was already pushing her way into the crowd. She shouldered her way through, calling out 'Excuse me!' and 'Could I just squeeze past, please?' as she went. Finally she reached the door, but Elsie and Frankie were nowhere to be seen. Where had they gone?

At the factory gates, a smartly dressed chauffeur stood to attention. He wore a long grey coat, peaked cap and leather gloves. Beyond the gate was a sleek black motorcar that took Hetty's breath away. From behind her she heard Mr Jack's voice. Surprised, she turned, in case he was calling her back into the room. But he was speaking to the tall, handsome woman who'd arrived late for the launch. He kissed her on the cheek, then she turned and swept away in a cloud of overpowering perfume towards the chauffeur at the gate.

'Take me home, George,' she ordered.

'Yes, Miss Dalton,' he replied.

Hetty walked across the cobbled yard. She spotted

Elsie by the door to the wrapping where Frankie had her pinned to the wall. She marched forward.

'Get away from her,' she yelled.

Frankie sneered when he saw her. He kept his hands against the wall, preventing Elsie from walking away. Hetty saw how worried Elsie looked, but she wasn't scared.

'You're just a bully,' she said.

'Are you still here?' Frankie said scornfully. 'I'm having a private word with my wife.'

'Frankie, leave me alone!' Elsie begged.

Hetty stepped forward bravely. 'You heard her, now go.'

Frankie dropped his hands, and Hetty saw Elsie's shoulders fall with relief.

'Are you all right?' she asked.

'I will be, once he's gone,' Elsie said, nodding at Frankie.

Frankie bared his teeth. 'Who's going to throw me out?'

'I will,' a man's voice said from behind Hetty.

'And I'll help him,' another man added.

'I'll call for a policeman to attend,' a third man said.

Hetty spun around, unable to believe what she saw. It was Stan who stepped forward first. He gripped Frankie's arms and twisted them behind his back, then pushed him up against the wall. Mr Jack was next, warning Stan that this was a matter for the police.

'A lowlife like him isn't worth you being cautioned for assault,' he warned. 'I'll ask Jacob to bring a policeman from Front Street to throw him out.'

Mr Jack walked away across the yard and disappeared

into reception. But it was the third man whose appearance took Hetty most by surprise. She watched in awe as Dirk stepped forward to help Stan control Frankie, who was now writhing like a wild animal.

She hugged Elsie, whispering in her ear. 'He didn't hurt you, did he?'

'No. But he was going to. If you hadn't found me when you did, I dread to think what might've happened. He's drunk, Hetty.'

Elsie pulled away from Hetty and they watched Stan and Dirk struggling with Frankie, trying to subdue him.

'I just wish he wasn't my husband. What was I thinking of when I married him? Oh, there's no need to answer that.'

'You married him for the right reason,' Hetty replied.

'I just wish I'd chosen the right man,' Elsie said sadly. Hetty saw that she was looking at Stan.

'Come on, lad, let's get you out of sight of the visitors. We don't want you bringing Jack's factory into disrepute,' Stan said, as he heaved Frankie away. Dirk grabbed Frankie's other arm, and together they frogmarched him off.

As the men walked away, Anne arrived.

'Hetty? The Mayor wants to speak to you in the canteen. Has anyone seen Mr Jack? Oh heavens, I wish I could keep tabs on that man. He sends my head spinning at times.'

Hetty explained what had happened with Frankie. Anne listened in horror, then she wrapped her arms around Elsie and hugged her.

'Are you sure you're all right, Elsie? Do you need the factory doctor to give you the once-over?'

'No, I'm fine, Anne, really. He didn't touch me. He wanted money, that was all, to buy beer. He threatened me, but he was too drunk to stand, never mind swing his fists.'

Anne hesitated, glancing behind her. 'If you're sure you're all right? I really must get back to our visitors.'

'I am, thank you,' Elsie replied. 'Mr Jack's gone to reception to ask Jacob to fetch a policeman. Frankie won't be back to bother me. Go, Anne, please. And when you find Mr Jack, thank him from me for being in the right place at the right time. If it hadn't been for him and Stan and that other man . . . Who was he, by the way? I didn't recognise him as a toffee man. And did you see that black suit he was wearing? Very stylish it was, with wide lapels. Was he one of today's visitors?'

Anne shrugged and looked enquiringly at Hetty. She felt unusually shy when she gave her reply.

'He's my Belgian friend, Dirk.' Her cheeks heated up.

'I think Stan had everything under control before Dirk offered to help,' Elsie teased.

'And I'm sure Mr Jack has called for the policeman now,' Anne added. 'Look, I'm really sorry, but I must go back indoors. I've got to keep the Mayor sweet. Speaking of which, if you're up to it, Hetty, could you join me in speaking to him? He's asking for you again. His wife is taken by the artwork and the tins.'

Hetty looked at Elsie. 'Are you sure you're all right?'

But Elsie was already heading to the wrapping room. She turned and gave a cheeky wink.

'Don't you worry about me. I'll be fine. Aren't I always?'

Satisfied that she was telling the truth, Hetty followed Anne back to the canteen. The first thing she did was to look around for Dirk, but was disappointed not to find him. She was confused about why he'd turned up for the launch after he'd told her he'd be teaching.

'Ah, Miss Lawson, the new Lady Tina!' the Mayor cried when he spotted her.

Hetty's thoughts about Dirk were put to one side as the Mayor and his wife chatted to her. Around her she was aware that the crowd was thinning out, the noise dimming and chatter ceasing. People were leaving with their boxes of Lady Tina. As the visitors drifted away, the women who worked in the canteen straightened tables and chairs, getting ready to serve lunch to the workers. Food left over from the launch was laid out on tables: plates of mince pies, sausage rolls and small glasses of sherry.

Hetty said goodbye to the Mayor, then headed to the door to return to the wrapping room. She picked up her own tin of Lady Tina and headed out into the cold day. Dirk was waiting by the gate, this time with a small bouquet in his hands. He stepped forward as soon as she entered the yard.

'Dirk!' she called. 'Frankie didn't hurt you, did he?'

'No, he didn't hurt me,' he said.

He handed the flowers over, a winter bouquet of green ivy with a sprig of white mistletoe berries, all tied with green ribbon.

'Why, this is beautiful,' she said. She took the flowers in her free hand and looked into his eyes.

'When I arrived and saw you having trouble with that drunken man, I handed the flowers to a man standing by the gate. He seemed surprised to be asked to hold them, but he did so nonetheless. I've just been to find him and thank him. He said his name was Peter Matthews. Do you know him?'

Hetty shook her head. 'He must be a visitor,' she replied. 'I'm so glad you're here, thank you for coming.'

'Well, my sister is teaching my boys this morning so that I could be here on your special day. I didn't want to miss it. But the bus from Birtley was late, and hence I arrived after the speeches.'

'You arrived in the nick of time to save my friend Elsie from the monster she married,' Hetty said.

'Monster?' Dirk said, confused.

'I'll tell you all about him sometime,' Hetty said. 'Oh, it's so good to see you, a wonderful surprise. But I really have to get back to work. I'm afraid I can't stop.'

He beckoned her to a corner of the cobbled yard. 'And I can't stop either. I have to go back to Elisabethville. May I meet you after work? Perhaps you might let me buy you afternoon tea at the Lambton Café on Front Street? My treat.' He smiled at her. 'See, I learn so much from you; you help improve my English. We should celebrate your moment in the spotlight now you're the face of Lady Tina. Although if I may say so, the lady on the tin is nowhere near as pretty as you are in real life.'

Hetty laid her hand on his arm. She thought for a moment, then she looked from Dirk to the bouquet. She knew that when she returned home, her mum wouldn't ask questions about the Lady Tina launch, as she'd shown no interest so far. However, she might be curious about the flowers. It flashed through Hetty's mind that she could lie to Hilda and tell her the flowers were a gift from the factory along with the free tin of toffee. But she decided otherwise. It was time to prove to her mum that she was an adult now, and she wanted to be treated as one.

'I would like to have tea with you, Dirk,' she said, looking into his honest, open face. 'But not tonight, and not at the Lambton Café.'

'Why not? I have been there before and enjoyed it. Although I found the waitress a little rude.'

Hetty smiled when she recalled the waitress who'd served her, Elsie and Anne when they'd taken tea there. It sounded like the same girl.

'How would you like to come for tea at my home, on Christmas Eve? Of course, I'd need to ask my mum first. We're becoming more than friends, Dirk, don't you agree?'

'Most definitely, yes,' he replied.

Hetty swallowed hard. 'Then I think it might be time for you to meet my mum.'

'I would love to,' he replied politely.

'I have to warn you, she can be tricky.'

'Tricky?' he asked, puzzled.

Hetty thought for a moment. 'What I mean is . . .' she said, searching for the right words. 'What I mean is that she might be even more rude to you than the waitress at the Lambton Café was.'

'It's not possible,' Dirk said.

She reached up and planted a kiss on his cheek.

'Mum is . . . well, she's narrow-minded. She doesn't know what goes on outside her four walls, and what she does know, she doesn't like.'

'She can't possibly be that bad,' Dirk laughed.

Hetty arched her eyebrow. 'Don't say you weren't warned,' she replied.

Chapter Forty-Six

That night as Hetty walked home, she ran through the day's events. Shaking hands with the Mayor and meeting his wife; having her photograph taken and being interviewed by the reporter from the Chester-le-Street newspaper. Seeing Dirk had been the cherry on the cake. The only bad thing had been Frankie. When she thought of the way Stan and Dirk and even Mr Jack had got involved to have him thrown out of the grounds and marched off by a policeman, she stifled a smile. She didn't think he'd be back to bother Elsie again.

So much had happened and the day had gone by in a blur. None of it seemed real. And yet it *was* real, for she carried her box of Lady Tina in one hand and her winter bouquet in the other. Before she reached Elm Street, she practised the words she would say to her mum about Dirk. It was time to be honest. She didn't want to keep him a secret when he was becoming increasingly important to her. However, she knew her mum wouldn't take the news well. Hilda's world was limited to the gossip she overheard from neighbours on Elm Street or on Front Street while shopping. As far as the Belgians and

Elisabethville went, Hetty knew she chose to believe what she wanted, which wasn't the truth. Now that Hetty had visited Elisabethville, however, and had seen it with her own eyes, she knew the people there were no different from her, Hilda and Dan.

Ah, Dan. Her shoulders tensed when she thought of her brother, wondering what trouble he was up to now. She wondered if he'd be at home when she returned. She hadn't seen him for a while. He was either sleeping in his room while she was at home or out with Tyler Rose conducting shady business. She wondered whether now was the right time to tell her mum about Frankie Ireland stealing from the factory, and about Dan being involved.

When she reached Elm Street, she paused on the doorstep to gather her thoughts. She'd need to handle her mum carefully. Not only did she intend to tell her the truth about Dirk, she also had to tell her about Bob. She pushed the door open and stepped inside. But the moment she did so, she could hear her mum yelling. She gasped. Was it Frankie Ireland? Had he returned to demand more money?

She raced along the hallway and into the kitchen, but when she saw who her mum was shouting at, she came to a sudden halt. It was Dan. Hetty was stunned. She'd never in her life known her mum have anything but good words to say about him, no matter what mischief or trouble he caused. She laid her tin of toffee and the flowers on the table. Hilda was red in the face and pacing the floor, while Dan sat at the table looking cowed. Hetty struggled to make sense of what she was seeing.

'What's happened?' she asked.

When Hilda didn't reply, she turned to Dan.

'What've you done to upset Mum?'

Hilda stopped pacing, put her hands on her hips and pointed at her son. 'He's only gone and signed up to join the bloody army!' she screamed.

'What? But he's too young to be a soldier,' Hetty said. She flew to Dan's side and sat down.

'Tell me what's happened,' she urged.

Dan shrugged, as if he couldn't care less. This enraged Hilda even more.

'It's like Mum says, I've signed up. I'm getting sent to the battlefield. I'm not scared, if that's what you're worried about.'

Hilda threw her arms in the air. 'He says he's not scared. Just listen to him. He's just a boy, *my* boy, and I won't let him go.'

Hetty leaned close to Dan. 'You know you're not old enough. It's not right, Dan. Whoever told you that you can go must have got it wrong.'

Dan sat up straight. 'Technically, I'm supposed to be nineteen.'

'See, I told you,' Hilda yelled.

'You lied to the recruiting sergeant about your age?' Hetty asked.

Dan shook his head. 'No. The sergeant told me the law doesn't prevent lads my age from joining. They're desperate for troops, so they'll take younger men. There was a queue of us down Front Street waiting to join. The sergeant gets two and sixpence for each lad he signs up as long as we're keen as mustard and look fit and well. He asked questions, I answered them, then he said he'd take me.'

'What about your height? I thought you had to be tall,' Hetty said.

'I'm five foot three inches, the minimum. I scraped in.'

'You're just a boy!' Hilda cried again.

Dan puffed out his chest. 'I want to be a man.'

'Oh, and the army will do that for you, will it?' Hilda snapped. 'You'll be dead on a battlefield within weeks. You'll go looking for trouble. I won't let you go, lad. With every breath I've got in me, I will not let you go.'

Hetty stood and walked to her mum. 'You've got no choice, Mum. It's his life,' she said gently. 'If it's what he wants, you've got to let him go. We've never heard him so determined about anything in his life.'

'But he's my baby,' Hilda sobbed.

Hetty pulled her mum to her. 'If he stays here, thieving for Tyler Rose, getting in with villains like Frankie Ireland, what good will that do him? He could end up dead here, never mind on a battlefield.'

Hilda pulled away from her embrace.

'I'm going, Mum. You can't stop me,' Dan said firmly.

Hilda sat on a chair by the fire. 'We've argued about this for hours. We've gone round in circles.'

'When do you leave?' Hetty asked.

'Christmas Eve, early morning,' Dan replied.

Hilda's sobs went up a notch. 'He leaves his own mother at Christmas,' she wailed. 'What sort of a monster have I raised? I've given him everything. Everything! I've given him my life, and this is how he treats me.'

Hetty fully expected Dan to rush to their mum's side, as he used to do when he was in her bad books as a child. But this time he stayed where he was. That was when Hetty knew he was resolute. She knew his decision was one he wouldn't apologise for, and she took strength from that. She too was determined not to apologise for her decisions about Bob and Dirk. However, looking at the state of Hilda struggling to take in Dan's news, she wasn't sure when the right time to tell her would be.

She busied herself putting the kettle on the coals to make a pot of tea. She pulled plates and a pan from the cupboard and began peeling potatoes.

'Did you buy ham today?' she asked.

Hilda dried her eyes on her apron. 'It's in the pantry.'

As Hetty began to prepare their meal, she looked at Dan. 'Are you staying for tea?'

Dan nodded.

'It feels like our last supper,' Hilda moaned.

'You've got a few days more of me yet, Mum,' he said, then he turned to Hetty. 'Where did Bob say he was in his last letter to you? Who knows, I might even get sent to the same place as him.'

Hetty stopped peeling. She felt her mum's eyes on her, and Dan's, both of them waiting for her reply.

'I've got something to tell you both about Bob,' she began. 'I haven't had any letters from him, just one card. That's all.'

'He's probably gone off you, and I can't say I blame him. Out of sight, out of mind. He was always too good for you,' Hilda sniffed.

Hetty gripped the potato she was holding, then dropped it into the bowl. She laid the peeler down too. She looked at her mum. Hilda's comments had stung her to the core, as always. It also hurt that she hadn't cared enough to ask about the Lady Tina launch. She must have noticed the toffee tin and bouquet by now.

'Our Hetty doesn't need Bob any more. She's got another fella,' Dan smirked.

Hetty glared at him. 'Shut up!'

'What's going on?' Hilda demanded.

Hetty picked up the peeler and jabbed it in Dan's direction. 'Shut up, Dan, I'm warning you. I'll tell Mum in my own time.'

'Tell me what?' Hilda asked.

Hetty thought for a moment. This wasn't how she would have chosen to break the news, but now that Dan had forced her hand, she had no choice. She glared at her brother.

'I've just defended you over your decision to join the army, and yet you do this to me. You're the worst, Dan Lawson. You might be going off to be a soldier, but you're immature and need to grow up.'

Dan shrugged. 'Go on, tell Mum about your Belgian friend.'

'What?' Hilda said, incredulous.

Hetty was ready for a fight, ready to hold her own and put her opinion forward, no matter what Hilda said. But when she looked into her mum's eyes, she didn't see anger or fear, she saw resignation. After her argument with Dan, she had no fight left in her.

'He's a teacher, he's called Dirk and I've been getting friendly with him,' she said matter-of-factly. 'Now, do you want these potatoes peeled or not?' She returned her attention to the bowl.

'She's kissed him,' Dan added. 'She was seen at a dance in the Belgian village.'

Hetty carried on peeling, seething with anger. She looked at Hilda, who sat open-mouthed, shaking her head.

'He's a good man, Mum. I wouldn't be friends with him otherwise.'

'You've kissed a Belgian man?' Hilda said, her voice coming out of her in little more than a whisper.

'Once or twice, and I hope there'll be a third time,' Hetty replied. 'Look, Mum, I'm being honest. Just as Dan has been honest about signing up for the army. We're not children any more, we're adults. Life has changed since war began. We need to take happiness where we find it. I can see who I want, kiss who I like.'

'Does Bob know?' Hilda said. 'Is that why he hasn't written?'

'I wrote to Bob to call things off once I knew I had feelings for Dirk,' Hetty admitted.

What a relief it felt to be honest, finally. She realised what a heavy weight she'd been carrying in her heart, afraid of her mum's reaction. And now she'd told her everything and Hilda hadn't exploded as she had feared. She hadn't threatened to throw her out, which Hetty had dreaded most. She'd already planned to ask Elsie if she could move in with her at her aunt Jean's if that happened. And yet Hilda had taken the news quietly because she had no strength left after Dan's shock. In a strange way, Dan's decision to join the army had done Hetty a favour.

'When Dan leaves on Christmas Eve morning, it'll just be the two of us,' she said carefully, gauging her mum's reaction as she spoke.

'What of it?' Hilda said.

'Well, I was wondering . . .' Hetty began cautiously. 'I was thinking . . . it might be nice for you to meet Dirk.'

Hilda crossed her arms and leaned back in her seat.

'Maybe he could even come for tea on Christmas Eve?' Hetty dared to ask.

She took an unusual interest in the potato she was peeling as her words hung in the air. Hilda didn't speak at first.

'You really like this fella enough to invite him here?' she said at last.

Hetty nodded. 'Yes, I do. I'd like you both to meet.'

There was another long silence.

'He's a teacher, you say?' Hilda asked, impressed.

'He speaks English quite well and he's very polite,' Hetty replied. She looked at her mum, who was now turning coal with the poker.

'All right, tea on Christmas Eve it is. But if I don't like him, or if the neighbours gossip, he won't be allowed back. Do you understand?' Hilda said.

'Only too well,' Hetty muttered.

Chapter Forty-Seven

Early the next morning, Elsie turned onto Front Street, heading to work. There was frost on the ground and she picked her steps carefully so as not to slip. A voice called out behind her.

'Elsie, wait for me.'

When she saw Stan's friendly face, her heart lifted. She waited for him to catch up. He too was carefully choosing where he placed his feet.

'It wouldn't do to fall,' he said when he reached her side. 'Let me walk with you. Here, grab my arm. It'll stop you from slipping.'

She hesitated a moment before putting her arm through his.

'Are you all set for Christmas?' Stan asked.

It was so cold that when they talked, they could see their breath in front of their faces. Elsie didn't know how to reply.

'If you mean do I have a turkey and gravy followed by pudding and sherry, then the answer's no. My aunt's not a great cook and she ... er ... she might be working anyway. As always, I'll be left to my own devices. But

I'm looking forward to having two days off work. What about you, Stan? What'll you be doing?'

Her foot slipped from under her.

'Steady on, girl,' he said, grabbing her with his strong arms.

She righted herself and they carried on walking.

'I'm not so keen on Christmas,' Stan said. 'It's a day for families, isn't it? But I don't have any family to share it with except my sister, who lives in Birtley, and of course my dog, Patch.' Elsie detected a note of sadness.

'I'm not keen on it either,' she admitted. 'We don't even exchange presents in our house. It's just a day like any other, except I won't be at work.'

'What'll you do, then?' he asked.

She shrugged. 'Read a book. I might go for a walk if it's not too cold.'

Stan looked ahead as he replied. 'Well, if you're free, I'll be walking Patch by the river about ten o'clock in the morning. You could join us if you like, although I wouldn't want to put you out. Just if you're passing, of course. Patch might like to see you again.'

Elsie held tight to Stan's arm as they crossed the main road.

'And I might like to see Patch,' she smiled. 'Just if I'm passing, of course.'

Once they were through the gates, she dropped her arm.

'Thanks, Stan. For everything,' she said.

He raised his cap. 'My pleasure. Do you know what? I'm really looking forward to today.'

'Oh? Why's that?' Elsie asked.

'Because I'm planning the seeds I'll sow in the New

Year. It's never too early to plan. And I'll be thinking of where to plant the rose bush in Anabel's memory. Her brother's chosen a red flowering rose; he said it was her favourite colour. Do you know, in some ways gardening is a lot like life.'

Elsie started to laugh. 'How?'

Stan held his cap in his hands and looked deep into her eyes. 'You need to get rid of nasty weeds to allow beautiful flowers to grow.'

And with that, he waved goodbye and headed to his shed at the back of the factory. Elsie watched him go, his broad shoulders, his straight back.

She was about to head to the wrapping room when Anne walked through the gates.

'Morning, Elsie. You all right?'

'Morning, Anne, I'm fine. How are you? Looking forward to Christmas?'

'I'm spending it with Mrs Fortune, my landlady. She's cooking beef and all the trimmings, so I can't complain. She's even made a plum pudding that she's been feeding with brandy for weeks. It's got so much alcohol in it, I feel tipsy just thinking about it. Anyway, I must dash. There's a board meeting this morning and I need to prepare. See you at lunchtime for our Christmas meal in the canteen.'

'See you, Anne,' Elsie said, then the girls headed off in different directions.

Anne walked into reception, where Jacob was at his desk. He didn't glance up when she entered, didn't even say hello, but she was used to that now. However, this time, instead of walking straight past him with her usual cheery

'Good morning', which she knew he'd ignore, she stopped. In the spirit of the season, she leaned across his desk, pulled a tiny sprig of mistletoe from her handbag and held it over his head. Before he knew what was happening, she'd gently kissed his cheek. For the first time in her memory, his face broke into a smile.

'Merry Christmas!' she called as she disappeared through the door.

'Merry Christmas!' he called back.

In the boardroom, she began arranging papers ready for the meeting. Then an idea struck. She went to the supplies cupboard and took out a box of Lady Tina. Opening it, she poured wrapped toffees onto a plate for the board members to enjoy.

'Ah, what the heck, it's Christmas,' she said out loud.

Soon each place at the long table had a complete set of papers set out in readiness. The coal fire warmed the room and sprigs of holly on the windowsill gave it festive cheer. Anne was pleased with how it looked. She returned to her office, happy to see Mr Jack arriving.

'Everything's ready for the board meeting,' she said gaily.

'Ah, yes. I, er . . . I need to speak to you about that,' he said as he removed his coat and hat. Anne walked towards him, ready to take them and hang them up as usual. But Mr Jack didn't look at her as he handed them over, his gaze trained on the floor.

'Is everything all right, sir?' she asked.

'No, Anne. Everything is not all right, I'm afraid. My father came to see me last night.'

At last he lifted his eyes, and when Anne saw his face, she knew something was wrong. It looked as if he hadn't slept. He appeared exhausted, done in. His eyes were bleary and heavy.

'What I'm trying to say, Anne, is that we need to set another place at the table today. We have a new member of the board.'

'Oh,' Anne said, taken aback. 'Is it Mr Burl's new assistant, Mr Gregory? I recall he was discussed at the last meeting.'

'No, it's not Gregory.'

'Then it must be your father. Has he decided to attend board meetings again instead of receiving the minutes by post?'

Mr Jack shook his head. 'It's Lucinda Dalton.'

Anne's mouth hung open in shock.

'It's my father's idea. He thinks, and of course I see his reasoning, that the factory might not survive this blasted war. I have to listen to him, Anne. Not only is he my father, but he owns more than fifty per cent of the business. Although he handed the reins to me when he retired, he still controls the power. This damn war, for heaven's sake! Sugar rationing will come, there now seems no doubt. It could put us out of business. My father and I had a discussion long into the night. He warned me that if I don't . . .'

He paused, defeated, and laid his hands on his desk. He looked up at Anne.

'He says that if I don't marry Lucinda and invest her family's money in toffee, we'll lose the factory before the war's over. Well, there you have it. There's no easy way to say it.'

Anne felt tears prick her eyes and a lump rise in her throat. 'Then Miss Dalton must join the board, of course,' she said, trying to keep her emotions in check. 'I'll arrange for the documents to be signed by all present today.'

'Thank you, Anne. I knew I could rely on you. You do understand, don't you?'

She swallowed hard. She understood only too well. 'Of course, sir. The toffee factory must always come first.'

Mr Jack walked to her and laid his hand on her arm. 'Thank you,' he whispered.

Anne looked deep into his eyes, and they held each other's gaze for a moment before he turned and walked out of the door. She still had his coat draped over her arm. She smoothed it with her hand, then placed it on a hanger.

'Come on, Anne, pull yourself together. You can get through this.'

She picked up her notepad and pencil. Alone in Mr Jack's office, she checked her appearance in a small mirror from her handbag. She smoothed her hair and straightened her glasses. Then she headed to the boardroom, where she was met by the overpowering scent of citrus perfume. Lucinda Dalton was sitting in the chair on Mr Jack's right-hand side. It was the chair where Anne used to sit.

On Christmas Eve, there was a festive lunch in the canteen of leek soup and roast ham, followed by treacle tart. There was a small glass of sherry for each woman and a half-pint of beer for the men. The factory would be closed on Christmas Day and Boxing Day.

Hetty was sitting with Elsie and Anne.

'This treacle tart is gorgeous, it's melting in my mouth,' Elsie said.

'It's delicious,' Hetty agreed, then she nodded at Anne's plate. 'Don't you like it? You haven't touched yours.'

Anne pushed the plate towards her. 'You have it. I can't stomach any more. The soup and ham were enough.'

Hetty shook her head. 'I shouldn't eat it. I've got plans for tea tonight.' She passed the plate to Elsie, then leaned forward to her friends. 'Dirk's coming to tea. He's going to meet Mum.'

'I hope she likes him,' Elsie said.

Hetty crossed her fingers.

'Did Dan get off all right this morning?'

She sighed. 'Yes, he's gone with the boys from the Durham Light Infantry. Mum saw him off. He said he'll write as soon as he can. He'll be on his way to Folkestone by now.'

Elsie dug her spoon into Anne's treacle tart. 'Do you think the war will go on much longer, Anne?'

'Sorry, what?' Anne said. Hetty noticed that she seemed distracted.

'I was wondering if you'd heard anything, you know, about the war and the factory. It's just that some of the sugar boilers say they're worried about rationing. They've heard rumours. Have you?'

Anne had heard more than just rumours. She'd heard distressing news at the board meeting that week. But she couldn't tell Hetty and Elsie. She couldn't tell anyone. The information about sugar rationing was under embargo for now. Mr Jack had asked her to keep it secret, and she was bound by confidentiality to the board. He didn't want word to get out to his staff and ruin their Christmas.

'No, I haven't heard anything,' she said, hating herself for not being able to tell the truth. Then she remembered something from the meeting that she *could* share.

'But I do have one bit of good news.'

Hetty leaned forward. 'Go on,' she said eagerly.

'It's Mr Gerard's idea. We're going to make special toffee for the war, to send overseas to our boys.'

'That'll keep us busy,' Hetty smiled.

'There's a lot to look forward to,' Elsie said. 'This awful winter weather won't last for ever, and before we know it, it'll be spring. Flowers will bloom and weeds will need picking.'

'It's not like you to be sentimental, Elsie Cooper,' Hetty teased.

She raised her glass of sherry.

'We should make a toast,' she suggested.

Elsie picked up her glass too. Anne, however, didn't move. She was still thinking about the board meeting, and about Lucinda sitting on Mr Jack's right-hand side.

'Come on, Anne. Don't be a spoilsport,' Hetty said. 'Let's drink a toast to the future.'

'And to us,' Elsie added.

Anne raised her glass at last.

'Here's to friendship.' Hetty clinked glasses with the others.

'To springtime and flowers,' Elsie chipped in.

'And to saving ourselves from dull men,' Hetty said.

They looked at Anne, waiting for her to add her own toast. Finally a smile came to her lips, and she raised her glass high.

'Here's to the three of us, the toffee factory girls . . . and all that our future will bring.'

We hope you have enjoyed reading
The Toffee Factory Girls.

To discover what happens next to Hetty,
Elsie and Anne look out for *Secrets of the
Toffee Factory Girls*, the second novel in this
exciting new trilogy, to be published in 2025.

And for a sneak preview of the first chapter of
Secrets of the Toffee Factory Girls read on . . .

An extract from
SECRETS OF THE
TOFFEE FACTORY GIRLS

Chapter One

January 1916

Anne Wright rented a cramped room on the top floor of a terraced house on Victor Street. Her landlady Mrs Fortune had an annoying habit of entering her room without warning. However, this time when Mrs Fortune tried to open the door, she was thwarted. Anne allowed herself a smile as she glanced at the bolt.

There was a knock, loud and insistent.

'Miss Wright!' Mrs Fortune yelled from the landing. 'Is there something wrong with your door? It won't open.'

There was more rattling of the handle before Anne slid open the lock. Mrs Fortune, red in the face with frustration, almost fell into Anne's arms when the door finally opened.

Anne, standing tall and straight, smiled serenely. 'Mrs Fortune, how nice to see you this Saturday morning. Was there something you wanted?' She knew she'd have to play it carefully with her landlady for she didn't want to risk being thrown out. Her little room wasn't plush, but it was the only home she had. However, she was fed up to the back teeth of her landlady barging into her room. Finally, she'd taken steps to ensure it didn't happen again. She'd fitted a lock to the door. Mrs Fortune breathed deeply, nostrils flaring, and narrowed her eyes.

'What happened to your door? Why was it stuck?' she demanded. She looked around the room. 'I hope you're not hiding something in here.'

Anne's shoulders dropped. She'd been living with Mrs Fortune for over a year and was disappointed that her landlady still didn't trust her.

'Mrs Fortune, I am not hiding anything, or anyone. I know you well enough by now to know you're intimating, yet again, that I have sneaked a gentleman in here. I have told you many times that I'm not that kind of girl. You know I'd never break any of your house rules,' she said firmly.

This, however, didn't stop Mrs Fortune's beady eyes from roaming the room and landing on Anne's pristine eiderdown. Anne could have sworn at that moment that Mrs Fortune looked disappointed not to have found evidence of wrongdoing.

Mrs Fortune was a peculiar woman, Anne thought. She was short with grey hair tucked under a small black hat which, from first thing each morning to last thing at night, she always wore. Anne had never seen her without it. 'Mrs Fortune, do you remember our conversations . . .' Anne began, then paused, thinking of how best to explain why she had installed the lock on her door without permission. 'Our *many* conversations about you, as my landlady, respecting my privacy, as your lodger?'

Mrs Fortune put her hands on her stout hips and looked from Anne to the door where the shiny new bolt finally caught her eye.

'What on earth is that?' she yelled.

'I think you know what it is, Mrs Fortune.'

'You've damaged the door,' Mrs Fortune said, running her fingers across the bolt.

Anne crossed her arms.

'I've done no such thing. As you can see. I've installed a lock, carefully and neatly.'

Mrs Fortune stepped forward and looked into Anne's clear, bright eyes. Anne stood her ground and pressed her sensible, flat shoes against the bare floor to steady herself. She knew she should have asked permission to put the lock on her door but, had she done so, she feared Mrs Fortune would have said no.

'If I'd asked you about installing a lock, you would have refused me,' Anne began, pre-empting complaints.

Mrs Fortune shook her head.

'You don't need a lock on your door. You don't require privacy in my home . . . unless you've got something to hide,' she said darkly.

Anne dismissed her comment with a wave of her hand.

'I do need privacy, Mrs Fortune. Everyone is entitled to it. I don't barge into your rooms downstairs, do I? And although I've asked you many times not to enter my room without permission, you've repeatedly ignored my requests. I'm a grown woman, not a child. While I've lived under your roof I've been a model tenant. I always pay my rent on time, I keep my room clean and I never . . .' Anne tilted her chin, 'I never bring back gentleman callers. And don't I give you free toffee each week from my work at Jack's factory too?'

Mrs Fortune's right eye twitched. Anne had expected more resistance from feisty Mrs Fortune. She'd even put money aside from her wages to offer to her landlady if she demanded compensation for installing the lock. However, she was both surprised and relieved when Mrs Fortune dropped her gaze. For the first time since she'd moved in to Victor Street, Anne felt she'd won a small victory. Mrs Fortune turned away and carefully inspected the lock.

'You installed this yourself?' she asked more gently now, impressed.

'Yes, I bought it from the Co-op in town, along with a screwdriver and all the fixings,' Anne replied.

Mrs Fortune spun around and her eyebrows shot up into the rim of her black hat. 'You know how to operate a screwdriver?' she said, astonished.

Anne nodded.

'Yes, of course,' she said. 'I'm a woman of many talents, Mrs Fortune. There's a lot you don't know about me.'

Mrs Fortune gave a wry smile. 'There are many things we don't know about each other,' she replied.

Anne immediately wished she could take back her words. Because if Mrs Fortune found out everything about her, Anne knew she'd be thrown out immediately. She'd shared her deepest secret with only Hetty and Elsie, her close friends at the toffee factory. They knew about her son who she'd parted with as a baby to be raised by Mr and Mrs Matthews, a well-to-do couple in Durham. That was where Anne had been heading that morning before Mrs Fortune had tried to enter her room. All Anne wanted to do was take a peek at her boy, just a glimpse over the fence of the Matthews' back garden. Some days the heartache of giving up her child wouldn't leave her and compelled her to seek him out, hoping for a glimpse of him through a window of the Matthews' large, impressive home. Anne kept other secrets too, things that she hadn't even shared with Hetty and Elsie. Things that she couldn't share with anyone. The truth was that she'd fallen for the factory owner, Mr Jack, who she worked with closely. However, he was promised to a society lady by the name of Lucinda Dalton and they were to be wed. To complicate matters further, Mr Jack had recently told Anne he loved *her,* not Lucinda. He'd even presented Anne with a jewelled Christmas gift, a silver brooch with precious stones in the exact shade of blue to match the toffee factory logo. Lucinda Dalton's father planned to invest in the toffee factory. So far, Anne hadn't dared allow herself to be swept up in the romance of Mr Jack's heartfelt words. If she did, his marriage to Lucinda might not go ahead. No wedding would mean no investment for the factory and, without investment, there was every chance the factory would have to close, particularly if the rumours of sugar rations were true. All the sugar boilers, chocolate enrobers, wrappers and packers, delivery men and stable men would then be out of work. She would lose her much-loved role as secretary to Mr Jack and every toffee factory girl, including her friends Elsie and Hetty, would lose their jobs too. No, there was no need for Mrs Fortune to know everything about her.

Anne bit her tongue as Mrs Fortune looked her all the way up from her sensible brown shoes to her black linen skirt and cream blouse with its patterned-lace collar. Anne's brown hair was elegantly styled in a bun. Aware she was being scrutinised, she felt herself blush and she pushed up her small, wire-rimmed glasses to the bridge of her nose. Mrs Fortune crossed her arms.

'I won't have you damaging any more of my doors,

Miss Wright,' she said. 'Or floors, or windows, or any part of my home. Do you hear me?'

'Loud and clear, Mrs Fortune,' she replied. 'Now, was there a reason for your visit this morning? I was about to go out.'

Mrs Fortune nodded quickly, then closed the door. She indicated the bed.

'You may wish to sit down, Miss Wright.'

Anne shook her head.

'Whatever it is, Mrs Fortune, I'm sure I can remain standing.'

Mrs Fortune began pacing from Anne's bed to the window. The room was so small that it only took the landlady three steps to reach the window and three steps to return. Anne wondered what was on her mind. She quickly glanced at her wristwatch. The bus to Durham was due soon and she didn't want to miss it. She hoped that her landlady would be quick. However, the clouded look on Mrs Fortune's face suggested otherwise.

'Times are hard, Miss Wright,' Mrs Fortune began, still pacing. 'This dreadful war shows no end and food prices have shot through the roof.'

Anne braced herself. Because of her privileged position at the toffee factory she knew exactly how much of an increase there'd been in food prices nationwide.

'I understand, Mrs Fortune,' she said.

Mrs Fortune stopped pacing. She looked at Anne.

'Of course you do, you're an intelligent girl. You wouldn't have been taken on at Jack's factory in such a senior role if you weren't.'

'How much more rent do you want?' Anne offered.

A smile came to Mrs Fortune's lips then she delved

into the front pocket of the apron that covered her skirt and blouse. She pulled out a small envelope and handed it to Anne.

'The new terms are in my letter. Please read this and sign it to say you agree, then return it to me on your way out.'

Anne took the envelope and placed it carefully on the mantelpiece.

'I'll read it when I return, Mrs Fortune. I really should go. I don't want to be late.'

Anne began picking up her handbag and gathering her coat, hat and scarf. It was blustery outside with a strong January wind and Anne needed to be wrapped up.

'There's something else I need to tell you,' Mrs Fortune added.

Anne didn't stop in her preparations to leave, hoping the landlady would pick up on the hint.

'Oh?' she said, thrusting her arms into her winter coat.

'I'm taking in another lodger,' Mrs Fortune announced.

This made Anne stop in her tracks. She blinked hard.

'Another . . .?'

'Lodger,' Mrs Fortune added.

'But where will they . . .?' Anne tried to form the question she wanted to ask. There were no more rooms in Mrs Fortune's house so where would another lodger live?

'Pearl will live downstairs in my front parlour,' Mrs Fortune said.

Anne was stunned. Not only was Mrs Fortune giving up one of her private rooms but she'd called the new lodger by her first name. All the time Anne had lived in Mrs Fortune's house, she'd been addressed as Miss Wright.

'Pearl?' Anne said, hoping that Mrs Fortune would share some more details about the new girl. However,

Mrs Fortune pursed her lips and headed to the door. She paused, holding the handle. Anne followed, knowing that as soon as she left the house she'd have to run to Front Street if she was to catch the Durham bus.

'One more thing, Miss Wright.'

'What is it now?' Anne asked impatiently.

'There's a gentleman to see you. I haven't invited him in, as the neighbours will gossip and I won't have that, Miss Wright. He's waiting outside on the street.'

Anne's heart skipped a beat.

'A gentleman? Who is it?' she asked.

'I didn't ask his name as I have no time for such callers. You know my house rules about gentlemen,' Mrs Fortune said sternly. Then she walked from the room and away down the stairs. Anne was confused, she wasn't expecting anyone. The only men she knew in Chester-le-Street were those she worked with at the factory. Why on earth would one of them come to her home? She racked her brains to think of who knew where she lived. The only person she could think of was Mr Jack himself, but surely it wouldn't be him? He wouldn't be so indiscreet as to visit her lodgings. She reassured herself that it couldn't possibly be him because Mrs Fortune would have recognised him. As the owner of the toffee factory which employed many in the small market town of Chester-le-Street, everyone knew who he was. Anne listened to Mrs Fortune's footsteps disappear downstairs, then she heard the door open into the landlady's parlour.

'Pearl, my dear!' she heard her exclaim before the door closed. Anne's head spun. She couldn't think straight. Another lodger in the small house was one thing to get her head around, especially one so familiar with Mrs Fortune.

And now a gentleman coming to call, well, that was another matter entirely. She took a moment to gather herself and calm her racing heart. She glanced at her watch again, realising she was too late to catch the bus and there wasn't another due for an hour. There was only one thing for it. She headed downstairs to discover who was waiting outside.

© Les Mann

Glenda Young credits her local library in the village of Ryhope, where she grew up, for giving her a love of books. She still lives close by in Sunderland and often gets her ideas for her stories on long bike rides along the coast. A life-long fan of *Coronation Street*, she runs two hugely popular fan websites and has written official TV tie-in books for the ITV soap opera. Glenda has both won and been shortlisted for multiple short story awards, and her stories have been published in the *Express, Sunday People, Take A Break* and *My Weekly*. Glenda was also commissioned to write the first ever soap opera, Riverside, for *The People's Friend* which publishes weekly.

For updates on what Glenda is working on, visit her website **glendayoungbooks.com** and to find out more find her on **f** **/GlendaYoungAuthor**, Ⓘ **@flaming_nora** and X **@flaming_nora**.

Don't miss Glenda Young's heart-warming debut saga

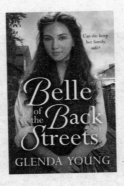

'Any rag and bone!'

Everyone recognises the cry of Meg Sutcliffe as she plies her trade along the back streets of Ryhope, having learnt the ropes from her dad after the War. When tragedy struck, Meg had no choice but to continue alone. Now the meagre money she earns is all that stands between her family's safety and predatory rent collector Hawk Jackson . . .

Many say it's no job for a woman – especially a beauty like Meg who turns heads wherever she goes. When she catches the eye of charming Clarky it looks like she might have found a protector and a chance of happiness. But is Clarky really what he seems? And could Adam, Meg's loyal childhood friend, be the one who really deserves her heart?

For further information visit:
glendayoungbooks.com

f /GlendaYoungAuthor
𝕏 @flaming_nora
⊙ @flaming_nora

9781472256584

HEADLINE

Read Glenda Young's emotional saga of love and loss

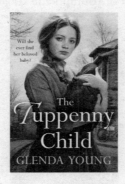

'She's not worth more than tuppence, that child!'

Those are the words that haunt Sadie Linthorpe. She is the talk of Ryhope when she arrives there, aged seventeen, alone, seeking work and a home in the pit village. But Sadie is keeping a secret – she is searching for her baby girl who was taken from her at birth a year ago and cruelly sold by the child's grandmother.

All that Sadie knows about the family who took her daughter is that they lived in Ryhope. And the only thing she knows about her daughter is that when the baby was born, she had a birthmark on one shoulder that resembled a tiny ladybird. But as Sadie's quest begins, a visitor from her past appears – one who could jeopardise the life she's beginning to build and ruin her chances of finding her beloved child for ever . . .

For further information visit:
glendayoungbooks.com

 /GlendaYoungAuthor
 @flaming_nora
 @flaming_nora

9781472256621

HEADLINE

Lose yourself in Glenda Young's romantic
saga of triumph and tragedy

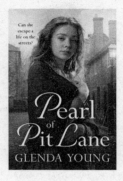

'*Put me to work on the pit lane, would you?*
Is that all you think I'm worth?'

When her mother dies in childbirth, Pearl Edwards is left in
the care of her aunt, Annie Grafton. Annie loves Pearl like
her own daughter but it isn't easy to keep a roof over their
heads and food on the table. Annie knows the best way to
supplement their meagre income is to walk the pit lane at night,
looking for men willing to pay for her company.

As Pearl grows older she is unable to remain ignorant of
Annie's profession, despite her aunt's attempts to shield her. But
when Pearl finds herself unexpectedly without work and their
landlord raises the rent, it becomes clear they have few choices
left and Annie is forced to ask Pearl the unthinkable.

Rather than submit to life on the pit lane, Pearl runs away.
She has nothing and nowhere to go, but Pearl is determined
to survive on her own terms . . .

For further information visit:
glendayoungbooks.com

f /GlendaYoungAuthor
X @flaming_nora
◎ @flaming_nora

9781472256669

HEADLINE

Don't miss Glenda Young's unforgettable, heart-wrenching saga

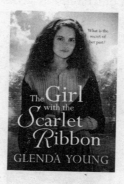

'*You deserve more than this, Jess . . . You deserve
to know the truth about the McNallys.*'

When a newborn baby girl is found abandoned with nothing
but a scarlet ribbon tied to her basket, Ava Davidson,
housekeeper of the wealthy McNally family's home, the
Uplands, takes her into her care. Sworn to secrecy about the
baby's true identity, Ada names her Jess and brings her up as
her own, giving Jess no reason to question where she came from.

But when Ada passes away, grief-stricken Jess, now sixteen,
is banished from the place she's always called home. With
the scarlet ribbon the only connection to her past, will Jess
ever find out where she really belongs? And will she uncover
the truth about the ruthless McNallys?

For further information visit:
glendayoungbooks.com

f /GlendaYoungAuthor
X @flaming_nora
O @flaming_nora

9781472268549

HEADLINE

Look out for Glenda Young's emotional family
saga of triumph in adversity

'She's just a paper mill girl.'

Ruth Hardy works long hours at Grange Paper Works,
with her younger sister Bea, and spends her free time caring
for their ailing parents. Their meagre income barely covers
their needs, so when Bea falls pregnant out of wedlock,
there are tougher times ahead.

Luck turns when Ruth is promoted, but the arrival of
Bea's baby girl ends in tragedy, and Ruth is left with no
choice but to bring up her niece herself. However, news of
Ruth's plan brings a threatening menace close. And although
Ruth's friendship with the girls at the mill, and the company
of charming railway man, Mick Carson, sustain her, ultimately
Ruth bears the responsibility for keeping her family safe.
Will she ever find happiness of her own?

For further information visit:
glendayoungbooks.com

f /GlendaYoungAuthor
𝕏 @flaming_nora
○ @flaming_nora

9781472268563

HEADLINE

Look out for Glenda Young's powerful family
saga of love and sacrifice

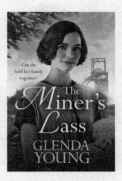

'*You're a Dinsdale lass, Ruby. Nothing
and no one keeps us lot down.*'

A life of poverty in a cramped pit cottage is all that
seventeen-year-old Ruby Dinsdale has known. Even with
her father and younger brother working at the coal mine,
money is tight. Her mother Mary is skilled at stretching what
little they have, but the small contribution Ruby makes from
her job at the local pub makes all the difference. So when Ruby
is sacked, and Mary becomes pregnant again, the family's
challenges are greater than ever.

When charming miner Gordon begins to court Ruby it
seems as though happiness is on the horizon, until she uncovers
a deeper betrayal than she could ever have imagined. But
although the Dinsdales are materially poor, they are rich in
love, friendship and determination – all qualities that they will
draw on to get them through whatever lies ahead.

For further information visit:
glendayoungbooks.com

f /GlendaYoungAuthor
X @flaming_nora
⊙ @flaming_nora

9781472268600

HEADLINE

Enjoy Glenda Young's warm-hearted festive family saga

'I hope this Christmas is better than last year's.'

Following a scandalous affair, wayward Emma Devaney is sent in disgrace from her home in Ireland to Ryhope, where she will live with her widowed aunt, Bessie Brogan, and help run her pub. Bessie is kind but firm, and at first Emma rebels against her lack of freedom. Struggling to fit in, she turns to the wrong person for comfort, and becomes pregnant.

Accepting she must embrace her new life for the sake of her baby, Emma pours her energy into making the pub thrive and helping heal the fractured relationship between Bessie and her daughters. She catches the attention of Robert, a gruff but sincere farmer, who means to win her heart.

As December approaches, thankful for the home and acceptance she's found, Emma is determined to bring not just her family, but the whole Ryhope community, together to celebrate – and to make one very special mother's Christmas dreams come true.

For further information visit:
glendayoungbooks.com

f /GlendaYoungAuthor
X @flaming_nora
@flaming_nora

9781472283252

HEADLINE